Review

For a sci-fi fan like me, one who has read many sci-fi series, this book is probably the one that appealed to me most. Reading Vučak's sci-fi novel does take some effort, and it would probably be better if you read the previous books first. But don't let me put you off reading this. If anything, *Guardians of Shadow* is still more than capable to be read as a standalone.

Readers' Favorite

Books by Stefan Vučak

General Fiction:
Cry of Eagles
All the Evils
Towers of Darkness
Strike for Honor
Proportional Response
Legitimate Power
Autumn Leaves
All My Sunsets
F/X-26
28th Amendment
Night Sirens
Broken Rose

Shadow Gods Saga:
In the Shadow of Death
Against the Gods of Shadow
A Whisper from Shadow
Shadow Masters
Immortal in Shadow
With Shadow and Thunder
Through the Valley of Shadow
Guardians of Shadow

Science Fiction:
Fulfillment
Lifeliners

Non-Fiction:
Writing Tips for Authors

Contact at:
www.stefanvucak.com

GUARDIANS OF SHADOW

By

Stefan Vučak

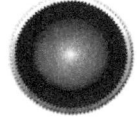

Stefan Vučak ©2013
ISBN-10: 0648473198
ISBN-13: 9780648473190

Dedication

To Chris … choosing life's faces

Acknowledgments

Image of the 'Crab Nebula' supplied courtesy of the National Radio Astronomy Observatory.

Cover art by Laura Shinn.
http://laurashinn.yolasite.com

Map of the Serrll Combine

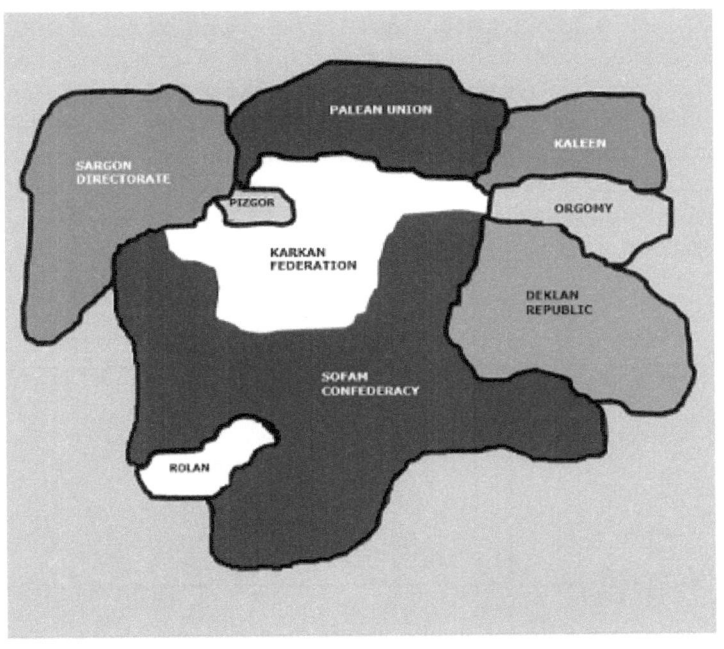

Composition of the Serrll Combine

The 247 star systems that make up the Serrll Combine is an association of six interstellar power blocks, split between two rival camps - the Servatory Party and the Revisionists. Each star system has a single representative in Captal's General Assembly from which members are elected to the ruling ten-seat Executive Council. Seats are based on a percentage of systems occupied by each power block in relation to the total number of systems in the Serrll Combine.

Name	No of Star Systems	Percentage of Total	Executive Council Seats
Sofam Confederacy	83	34	4
Deklan Republic	19	8	1
Palean Union	28	11	1
Karkan Federation	46	19	2
Sargon Directorate	32	12	1
Independents:		15	1
- Kaleen	8		
- Rolan	5		
- Orgomy	6		
- Pizgor	3		
- Other systems	17		
General Assembly	**247**	**100**	**10**
Outposts	40		
Protectorates	34		

Principal political blocks:

Revisionist Party:	Palean Union
	Deklan Republic
	Sofam Confederacy
Servatory Party:	Karkan Federation
	Sargon Directorate
	Nonaligned Independents

Composition of the Executive Council:

Security Council	Bureau of Colonial and Protectorate Affairs
	Bureau of Defense
	Bureau of Cultural Affairs
Administrative Council	Bureau of Administrative Affairs
	Bureau of Justice
Economics Council	Bureau of Economic Affairs
	Bureau of Technology and Development
Central Planning Council	Bureau of Central Planning and Development

Prologue

"Who are you?" Teena whispered, her face lost and tragic.

"I am the harbinger of eternity," Terr said, but the god of Death in him provided the words.

He could see her bite her lip, trying hard to keep back the tears of doubt and indecision. Something tore inside him and he wanted to embrace her, say the healing words, but he stood rooted. They had reached a cusp, and this time, *she* needed to close the chasm that separated them.

"And can I love you, my lord of Death, as much as I love him?" she choked, her words a whisper, almost too low to hear, the pain in them poignant.

Unbidden, like invisible gossamer, the hand of Death settled about him and he stood in its shadow. The flicker of small lightnings in his hands did not writhe in anger. Blue softness enveloped him as he opened his arms to her and waited. She now saw the real him, Death manifest, and she had to accept him on those terms. Her steps were hesitant and she stopped short of the shimmering aura surrounding him.

Terr stood still, waiting for her to decide. She must want to cross the barrier that would otherwise always stand between them, but she must do it willingly. Then she was in his arms, her body hot to the touch, head on his chest.

"There has always been only me to love," he murmured into her soft hair with relief as he closed his arms about her and held her tight. "Only me."

As he stood there, time did not matter, the soft shipboard noises hardly audible. It was enough being one with her. He needed to tell her so many things, but the words could wait. She made her choice and he felt fulfilled. Wrapped in blue light, he cupped her small oval face between his hands. He leaned forward, brushed away a strand of hair from her forehead, and gently touched her full lips with his. After a moment, she let out a soft sigh and her arms circled his neck, pulling him down.

"I thought I'd lost you," she moaned and her lips parted.

"I shall always be with you, my pet. For all time," he said gruffly and brought his mouth hard against hers. Gods, how he cherished this woman!

She held him tight, trying to burrow into him as their tongues danced. They were one, body and soul, and he would never let her go. It would take time to fill whatever void still separated them, but neither were short of time. Besides, it was only a small void.

Cloaked in the shadow of Death, removed from a reality she did not fully understand, he feared his display of raw power when he destroyed the Celi-Kran ship may have driven her away. She saw him wield the lightnings before, but not like this, not with such devastating consequences. To an extent, he shared her shock because he had not thought it possible either. He never heard of a second-level Discipline adept capable of such a thing. To reach out with his hand and spear the Kran ship like an insignificant insect...

He would think about it later, wishing he could talk to Sidhara. His master would know what happened, how he managed something seemingly impossible, but the venerated Wanderer was hundreds of light-years away on Anar'on in another reality. A place Terr wouldn't mind being right now. He needed a moment of peace to pull it all together.

As he held her in his arms, enclosed in her faint citrus fragrance, his hand stroked her flowing black hair and he felt complete, his reservations banished. He should not have doubted her, doubted her love, but he guessed that living with someone able to summon a god could not have been easy for her. Sometimes the realization did not sit comfortably with him either, but she knew what he was. She had glimpsed something of what lurked within him when she stood before the silent, towering red cliffs of Athal Than, surrounded by Saffal's rippling sands, feeling the pull through him.

Fates brought him back to Anar'on, and his brother Dharaklin, whom he almost killed in blind revenge for taking Teena from him. Reconciled, Terr wanted to share with her something of its sweeping deserts and amber skies—and where the god of Death restored his sanity and gave him the power to walk in his shadow. Naturally curious, she wanted to see Athal Than. It meant oblivion for her to enter one of the gaping dark fissures that led into the Keep of Death, but the pull could not be denied. When she started to walk toward the cliff, he barely reached her in time to hold her back, sharing her terror at what almost happened. In that fleeting moment of connection, she had glimpsed the naked face of his god, and it haunted her ever since.

The blue radiance around them slowly faded. Although visibly gone, power still surrounded him, but it now embraced Teena. Part of him, the god accepted his duality as she had accepted him.

He smiled into her large green eyes. "Come."

Her face clouded as she pulled away and her eyes turned dark. "Between you and your god, living with you is hard. I don't know if I can take it. Do you have any other surprises you'd care to tell me about?"

"I'll need to show you," he said and pulled her toward the Personal Transport alcove.

"Beast," she murmured tenderly and a dimpled smile wiped away the shadows from her face. "You're crude."

"Always, my pet."

As he stood in the alcove, his arm around her waist, he gazed through the transparent hull of the darkened Observation Deck. In a burst of white scintillation, *Tapal* left Devon 3-VL4's moon and the Kran cruiser lying shattered on its surface, and slipped into subspace, cleaving its way through thick strands of yellow and brown gravity waves induced by Devon's sun. It would take *Tapal* fourteen days to reach Tureen's Star on the edge of the Moanar Nebula more than two thousand lights away, bearing them toward an unknown destiny among alien worlds. From Line Tracking Station 3, with Teena and Dhar, they would be transported to Orieli space where his mission would begin, a mission to understand the vast interstellar union…and find out whether the Serrll can accept them as friends. That's the plan Anabb Karr, head of the Diplomatic Branch on Taltair outlined, but no one anticipated Terr would destroy the Celi-Kran invader before the mission even started. Now, he did not know whether he still had a mission. If he did, it might be executed under different parameters. After display of Terr's awesome power, the Orieli would understandably want to know all about Anar'on and its Wanderers, and the uneasy relationship they had with Captal, governing center of the Serrll Combine. If more Krans came, Captal would also be keen to know if Anar'on would help the Serrll Scout Fleet repel the invaders.

Nightwings, the shadow who walks at night…

A tall figure stood proud on the sharp crest of a sand dune, the brown cape of his surtaf stirred in a light wind, the red hood thrown back. Shielded by prominent eyebrows, the orange eyes, protected by transparent membranes, gazed steadily at a far horizon as it merged with an amber sky. Strands of thick tarad grass bowed before him. Looking at him, no one could mistake his mastery of everything he saw.

That's how Terr pictured Dharaklin, his Wanderer brother.

He would need to talk to Nightwings about what happened in *Tapal's* Primary Flight Control. There was no rush, and Dhar would understand his need to bridge the gulf with Teena first. After all, he and Dhar walked under the same shadow. Different certainly, and alien, they still shared each other's very essence. He still found it incredible how the fates brought them together.

Assigned as Envoy Rayon Tantour's military aide on Elexi in the Four Suns to investigate alleged slavery, Terr fell afoul of Kapel Pen, Controller of Elexi. She planned to cede the Four Suns to the Karkan Federation, which would have been a PR disaster for Captal. Pursued by rogue Scout Fleet M-3s all the way to Anar'on, Terr's survival blister crashed in the deep desert. After two days, the nomad Wanderers found him and nursed him back to life, but the desert trek left him without his memory, unable to talk. Dharaklin entered Terr's mind to pull him out of his madness and the two merged into a single personality, forever brothers.

The stars crawled in the black deeps, so far away and so indifferent.

"Quarters," Terr commanded.

A scimitar of cutting blackness, infinite and cold, swept through his body, accompanied by an instant of unbearable pressure. He had a moment of irrational panic as he crossed the interdimensional threshold, but his senses settled when he found himself in another alcove, now deep within the ship. He waited for the transceiver's aftereffect tingle to subside and glanced at Teena. Her hand in his, they quickly walked through the brightly lit lounge of their quarters toward the bedroom, both felt the urgency to be close, share and renew, and perhaps even forget a little.

After a frenzied moment of passion and release, they lay on the bed entwined. The thick carpet glowed faintly green, enough to keep the darker shadows at bay. His left arm wrapped around her, Terr slowly stroked Teena's smooth side, her head resting on his chest. Everything was all right now and he finally had peace. She finally accepted him and his duality. Accepted or given in to the struggle, it did not matter. They were one; nothing else mattered.

She shifted and looked at him, eyes searching in the semi-darkness. "I love you desperately, but you don't make it easy sometimes," she whispered and her head sank into the crook of his arm. Her fingernails slid playfully across his chest and left trails of exquisite fire.

He kissed the top of her head and stroked her silky back, marveling at the softness of her skin. "I wield death in my hand, my pet. It is a destroyer and demands sacrifice. That's all there is to it."

"Between you and your god, you two make a pretty powerful combination. No wonder you frightened everybody, including me. I still get the shivers when I think about it."

"I don't know what happened," he said slowly, amazed at the vivid memory still crowding him as though he were standing there, hands raised, the lightnings crackling between them. "When the Kran ship fired at the M-4, knowing it posed no threat and unable to offer resistance, I simply reacted. It did not have to destroy the M-4, but the *Daktar's* central nexus did it anyway. Whatever logic guided the thing did not operate along any line I understood. It was wanton destruction and I needed to remove the blight from my sight."

Pursued by *Tapal*, the Kran cruiser came to Devon 3-VL4 to affect repairs. How it managed to evade the Orieli LTN stations was something Orieli Space Command and the Serrll were even now looking into. Ordered by CAPFLTCOM, Captal Fleet Command, not to interfere since *Tapal* had crossed into Serrll space, Karhide Arlon Dee waited for Scout Fleet forces to arrive and neutralize the Kran ship before it could lift. Instead of an M-6, a single M-4 confronted the *Daktar*.

Her fingers marched playfully across his chest. "When you loosed that bolt of light…I didn't know who you were or what you were. You simply reached out and the Kran ship died," she whispered in awe. "The bolt went right through *Tapal* without harming it. I feared you then."

"And now?"

"I was shocked and surprised, but I'm over it now, I think." She snuggled against him, her arm thrown across him. "You need to give me time, but I kind of like having a god at my bidding. It could come in handy."

"If only I were a god."

"Close enough," she murmured happily. "What will happen now? Karhide Dee will report the incident to his superiors. It could mean the end of our mission."

He allowed the silence to cradle them for a while.

"This was bound to happen sooner or later, perhaps not in such dramatic fashion," Terr conceded, not sure whether to reveal Zor-Ell's secret how the Orieli conducted alien contacts by superimposing an Observer's personality onto a native. In the end, he decided it was not his to divulge. The Orieli Observers, open and clandestine, would find out soon enough about Anar'on and the Wanderers. Their reaction would shape Serrll and Orieli relations for centuries to come. "Perhaps it's better this happened now. More Kran ships will come and we must face them together."

"And can we face them?"

"I don't know, my pet, but we'll have to."

"If the Krans do come, will Anar'on stand with us?"

Terr sighed. "I don't know that either. With all the power maneuvering between the Revisionists and the Servatory Party, Captal hasn't given Anar'on much reason to get involved. It's all speculation anyway, and the Krans might never come."

"But you don't think so."

He leaned forward and kissed her forehead. "I don't want to talk about the Krans or the Wanderers now. I want to talk about us."

Terr took on his aspect and blue light flooded the bedroom as he gathered her in his arms. She squealed as his mouth sought hers, small fists beating against his chest.

Chapter One

"Come in, Alkarh," Enllss-rr said cordially and waited for his important visitor to walk through, pleased to see him again. He glanced at Landa, his confidential assistant, and she nodded. There would be no interruptions.

His bearing determined, Zor-Ell strode purposefully into the spacious office and glanced at the Wall communications station opposite the wide executive desk as it pooled through shifting, merging colors. Enllss caught him at it and grinned as he sat down. Bright sunshine streamed through the window screens behind him. Overhead, layers of crisscrossing lines of traffic made checkered patterns in a clear sky.

"My mind bender tells me it's therapeutic," he said. "I don't know. Maybe it is, although I don't have much time to appreciate its therapeutic qualities. Make yourself comfortable." As the Zaronian lowered himself into the formchair, Enllss smiled broadly. "I must congratulate you on your promotion."

The last time they spoke, Zor-Ell commanded all Line Tracking Net stations. With LTN-12, the last link in the chain of stations completed and fully operational on Earth's Moon, additional resource commitments by the Orieli meant greater responsibility. Who better to fulfill that role than the person who made first contact with the Serrll, now five years ago. Where had all those years gone? From what Enllss heard, other survey ships had encountered intelligent life, but none came across an interstellar block such as the Serrll Combine. Zor-Ell also had an unusual personal interest in the Serrll—Earth, anyway, if he believed Terr's yarn about Orieli Observers.

Guardians of Shadow

During an informal gathering on the eve of Zor-Ell's departure after he explained to the General Assembly the existence of the Celi-Kran and their mindless war against all organic intelligence—it hardly seemed real it was only a week ago—mixing it with a small group of Executive directors and several lesser lights, the alien told Enllss blatantly that within three years the Serrll would be actively repelling a Kran invasion or they'd be overrun. Having just sipped a fragrant white wine, the declaration left Enllss spluttering, fighting for control. Ultimately tactful, Zor-Ell ignored his moment of discomfort, but the comment he made was not at all comfortable, and set off a chain of thoughtful speculation within the Security Council, and the Bureau of Defense in particular.

Enllss took solace that it wasn't his problem, not directly at least. As commissioner for the Bureau of Colonial and Protectorate Affairs, he had to be aware of all Executive Council policies even if he did not necessarily need to act on them. Responsible for forty outposts and thirty-four protectorates, he had to fight for his share of funding and resources, navigating through layers of obfuscating bureaucracy and political vested interests. It paid to be well informed, and his contacts in the Bureau of Cultural Affairs made sure of it. Information gathering was not done only through formal channels, and accurate information was lifeblood in his job.

At least Serrll's contact with the Orieli went smoothly, even if no one else would say it, and he had his army of detractors. Exchange of cultural missions arranged, and two Orieli investigation teams now safely quartered, ready to do whatever it is they did. He refrained from asking about their Observers, afraid he might be told. Outrageous as Terr's idea was, it did make a screwy kind of sense. No matter how good, Orieli's two four-man teams could not hope to cover the Serrll in any depth within the two-month timeframe they requested, regardless how sophisticated their data collection techniques. Still, planting hidden observers able to move freely among the population

Stefan Vučak

as Terr suggested, took some swallowing. For his peace of mind, Enllss did not want to think too much about how they might go about doing it, and refrained from discussing it with his boss. Illeran had enough on his mind setting policy. There was no need to bother him with detail, which rightly fell within Enllss' sphere of responsibility. The man kept busy marshaling Karkan resources for the general elections in two years' time. A Karkan and a senior Servatory Party wheel, Illeran was a nominal political enemy. Although a good system, power sharing got a bit complicated sometimes.

"Thank you, Da Commissioner, although I occasionally think it is punishment for past sins."

Enllss laughed. "I sympathize, but you'll get used to the mantle of power, and you carry it well."

Zor-Ell's mouth twitched. "It does give me a degree of freedom to act, with correspondingly higher penalties should I stumble."

"By damn! You're right there. Authority can be a dubious honor."

Zor-Ell crossed his legs. "I miss having my own ship, though. Deskbound these days is living in uncharted territory."

Just short of average height, he seemed to dominate all the space around them, and his brown eyes shone with intelligence. His skin had a beautiful shade of blue-green, growing black around the eyes and powerful mouth, head covered by short black hair. On the left side of his chest, he wore a small gold-bordered Cluster-and-Circle emblem, a densely packed conglomeration of yellow stars representing the Orieli globular cluster. At fifty-one, he was young for his rank, given a life expectancy of one hundred and sixty. Past sins? Enllss did not think so.

Relaxed, legs stretched, he appreciated sharing confidences with the alien, and an opportunity to glimpse a depth of cultural richness he represented.

"The stars were never a magnet for me, but talking to my

nephew Terr, I can understand what draws him out there. My brother also lusted after the stars and I guess he passed it to his son."

"Terr…a unique individual, Da. In a most unusual way."

"His aspect? Remarkable indeed, and I hope I'm never on the receiving end of his displeasure."

"A Discipline adept, and apparently the only non-Wanderer."

"A mission gone wrong. I'll tell it to you sometime."

Zor-Ell nodded. "I'd like that."

"Do you have any family, Alkarh?"

"A brother. He is also a politician, member of the Klanina Caucus on Zaron. Both my parents are still alive and I visit when time permits."

"I know what you mean. Our jobs own us."

"I also have a younger sister. She recently obtained command of a sweeper, a general purpose support ship."

Enllss chuckled. "Funny you should say that. We call our M-3s the same thing, and for a similar reason."

"Talking of jobs, I appreciate how seamlessly you integrated our investigators."

"It's not like you didn't give us any warning. I trust they're satisfied with the arrangements?"

"More than satisfied, thank you. Your willingness to give us restricted access to your library networks will greatly assist our investigation of the Serrll Combine."

"I'm glad to hear it. Our personnel are ready to board your ship as soon as you clear them."

"I understand the embarkation is already happening, Da Commissioner."

"I wouldn't mind going with them," Enllss murmured, also chained to his desk. As an administrator, he had a keen desire to understand how the Orieli ran things, and perhaps pick up ideas to help the Serrll. Well, that's what Serrll's exchange teams sent into Orieli space would hopefully find out.

11

No longer a ship commander, Zor-Ell now focused his attention on broader aspects of Orieli's presence on this side of the Moanar Nebula, and the Serrll in particular. However, his pointed reminder that building the LTN stations was not done to benefit the Serrll, but to extend a security buffer for the Orieli, had not gone unnoticed by the Executive Council. True or not, the Orieli did not have to build LTN-12 on Earth's Moon to achieve their strategic objective. As a tactical barrier, the chain of stations was effectively complete at LTN-10 without having to enter Serrll space.

Although reluctant to admit it, Enllss acknowledged that Terr could be right. The boy was smart and thought things through. The Orieli had found something fascinating on Earth and were prepared to sit on the Moon scratching the itch, even if it meant imposing themselves on a protectorate, which no one in the Executive liked much, including Enllss, but were forced to swallow their indignation. There were overriding strategic considerations to consider with their Orieli friends. Revealing to Earth existence of a Serrll base on the Moon, and now an Orieli one, stirred too many uncomfortable memories within the General Assembly; memories of genetic engineering done thousands of years ago, a past everyone preferred to forget. When keeping old skeletons, they sometimes rattled when exposed to a breeze.

"When are you departing?"

"Within a few hours. Commissioner Katan from the Bureau of Defense requested to see me and I wanted to make a courtesy call on you, otherwise I'd be on my way to LTN-5 now."

"Where the Kran cruiser emerged," Enllss mused, the incident that started all the recent troubles.

"We're still looking into sensor logs to understand how the thing managed to slip past the first four stations. It shouldn't have been possible." Zor-Ell paused and stared at Enllss. "About Devon 3-VL4—"

12

Enllss raised his hand. "Arlon Dee made the correct decision to engage the Kran ship after it destroyed our M-4, and the Executive Council shall state so to Orieli Space Command. As for violating our territorial integrity when he entered Palean space in pursuit of the Kran ship, you need not harbor any concerns. If anyone needs castigating, it's our Scout Fleet for not able to contain the threat. Karhide Dee's action prevented what might have been an appalling loss of life and destruction of infrastructure in nearby systems had the Kran ship gotten away."

"But Arlon Dee didn't destroy it, Da."

"No, he didn't, but you need not be concerned about any diplomatic fallout."

"Master Scout Terrllss-rr...I understand he is Head of Mission of one of your cultural exchange teams."

"Do you intend to revoke his accreditation?"

"No, but you can appreciate why we might be somewhat reluctant to allow him and his brother Dharaklin entry into our space. With their apparent power..."

Enllss smiled. "The young scamp doesn't do things by half, does he?"

"However unconventional his means, he did neutralize the Kran cruiser and removed a serious threat to worlds near Devon 3-VL4."

"I'll say it was unconventional, and perhaps rash."

"Terr could not know that Arlon Dee was capable of dealing with the situation."

"And was he?"

"Definitely."

"You seem to be defending my nephew."

"He revealed a new force we'll have to consider carefully. These Wanderers, we will want to know all about them."

Enllss noted the subtle change in Zor-Ell's tone. He was not making a request, but a demand. Under the circumstances, not an unreasonable one. In any future confrontation with the Krans, the Serrll would need Orieli support badly. It was always prudent being polite to someone giving a helping hand, even if it stuck in the craw, and it certainly stuck with some Executive Council Directors, uncomfortable with the notion the Serrll Combine could not manage its own security. Facing a probable Kran incursion at some point, the Serrll should be glad to have someone like the Orieli for a friend, if they were genuine friends, yet to be determined.

"All pertinent data will be made available to your investigators, Alkarh," Enllss told him formally.

"Inhabitants of an entire world able to link with what they claim are gods," Zor-Ell mused and shook his head. "Tell me, Commissioner, what is Captal's relationship with Anar'on and the Kaleen group?"

"You mean, should the Krans invade, will the Wanderers help us?"

"We've been engaged with the Krans for five years now. So far we managed to contain them, but the situation is fluid and we still know very little about them."

"With their Discipline adepts, Anar'on will undoubtedly protect themselves, but I cannot say if they will commit to protect the rest of the Serrll. That's something I'd like to know myself. We're discussing it at the diplomatic level with Anar'on. Should the Wanderers ever decide to march on Serrll worlds, we would not be able to stop them. Let me say that Captal treads carefully when dealing with them."

"The vagaries of politics, Da. No one can tell when past transgressions will catch up with us."

"If they choose not to support us, we'd only be getting what we deserve," Enllss said dryly and Zor-Ell grinned.

"The Kran ship on Devon's moon, study it, but take care. You'll be dealing with very advanced nanolite constructs, nanobods as you call them. The ship's central nexus core may be dead, but not necessarily all its systems or mobile units, although Arlon Dee has not detected any residual energy signatures."

"Our investigators on site haven't either, but your warning is noted."

From what Katan told Enllss without bothering to hide his excitement, the Bureau of Technology and Development were salivating with eagerness to pick over the Kran ship, although it would probably take years before any alien technology might be applied within the Serrll.

Zor-Ell rose. "Thank you for seeing me, Da Commissioner, and please feel free to contact me at any time."

Enllss stood. "I should be thanking you, Alkarh. Have a safe return home."

He escorted his visitor out and returned to his office. With a heavy sigh, he walked to the floor-to-ceiling window screen and gazed at Celean Park below. Taking advantage of a bright, sunny spring day, the citizenry were out in force, looking like insects from this high up. He would not mind stretching his legs either, but his position forbade any such indulgence. Although superbly appointed, including surround holoviews, using the in-house gym just wasn't the same. He wielded enormous power and capacity to influence the course of worlds, but he could not go out for a simple walk. What use power if it limited his freedom?

A somewhat rhetorical question, one he'd answered a long time ago. He was a driven man who liked power and what it could do. He had the temperament for it, someone told him, but could not remember who. Not only temperament, but also judgment to apply it properly without having it overwhelm him. Many newcomers to Captal fell by the wayside when they failed to cope with that duality. The General Assembly was not a place for budding megalomaniacs, although a few did try sneaking in from time to time, like Ed-Kani Takao, Executive Director for the Bureau of Economic Affairs, senior Sargon member in the General Assembly, and the Alikan Union Party's Provisional Committee powerbroker—a general pain in the butt.

Enllss would not be sorry to see the last of this particular political opponent. He could picture him right now: standing rigid, completely hairless, his bony face etched with deep character lines, icy blue-white eyes devoid of light, the man was someone to be reckoned with. His vision of how the Serrll should be run differed radically, but in his own way, Ed-Kani lived by a code and with honor, and could rise above parochial interests when required. Honorable or not, it didn't make him a likeable character.

Enllss looked down at the city. There were no regrets. He had worked hard to reach his position, and he meant to keep it. In two years, when the general electoral session swept away old enemies, bringing in new ones, of course, he would be an Executive Director and at the absolute pinnacle of Captal power, with awesome authority and crushing responsibility. He wielded both to a large degree already, and felt comfortable with the prospect of stepping up a notch. He was not a manager, but a policymaker, a crucial difference.

As he thought of his visitor, Enllss chewed his lip. Zor-Ell was right, past sins do eventually return to demand an accounting. Did they now return in the shape of Kran invaders? If so, they were not Serrll sins. If anyone was responsible for the current mess facing everybody, the blame lay with the Orieli. Their survey ships stumbled on the Krans and the mindless things were now on a rampage. In reality, no one was responsible.

Contemplating a possible Sargon/Palean merger—another potential nightmare for the entire Serrll—containing raiders preying on merchant shipping, maneuvering to secure Anar'on's Unified Independent Front support, he did not need the Krans souring his day. He was being unreasonable and knew it. Blaming the Orieli for dragging the Serrll into a possible interstellar war wasn't their fault. Unpleasant things sometimes simply happened when exploring, but it did not stop Sargon from exploiting the development. No one could have foreseen Orieli survey ships bringing the Krans from wherever they came from. Politics...he'd often wondered whether it was all

16

worth it.

The comms alert beeped and he touched a glowing pad on the inlaid console in his desk, diverting him from descending into morbidity, never a comfortable environment.

"What is it, Landa?"

"Executive Director Illeran is calling, sir."

"Very well," he said impatiently and tapped another pad, not in the mood to discuss political entanglements, but enjoying his work was not part of the job description. He won't be sorry to see the last of Illeran either, come the next elections. Two more years...

He sat down and waited for the Wall to clear. Illeran looked up from his desk and sat back.

"I hope I'm not interrupting." Hiss.

"Would that worry you?" Enllss demanded amiably and Illeran chuckled. Beneath the façade of political infighting, they were really good friends. Although the Karkans would love to topple Sofam's hold on the government's policy apparatus, and they worked hard at it, they did not seek to do it by creating social discord, unlike their mutual Sargon headache, Ed-Kani Takao.

"Not particularly."

Broad pale green scales covered his wide, slightly flattened head, glinting faintly under bright ceiling light. Beneath a thin ridge of darker scales, fishy black eyes stared from horizontal slits. A sharp pointed tongue flickered between thin, dark lips. Around him, lush greenery and potted plants decorated the humid room, reflecting the tropical nature of his native Karkan. Enllss could see a large fish tank flush against one wall. In the gloomy interior, shadowy shapes glided with myopic eyes.

"Your alien visitor gone?" Illeran asked and tilted his long delicate neck.

"And curious about what happened at Devon and what position Anar'on will take," Enllss told his boss.

"I'm not surprised. We're still to hear from Prime Director

Marrakan."

"The Devon incident has given him a lot to consider."

"And everybody else. The thought that we might need Anar'on to protect us is galling. Anyway, I didn't call to talk about Anar'on, fascinating as the Wanderers are. Ed-Kani saw me a little while ago, as did that Palean slime worm, Ti Inai. Both expressed outrage at how our mighty Scout Fleet were left wanting and we needed to depend on the Orieli to defend us in a grave crisis."

"Grave crisis? It was one ship!"

"Not my words, Enllss. Still, they do have a point of sorts. Katan at Defense has some awkward explaining to do why Devon wasn't properly supported."

"By damn! It's an ecoforming world, not a military base."

"Agreed, but that M-6 wasn't around when we needed it. The Scout Fleet took too long to respond."

"If Ed-Kani has a problem with our defense posture, he should be beating up on those comfortable Prima Scout chair warmers at COMPALOPS, not us. They're the ones who let everybody down. Why are you involved?"

"Because Devon is an ecoforming world, which makes it my business…and yours."

"Look, Illeran. The Devon thing has given the Alikan Union Party Provisional Committee some temporary oxygen to trumpet the merger, but they're a long way from achieving it. Coercion of independent systems to secede into their camp isn't played anymore. Not openly anyway."

"It's making the Palean Congress nervous. It made Tao Karam's faction nervous, perhaps enough to start thinking that a Sargon/Palean merger might not be such a bad thing after all. Especially if more Kran ships show up and the Fleet is polishing its hulls instead of using them properly. It's a ridiculous proposition, I know, but we're talking about public perception, not reality. If you don't count the loss of billions of credits when Devon's ground stations got shredded by those Kran things, and you'll be hearing from BueAdmin about that, it highlighted the vulnerability of every protectorate and outpost in Palean space."

"Including Deklan, Kaleen and Orgomy space. You don't need to tell me, but the Palean Union won't be paying to clean up the mess on Devon."

"You're missing the point. Instead of landing at an eco-forming world, the Krans could easily have hit an inhabited system. Everybody was lucky this time. What about the next time? The Paleans are pitching the emotional angle. It doesn't have to sound reasonable for people to start worrying."

"I am aware of all that, Illeran, and I didn't miss the point. What did Katan say?" Enllss knew Katan, of course. Rather young for a commissioner and running an important bureau such as Defense, but the Karkan worm handled the job well enough.

"The M-6 is on location now, which is really terrific since the Kran cruiser is destroyed and the Orieli ship is gone. Not a good PR image, and Ed-Kani made sure everybody knows it." The tongue flickered again.

"What does he want? Place M-6s along our entire frontier? He might be able to stir some public sentiment with such a stunt, hoping it'll score points for the Sargon/Palean merger, but when things calm down, people will see through his rhetoric."

"That's been the pattern so far, but things may not settle down."

Enllss shrugged. "Nothing we can do about it. Besides, even if we wanted to, we don't have that many M-6s to deploy."

"We may need to commission some of our mothballed hulls."

"That's Katan's problem. Talking of our Sargon colleague, I saw him the other day with a brand new hand."

Always impatient, Ed-Kani sought to intervene directly af-ter failing to woo Pizgor's three systems and two outposts into the Sargon/Palean camp, giving the Alikan Union Party the required number of General Assembly representatives to claim one additional Executive Council seat and threaten Sofam's control of the government. When Marrakan, Controller of Anar'on and Prime Director of the Kaleen group of stars, learned of the plot to assassinate Kernami Asai Tainam, Pizgor's Prime Director, he attempted to persuade Ed-Kani to desist. It required a small demonstration, resulting in Ed-Kani possessing a stone hand. How the Wanderer could reach from Anar'on to Captal astounded Enllss, but it achieved the desired effect. With modern genotherapy, Ed-Kani had his hand regenerated, but every time he looked at it must have brought less than pleasant memories.

It could not have happened to a nicer guy, Enllss thought comfortably.

Illeran snorted. "Marrakan stopped short. Everyone would have heaved a huge sigh of relief had Ed-Kani joined his ancestors as a block of stone."

"For sure, but you're overreacting," Enllss told him bluntly. "Over the last two years the Provisional Committee hasn't stirred. The merger is a background annoyance fueled by diehards like Ed-Kani and Ti Inai."

"And you refuse to see the threat," Illeran snapped. "As a prospective Executive Director, you need to focus on the strategic, a point I made before. Ed-Kani is a tormented man. He has two years within which to leave a lasting legacy as someone who changed the course of Serrll history. Things may be quiet today, but that's only because we're in the storm's eye, not that the storm has passed. He's not someone who'll give up. I'm surprised at your casual attitude, Enllss."

He shrugged off the criticism, figuring that Ed-Kani Takao was not the only tormented man. Also in his last ten-year term, after almost thirty years of unbroken service in Captal, Illeran would return to Karkan a respected maluran, but one haunted by unfulfilled dreams. As the senior Servatory Party coalition partner, the Karkan Federation constantly fished for gambits to unseat Sofam's hold on the Executive Council. They faced serious impediments, which Illeran spent a lifetime trying to overcome. He too wanted to see Karkan rule the Serrll Combine rather than an Alikan Union, but it wouldn't happen in his lifetime. Enllss almost pitied him.

"Come on, Illeran. You're cutting it a bit deep, aren't you? I'm aware as you are how a Kran incursion could fuel Ed-Kani's ambitions, and what it could mean for Tao Karam's wavering supporters. I wasn't grown in a jar. Should his faction lose control of the Palean Congress, Ti Inai's faction would move in and the merger might assume a different and more aggressive complexion. But we're mitigating the threat, or Sill-Anais is, which is saying the same thing. If those Kran things decide to strike, we have public information conditioning programs in place to neutralize whatever Sargon or the Paleans might come up with. We're prepared for what we know. By definition, the unknown is a surprise."

"That's what's worrying me, you Sofam heathen," Illeran murmured, his tongue flickering.

"You're twitchy over nothing. If another Kran attack does come, it's likely to be Kaleen and Orgomy, not the Paleans."

"A supposition only!"

"They're much closer to Kran space. I've asked Katan to provide additional Fleet coverage along the borders of both."

"You talked to him without clearing with me first?"

Enllss straightened his shoulders. "Look, I did my job. If you're worried about the Krans, talk to Director Bakral. He runs the Security Council. If you want to know what Ed-Kani and the Provisional Committee are doing, talk to Ed-Kani Takao. Sargon is your coalition partner, not ours."

"No need to be testy, Enllss. You used your initiative and it's something I'd have approved anyway, but you don't go out of your way to make life easy for me. I'd like nothing better than to slit your political throat, and maybe my successor will do it. One day we hope to see the Sofam Confederacy humbled, and the Karkan Federation will rule, but not at the expense of destroying Serrll's social fabric, which is what the Alikan Union Party would do if Sargon and the Paleans unite."

Enllss could not help smiling at the thought of poking some fun at his friend, although a political opponent. "Tell me. Hypothetically speaking, of course. If those two merge, would the Karkan Federation join with us to marginalize them? That is if you value Serrll stability as much as you say."

Illeran grinned and shook a finger at him. "That's treasonous talk and you know it. Even if such a blasphemous idea did enter my mind, it's not something I could commit the Karkan Federation to doing, and you're being obtuse as usual."

"I'm being realistic, that's all. Nobody wants the merger, even if one would give you partnership in government."

"The Karkan Federation is already in government," Illeran hissed, cut the connection and the Wall resumed its color pooling.

But not its most important policy-making machinery, my friend, Enllss mused.

Essentially, Illeran was correct when he said the Karkans were in government. Executive directors were posted according to the number of seats each interstellar block held as a percentage of total Serrll voting systems. Power sharing avoided many political complications, and defused possible unrest by blocks who might regard themselves disenfranchised. It wasn't an ideal system, but it worked well enough and everyone was represented. However, the arrangement did sometimes produce odd relationships, like the one Enllss enjoyed with Illeran, a senior Servatory Party member.

Still, the Karkans and Sofam in coalition? Entertaining as the idea was, he really did not want to test it. Nevertheless, it was a titillating thought, worthy of canvassing at cocktail gatherings. Who knows, Ed-Kani might get to hear an outrageous rumor and start wondering about the solidity of his support.

Having Ed-Kani walk around with a concerned frown on his sour face was always a good thing. A doubt cast is like a pebble thrown into a still pond. There is no telling what the ripples would disturb, or uncover.

Would the Karkans really side with Sofam if they were forced to choose between stability or upheaval? Given the stakes everyone was playing for, it might be worthwhile to find out. Enllss needed a serious strategy chat with his First Assistant. He leaned across the desk and tapped the comms pad.

"Landa, get Tariq to see me."

As a commissioner, looking after Sofam's interests was not always a matter of worrying about protectorates and ecoforming projects.

* * *

Renlow sat in the contoured couch, hands clasped behind her head, and allowed her gaze to drift across the towering expanse of the nebula. Lit from within by furiously burning young stars, columns of brown and orange gas loomed above a darker sullen mass of green. Alien stars glowed against the black deeps, indifferent to the architectural majesty the Karina shaped. Perhaps the only majesty came from her own mind, she decided ruefully. Introspection was not something a hard-bitten commander should indulge in, but it did make for a diverting moment. Besides, it was a pretty vista, deadly but pretty.

Instead of wasting time gawking, she should be studying anomalous tracks that appeared four days ago, identified by the Burlig scanners sown along the nebula's edge in LTN-2's forward area. Cent Comp's analysis proved inconclusive, but she could not shake off the feeling the Krans were testing the limits of her defenses, although why launch a strike now puzzled her. After five years trying to penetrate the Line Tracking Net, they had to know the station defenses were impervious. Pattern analysis of their forays to date suggested their heart wasn't really in it, which was inexplicable. Accepting the futility of attempting to understand what drove the machine intelligences—more capable brains were working that problem—she indulged herself by studying the nebula. Not professional behavior at all. Still, she needed something to divert her mind from duty.

Without warning the image jerked and she looked at three bright blue pulsing dots moving swiftly toward her station a bare half a light off. Beside each dot, a small window displayed available information on distance, timings and speed, but she did not need to see the data to know what those dots were. The infernal objects probably made a blind portal jump to appear so suddenly. Otherwise, LTN-1 would have picked them up if the Kran ships tried sneaking through the nebula, a costly option they discovered before. Jumping blind was risky, but tactically very sound, especially if the intention was to arrive unannounced and in force. An operational departure from their normal behavior, it caught her attention. Far on her right, two orange dots representing Orieli pickets were already shifting course to intercept. She nodded with approval.

However unusual the arrival, in one respect the Krans were operating predictably. The three ships were bunched close for mutual support, giving them the ability to tandem their fire control, something the Serrll seem to use extensively. By channeling each ship's projector emission into a single collimated beam, the combined power was devastating, which the Orieli found out the hard way. Reaction, counter-reaction, counter-counter-reaction...

"Opturkarh Renlow?" Cent Comp's firm masculine voice prompted diffidently through the VI coupling.

She sat up, washing her mind of distracting Karina images, focusing on the approaching threats. At the rate of closure, she had almost seven minutes to get ready before things started getting intense.

"I see them," she responded instantly. "Execute condition three and inform MC that I'm on my way up."

24

"Acknowledged."

She took in the immediate tactical profile, confident that *Trailer* and *Marin* were more than capable taking care of three Kran *Daktar*-class cruisers. Tandem fire control worked fine in a sustained bombardment scenario, but not so good against fast maneuvering targets. Moreover, tandem fire forced the triad to maintain formation, not a good thing in a rapidly evolving environment where individual maneuvering might be required. From the Kran attack profile, she was confident in the station's ability to defend itself. Nevertheless, a twinge of uncertainty lurked in the background of her mind. It wasn't exactly fear, more like puzzlement, she told herself, forcing her stomach to relax. The Krans were not ordinary aliens, and she needed to be ready for the unexpected, which of course, was a contradiction.

As Renlow watched the projected tracks, she realized the Kran vessels would approach uncomfortably close to LTN-2 before her pickets could engage. It would be up to the scanner array to eliminate the threats before the Krans could come within an effective firing envelope of her station.

She stared at the crawling dots and bit her lower lip. Something wasn't right here. If the Krans were serious about neutralizing her station, they must know that sending three ships, although powerful units, would not be up to the job. With their interceptor nets fully modulated, the Orieli warships were effectively immune from detection and able to close with lethal effectiveness, largely negating any tandem response. The Krans found that out to their cost in previous probing incursions, and they never repeated a mistake. There must be more of them lurking somewhere.

Draw away her forward pickets and attack from an exposed quarter? With the vast expanse of the Karina on her port flank and the deep emptiness everywhere else, she could not see where another threat could emerge. If this was an attack in depth, the Krans should have thrown in more triads to saturate her defenses; an ineffective tactic with the scanner grid array providing a screen one billion ampirs deep around the system's primary.

It was not like the Krans to throw away ships in a futile gesture. Watching the blue dots drawing closer, the bright red line of their projected trajectory taking them toward KSN-013D, a ringed blue-green gas giant one point-three billion ampirs from the primary, she felt uneasy. It didn't make sense going there. How could the Krans threaten LTN-2 with such a maneuver? It worried her. She could not do anything except wait for the tactical situation to develop—and be prepared.

"Operational caution," the computer announced. "LTN-3 advises they are under attack by two Celi-Kran *Daktar*-class cruisers and two *Sandar*-class battlecruisers."

Renlow frowned. There it was again. The Krans could not possibly hope to disable LTN-3 and its transport portal with such a small strike package. By wiping out the portal with Perilia, the link to Orieli space on the other side of the Karina Shield Nebula would be severed, disrupting a strategically critical logistical gateway and communications relay. The Krans recognized the portal's importance and mounted attacks before, using different tactical scenarios, none of which worked. A variation on the same theme? What they were doing simply did not make any tactical sense.

Small force or not, with her pickets engaged, she could not support LTN-3 even if there was time to do so. Likewise, they could not help her for the same reason; they were simply too far away from each other in distance and time. Clearly, the Kran ships had made another blind portal jump to avoid detection. A disturbing tactic for PERCOM to ponder, but she had enough on her hands without worrying about grand strategy.

It looked like the Kran foray was an attack in depth after all, but what *kind* of attack?

"Anything from LTN-1?"

"Negative."

As the first link in a chain of security outposts, the station was heavily armed and defended by three battlecruisers. Why didn't the Krans choose to take it out? If their intention was to neutralize the transport portal, why go after LTN-2? She could not comprehend their thinking, which also concerned her, but she'd been concerned ever since getting command of LTN-2, a fast track to her own cruiser, something she'd yearned for ever since deciding to join the Orieli Space Arm. Put on the prospective commanding officer list was an honor in itself and a sign of Orieli Space Command's approval of her abilities and potential. So far, she had not done anything to disappoint that trust.

"Detach VI coupling."

She issued a mental order and blinked hard as the link with the computer severed and reality crashed into her senses, revealing the lounge around her. She could manage the current situation from her couch without having to be physically in Mission Control, but as the station commander, her presence was mandatory. Cent Comp ran everything and would execute any engagement, but under her direction. In theory, there was no need to man any of the LTN stations, the computers well able to look after them in any scenario, but OSCOM had not become that sterile yet. Besides, scientific research programs helped keep everybody motivated. She straightened her dark indigo one-piece tunic and hurried toward the PT alcove. Turning, she clasped her hands behind her, projecting a recruiter's image of a competent officer, which amused her intensely.

"MC."

The aftereffect tingle faded and she swept her eyes around the spacious control room. The concave ceiling glowed dull red, reflecting the increased readiness of the station. She faced three full-dimensional interactive holoview displays projected above a curved console covered with flickering touch-sensitive color pads—backups should the virtual interface coupling and voice command links fail. In front of each four-kanampir-wide display was seated a watchstander in a broad reclining couch, monitoring his area of responsibility, ready to act as ordered. Set farther behind them were two command stations.

Taroptur Ghere turned his head and nodded as she took the right seat. Another competent officer, she thought approvingly. Young, still yet to gain experience—that's why he drew this assignment—his enthusiasm and infectious humor made up for any awkwardness. Liked by everyone, he needed to work on gaining respect, something only time and attention to duty would earn him. On reflection, she had not been all that different, now seemingly a lifetime ago.

"*Trailer* and *Marin* will close the triangle with the Kran cruisers in eight minutes and thirteen seconds, Da. If the *Daktars* maintain their heading, they'll never enter our effective engagement sphere. We're at condition three and ready to play. Interceptor nets are modulated and the scanner array is on active standby. Cent Comp is maneuvering the array to unmask the targets and keep them in line of sight."

Although the defensive screens made the small moon on which LTN-2 was built effectively invisible, making targeting the station more difficult for the Krans despite knowing its spatial location among the six other moons circling 013B, the large rocky planet looming above them, they were not invulnerable. Nevertheless, every tactical advantage counted. Long before the *Daktars* could come within firing range, the scanner grid array mounted outside the star's distortion field limit would provide covering fire in depth. Discovering the array's one-billion-ampir envelope had cost the Krans dearly and they learned to stay away. So why send only three ships, and why head for 013D?

"No other threats?" Renlow demanded, her voice even and pleasant. Everyone was apprehensive enough without her adding to the natural tension by appearing flustered.

"None detected, Da, but there is a possible problem,"

Ghere said and nodded at the tactical holoview display.

For a moment, she couldn't see it, and then frowned. The full-dimensional projection showed orbital paths of all planets, and right now 013D stood directly behind 013B, effectively occulted from the system's star and the orbiting scanner array. What significance that had, she could not say, but could not fight off the feeling something was very wrong. The *Daktars* would not place themselves behind the gas giant without an objective in mind, one designed not to make her happy.

Chin in hand, she stared at the displays and felt mounting uncertainty coil inside her.

Excitement slowly built in MC as the minutes dragged on interminably. Everyone waited to see what the Krans would do, unable to do anything else. They'd been through this before and were blooded, figuratively only, of course.

Just outside the gas giant's distortion limit, the *Daktars* dropped relational normal and stopped. Renlow leaned forward and stared at the alien ships holding position 650 million ampirs from her, comfortably out of the scanner grid's range. Almost immediately, each ship launched two projectiles at an estimated closure rate of nine times light speed, using Orieli measuring system. Whatever those things were, they would reach 013B in two minutes and sixty-six seconds—and it did not look like the scanner array would be able to intercept them when they *did* come within range, not with the massive barrier of 013B between it and the objects.

It became painfully clear why the Krans positioned themselves behind 013D.

Cent Comp anticipated the threat and moved the scanner grid below the planetary plane to bring its projectors into line of sight with the incoming missiles. Barely clearing the orbital path of 013B, it fired almost continuous bursts, leaving behind four tracks of vivid blue ionization decay as the deadly beams traversed the distance through subspace. It took a prodigious amount of energy to fire at such range, but the star to which the scanner grid was anchored provided an unlimited supply to power its quantum point singularity used to open an interdimensional rift, the scanner's actual energy source.

Apprehensive, not certain how missiles of all things, no matter how fast or type of warhead they mounted, could threaten her, Renlow exhaled softly as the array obliterated four of the incoming objects. Two missiles managed to evade and continued their headlong rush toward 013B. Whether LTN-2's modulated interceptor net confused one or it could not maintain target lock due to the growing gravitational density induced by 013B's mass as it reached the planet's distortion limit, a forced collapse of its drive caused it to drop into normal space and it detonated instantly in a sphere of white radiance as LTN-2's layered defenses took it out. The last missile closed with the orbiting moon on which LTN-2 was built and spontaneously exploded.

Even as the deadly exchange took place, the *Daktars* were shifting position, moving above the planetary plane to bring themselves behind 013B again, blindsiding the scanner array. Six more projectiles streaked toward LTN-2. In the narrow window where the Kran ships fired and the missiles entered its acquisition cone, the scanner array reduced three to molecular dust, but three managed to get into 013B's shadow. Two detonated as they entered the planet's distortion limit, but the remaining one found the moon.

Not overly concerned that a single missile represented a credible threat to her station, Renlow watched it impact the moon's secondary interceptor net in a brilliant display of slithering discharges. Some fragments survived, hurling hypervelocity debris against the primary net, only to flare into incandescence. A tremor ran through her feet as the station rocked under the strike. Whatever hit her, she could not see how a few fragments could cause a tremor. Even if the missile itself detonated against the surface, such bombardment was not a threat unless one of those infernal things struck LTN-2 directly. The missile's nine times light speed came as a shock, but apart from scattering some rocks, even an antimatter warhead would be ineffective against her.

In the tactical plot, she watched *Trailer* and *Marin* close with the *Daktars*, still undetected. They'll sweep away the threats and life could return to normal.

The Orieli Sardan-built *Tangar*-class battlecruiser had an effective range of 300,000 ampirs. The ship could project a maximum of 320 TeV in almost continuous single or variable bursts of up to twenty-four milliseconds. Saturated with that much energy, matter was literally torn apart into its constituent quarks as the binding forces were released.

The Kran *Daktars* were caught completely unprepared when the two Orieli ships dropped normal critically close to the gas giant's distortion limit and fired into them from point-blank range. They concentrated their fire on the larger trailing segment of the leading Kran ship and internal explosions broke the segment from its forward component. An instant later, a pencil-thin blue-white spear of light shot through the opposite sides of the hull and faded as the quantum singularity power grid failed, which left the segment drifting. The severed forward component drifted lifelessly.

The two remaining *Daktars* responded with intense fire, using the decaying residual tracks from the Orieli ships fire as targeting guides, but the layered interceptor nets kept out the deadly beams. A second Kran ship was disabled and the third did not wait to share the fate of its consorts. In a flash of white scintillation, it transited into subspace and fled. *Marin* transited immediately and streaked after it.

Another severe tremor rocked LTN-2 and Renlow grabbed the armrests, not liking what was happening. A second missile hit? How could a mere missile generate such a disturbance?

"Cent Comp? Analysis!"

"A gravitational instability locus is forming around the secondary net impact point," the computer announced and displayed a graphical image in the holoview plot. It looked like a twisted sink into which the force lines of the two defense screens were wound, pulling in surrounding moon matter. Renlow stared at the image and felt her face drain. She was looking at a singularity interference point, which could not be possible. Another prolonged tremor shook the station as the moon's structure fractured and deformed under intolerable stresses. The secondary net failed and the ceiling immediately flashed pulsing orange.

"Emergency evacuation procedure now in effect!" Cent Comp blared. "Emergency evacuation procedure now in effect!"

Renlow understood what happened, although she did not comprehend how it was done. Her station faced mortal danger. She bellowed an order to the three watchstanders.

"Out!"

They did not need urging and scrambled toward the two PT alcoves behind her. She turned and watched as they entered and vanished. When they were gone, she jerked her thumb at Ghere. Alone, facing an imminent loss of her command, she cast a glance around the control room. Sidetracked for a moment, she wondered how the incident would look on her record.

"Confirm evacuation complete," she demanded to make sure, forming the words mentally.

"All forty-six personnel extracted," the computer declared.

Satisfied that everyone was safe, she stepped into the alcove and reality changed. She opened her eyes and found herself on an RV/6 dart's flight deck, already launching. Without hesitation, she walked out of the PT alcove and slipped into the front couch. Looking somewhat uncertain, no longer totally confident, Ghere monitored the tactical station beside her, the only other crewmember required on the command deck of the small ship, his demeanor grim, the joviality gone.

"Just like a drill," she told him softly. He gave a small smile in return.

"VI enable," she snapped and the onboard computer linked with her through the virtual interface. Her station might be destroyed momentarily, but she needed to maintain an image of total control even when everything around her was chaos.

Remnants of the primary and secondary interceptor net screens shielding the moon were torn apart, white arcs discharging along the force lines. Although the station below her was still intact, on the starboard horizon, the moon's distorted surface crumpled and caved in on itself. A hellish blue glow made the stars beyond ripple and waver. She switched quickly between sensor modes, relieved to see two darts stationed on her. They all made it out safely.

"Open a channel to *Trailer*."

Almost immediately, Karhide Ari-Ann's face solidified in her mind.

"Da, I'm going to lose the station, but we managed to get away in one piece."

"KSN-013B3 is breaking up, Opturkarh," Ari-Ann replied heavily. "It is literally collapsing into a gravitational hole, and there is a growing energy field building around it. Whatever hit you is swallowing the moon. Without knowing how far the effect can reach, I suggest you put some distance from it and stand by for retrieval."

If the phenomenon was some type of point singularity, would it continue to suck in matter and grow, establishing a genuine subspace anomaly locus? In such an event, the rocky planet hovering above her could itself be in danger. It explained why the Krans made this type of attack. Unable to get close enough to prosecute her with their ships because of the scanner array, those cursed missiles of theirs gave them a potent stand-off capability, which they exploited exquisitely. No one said the Krans weren't smart.

"I read you, Da. Anything from LTN-1?"

Ari-Ann frowned. "I've lost contact with them and its three pickets."

Renlow sagged in the couch and pursed her lips. So, the Krans did not neglect the station after all. A mess. Fifteen minutes, that's all it took to wipe her out, and maybe LTN-1 as well. She did not think it possible. Perilian Sector Command had much to reconsider; glad it wasn't her problem.

Did all the LTN-1 personnel make it off safely? She had a friend there. Nothing romantic, Tuval was just someone she felt comfortable with. Not dashing or brilliant, or anything, he was simply nice to be around. She would not mind if their friendship turned into something more serious, but there was no hurry. The few times they'd been together were pleasant. He had an easy way about him, completely unselfconscious, with a droll sense of humor she loved. Now, that connection might never blossom, and she wondered if he got out. A future that once had possibilities might now remain only a passing dream.

"LTN-3 reports receiving fire from unknown type of projectiles, presumably the same things used against you," Ari-Ann added, his features drawn. They were all having a very bad day. Looking unbearably weary, he sighed. "And I've just lost contact with *Marin*."

"Thank you, Da," she said softly and cut the link, suspecting she knew what happened. Did *Marin* fall to a Kran missile?

She took in the visual sensory input and watched the image of the small moon receding behind her flare as blue radiance enveloped it. She could vividly imagine the torturous grinding of rock as the moon was consumed. Did they scream in agony even when there was no atmosphere, and no one could hear it? Abruptly, in a flash of blinding white light it vanished, leaving behind total blackness. Sensors did not detect a residual gravitational sink. Whatever swallowed her station was not a point singularity, that being the dubious good news.

She glanced at Ghere, but had no strength left to give him.

Tense, shock setting in, she waited for *Trailer* to close.

Guardians of Shadow

* * *

With the massive wall of the Karina Nebula splitting the sky on the port side—Terr had to remember to use Orieli nomenclature—*Tapal* slowed to half standard boost, the white star in front of it still merely a bright point among the profusion of other stars. Hooked into the VI, he marveled at the glory of creation as he stared at the twisting columns and buttresses of dense gas, lit from within by young stars and ghostly glows from pockets of condensing matter, which in eons to come would give rise to new light and perhaps new life. He'd seen images of the nebula taken by Serrll survey ships, but they did not convey the sheer size and magnitude of the impenetrable barrier. Nature certainly displayed some truly awesome wonders.

The system they were approaching still young, not yet a billion years old, and still in the process of planetary formation. According to Cent Comp, apart from three gas giants sweeping up planitesimals from the outer reaches of the system, twelve protoplanets of various sizes traveling in chaotic orbits were competing for dominance. Eventually the larger would swallow their smaller rivals in cataclysmic collisions until only three or four inner planets remained and the system would stabilize. Right now, everything was bombarded by remnants of planetary formation, leaving the infant planets glowing red from impact craters and heaving, belching volcanoes.

A living stellar laboratory, the system was a scientific marvel and a terrific tourist curiosity, but hardly a place to set up housekeeping. Yet that's exactly what the Orieli did, placing LTN-3 on one of the smaller planetoids, protecting the minute world barely 1,500 ampirs in diameter from wildly orbiting remnants with powerful screens. In something like two-and-a-half thousand years—a blink of cosmic time—the planetoid would collide with its more massive neighbor when their orbits eventually intersected, but that was something comfortably far away in the future to worry the short-lived creatures who occupied it now.

Were the Orieli interfering with the natural development of the new star system? Terr did not think so. Nothing anyone could possibly do would make the slightest difference to the eventual composition of this star's planetary members. The forces involved were simply unimaginable compared to the puny powers of man. The Orieli could destroy entire worlds, but they were powerless to shape them.

"Tactical caution," the housekeeping computer announced, replacing the scene of the Karina in Terr's mind with a grid overlay of the system. "Two Celi-Kran *Daktar*-class cruisers and two *Sandar*-class battlecruisers detected. Distance, two point-three light-years. Closure rate, six light-years per hour. Intercept in thirty minutes under current flight parameters."

Although the message was not directed to him, hooked into the command net, he received it—an unwelcome development.

"Detach VI coupling," Terr ordered immediately and blinked hard as another reality shifted around him.

Rit!

On the couch beside him, shapely legs curled beneath her, Teena looked up from the holographic display she was using to indoctrinate herself about the Orieli; a lot of material to cover, as Terr knew from his sessions, but necessary research if they were to undertake their mission effectively.

"Anything the matter?"

"I don't know. Probably nothing."

"What is it?" she demanded more sharply, putting on her official analyst face.

"Four Kran ships just entered the system." Not something she would relish hearing, but she had a right to know. Besides, it wasn't as if he could keep it secret. He stood up and pulled down the front of his working grays. "I'm going to PFC. You stay here, my pet."

She frowned prettily, her large green eyes darkening. "Krans here? But you said—"

"I know. It shouldn't be possible. I wouldn't worry, though. LTN-3's pickets will take care of them. We'll be through the portal and heading for Perilia within the hour."

She smiled impishly, a dimple forming on her right cheek. "Then why are you looking so worried?"

He paused and brushed her long hair. "I'm not. Just considering the possibilities."

"Unpleasant ones, judging by your expression." She uncurled her legs and stood up. "I don't like this, Terr. We weren't supposed to face any Krans. Our job is to investigate the Orieli, not get involved in their war."

"Right now, the two are one and the same," he said sternly, not liking it much either.

"This is not our war!"

"It might be."

He walked to the PT alcove set into the lounge wall and stepped in. When he turned, her eyes were fixed on him and her mouth tight, but he had no time for an argument. Nevertheless, he could not help feeling he was somehow running out on her.

"PFC."

As the aftereffect tingle passed, he strode out of the alcove and automatically swept his eyes around the ellipsoid of Primary Flight Control, taking in information from ceiling-high full-dimensional interactive holoview status displays running the length of Command level. A protruding platform curved along the long axis halfway up the chamber wall. Swivel-couches faced repeater readouts from operations stations below.

Operations was some three kanampirs—using the Orieli unit of measurement—below the command platform. A flattened bowl, its inner surface mounted one continuous backup console above which were projected three-kanampir-high holoview ship status images.

On his left, two watchkeeping officers briefly looked up from their repeaters. On his right, three couches were set against the curved wall. Color-coded pads covered the broad armrests. Seated in the center couch, Arlon Dee saw him and grinned. His pale pink tongue ran across fleshy lips.

"Come to watch the excitement?" the tall Cetan demanded pleasantly in perfect Serrll interlingua, his deep voice resonating. Dark brown skin covered a very reasonable solid, angular human face. His red eyes were cold, with an impersonal touch, eyes that had seen everything and understood everything. At least it was an image the alien projected. Projected or not, Terr found him somewhat intimidating. A spacefaring history of over twelve thousand years lay behind those eyes. A wealth of knowledge also lay behind them, but was it tempered by wisdom? One of the things his mission was supposed to find out.

In the right couch, Opturkarh Tavac, *Tapal's* executive officer, nodded to him with a slightly vacant look of one hooked into the virtual interface. A Zaronian, just short of average height, his skin had a beautiful shade of blue-green, growing black around the eyes and powerful mouth. Somewhat distant and reserved, Terr liked his sardonic sense of humor. In their fourteen-day journey, there had not been much time for familiarity.

He sank into the left couch, not bothering with formalities. Although detached to the Diplomatic Branch, he held the rank of Master Scout in the Serrll Scout Fleet, equivalent to a karhide. Arlon Dee did not stand on formalities either, or was simply making allowances for Terr's provincial attitude, and probably too sophisticated to care. Right now, Terr didn't care either.

"You couldn't keep me away, although I never expected to see those things here."

"Neither did I, but there they are. An interesting start to your mission, wouldn't you say?"

Terr chuckled, although he did not care for the words. "One I could have done without. Do the Krans mount frequent incursions? I thought LTN-1 and LTN-2 were there to make sure none got this far."

"They blind jumped through a transport portal," Arlon Dee declared.

Terr stared. "You mean, it is the first time they used this tactic?"

"Sensor logs indicate the *Daktar* that hit Devon 3-VL4 may have done the same thing. Not a pleasant development, and raises many questions about their technology."

Terr frowned and rubbed a scar above his left temple. He wanted answers to a few questions of his own. "But with such capability—"

"All the worlds on our side of the Karina are vulnerable and the Line Tracking Net stations are tactically useless," Arlon said harshly without any trace of bitterness. He was merely stating a fact. "Setlan Eleven, Kardush, Heplon, they're all exposed if the Krans decide to look for us there, and those systems are much closer to the inner galactic arm where we suspect those infernal things come from. We expended considerable resources building the LTN stations for no tactical gain at all."

"Perhaps not. The Krans may be able to jump out, but to withdraw to their space still means using a conventional transition drive. Getting home could take them a long time, wherever home is. Not the best way to wage war."

"Laying waste to our border systems might be worth the price, and perhaps that's what the Krans intended—lure us into a false sense of confidence."

It would also divert attention away from the Serrll, Terr told himself coldly. Not wishing disaster to befall the Orieli, but looking at the situation objectively, they were far more capable handling the Krans. Were those things to confront the Serrll anytime soon, he feared destruction on an unimaginable scale, unless the Orieli extended its protective umbrella over them, something not altogether certain. From what he'd learned, factions within the Klanina Caucus wanted to seal the Karina breach and pull back, leaving the Serrll to its own devices. Strategically sound, although unlikely in the current political climate. Were the Krans to launch a strike against Setlan Eleven or some other border system like Arlon said, and perhaps seek to establish a launch point for strikes deeper into Orieli territory, such a withdrawal might very well happen.

He glanced at the mainframe tactical plot. Three orange dots were moving to intercept the oncoming intruders, but at the current closure rate, the Krans would reach the inner system before the pickets were able to engage. Given the awesome power of the Orieli Space Arm warships, he could not imagine the Krans getting close enough to LTN-3 to do any damage. Wouldn't they understand their position as well? It worried him.

"Why reveal this capability now?"

Arlon Dee shrugged. "Prelude to a prolonged thrust against our stations?"

Terr did not need reminding. Ever since Karhide Zor-Ell's survey ship five years ago tripped a dormant beacon, the Krans were looking for the intruder—and found the Serrll instead. Even they found the Karina impenetrable, denying them access into Orieli space. As he told Teena, this made it a Serrll war, hopefully not one they would have to fight anytime soon.

"Whatever they're up to, your pickets should be able to dispose of the unwelcome visitors."

Arlon Dee did not say anything. In any engagement, the uncertainty principle had a large say in what happens.

"You have a family, Karhide?"

"A wife and two grown daughters. I missed seeing them grow up." The alien stared hard at Terr. "Don't let that happen to you and Teena."

"It almost did," Terr said softly. "We became too comfortable with each other and drifted apart without knowing it. I allowed us to drift apart."

"Sometimes, life's priorities can get blurred."

"Operational caution. LTN-2 advises they are under attack by three *Daktar*-class cruisers. LTN-3 Mission Control has initiated condition three. Status. Ship at condition one. Interceptor net now modulated at full EMCON."

In a way, Terr was glad for the interruption, his thoughts straying into corridors best kept shut. He was still repairing the damage of his thoughtlessness.

"Very well," Arlon acknowledged bleakly. "Initiate condition three." He glanced at Terr. "Perhaps now, we'll find out if our pickets are up to the job."

The domed ceiling above PFC changed from soft blue-gray to pulsing red, accompanied by increased inter-deck comms. Modulating *Tapal's* interceptor net was a prudent tactical response, rendering the ship invisible to Kran sensors. However, Terr did not relish the prospect of going into action even if the risk was minimal, which in this case it wasn't. Clearly, the Krans seem to have mounted a coordinated strike against the Orieli, not something that gave him a warm fuzzy. But if they were serious about taking out the transport portal and LTN-3, why send only four ships? That little piece of datum worried him.

"Condition three commencing. Primary fire control active. Auxiliary Flight Control active. Interceptor net now at level three. Status. Condition three active." The ceiling faded to soft red. Two additional watchstanders manned operations stations and the interactive holoview displays rippled through a cascade of tactical images.

For a vessel not a warship, the increased readiness status made Terr wonder what a real fighting platform was capable of. Even so, he would love to command a ship like *Tapal*, but Arlon's words troubled him.

As he stared at the mainframe tactical plot, coordinated strike or not, he did not understand what the Kran ships hoped to achieve, or what was their exit strategy. Powerful as they might be, they could not match themselves against *Ballard*, an Orieli *Nasor*-class assault monster, even without its two accompanying *Tangar*-class battlecruisers. With their screens modulated, the Krans would not even be aware of their presence until they were hit. The alien horrors were a lot of things, but from what he'd learned, they were not suicidal. He looked searchingly at Arlon.

"This doesn't feel right, Karhide. Those things are up to something."

Arlon pulled at his chin as his tongue went around his lips. "I tend to agree, but until they make their move, we can only wait and watch. Anyway, *Ballard* will be in range long before the Krans can engage. The station and the portal are in no immediate danger."

An assault ship on the prowl was good, but Terr still did not feel reassured as he followed the four blue blips crawl unwaveringly toward LTN-3. The Krans surely knew the station was protected, but it did not seem to bother them. He sensed someone beside him and turned…and his heart lifted. Smiling, towering over him by a full head, the Wanderer reached with his hand palm up and touched Terr's chest. Something flowed between them and he was reassured. After his display of power at Devon 3-VL4's moon, which shocked him as much as it did everybody else, he had seen the stricken look on his brother's face and did not know if Death now held a barrier between them. Terr had done something, which according to the Discipline should not be possible for a level-two adept. On the way to LTN-3, they spoke briefly, but both avoided the moment when the air needed to clear between them. Barrier or not, his heart sang at the sight of his brother.

Dharaklin's reddish hair framed a long, narrow face before it spilled across his shoulders. He was thin and wiry like all desert nomads. The yellowish skin was drawn tight over the bony ridges of his face. The orange eyes with their vertical red slits were warm with understanding.

"Sankri," he said, his voice a rumble from the sandy deeps.

Terr stood, raised his arm and touched his brother. "Nightwings."

There was no need for words; that would come later. It was enough being together, to be one. Dhar nodded and turned to Arlon Dee.

"Karhide."

Terr noted the Cetan watching the exchange with obvious curiosity, but was intuitive enough not to intrude into the moment. Arlon tapped a glowing yellow prism on his armrest and another couch slid out from the wall.

"Make yourself comfortable, Opturkarh," he invited, using Dhar's honorary OSA rank.

Terr knew Dhar secretly relished his recent promotion to First Scout, although he would never admit it openly. According to the *Saftara*, display of pride is hollow indulgence. The problem with the Wanderers, Terr mused, they lacked a sense of fun. Then again, the harsh life in the Saffal gave them little opportunity for joviality.

Dhar eased himself down and allowed the couch to mold itself around him. "I was hooked into the VI when Cent Comp issued the alert."

"So was I," Terr said.

Dhar studied the mainframe plot and frowned. "I don't understand what the Kran ships are doing."

"And neither does anybody else," Terr agreed as he observed the Orieli ships close the intercept triangle.

Not unexpectedly, one point-two billion ampirs out, the Kran ships dropped normal and the *Sandars* swung toward the transport portal, keeping it between themselves and the scanner grid. The attack tactic slowly became clear. Still, he could not see how such a move would help them reach the portal or the station. The scanner grid's defensive envelope should be impenetrable, that's what he knew anyway.

In orbit around Tureen's Star, the array maneuvered to keep the oncoming targets in line of sight and still be in a position to cover LTN-3. *Ballard* maintained closure on the *Sandars*, a more credible threat, leaving the smaller cruisers to the *Tangars*.

Terr waited, expecting to see the Kran ships blasted into iron filings at any moment. The *Sandars* maintained their separation from the array and began launching salvos of two projectiles at the transport portal, the sixteen missiles traveling at a staggering nine times light speed. Flight time, just over five minutes. Immediately, the two *Daktars* also launched, targeting LTN-3 with almost identical flight times, the portal positioned one hundred thousand ampirs from the station. Missiles in an age of energy weapons? A rush of prickles along his skin made his palms sweaty as a sense of deep foreboding overtook him. Those things must be more than conventional warhead missiles.

"Cent Comp, analysis!" Arlon Dee snapped at once, clearly concerned.

"Unknown, Karhide. LTN-2 reports they're under attack from same type of objects. One moment...Operational caution. LTN-3 advises KSN-013B3 was struck by a projectile which released an interdimensional disruption field, collapsing the moon's structure. Evacuation protocol was initiated."

The situation appeared to be deteriorating and Terr looked hard at *Tapal's* commander. It explained why the Kran ships did not need to approach within the scanner array's acquisition envelope to launch their attack. Despite the colossal closure rate, it still gave the array plenty of time to neutralize the missiles once they got within its one billion ampirs range. It sent streaks of energy through subspace at the oncoming threats, leaving behind blue-white lines of ionization as the emission residuals decayed into normal space.

Two white blips came uncomfortably close to the transport portal before they were obliterated. By now, the

Sandars were positioned behind the portal and launched another salvo. Aware of the threat, the scanner array moved to maintain line of sight and maintained fire at missiles targeting LTN-3. Clearly intending to compromise the array's tactical response capability, the *Daktars* also launched another salvo.

Opturkarh Tavac slowly looked up. "Looks like the gunk is about to hit."

Terr smiled at the obvious, but it wasn't with humor, his eyes on Arlon Dee. "Singularity generators, Karhide? Is that possible?"

The Cetan pursed his lips and shook his head. "I doubt it. Although the Krans use a quantum point singularity to power their ships, the energy required to generate a gravitational sink able to collapse a moon would be prodigious, not a package one can fit into a missile."

"Then what are those things?"

"An interdimensional interface?" Dhar ventured, his voice heavy. "Like your power source."

When Terr first met Zor-Ell five years ago, he learned that the Orieli also utilized a quantum point instability, but not as a direct power source. Its energy was used to induce a rip in the fabric of the multi-dimensional spacetime continuum, allowing it to momentarily fluctuate in place. The resulting energy discharge harvested conventionally, although not so conventional to him. However, it gave the bulging brains at the Bureau of Technology and Development on Captal something new to scratch their heads. The Orieli Personal Transport system also presented a theoretical and engineering problem, utilizing one of the closed dimensions, which neatly sidestepped traditional difficulties associated with matter transfer, requiring an object to be destroyed during patterns analysis, and then reassembled at another location.

"Perhaps, but whatever they are, the portal is in trouble."

Terr looked at the mainframe plot and nodded in agreement. It was eerie being a spectator to an unfolding disaster. By entering the engagement area, he wondered if *Tapal* now faced danger.

The scanner array easily picked off most of the incoming missiles, but two were now in line of sight with the portal and immune from the array's fire. The white dots merged with the pulsing orange square of the portal. A ring of energy flared around the portal. It only took a minute for the square to shrink and vanish.

Terr turned and looked at Dhar's impassive face. The Orieli were stranded on this side of the Karina nebula until a new portal could be built. They were still able to traverse the breach through the enormous gas cloud they discovered years ago, but it presented a dangerous option, since the rift appeared to be closing as the gas streams shifted.

Not counting the nineteen hundred occupied systems in the Orieli Cluster twelve thousand light-years above the galactic plane, thirteen hundred unified systems lay beyond the Karina Shield Nebula, as the Orieli knew the Moanar gas cloud, one of nine super gas filaments girthing the outer galactic core; a 6,800 light-year-long impenetrable barrier. A staggering collection of disparate cultures compared to Serrll's 247 systems. Normally, transiting through any nebula is not a problem, basically a vacuum, but given the Moanar's average thickness of almost four hundred light-years and its unusual composition, the mass profile invariably begins to interfere with the ship's shield grid as it penetrates the cloud, causing the field precursor to decay and collapse. Forced to drop normal, the surrounding mass prevented transition into faster than light speed and the ship is stuck, as Serrll surveys found to their cost.

Loss of the portal was a severe tactical blow for the Orieli, and his mission may have effectively ended before it began. Right now, he was not thinking about his mission.

"Cent Comp? Maximum boost for LTN-3. Position *Tapal* between the station and the *Sandars*," Arlon ordered, which made Terr wince, not relishing the prospect of going into combat.

"Acknowledged."

Ballard saw what the Krans did to the portal and accelerated its closure rate with the *Sandars*. It might not be able to do much against the projectiles, but it could certainly deal with the Kran ships that fired them. The *Tangars* were also closing with the two *Daktars*.

With the portal destroyed, the Kran ships coordinated their attack, launching a salvo at LTN-3, maintaining their position outside the scanner array's acquisition envelope. Terr noted the frown of frustration on Arlon's face and sympathized. He could not see what the Orieli could do to neutralize the threat, except hope the Krans would run out of those infernal missiles.

Even as *Tapal* maneuvered, it was not clear how it could counter something traveling at nine times light speed, and it had to counter in normal space in order to engage the Kran ships, also normal. In subspace, the missiles were tactically useless, given the speeds used in transit. *Tapal's* 250-thousand-ampirs acquisition envelope would at best allow it to get off one burst before the missile flashed past or struck. If they got too close to one of those things, it could interfere with the scanner grid's firing solution.

However, Terr's opinion was not asked. He was merely a passenger, albeit a very concerned one. When he agreed to head one part of the Serrll cultural exchange mission to investigate the Orieli culture, a prelude to establishing full diplomatic and trade relations, he had not bargained on confronting the Krans, certainly not with Teena on board. He wondered if she was also watching the developing confrontation through the VI. Probably, and he could guess her outrage, but there was no time to indulge her, not right now. Nobody planned this to happen, except the Krans, of course.

A *Tangar* dropped normal close to a *Daktar* and opened fire. The Kran ship immediately launched a missile. With no

Stefan Vučak

time to evade, the *Tangar* was struck and its interceptor grid
flared in bright discharges. The battlecruiser immediately
stopped, dead in space.

"Operational caution. OSA *Rangen* advises they're aban-
doning ship and taking to escape modules," the computer announced remorselessly.

Terr bit his lip. If a *Tangar*-class warship could be dispatched this easily, he doubted the wisdom of sending *Tapal*
into the fray. Although armed, it was not a fighting platform,
and its defense screens were not designed for prolonged combat.

"Karhide—"

"I appreciate the tactical situation, Terr, and the diplomatic
nature of your mission, but I must honor the threat...Cent
Comp? Head for the nearest *Daktar*."

"Acknowledged."

In the plot, the surviving *Tangar* resumed its base course to
close with the *Daktars*. Terr understood the reasoning immediately. With the transport portal destroyed and their inability to
counter the missiles, the Orieli were going after the launch platforms. Eliminate the enemy warships and you eliminate the
missile threat. The scanner array would protect LTN-3 as best
it could, which it seemed to be doing well enough, having destroyed every missile targeting the planetoid. However important the station, trading an Orieli warship for its sixty-four
personnel was not good arithmetic. If necessary, it could always
be rebuilt.

He glanced at Arlon and realized the Karhide was hooked
into the VI. Too much went on to exercise control using
holoview displays only, interactive or not. He wondered what
exchange Arlon was having with the other Orieli ships and
LTN-3, *Tapal's* maneuver far too coordinated for an individual
act.

Ballard closed with one of the *Sandars* and dropped normal,
which momentarily exposed its position to the Kran ship, and

opened fire. Maneuvering, *Ballard's* interceptor net fully modulated, the Kran ship could not hope to escape. About to be destroyed, it fired two missiles at the assault ship along its residuals tracks. Dismayed, Terr watched as one of the missiles detonated against *Ballard's* secondary net. A cloud of escape modules immediately fled the stricken starship even as it was consumed within a gravitational point. The orange dot faded and vanished. It died, but it claimed the Kran ship with it.

From a seemingly overwhelming position, the Orieli were now critically exposed, with only a single battlecruiser against three powerful Kran units. Undeterred, Arlon Dee kept *Tapal* on its course, and Terr frowned. Logically, with the portal destroyed, the Orieli ships should withdraw within the scanner array's acquisition envelope, daring the Kran ships to go after them. It made little sense to engage the Krans in an environment where they held the tactical advantage.

Not good. Not good at all.

Terr glanced at his brother and saw the same concern reflected in Dhar's eyes.

"Sankri…"

"I know. We're about to be hammered."

In range of a *Daktar*, the surviving *Tangar* engaged. The *Daktar* immediately fired one of its missiles. Although the Orieli ship was effectively shielded from sensor detection, its emission residuals were not and the missile used them to track against. Terr gripped the armrest and wondered if he was about to witness another disaster. Aware of the threat, the *Tangar* maneuvered, causing the missile to lose lock and overshoot. After a few seconds, failing to find its target, the missile detonated.

The Orieli ship positioned itself behind the Kran vessel and resumed firing. In a series of explosions that tore it apart, the Kran vanished in a blinding detonation, which sent huge sections of hull hurtling into space. Out of the debris cloud, a missile streaked toward the *Tangar*. The ship made a desperate move to evade just as the missile reached it. Terr saw a rippling flash, but could not tell what happened.

"Operational caution. OSA *Latva* advises they lost interceptor net integrity and are engaging the remaining *Daktar*."

"Cent Comp, order *Latva* to break off. *Tapal* will engage the *Daktar*."

"Acknowledged."

Although more powerful, without fully operational defense screens, it made no tactical sense for *Latva* to attempt prosecuting the remaining *Daktar*, especially if the Kran ship mounted more missiles. It certainly could not hope to face two threats, with the *Sandar* closing on its consort even now.

The *Latva's* commander understood the tactical situation and maintained position. Terr wondered why it did not go after the escape modules heading for LTN-3, when the answer became obvious. If *Latva* were destroyed, those modules would go with it. Protected by the scanner array, they were better off landing at LTN-3.

Terr turned to Arlon Dee. "How did he evade?"

The Cetan's expression was grim. "*Latva* pulled off a smart move. It pulsed its secondary interceptor net at the last second and dropped the primary one. When the missile struck, the gravitational sink couldn't latch onto the ship. Not enough to snare it anyway."

Terr watched the situation unfold. Even with the power of Death in his hands, he felt helpless. What he did to the Kran ship at Devon was extraordinary, but could he hope to do it again? There, he was forced to act through a complex set of emotional reactions that surprised him as it did everyone else. As *Tapal* closed with the *Daktar*, he simply did not feel the rage and sense of evil to act. If he loosed Death in a moment of hubris, he could very well seriously damage PFC without achieving anything.

He clenched his fists and gritted his teeth. Unable to help, he watched the situation unfold. It looked like the Orieli would need to fight the battle alone. Destiny or a lesson to be learned?

"Cent Comp? Issue an advisory abandon ship," Arlon commanded. "All non-combat personnel to their assigned escape modules."

"Acknowledged."

Terr sat up with a start as an awful realization struck him. "Teena!"

He was about to leap to his feet when his brother's powerful hand held him down.

"There is nothing you can do for her now, Sankri."

Arlon glanced at him. "He's right, and you two don't belong in PFC either."

Terr wanted to rush to her and comfort her, make sure she was safe, but he understood that she was safe enough. Safe as anyone can be in a fast deteriorating situation.

"If you don't mind, Karhide, I'd like to see this through to the end."

After a searching moment, Arlon nodded. "Very well. Cent Comp? Target the *Daktar*. Autonomous tactical control."

Giving the ship's computer tactical authority made sense. Human reactions simply were not fast enough in a millisecond environment.

The Kran *Daktar* closed on the exposed *Latva* when *Tapal* dropped normal to engage, but could do nothing to avoid the raking fire that traversed its bulbous insect-like rear segment. Its screens flared in blue-white discharges, and backsurges licked the exposed hull. Plating melted, showing gaping skeletal frames. The *Daktar* fired and *Tapal* trembled violently under the bombardment. A brilliant sphere of white light suddenly consumed most of the Kran's rear segment and its screens failed. It immediately fired a missile. There was sufficient separation between the two ships to enable the precursor field to form and the missile transited. Its flight time was instantaneous to cover the 200 thousand ampirs to *Tapal*. The missile detonated as it struck the secondary interceptor net screen. A blanket of blue radiance crawled along the screen's force lines, sucking all energy as space itself distorted. Arlon bit his lip, but didn't hesitate.

"Cent Comp! Issue abandon ship!" He glanced at Terr and pointed at the two PT alcoves set in the wall. "Time for you to go."

In Operations, watchstanders were already scrambling to get out. Arlon Dee glanced at Tavac and stood up.

"Tactical caution. An emission trace from a Fernai vessel detected one point-two light-years in our rear starboard quadrant."

Terr looked sharply at Arlon. Who the hell were the Fernai?

"An encounter we had five years ago," Arlon said. "I'll fill you in later."

"Caution. The *Sandar* has picked up five escape modules and is preparing to transit. The damaged *Daktar* is pulling away."

A clawing dread churned Terr's stomach, which made him wince with pain. Teena! Horror in his eyes, he turned to Dhar.

"What are the odds, my brother?" Dhar rumbled as he stood up. A violent shudder ran through the ship.

"Move!" Arlon barked.

Feet heavy, Terr made for one of the PT alcoves. It was irrational, but he knew those mindless machines had taken her. He could not explain it, but he couldn't shake off the feeling as he stepped into the alcove. He should have gone to her!

Rit!

A moment of cutting cold and blackness, he found himself in a large, brightly lit capsule. He stepped out of the alcove and Dhar appeared. Terr shook off the momentary aftereffect dizziness and sat down on one of the padded benches that ran along both sides of the cabin. In quick succession, Arlon appeared and immediately walked toward the pilot's couch positioned next to Tavac's. Cent Comp launched the module. Terr did not feel the rush down the tube, but suddenly, they were in space. Arlon Dee was already at the controls.

"Cent Comp, status?"

"Escape modules in sections four-eleven to nineteen-eight are disabled due to ship's mass collapsing into an interdimensional anomaly. Personnel distributed among remaining modules. No casualties."

Under abandon ship protocols, Cent Comp controlled where someone would end up when entering a PT alcove. It saved people having to scramble to a particular escape module—provided there was power to operate the PT system. Buried deep within the ship, it would take a catastrophic detonation to damage the power core or the central housekeeping computer.

"Status of the Fernai vessel?"

"Approaching OSA *Latva's* position. Kran hostiles are withdrawing. Status. Transmitting technical information on the gravitational anomaly to LTN-3 and Perilian Sector—"

With transmission suddenly severed, Terr glanced at Dhar, not having to say anything. *Tapal* was gone, destroyed by whatever thing had swallowed the other ships. The bruising encounter with the Krans had left the Orieli badly battered. Two capital ships wiped out, another severely damaged, and probably lives lost as well, and he wasn't even counting possible losses at LTN-1 and LTN-2. Considering themselves secure behind the Line Tracking Net stations, the entire Orieli strategy to contain the Krans appeared to be in tatters. Until the Orieli developed an effective countermeasure response to the deadly projectiles, every station was vulnerable, as were its picket ships. And if the Krans became aware of the Serrll worlds and mounted a strike in force? He suspected there would be devastation on a horrible scale, as the Scout Fleet had nowhere near the capability of Orieli ships. It did not bear thinking about.

Right now, the possible loss of billions of lives did not concern him, his thoughts on only one life that mattered. The image of her lost sent him into panic, unable to think, but that was exactly what he could not afford to do. He must keep focused, evaluate the situation and get to her somehow. By sharing everything with her and what he did, he had not meant to expose her to danger or threatening her life. He was on a diplomatic fact-finding mission where the only danger she should have faced was ruining her figure through overindulgence at cocktail parties.

She was alive, he could tell, and kept him from working himself into a state.

Arlon Dee swiveled his couch and faced them, his tongue massaging his lips. "Although I'm not questioning our luck, I don't know why the Kran ships withdrew. We were beaten. The sudden appearance of the Fernai perhaps? There is no way to tell. Our visitor is waiting. For what, I cannot say. *Latva* is proceeding to recover *Tapal's* escape modules. Once done, they'll be coming after us." His face clouded. "I've taken inventory of all personnel. Thirty-eight were in the five modules taken by the Kran *Daktar*. Teena-raye was among them. I'm sorry, Terr."

Something cold materialized in his belly and Terr swallowed hard. He clenched his fists until the fingernails bit into his palms.

"Thanks for letting me know, Da." It was a hollow, trite thing to say, but he was running on automatic.

Alien monstrosities had torn from him everything he loved and his world had caved in around him. In a living nightmare, he hoped to wake up and find her beside him, smiling, her cheek dimpled, ready to come into his embrace. That something indefinable bonding them, the tenuous link between their souls, still there and gave him comfort. Until that link was broke, he would go after her with Death in his hands, no matter how long or where it took him.

Dhar reached across the space between them and touched his shoulder.

"Sankri…"

Terr covered the hand with his. "It's not over yet, my

54

brother."

* * *

The encounter with the *Daktar* left *Latva* carrying damage, mostly to its circuitry, and the autonomous repairs were already underway. Thankfully, she suffered no casualties. Assembled in her PFC, Arlon Dee and Bearn, *Latva's* unsmiling, heavyset commander, conferred. Given their grim expressions, Terr figured they had a lot to confer about, none of it pleasant.

The black tetragonal-bipyramid Fernai ship showed no sign of life as it hung 2,000 ampirs off their starboard quarter. It was not emitting and did not maintain any defensive screens Cent Comp could identify, although a fuzzy envelope of *something* surrounded the strange thing. At eighty-four thousand teridines, the vessel was large, equivalent to a *Nasor*-class assault ship.

"Never seen anything like it," Terr murmured to Dhar and shook his head, glad for the distraction, if for a moment. An alien contacts were always interesting, and it seemed another one for the Orieli as well. Despite his worry about Teena, he was curious to see how the Orieli would handle this—being masters of first contact procedures as it were.

"Something about that ship...tah, the gods will tell," Dhar said absently.

"A memory?"

"I don't know. Just a tale I heard as a child. Village stories."

Arlon Dee walked to them and stopped, studying the mainframe plot. "Unique design. One of our survey ships ran into one just like it five years ago when we transited the Karina."

Unique design indeed, Terr noted. "First time meeting someone superior, Karhide?"

Arlon stared at the plot, not say anything for a while, but his sliding tongue said it for him. Then, "No, no quite. A long time ago the old Concordiat sent survey ships to the adjacent

55

galactic arm. It's where we learned our limits. With the Fernai, we were warned off without incident." After a while, his features firmed and he was a commander again. "We'll try to raise them. You two can link into the VI and follow the proceedings."

Terr hooked into the interface, certain that more than a simple alien contact occurred in that distant past and he promised himself to check. With active spaceflight spanning many thousands of years, the Orieli must have seen a lot, clearly not all of it to their liking. Then again, given the galactic vastness, it would have been remarkable to find the Orieli masters of everything they saw.

"Fernai vessel, this is the Orieli Technic Union cruiser *Latva*. Please respond," the comms officer declared.

"Intruder alert!" Cent Comp announced immediately. "One alien lifeform in the Observation Deck."

Terr exchanged looks with Dhar and smiled. For a dramatic entrance, it was unequalled. The alien had style, but would the Orieli be amused, given they hadn't had much fun lately? And how did the alien manage to transfer through *Tapal's* interceptor net? A demonstration of superiority? Bearn turned, strode past them wearing a scowl and entered a PT alcove. He at least did not see any humor in it. Arlon gathered Terr with his eyes.

"You two come with me."

The Observation Deck, smaller than *Tapal's*, was brightly lit and Terr blinked as he stepped out of the alcove. From floor to ceiling, the transparent hull allowed harsh white light to flood in from the system's primary. Soft couches and sofas were arranged seemingly haphazardly around low tables, screened by discreetly positioned broad-leafed plants. In the background, he heard running water. The deck emitted a soft dark green radiance. Combined with the slowly shifting patterns in the deep blue ceiling, the ambient atmosphere was tranquil, but Terr doubted that anyone was relaxed just now.

Bearn and Arlon Dee faced a stocky figure, powerful and

relatively short, about 160 minampirs as far as Terr could tell, clad in single piece maroon uniform with four slanted black stripes above the wrists. Mounted on a heavy neck, his head was bald and completely spherical, with skin a rich sheen of dark aged wood. He came from a high gravity world, something immediately obvious.

He held out his arms palms down and bowed slowly.

"I beg you to excuse the abrupt nature of my arrival." He spoke perfect Orieli interworld standard in a deep, strong voice used to command and unquestioning obedience. His small black eyes were clear and searching.

Bearn glanced at Arlon Dee and gave a small nod, deferring to his superior. Arlon returned the alien's bow.

"Welcome aboard, Da. I am—"

"Karhide Arlon Dee of the Orieli survey cruiser *Tapal.* I regret, Da, that our arrival could not be more timely to prevent the tragic loss you suffered. However, I fear for the safety of your people taken by the Krans."

The alien did not explain. He did not have to. A lot of sophistication underpinned those simple words. They had clearly monitored the comms channels between the Orieli ships and kept an eye on Orieli worlds to understand the common working language and cultural nuances. But subspace channels were supposedly untraceable. Evidently, it did not look like it. This reminded Terr of his first meeting with Karhide Zor-Ell and the feeling of inadequacy when *Valon* materialized above his M-1. Fates turning full circle for the Orieli?

"Thank you for receiving me on board your fine ship, Karhide Bearn," the alien added smoothly, totally confident in what to him were not quite strange surrounds. A ship's interior could be molded in a very limited number of functional ways. "To allay your fears about possible biological contamination, I am an isomorphic projection."

Terr exchanged glances with Dhar and grinned. It explained how the alien was able to bypass the ship's screens. A comms channel data feed was not a threat, although realistic enough to trigger an intruder alert. *Latva's* commander took it in stride.

"Your appearance caused the Krans to withdraw rather abruptly. Your doing? Meaning you met them before?"

The alien laughed, a rich booming sound. "Nu. A long time ago, Karhide. They have cause to fear us. Permit me to introduce myself. I am First Commander Shah Pak of the Fernai cruiser FN *Itaiah.*"

Terr stepped forward and stood beside Arlon, who extended an arm toward him.

"Terrllss-rr, Head of Mission—"

"Representing the worlds of the Serrll Combine," Shah Pak said slowly, looking puzzled as he stared curiously at Terr. When he saw Dhar, he gaped and bowed deeply.

"My lord, I crave your blessing!" Shah Pak's low voice trembled with undisguised reverence.

Terr simply stared. In some distant past, the Fernai visited Anar'on and met the Wanderers. Not only met them, but knew what they were. He would need to talk to Dhar, but his brother's expression suggested he might not know anything.

Frowning, Dhar walked to the alien and briefly touched the alien's head with his right hand, not flinching when his hand went partially through the projection.

"You have my blessing, but I fear—"

The alien straightened and smiled happily. "Nu. It's been a long time since anyone from our worlds walked in the footsteps of a lord of Death."

Touched by the gesture, Terr experienced a stirring of power course through his body. Shah Pak's head snapped around in astonishment.

"It's not possible," he whispered in shock and bowed again. "Lord!"

Terr's momentary embarrassment at this emotional display vanished as Death settled on his shoulders. How the alien could tell that he walked in a god's shadow was a mystery, but the power he wielded swept away his flash of discomfort. Small blue sparks crawled over his arm as he reached out and touched him.

Bearn looked like he waited to ask a million questions. Arlon Dee's expression was thoughtful as the alien straightened. Explanations would wait.

He cleared his throat. "Terr's associate Dharaklin, whom you seem to know."

"Know of, Da," Shah Pak corrected. "A debt we owe from a long time ago…a long time." He turned to Dhar. "My lord, with your power, why didn't you destroy the Krans instead of allowing this tragedy to unfold?"

"Unfortunately, I don't have that ability, First Commander," Dhar said, heavy with regret.

"But—"

"If I may, First Commander, our discussion will be made easier if we were all more comfortable," Arlon said firmly, bringing everyone to the reality of the moment.

"Of course, Karhide. You're quite correct," Shah Pak murmured absently, still looking with wonder at Dhar.

As they seated themselves on soft couches, the ship whispered around them. Terr studied the alien, easily ignoring that he was only a projection, so real was the effect. A strange encounter, but it appeared his god also knew the Fernai. More importantly, the Ferani did not appear hostile. Right now, neither the Serrll nor the Orieli, he imagined, would relish the prospect of facing another flanking threat. Given the Kran's swift retreat, a friend could be very useful—if the Fernai were indeed friends. Non-belligerence did not necessarily imply comradeship. They were not shooting at each other, and that wasn't so bad.

"Your presence has prevented the destruction of this ship, and possibly our station," Arlon Dee said gravely. "You have the grateful thanks of the Orieli Technic Union, First Commander."

Shah Pak crossed his legs and leaned back. "Nu. I can answer some of the many questions you want to ask, Karhide Dee, but only some. I must point out that my presence here is not a prelude to establishing formal relations with the Orieli, nor the Serrll Combine."

"You warned our survey ship to stay away. Why did you appear now?"

"Suffice to say the Celi-Kran needed a timely reminder. We encountered them some 2,800 years ago when they began expanding into this part of the galactic arm. They caused much damage before we compelled them to withdraw. Your survey ships saw the devastated worlds left in their wake."

"Like us, you appear to be maintaining outposts here."

"To discourage further Kran adventurism, which they tried only once. We observed you for a long time and avoided contact, until now. Likewise, the worlds of the Serrll Combine are also known to us, and your progress is monitored with interest, my lords," he said with a small bow. His eyes locked briefly on Terr and shook his head, still not able to resolve his puzzlement. That an alien, not a native of Anar'on, could wield the hand of Death was clearly a gnawing mystery for him. Terr sympathized.

"Unfortunately, one of your survey ships, Karhide, tripped an old relay which brought the Krans back. You fought them for five years and thought the string of LTN stations you built would keep you and the Serrll safe. Today's demonstration was meant to expose your vulnerability and send you a message. They're coming. In their eagerness to confront you, they have forgotten their history, or chose to accept a possible confrontation with us. My presence was a reminder that we did not forget."

Arlon licked his lips and leaned forward slightly. "From their reaction, not a comfortable encounter for them."

"Nu. Although totally hostile, the Krans are also pragmatists. They will not pursue a no-win scenario."

"Unless they can alter some of the variables."

"Existence implies constant change and we need to be prepared. They are relentless and will one day return if they believe they can sweep us away."

"If you're watching everything, why didn't you act to eliminate them? You appear to have the capability."

"Capability, yes. However, the Krans are not a threat to us. Regardless how inimical they are to all intelligent life, we're not the galaxy's protector. This may sound harsh, especially when inaction continues to result in civilizations lost and worlds denuded of life, but space is vast and all those who venture between the stars must accept the possibility of hostile encounters. Unfortunately, encountering the Krans is often terminal."

Arlon Dee frowned deeply. "Pardon me for saying, but your attitude *is* harsh. Aren't we all men facing a common threat? And those who are able, don't they have an implied responsibility to protect those who cannot do it themselves?"

"A recognized ethical dilemma, as is your suggestion that in some distant future we may not be able to stop them. Let me say this. Although we're not involved, we do watch. As for the implied responsibility, we covertly seed ideas and nurture technology, but our resources are not limitless, and there are many stars. Like any entity, preservation of self takes precedence over any other consideration."

Terr glanced at Dhar, both thinking the same thing. Did the Fernai employ the equivalent of Observers, able to infiltrate and study a society undetected? Not only study, but apparently influence. He was certain the thought had occurred to Arlon Dee, and would be an ironic reversal of roles.

"After 2,800 years, you still practice isolationism?" Arlon gave a hiss of annoyance and bowed. "Forgive me, my words were unpardonable."

"I am not offended. Although understandable, your words

are spoken from lack of knowledge."

"Of course, and I did not mean to judge. Tell me. If you wanted to send the Krans a reminder, why choose to appear now rather than five years ago?"

Shah Pak smiled. "It was not because of any benevolent desire to protect the Orieli, Karhide. We acted now to protect our own space. Hoping the Krans would stop their forays, your presence and construction of the LTN stations were simply too alluring. Their withdrawal today does not mean they will cease to seek you out, or the worlds of the Serrll, my lord Terr. They simply won't be doing it from here. My appearance will stop them encroaching into this part of space, which is sufficient for our purpose."

"For how long, First Commander? You must realize that sooner or later they'll return in force since this is in their nature. Why not eliminate them now and forestall what might be untold destruction?"

"Simply because we're able to, should we?"

"As you said, an ethical dilemma. Can their behavior be changed?"

"Nu. Although machines, they have developed self-awareness, at least the command cells and the ship central nexus cores are sentient. Their ancillary units are indeed merely functional constructs and any intelligence they exhibit is purely a byproduct of their link with a central core, ship or land-based nexus. We have communicated, but their behavior is regulated at a fundamental level that prohibits change in basic patterns. Intelligent organic life is something they're compelled to destroy, however illogical the imperative seems to us."

Terr wanted to ask the obvious, when an equally obvious answer presented itself. The Krans were nanometric constructs, which implied a creator, but however powerful, the Fernai did not know who that was, or were never seriously tempted to find out. It looked like overwhelming superiority also induced selective blindness, although he was not about to say so. Anyway, he was in no position to judge, not after a single meeting.

"Unless checked, they will continue to expand and destroy everything they encounter," Arlon Dee warned.

"Simply because we possess superior capability does not convey on us authority to wipe out an intelligent species, even though created inimical. Don't your own contact protocols demand similar behavior?"

"Against wiping out life."

"What is life?" Shah Pak asked. "A question we all debated for a long time. We still do."

"Are *we* intruding?" Arlon demanded gently, sidestepping a complex philosophical problem and the alien smiled, completely friendly.

"Not yet, but by establishing a presence on this side of the Karina, intentionally or not, you took upon yourself the role as protector of the Serrll Combine, something we welcome. Moreover, given your social and cultural matrix, not unexpected."

"Had we not appeared, were you prepared to protect the Serrll?"

"Nu. Cause and effect, Da. Your survey ships brought the Krans here."

Arlon Dee smiled. "A problem of our own making."

Terr keenly observed the exchange, trying to extract information from words not said. Arlon and Shah Pak were interacting at a level that implied an understanding of cultural and sociodynamic processes outside his experience. He wondered whether he was really suited to undertake an in-depth study of the Orieli. By sending him out here, did Anabb seek to rid himself of a troublesome agent? He wouldn't put it past him, but it was a dishonorable thought. Too much was at stake for Anabb to descend to such manipulation. On the other hand, it did not mean he was not pursuing both objectives. The evil old fart could be tricky like that.

"There is one thing that puzzled us since our initial contact with the Krans," Arlon mused. "Before attacking, they transmit a long modulated signal. We were never able to makes sense of it or why they do it. They must know it meant nothing to us."

"Nu. It's a byproduct of their programming, Karhide. They know the futility of sending the signal, but they're nevertheless driven to do it."

"And what is that signal?" Bearn asked.

"A request for a failsafe code."

Arlon stared at him. "You understand their machine language?"

"We do, although it hasn't helped us. We don't know the correct response."

"An IFF…"

Bearn snorted, dismissing the conversation. "In your encounter with them, did they employ their gravitic weapon against you?"

"As you so painfully learned, the Krans are very advanced, but in many ways simple and predictable. Had we not repulsed them, I fear the Orieli would have encountered them a long time ago with drastically negative consequences."

"Slow to evolve, eh?"

"Nu. However intelligent, machines are not subject to normal evolutionary processes, Karhide, as you undoubtedly realize. If a pattern of behavior works, change occurs only through external influence."

"Such as contact with a superior force. Can you tell us what exactly are these projectiles?"

"As you already surmised, the devices generate a rift through one of the closed dimensions, but unlike the one you employ to power your ships, the rift channels energy, and matter is simply a concentrated form of energy. As you've seen, the effects in normal space are particularly destructive."

"However, the weapon has limits," Arlon Dee mused. "The burnt-out worlds our survey ships encountered…they were not subjected to such bombardment."

"The answer should be obvious," Shah Pak said dryly.

"The rift cannot be formed in the presence of a strong spacetime displacement field induced by a planet or star, or the Krans would have used the projectiles."

"That is indeed correct, Karhide. Kran technology is formidable, but they too are forced to obey physical laws."

"Wait a minute." Bearn raised a finger. "One of our picket ships reported the moon on which LTN-2 was built destroyed by such a weapon. Its distortion limit caused the missile's drive into a forced collapse and dropped it into normal space."

"The moon must have been small."

Frowning, Bearn nodded. "It was indeed small, only 194 ampirs in diameter."

"Which wouldn't give it a large distortion limit, perhaps eight ampirs. Not strong enough to prevent the missile from forming the interdimensional rift."

That made sense, Terr figured. Of course, an object's distortion limit is not only a function of size, but mass, a much more important parameter, which results in a power curve when calculating the distortion limit. It is why a singularity, although very small, has such a brutally large gravity well.

"If we're to protect ourselves and extend an umbrella over the Serrll, knowing how you countered the threat would be extremely helpful," Bearn said.

"Nu. That must also be obvious."

"You're able to somehow modulate your interceptor net frequencies and detonate the missile before it can generate the rift."

"You are only partially correct. We cannot prevent the rift from forming once a missile strikes, but we induce a sufficiently strong localized spacetime displacement sink that collapses the rift. Before you ask, Karhide Bearn, we cannot share the technology involved with you. However, I told you enough to develop it."

"At a possible cost of more devastated worlds while we do so," Bearn growled, not pleased at all.

"Nu. That is a price we all must be prepared to pay when venturing into the deeps, Da."

"An alien first contact protocol, First Commander?" Arlon Dee asked wryly.

"Somewhat. Like you, we don't interfere and we will not involve ourselves in your war. My presence has achieved its objective and the Krans will not return anytime soon, which is sufficient for our purpose…and will give you time to rebuild."

"You could have achieved your objective without making contact with us, First Commander," Arlon pointed out, a ghost of a smile tugging at his mouth. "Yet you chose to interfere."

Shah Pak's neutral face gave nothing away. "Under a purely fortuitous set of circumstances, Da."

Terr smiled. Arlon's expression suggested he didn't believe it either.

"There is something I don't understand," Bearn said with a scowl. "If the Krans possess such a weapon, why didn't they use it earlier when we were more vulnerable?"

Shah Pak smiled. "Forgive me, but you're launching your argument from an incorrect premise. You're assuming the Krans see you as a major challenge, thereby forgetting that they also have operational priorities and logistical constraints. By electing to strike now after you expended considerable effort and resources on your Line Tracking Net, they achieved a maximum desired outcome with a minimum expenditure of resources. Destroying your stations and transport portal, they are forcing you to withdraw from here, denying you a tactical forward strike position."

Bearn's thoughtful expression made it clear he did not like what Shah Pak said. Thinking about it, Terr admitted it was an obvious observation. Arlon smiled faintly.

"And what of our presence? If we are encroaching into your space, do you require us to dismantle our remaining LTN stations?"

"We would not have allowed you to build them were you

encroaching. They form a natural border between us and are still needed. All the stars on this side of your defense line are yours to share with the Serrll. Do not venture beyond it." Shah Pak rose and bowed. "The Orieli Technic Union recognizes the threat it faces, as does the Serrll Combine. Help each other and you may survive. I wish you both well."

A green radiance sprang around him and he began to fade.

"Wait!" Arlon Dee cried jumping to his feet, but he was gone. He muttered a pithy word Terr didn't catch, but could guess.

After a moment, Arlon turned with a wry smile. "You probably said something similar when I appeared on Salina."

"More or less," Terr agreed dryly and Arlon laughed.

How many months ago was that? It seemed to have happened in some other time and another place. Reflecting on the Orieli's mission to build LTN-12 on Earth's moon, their overbearing confidence and unstated arrogance was somewhat galling. Of course, Arlon had not been haughty or condescending at all. He simply appeared to know everything, and nothing was outside his capacity. The appearance of the Fernai served as a salutary lesson—the Orieli were not all-powerful.

"Operational caution. The Fernai vessel has transited. Unable to track."

"Unable to track it? Don't tell me they're not using subspace, damn them," Bearn growled, stood up, clasped his hands behind his back and began pacing. After a moment, he stopped and exhaled loudly. "They could have told us more about how to fight the Krans." He stared pointedly at Terr. "Lords of Death? Able to snuff out the Krans?"

Arlon Dee cleared his throat. "I'll fill you in later."

"How about right now? If they possess such power, it would be something useful to know, wouldn't you say?"

Terr slowly rose to his feet and sensed Dhar doing the same. "Da, my brother and I are initiates of the Wanderer Discipline, which gives us certain abilities."

"Brother? Wanderer Discipline?"

Terr wanted to raise his arms, lightning crackling, and show the mortal. Instead, he imagined himself standing on a tall dune, the cape of his brown surtaf fluttering behind him as the sands whispered beneath his feet, the amber sky turning indistinct as it merged with a distant horizon. The Saffal, unrelenting and unforgiving to anyone caught unprotected, was nevertheless a friend if one knew its ways. He needed to be there now, to replenish his resolve, which he knew he would need if he were to get Teena. He looked at the alien and shrugged.

"It's complicated."

"Then unravel it, Mister! If you and others like you can indeed neutralize the Krans, who threaten the Serrll as much as they threaten us, OSCOM needs to know. You want those things rampaging through our worlds, or yours?"

Terr bridled at Bearn's pushy attitude, but that quickly faded when he recalled what happened today. *Latva's* commander had a lot on his mind.

"They will know, but I submit, such a discussion would best be done with appropriate Orieli authorities."

What the alien wanted was a solution to an immediate tactical problem, forgetting the broader strategic implications facing everyone. Unfortunately, Terr did not have a neat solution. There were possibilities he could discuss, but they would be explored at a diplomatic level with Captal, and of course, Anar'on. Would the Rahtir Council agree to send Discipline adepts into Orieli space to confront the Krans when those adepts may be needed to defend the Serrll, even if Anar'on were predisposed to do so? Too many variables were involved and he could only draw attention to them. He lacked plenipotentiary powers to make commitments on behalf of Anar'on or Captal, even though he was a Wanderer, albeit an adopted one through strange circumstances.

Bearn realized the situation, pursed his mouth, then exhaled. "You're right, of course, and PERCOM must be involved. Please accept my apology, Da Terr."

"The Fernai," Arlon Dee mused, sidestepping an awkward moment. "I would have loved being there when they first encountered the Krans."

Bearn shook his head. "To perdition with them! LTN-2 destroyed, three ships lost here, our portal gone and we cannot establish contact with LTN-1 or its pickets...not good. And we don't know anything about them, except for their warning to stay away."

"Agreed, but we can infer a lot. Whether we like it or not, I can understand their non-interference position," Arlon said.

"So can I, but they could have helped a *little*!"

"They did."

Bearn pursed his lips. "They did tell us how to neutralize those missiles, didn't they. It will take us a while to develop the technology, but it's better than nothing, I suppose. Anyway, it's one headache I'm glad not to have. While everybody chatted, I updated PERCOM. We lost *Marin*, and *Trailer* was ordered to check out LTN-1 and pick up possible survivors. We're instructed to wait for her, take on board her survivors, recover our escape modules and return to Perilia. She'll remain on station here. The Kran strikes really stirred things up with OSCOM, as you can imagine." He glanced pointedly at Terr. "I have no orders concerning you and your mission. That's probably handled at the diplomatic level with Captal. It looks like you two are coming with us."

Terr realized Bearn was hooked into the VI even now and multitasking. He turned to Arlon Dee, face grim.

"My mission now, Karhide, is to find Teena."

Arlon's red eyes gave nothing away. "And how would you suggest we go about doing that?"

The enormity of the simple question was not lost on Terr, or the degree of difficulty trying to mount any kind of rescue effort. At least his link with her was still there. As long as she lived, he would go after her and Death would march against anyone who stood in his way.

"I'm not unsympathetic, and I lost people as well. I want them back as much as you want your Teena, but we need to consider our options, if there are any, against what the Kran strike and appearance of the Fernai means, not only for us, but the Serrll as well."

"There is one good thing about all this, if you can call it that," Bearn said heavily. "The Krans have not found the breach in the Karina."

Although his guts were churning and he wanted the Orieli to go charging off right now, Terr accepted the wisdom of Arlon's words. Much needed to be considered and done before anybody could do anything.

Chapter Two

Nothing existed except the ship and the Karina deeps, a deadly cradle whose embrace *Latva* must avoid. Should it succumb, there would be no returning. Outside, darkness ruled, having swallowed all light. An occasional glow lit towering columns of gas, stacked into twisted architectural forms where a protostar was forming. Long filaments of green sometimes stretched on either side of the ship, smeared with patches of brown and blue, betraying the elements released from previous supernova sheddings and neutron star collisions, marvels of tortuous creation.

A stellar nursery of staggering proportions, full of ices, organics and metals, highly charged and extremely reactive plasma flows churned by unstable magnetic fields, Karina was a giver of life, but it also took it. Stars were born quickly here, but lived and died just as quickly, their remnants giving rise to more stable, longer-lived systems. However, the very nature of this environment dictated instability.

Over the last three days as *Latva* hurtled through the breach, the ship shuddered violently when the surrounding gas density became critical enough to influence the distortion field precursor, threatening a collapse that would dump them into normal space, which would strand the ship within Karina's deeps. The incredible 411 light-year tunnel through which they were rushing had an average cross-section of four million ampirs, but in places it narrowed to only a hundred thousand or so, dangerously narrow, and becoming more so. Soon, perhaps within a year, the breach would become impassable as the clumps of gas within the nebula shifted, visibly demonstrating the need to rebuild the LTN-3 interdimensional portal.

If it wanted to, Perilian Command could make blind jumps now using its own portal to transport required personnel and materiel to LTN-3 and begin reconstruction. They recognized the strategic need and were ready to do so—once OSCOM developed a defense against Kran gravitic missiles. The appearance of the Fernai caused the Krans to withdraw, but would they attack again if the Orieli began to reestablish their presence on this side of the Karina, unable to resist whatever imperative drove them to extinguish all intelligent life?

Hooked into the VI, the computer-generated image of the Karina all around him—in subspace the only thing one could see were streaming gravity waves and mass-density fields induced by the nebula—Terr reached out with his mind, following the elusive link that bound him to Teena. After a moment, her form appeared before him, a white, shifting manifestation of her spirit. Unlike other times when he conjured her, this apparition had no awareness, like she had gone somewhere else or was resting. It was not sleep, he could tell. More like a suspension of everything as if she were in stasis. Where, he couldn't tell, but she lived and that's all that mattered.

He almost cried out with longing when she dissolved into nothingness. His power can do a lot, but it could not bring her to him. He wasn't a god, merely a shell the god used to amuse himself. Terr dropped his arm and stared into the darkness surrounding him.

"I'll be coming, my pet," he whispered the words with grim resolve.

"Sankri?"

Dhar's deep voice returned him to reality and he cut the VI coupling. *Latva's* empty Observation Deck took on solid form and the ship around him became alive. On the other side of the transparent bulkhead, lines of brown and yellow gravity waves coiled in the wake of the ship's passing. Emptiness hid everything else, a murky churning that reflected Terr's thoughts. He would get her, no matter what it took. Those who stood in his way would feel his wrath as he loosed the lightnings.

Terr turned the comfortable couch, not unlike the form-chairs he was more used to, forced himself to smile as his brother seated himself, and felt some of his burden lift. A Wanderer and an alien, Dhar nonetheless was an island of stability in his life, a life often turbulent and torn with doubt and excesses. The force of the Discipline coming through? Terr could not tell and simply allowed Dhar's powerful calming presence to envelop him. His brother was an anchor in an otherwise tempestuous sea of life, an anchor that saved him more than once.

"Nightwings, your presence gives me peace."

"Yet your heart is troubled and I feel your pain," Dhar responded gravely, his orange eyes unblinking, the protective membranes that kept out fine sand now pulled up. Joined far too long for anything to escape him, he naturally sensed Terr's dilemma, and his helplessness. Although this time, it did not take much effort.

"A black void sits in it, my brother, and I need to fill it."

"You harbor what might be a hopeless yearning, and the terrible truth is, you know it."

"Perhaps, but not as long as I can feel her. While she is alive, she will keep me alive." Terr reached across the space separating them and touched Dhar's knee. "Forgive me, I didn't mean I would shut you out—"

"Nothing can come between us, Sankri. We are one, but however painful, you must reconcile yourself to the possibility that you might never see her again."

"I can't. Not yet." Memories and images of her churned through his mind; her impish smile, the way she pulled back a rebellious lock of hair, her deep green eyes that could be soft and dreamy, or dark with anger…her unstinting love. "Remember when she and I were at Katai Than at our little hideaway? You called me, saying Anabb wanted to talk to me. Right then, given what he did to me, he was the last person I wanted to talk to."

"I remember," Dhar said after a while. Terr could see him reflecting on what might have been, on what was.

Lost in his memories, he clearly pictured the dark cliffs sheltering a grassed valley floor and a still pond surrounded by a wooded glade of gently swaying peelath. Taklan moss-palms leaned over dark, still waters. Long strands of moss hung limp from the branches and nodded at their reflection. In that dreamy, almost magical setting, it was easy to forget and just drift, letting go of everything, if only for a little while.

"We sat on white sand beside the glassy brown pool, content simply to be close. I wanted to share with her the world you and I had. Share some of the wonder the Saffal held for me, wanting her to understand a little of that land. Then she asked me to take her to Athal Than."

Dhar inhaled sharply. "She—"

"She almost did," Terr said and smiled faintly. A woman faced death to enter the domain of the gods. Jealous of life, women were an anathema as they are givers of life. "She wanted to see where the gods reside. After all, that's where I was transformed and she could not resist the opportunity to see it, a curiosity that almost destroyed her. Like a fool I am, I allowed her walk toward the cliffs, and before I knew what was happening, I could feel the pull. We are one in spirit and somehow, she felt it through me and began to make her way toward a fissure. Panicked, I barely reached her in time, but I tell you, it frightened the hell out of me and left her badly shaken."

"A dangerous indulgence, my brother."

"Yeah."

Gravity waves snaked around them and Terr's thoughts wandered, but like those waves, they had no turning. Life only went forward, and there was no undoing what had been.

"Later, I told her I would never leave her, and now, that's exactly what I did," he whispered brokenly.

"Sankri, even if the Orieli mounted a rescue mission for *Tapal's* crew, where would they search? Space is deep and the

Krans own it all. If that weren't enough, how would they get in? Powerful as their ships are, until a defense is developed to counter the gravitic missiles, it would be suicide. I do not question their ethical imperative to get their people, but there is an issue of pragmatism. Your pain is caused by this realization and your refusal to accept it."

Terr looked at him, his eyes hard. "Maybe, but how many does it take; a hundred, a thousand, before the effort is worth it? Isn't every life precious? If all action is controlled by impersonal expediency, what is the value of preserving their social fabric, any social fabric? All their noble words, all the blood shed over their tortuous history, the suffering and destruction endured by unknown millions to achieve what the Orieli have now, it's all a hollow lie unless they're prepared to follow the ethical code they profess to believe."

"It's a dilemma every society faces, my brother, and one already solved, which you know very well. You're allowing personal consideration to override your judgment. Regardless how compelled the Orieli might be to act, or the ethics driving them, they will not throw away men and ships in a futile gesture. No rational social order would or can. However agonizing the alternative, there must be something on the other side of the equation, a level of certainty the effort will succeed. Right now, there is no prospect of success, something you also know. Suppose they gave you a ship, you will not help Teena if you throw away your life on a hopeless quest. If not dead, you could end up where she is."

Cloaked in silence, not even the background whisper of machinery to intrude into his thoughts, Terr felt lost. It tore his insides to admit it, but Dhar's cold words rang with truth, which he'd known all along, just as his brother said. Rushing into the unknown might be brave and romantic, but it wouldn't achieve anything. To help her, he needed overwhelming force to back him up, which he did not have at his command.

"Still, it sucks," he declared and Dhar smiled faintly.

"Yes, it does."

Frustrated, Terr extended his arm. "If I could reach out, I would crush them, gravitic missiles or not."

Puzzled, Dhar leaned forward. "We haven't talked about it, but as a second-level adept, you should not have been able to destroy that Kran cruiser at Devon."

"I know, and it's troubling me."

"It is also troubling me, Sankri."

"You understand well why it happened, Nightwings. You simply don't want to accept it. Remember when you joined with me and brought me out of my madness? After surviving my crash, wandering the Saffal sands, the desert took me and you brought me back, if only partially."

"I remember," Dhar said, the memories clear on his stern face.

"You released me from my madness, but by joining, you left your shadow in me, and you walk in the shadow of Death. You thought you left Death in me, and you blamed yourself for that, but the power was already there, my brother. You just intensified it, and what's more, you always knew it, just as Sidhara knows. As I walked through the Saffal after my crash, that's when Death touched me. Sidhara's problem is, he cannot comprehend how that was possible. Athal Than merely wakened me and made me aware of what I inherited."

Dhar was silent for a moment. "Perhaps he understood and that's why he feared what I wanted to do. Our master told me not to join with you, but I wouldn't listen. Strong and proud, I felt I could do anything, ignoring the danger of what I intended. I could not allow you to remain insane, Sankri. You must believe that."

Terr smiled and touched Dhar's arm. "It was fated, my brother."

"What I often wondered later, why didn't Sidhara reach into you? He would have known what to do, and maybe avoided the mistake I made."

"Whatever his motive, you delivered me from a hell of my madness. You don't need to reproach yourself for anything. The turbulence I endured since by using my gift, or abusing it if I want to be honest, was of my own making. I'm not saying I am a third-level adept, I'm not that arrogant, but I am more than I thought I was. What happened at Devon could have been a once-off inexplicable event, a reaction to a unique circumstance as my recent failure demonstrated. When *Tapal* confronted that *Daktar*, I tried to blot it out, but Death wouldn't come. Fates again, my brother?"

"Tah, the gods will tell," Dhar murmured fatalistically.

"There is one way a rescue could succeed," Terr said slowly, a mischievous twinkle lighting his eyes. "If Sidhara were with us, or some other fully-fledged adept."

Dhar slowly lifted his head, his mouth open in wondrous surprise.

* * *

Latva burst through the Karina breach and immediately set course for Perilia, a little over six hours at maximum boost. It took the ship five-and-a-half tense days to traverse the nebula, days of loneliness and introspection for Terr. Dhar was always there, and also wise enough to understand his need for solitude and did not intrude. Terr went on missions that meant separation from Teena for some time, but even then they were never truly apart. He always the Wall to keep them in touch and exchange gossip that provided density and texture to their relationship.

Even though he knew she still lived, the impenetrable silence he now endured was a new and unsettling experience. Intellectually, he knew nothing could have prevented her capture, but it did not stop the demons of guilt from nagging him. He should have gone to her when Arlon Dee went to heightened alert. Suffering from a natural psychological reaction, it wasn't the reason why he preferred to remain alone. Brooding never solved anything, being a self-fulfilling indulgence, and Terr never believed at feeling sorry for himself. Not much anyway.

As he sat in his quarters, reclining in a comfortable couch, hooked into the virtual interface, he watched as *Latva* closed with Tavor's Star, still only a yellow point in a backdrop of other lights. Three rocky planets occupied the inner system and two gas giants huddled in the cold deeps. A disk of icy remnants left over from the time of creation extended almost a quarter of a light from the system. An ordinary star, an ordinary system, except that it lay in Orieli space.

The ship crossed the rocky belt and slowed to half boost. Immersed in the vista, he contemplated and weighed options available to him when he confronted the reputedly formidable woman who directed Perilian Sector Command. His mission, with Teena and Dhar, was to provide an overall perspective of the Orieli and what they were all about. Of course, his was not the only team going in. Two groups of sociodynamicists would gather the raw numbers against which refined computer models would generate profiles of the Orieli for the Serrll Executive Council to deliberate on, setting policy for future exchanges. Why then send him, a non-specialist? According to Captal chair warmers at the Bureau of Colonial and Protectorate Affairs, the answer was simple.

Terr would provide the human perspective, something the experts with their cold figures never quite got right. No matter how sophisticated the analysis, some things could not be reduced to their numerical value and retain the essence of the experience. Feelings, perceptions, the quality of suffering, joy and despair, a multitude of other nuances, by their very nature, they must be experienced within the cultural matrix of a social structure being studied. Who better for such a task than a group of non-specialists, but someone still aware enough to recognize the processes involved. Whether it was Anabb ridding himself of a troublesome agent or an impersonal directive from the

BCPA, Terr relished the challenge. Half the Scout Fleet officers would kill to be in his shoes.

Teena may be gone, but his mission was not over. Faced with a crisis where everything they stood for would be tested in a crucible of conflict that could result in their annihilation, it presented an ideal opportunity to study and evaluate the Orieli. He operated under a caveat, though. Anabb didn't have to explain, something Terr learned in the vastness of the Saffal. *Refrain from judging, for there lies temptation*, his master Sidhara told him more than once while gazing at the shifting dunes, listening to the whisper of the sands. *If forced to judge and act, judge by deeds, not words.* A simple philosophy, but also deceptively complex, especially when an act could unleash Death on the recipient in final retribution. It became even more complex when taken off Anar'on and applied to the multifaceted structure of the Serrll and its multiplicity of behavioral norms. To judge meant having a superior moral position, and who was he to set the yardstick when his own ethical defects almost cost him his soul.

Terr felt prepared and happy to observe without judging. He would compare and note differences. In an alien environment, a byproduct of his cultural upbringing, he would not be an arbiter. He would provide opinions, a primary input the highbrow analysts on Captal were looking for. No, his days were not spent in solitary brooding. He did not pretend to know everything about the Orieli, or understand their cultural and social drivers, not in five days, but he had built a framework he was comfortable working with. Although they commanded awesome technology, had a strong social ethic, far superior to what the Serrll professed to observe, their culture resonated at a familiar level. There was also discord, not unexpected in a union of over 3,200 systems. It was not a homogeneous society and sometimes conflict caused pain and horror. Nevertheless, it had flavor. Overall, he figured Sidhara would enjoy discussing some of life's multifarious philosophies with Arlon Dee.

Powerful and socially advanced, the Orieli were a conglomeration of races who over millennia learned to coexist and prosper. Not unlike the races that made up the Serrll Combine, Terr did not want to push the analogy too far. They could be understood, which meant they would easily understand the Serrll...and him. So, if he made a verbal or behavioral gaffe, he was certain it would be overlooked. He counted on this when he faced Alkarh Tertulion. After all, he was merely a backward provincial.

Thirty light-minutes from Perilia, *Latva* dropped normal and headed in on secondary drive. From a blue-green crescent, the planet's features resolved as the ship slanted down toward the terminator past squadrons of assembled warships. Clusters of lights flickered along dark ocean shorelines, extending into continental interiors in sprawling profusion. Dawn broke as *Latva* descended toward the Space Arm facility eighty ampirs north of the capital Tetra.

Despite his concern over Teena, Terr was excited to look at a world no one from the Serrll had seen, truly an alien first contact. Not only a new world, but an entirely different social system; parallel in some respects—all advanced social organisms obeyed fixed cultural laws—and undoubtedly different at many levels. His mission was to discover those differences.

He broke the VI link and decided to shower and put on a fresh uniform, his wardrobe left behind when *Tapal* was lost, figuring he'd be spending a lot of time in meetings. Sightseeing would have to wait.

He ran a comb through his hair and stared at the reflection in the holographic mirror. Strong features matured by the burden of command, brown-black hair that needed cutting partially concealed a ragged scar above the left temple near the eyebrow. The slight cleft in his chin emphasized determination, as did the cold gray eyes above an aquiline nose. Looking at himself, he decided the plain indigo uniform, devoid of any rank insignia, sat well on him. Everybody better the hell be on the ball, because he was coming, ready or not.

"Da Terrllss-rr?" Cent Comp inquired diffidently.

"What is it?"

"You are requested to make ready for transport to PERCOM where you will meet Alkarh Tertulion."

Terr almost asked the obvious, when the equally obvious answer presented itself. Of course Dhar would be alerted, probably under orders from Karhide Bearn or Arlon Dee. He figured all four were going. This was one disconcerting aspect dealing with the Orieli; the ones he'd met anyway. They seemed to grasp and understand things so quickly, removing the need for redundant dialogue. Even Cent Comp assumed he would understand without clarification, although he felt certain it would provide one if asked. Despite his resolve, he wondered whether he was up to this. What comforted him, a little at least, was the realization that not *everyone* could be so smart. However, the people he'd be interacting with undoubtedly would be. He took a deep breath and straightened his jacket. He only needed to be himself and to the pits with everybody else.

"I'm ready now."

"Please enter the PT alcove."

So, no shuttle flight to the capital, or whatever they used to get around? Then again, why waste time flying about when there was a much more efficient system, although a gut twister. He wanted to see Perilia and its inhabitants, and experience for the first time how a normal Orieli citizen lived and what he thought. So far, all he had to work with were impressions gained from Arlon's crew and *Latva*, a warship, definitely not a representative cross-section of normal Orieli society, whatever normal meant here.

He strode toward the alcove and stepped in. "Transport," he said gruffly and waited.

When the aftereffect tingle subsided, he blinked and looked around with intense curiosity. Slender wafer towers in single columns, or joined in pleasing geometrical shapes, clawed into a greenish sky. From what he could see of the city through the transparent wall—the entire floor was one open panorama—was more green than dwellings. Not unlike some Serrll cities, but something different about this landscape teased him.

"Da Terrllss-rr, I want to welcome you to Tetra and the Orieli Technic Union," a strong feminine voice declared behind him through the VI translator, bringing a sheepish smile to his face as he turned.

Tall, perhaps 170 minampirs, slim, she carried herself with authority. Her black hair short, it framed an elongated face. Large brown eyes set off a delicate nose and small, but full lips. Her deep yellow skin showed few wrinkles, belittling her eighty-nine years. He'd studied her record. She wore a perfectly cut unadorned dark indigo one-piece uniform. On her left breast was a small silver Cluster-and-Circle emblem packed with a dense conglomeration of yellow stars representing the Orieli Cluster. He recognized the emblem of a full flag officer.

"Thank you, Alkarh. I am honored to be here. An incredible view."

Without willing it, his legs carried him to the edge of the wall and he simply stared, trying to figure it out. Then it hit him: pattern destruction. Most cities had an ordered pattern to them, whether filled with low dwellings, towers, parks or lakes. The regular patterns invariably intruded into the landscape, dominating its surrounds, forcing inhabitants to live on its terms. As he gawked at the city with bemused wonder, he realized that Tetra *was* the landscape. It projected a soothing element he could not quite pin down. Far in the west, a wall of green hills cradled the city. He decided life would be pleasant down there. If all Orieli worlds were like this, he needed to prepare himself for ongoing cultural shocks.

"Forgive me," he said and walked toward an elongated oval black table surrounded by soft, rounded chairs. Apart from the glowing cream ceiling and walls, the room was otherwise empty. A full-dimensional interactive holoview image hovered above the table showing the Karina nebula and what he assumed were the first three LTN stations, what was left of them. "I was startled."

Across the table, seated beside Dhar, Arlon Dee and Bearn looked at him with amused tolerance. Was there some meaning to him arriving last?

She gave a pleasant laugh, allowing him his distraction. "Even with us, visitors often find Tetra a double-take. However, not all our worlds are gardens, which you will undoubtedly see for yourself. Permit me to introduce myself. I am Alkarh Tertulion. We did not intend that I meet you, a military officer. However, countervailing circumstances dictate I do so, which will impact on the parameters of your mission while you're on Perilia. Please, make yourself comfortable."

The ring of command in her voice unmistakable, Terr nodded. Somewhat curious to see her alone, he'd expected a packed delegation of inquisitive onlookers, he took a seat opposite Dhar and nodded to the others. Perhaps the delegation was yet to come, or this was merely an introductory session to ease him into things. Then, perhaps not.

Rit!

He should not be looking for subtlety that might not be there. Using the VI link, Arlon and Bearn probably told PERCOM everything already. They had five days within which to do it and pick over the bones. The meeting, he decided, was for his benefit.

Tertulion sat down, folded her arms in her lap and leaned against the seat, her eyes appraising him, totally in control. Kindly eyes, but also determined. He figured Anabb would relish sparring with her.

"Allow me to express my sadness at your loss; unprecedented, as the Krans never bothered taking captives before," she mused, her eyes searching. "However, not entirely unexpected. Their need for intelligence must be as great as ours. I am told you believe Teena is alive."

"She is alive, Alkarh," Terr said firmly, not bothering to explain. If Arlon had spoken to her, which was almost certain, he probably mentioned his link with Teena. If they expected him to read between the lines, so could she.

"And you want her back, no less than Karhide Dee wants his people. Or I. However, without belaboring the point, you must be aware of the practical difficulties involved in any attempt to retrieve them, even if we knew where they were."

"I believe they're in stasis. Once wakened, I'll know where to look."

"Your special abilities. We must talk about that sometime, and the Wanderers, able to meld with a supernatural entity? I find the total concept incredible, although it is apparently very real. As for a possible rescue mission, you speak as though the matter is settled."

He did not break contact with her probing large eyes. "Please excuse me if I sound presumptuous that you would automatically help me."

"But not apologetic." She smiled faintly and gave a small nod. "Karhide Dee did say you were determined, as did Alkarh Zor-Ell, something I admire."

"*Alkarh* Zor-Ell?"

"A deserved promotion. He commands all the LTN stations and support ships."

Terr's mind whirled. It appeared the years had caught up with his alien friend. As he reflected on that fateful first contact and the somewhat raw veneer Terr must have projected, he had come a long way himself.

"It's regrettable that as one of Serrll's Head of Mission, you're meeting us under such adverse conditions."

"On the contrary, Alkarh. These are perfect conditions to undertake my mission."

Her eyes widened for a moment, then she smiled broadly. "I was also told not to underestimate you, Da, and I shall not."

"Just Terr, please."

"As someone who understands fully what you must be feeling…Terr, and I do, I would give you a squadron of *Nasors* to get your partner and our people, but as PERCOM, I cannot do that, and you must appreciate why."

"I do. You don't have the capability now, but the Fernai told you how to achieve it. May I ask if it is possible to augment the operation of your interceptor net as they intimated?"

At the mention of the aliens, the holoview image changed, showing the strange shape of the Fernai ship.

"They've done it, so it's clearly possible. That they should choose to reveal themselves now…a lot for us to think about."

"Any idea how much time it might take to develop such a shield?"

"Terr, we're not magicians. Rather than emulate their technology, we're looking at a simpler solution that's within grasp of our existing capability. We'll turn each ship into a portal. We're experienced at manipulating closed dimensions. Creating an interdimensional interface around a ship is far easier than reducing a field theory to an engineering application, which we know how to do already."

Terr gaped as the possibilities challenged his imagination. "Anything striking the field will simply vanish, but the power required to do it?"

Tertulion shrugged. "It will demand upgrading the reticulation grid. Not a major challenge."

"But if the ship is enclosed in such a field, your interceptor net won't be able to discharge."

"It's a question of polarity. The field will translate any energy or matter stream that impacts it, but within the field, normal spacetime should still operate—we think. We haven't tried it with spherical containment as the novel application never occurred to us."

"Where would this *anything* end up?"

"That's one of the many variables under consideration and

will be tested."

Terr lifted his eyebrows as an idea bubbled up. If the Orieli could apply this technology, their ships would be virtually invulnerable. At least the larger ones would be. He could not see them installing such a system to every ship in their inventory.

Tertulion smiled approvingly. "I see you've worked it out. Indirectly, the Fernai did indeed help us. Their isolationist policy will need careful analysis and evaluation. Not only for the impact on us, but the Serrll as well, as it appears they visited you in the past," she said and glanced at Dhar. The holoview changed to show the Karina, and in the distance, the cloud of Serrll stars highlighted in pearly yellow.

"First Commander Shah Pak clearly has knowledge of Anar'on and the Wanderers, Alkarh," Dhar acknowledged gravely. "But that knowledge came from our distant past, as the Rahtir never spoke of it, at least not to me. I've heard childhood tales and little else."

"Rahtir?"

"Senior initiates of the Discipline, Dapata. Village elders, if you will."

"Able to destroy the Krans, so I'm told."

"Or a world."

She frowned, digesting the information. "Which you claim is beyond your ability. Yet Terr destroyed a Kran *Daktar* at Devon 3-VL4."

"Only a third-level adept can direct his thoughts, focus on an object and act. My brother and I are only second-level adepts. We cannot project through solid matter or an object we cannot see."

"Your brother...I would love to hear more about that. Nevertheless, he did destroy it."

"Done under a unique set of circumstances," Terr interjected. "However, our abilities do open a window for a rescue mission. Short of getting someone from Anar'on, by no means a certainty, and the intermediate negotiations could take some time, which we may not have, Dharaklin and I can provide what may be a decisive balancing factor."

"Against Krans ships and gravitic missiles standing in your way?" Tertulion pointed out quizzically. Sensing her amusement, Terr wasn't willing to give up the concept.

"Those risks can be mitigated if we make a precalculated portal jump to wherever Teena and *Tapal's* people were taken. You cannot defend yourselves against their missiles, but your modulated shields provide a definitive tactical advantage. Perhaps an adequate one."

"Not necessarily," Arlon Dee said, fingers locked on the desk. "Their sensors cannot detect our ships, but our emission residuals gives them an aiming point, and we may have to fire sometime. We can withstand their projectors, but we cannot maneuver fast enough to avoid a missile traveling at nine times light speed, not while we're in normal space."

"I concur, and wherever they were taken, the location will undoubtedly be heavily defended. As we've seen with LTN-3, in any prolonged engagement the Krans will prevail."

"We won't jump in with projectors blazing. We'll come in stealthy and carry out an onsite reconnaissance to confirm the viability of getting them out, and us," Terr said, desperate to find a way to convince Tertulion to proceed.

She shook her head. "You make a logical, but weak argument, Terr. Let's say we proceed. Are you able to determine with sufficient accuracy the target location to make a portal jump calculation possible?"

Terr felt torn between his desire to act and a definite uncertainty. "I don't know, Alkarh. Once I sense when she is awake…maybe."

"A lot of uncertainty to risk a ship's crew. Perhaps more than one ship, but I appreciate your honesty," Tertulion murmured. After a moment, she lifted her chin, her eyes drilling him. "We'll wait until you *can* sense her. I cannot promise more now."

Terr fought back a rush of gratitude. At least, she hadn't rejected the proposal out of hand.

"Thank you, Dapata."

"No, Da Terrllss-rr, I should be thanking *you*. Rescuing your Teena, we'll also be recovering our people. We don't abandon anyone if there is even a shred of hope of getting them. If Teena is alive, perhaps the others are also. Besides, it's our duty, and that's a powerful incentive to act." A whimsical smile played around her mouth. "You won't hold it against us if an attempt is never made?"

Terr sensed her effort to lighten the mood and broke into a broad grin. "Let's see what happens, shall we?"

Her laugh was infectious and Arlon Dee chuckled, running his tongue across his lips. Bearn appeared unwilling to see the humor in it, his face impassive. Did Tertulion blame him for not engaging the *Daktar*? Terr could not see why she would, but he didn't understand how the Orieli Space Arm operated. He was glad the alkarh was prepared to follow up on her principles.

Arlon Dee leaned forward. "Dapata, if my crew are alive—"

"I know. Once they're wakened, they'll likely be interrogated and the Krans will know all about us. It is almost certain to have been the primary reason for taking them. Anything they learn could be catastrophic for us. It might be too late to act even now."

"If you decide to mount a recovery, I want to command it."

"I shall take it under advisement, Karhide. Terr, you mentioned getting a Discipline adept to help you, but I need to look beyond any personal considerations. You experienced firsthand what a Kran invasion could mean for everyone. Would the Rahtir assist us?"

Terr looked at Dhar. "You want to handle this one?"

Dhar bit his lip. "The simple answer is, I don't know. The

Rahtir Council has debated the issue ever since Anar'on became aware of the Kran ship on Devon 3-VL4's moon, but I cannot say if a resolution was reached. Because of historical events involving our relationship with Captal, I do know the Rahtir would be reluctant to interfere, regardless of the threat, but the Celi-Kran are a menace against all life, and not merely another political adversary. Our obligations under the *Saftara* may be the deciding factor."

"They might help, then?"

"I suggest you contact Captal and ask them open a dialogue with Controller Marrakan. I am sure the Executive Council would be just as interested to know."

"Yes, the Serrll worlds are also threatened, and I suspect that dialogue has probably already begun. I will inform OSCOM and they'll refer the matter to the Klanina Caucus." She paused, her expression thoughtful. "Terr, as part of your mission, you and your party were scheduled for transport to Zaron. However, given current developments, it was decided not to do so, at least not immediately. Accordingly, you and Dharaklin will remain on Perilia until a response is received from Captal regarding continuation of your mission. Both of you are granted diplomatic immunity and are now recognized by the planetary VI net and can use the Personal Transport system to go anywhere. Quarters are provided. Simply instruct Cent Comp to transport you."

The holoview showed an aerial view of Tetra, panning over the city.

"Thank you, Alkarh."

"I understand your anxiety and desire to get Teena. Until we formulate a clear action plan, it will be in everyone's interest to keep you occupied. To start your assignment, some of Tetra's citizenry are holding a reception this evening. I trust you will be available?"

Terr tried to hide his dismay. He wanted to blend seamlessly into the city, not be exhibited like a quaint curiosity. Still, it wasn't entirely unexpected, and he would just have to deal with it. He had a mission to execute after all, and formal evenings were part of the package.

"We're at your disposal, Dapata," he replied formally.

Tertulion sensed his discomfort and smiled. "Rest assured, Terr. This will not be a cocktail party to rub elbows, but a serious exchange where all of us can learn from each other. Although you *will* have an opportunity to sample some of our vintages," she added with a grin.

"That will help," he said with a straight face, ignoring Dhar's disapproving frown.

"When you do go out into the city or anywhere else, you'll undoubtedly be recognized. We're just as interested to learn about the Serrll as you're to learn about us, but you'll not be mobbed by our media. Not directly anyway. However, and I apologize in advance, the loss of Teena is a human-interest story that's highlighted awareness of your arrival. We're not cold or impersonal, Terr, and everyone loves to indulge in idle gossip."

"I shall try to cooperate."

"Good. And if you could cooperate a little with me, I would appreciate it. Before I can communicate with OSCOM, I need information. Although the data pack you provided Alkarh Zor-Ell five years ago was helpful, out of necessity, it is purely factual. What I and the Klanina Caucus need is a personal element to understand the Serrll Executive Council and how best to approach them...and their relationship with Kaleen and the Unified Independent Front."

Terr blinked. The lady had studied, but he expected nothing else.

"My instructions from the Bureau of Colonial and Protectorate Affairs were to cooperate fully, with minor reservations."

Those instructions were not given easily. He'd had a sharp exchange with Enllss-rr before he made his uncle realize the Orieli cultural exchange teams would find out whatever they wanted, regardless of any attempts to curtail them. The Executive Council may not like having Observers roaming about, but it wasn't something anyone could do much about, and trying to extract a promise from the Orieli not to use them would likely be a futile gesture. A question of ethics? Terr was not prepared to wade into that quagmire. In the end his uncle got the message.

"In that case, if you and Dhar could meet me later in the morning, we'll discuss it further. I'll make up for any inconvenience with lunch."

Terr took this as dismissal and stood up. "Thank you for everything, Alkarh, and your welcome."

"Perhaps you should wait before thanking me."

* * *

Teena woke with a start, blinked and looked around. She gasped and the gag reflex cut in as she fought for breath and convulsed. When she realized she wasn't drowning, she gulped and forced down an instant of irrational panic. After a moment, her body demanding air, she took a tentative breath, willing herself to stay calm. She inhaled the oxygenated emulsion, apparently suspended in the stuff.

It was strange sensation breathing liquid, her lungs having to work a little harder, but not too uncomfortable. She lifted her arms and looked at them, the liquid around her completely clear. She glanced down at herself and a wave of embarrassment flushed her cheeks at seeing her naked body. Unable to do anything about it, she bit her lip and took stock of her surroundings. Although difficult to judge size, she seemed suspended in a transparent sphere some three kanampirs in diameter. As she moved, the lower left section flickered yellow-orange. Intrigued, she lifted her knees to her chest. Additional panels flickered into life.

Bemused, her fear gone, she looked up and gaped. Arranged in an array above her were other spheres, some transparent, others black. She placed a clenched fist against her mouth and turned. Spheres lay all around her, she could not tell how many, suspended in a vast chamber lit with soft green light. She could not conceive how they were kept in place. What shocked her were the alien creatures held captive inside, all frozen in a fetal position. Many looked purely animal and she wondered why the Krans would be interested in fauna.

She noticed movement in the sphere next to her and sucked in a lungful of fluid. The naked figure inside smiled at her and waved. Numb, she slowly waved at the young Zaronian taroptur who commanded her escape module. All about her, *Tapal's* crew looked at each other, sometimes gesticulating, hands spread as if to say 'I don't know either', but communication was impossible. She didn't know where they were, but at least the Krans had not killed them outright. The possible reason why she and the others were alive did not sit comfortably with her.

She remembered a panicked scramble for the PT alcove when Cent Comp announced abandon ship. That such a large and powerful vessel could be mortally stricken came as a rude shock. Hooked into the VI, she saw how the Krans mauled the Orieli ships, but was still rather surprised to see *Tapal* hit, not believing it could happen. As she reached the alcove, she skidded to a stop and asked Cent Comp to locate Terr. The computer calmly told her he was in Primary Flight Control and safe. Somewhat reassured, preferring to be with him, she stepped into the alcove and immediately found herself in an escape module.

Things happened quickly then. The awfully young-looking officer up front appeared to study the holoview plot that took up the entire forward bulkhead, his fingers tapping color-reactive touch pads. He turned and told everyone to take their seats. She barely noticed the five ratings around her as she watched the bulbous insect-like Kran ship blot out the stars before them. A flare of orange light filled the interior of the module and darkness enveloped her mind.

As she glanced at the occupants surrounding her, they were clearly all prisoners. She didn't complain being alive, but everything she'd studied about the Krans from *Tapal's* vast database indicated the alien monstrosities never took prisoners. As she looked at the columns of spheres, she figured that piece of information needed updating.

She should feel fear and apprehension at not knowing where she was, or what would happen to her, but she forced that part of her irrational mind back. Worrying about a condition she could not control, however dire the possibilities, would only send her into hysterics. To remain sane in a seemingly insane environment, she needed to keep calm and resolute. An analyst with a Scholar's degree, whatever information she managed to glean from this experience may come very useful if she ever got out of here.

Terr!

Several panels around her flickered wildly.

A flutter of trepidation gripped her heart at the thought of him dead. He *had* to have gotten away. Was he here, suspended in one of the spheres somewhere? She had no way of telling. She forced herself to calm down and reached for him. The indefinable that linked them still pulsed with life and fire. He was safe. Relief flooded her and she took in a deep breath of liquid. She did not care about herself, or what might happen to her, as long as he was safe. All she needed to do now was wait. He would come for her. She never doubted it for a moment. But could he? She had no idea where she was. Even if she knew, she could not communicate with him. She fought down despair and willed herself to be reasonable. There might not be anything she could do now, but if she lived, time may provide an answer.

The analytical part of her mind took over and she turned

her attention to the sphere. She reached out with her right hand, palm open, and touched the transparent wall. It yielded slightly before firming into a hard surface, her movement causing two panels at her feet to flicker with light. Whatever held her seemed attuned to her mind. There were no fittings or life-support machinery. Blinking, she realized she wasn't hungry or thirsty. Did the liquid provide nourishment? It would be logical. And her wastes? She spent a moment marveling at the technology able to do this.

Two columns in front of her, a sphere began to ripple all over with color. The crewman inside opened his mouth in a silent scream and clutched his head between his hands. A halo of white light surrounded his shoulders and head. She didn't know how much time passed, probably only a minute or two, although it seemed an eternity. The crewman convulsed, shuddered and was still. Gradually the sphere turned black and she knew he was dead. What did the Krans do to him?

Grief stricken, she watched helplessly as another crewman suffered the same fate. When the taroptur beside her stiffened and became still, she feared for him—and herself. Tears welled in her eyes as a white halo enveloped him, expecting him to die. She wanted to strike out at the mindless things that held her, but only managed a strangled sob. Suddenly, the light around him faded and he looked dazed. When he saw her, he smiled weakly and nodded.

A tingle spread through her and she gasped. She felt gently but firmly gripped, and she lost all sensation.

"You are not like the others," a decisive masculine voice sounded in her head. "What are you?"

The command imperative overwhelmed her senses and will, and like watching a Wall, images of her home on Taltair, her work at the Diplomatic Branch, the grumpy old Anabb Karr barking at people; it all came flooding out, unstoppable.

"Where do you come from?"

First, Taltair as seen from space, then the view expanded

to encompass the rest of the Sofam Confederacy and the bordering blocks of the Sargon Directorate and the Karkan Federation until the whole Serrll Combine lay open before her in stark three-dimensional relief.

"How did you come to be with those others?"

Immediately, she was in an M-1 with Terr and Dhar. Devon 3-VL4 came into view, then *Tapal*. She saw the crippled M-4 trying to get away from the Kran ship, then blasted by ravening energies that reduced the once proud vessel into a battered, drifting hulk. Terr, standing in *Tapal's* PFC, arms leveled, spearing the Kran ship with a single bolt of golden light. Teena tried desperately to block the flood of images rushing through her mind, but she could not control her responses. Aware of what was happening and what this information meant to the Kran voice, she could only watch in horror as her mind betrayed not only Terr and her, but also the Serrll and the Orieli.

"Why did you come to LTN-3?"

She blanched. The voice knew everything, presumably from other crewmembers it interrogated. The images returned.

A Diplomatic Branch threats and intentions analyst, her ordered thoughts went swiftly over Terr's mission to study the Orieli. When she saw the transport portal destroyed, realizing the only way now to cross the vast expanse of the Moanar Nebula—Karina Shield, as the Orieli called it—was through the breach, her betrayal became complete. Distressed, she wanted to cry out for it to stop, begging for release and death. It didn't help that the voice probably knew everything already. Her guilt and shame at not able to stop herself burned silently within her.

"What is Terr?" the voice demanded after a moment of blessed silence and darkness.

She saw Terr as he was on that fateful night when they both stood on a hill overlooking the lights of Barden, the smell of rain fresh in the air. It seemed such a long time ago now. Hands held high, enclosed in a cocoon of blue light, he chanted the litany that would invoke the god of Death to join with him.

Head back, he loosed the lightnings at the turbulent heavens. She stood awed before this unworldly being who loved her, and someone she almost drove away.

Although she could not move, she imagined herself standing tall and proud, chin lifted in defiance, her green eyes blazing with fury.

"He is a lord of Death, and he will come for me."

"Uncorrelated. Explain."

Blurred, confused images flashed through her mind. How could she explain to a machine what and who Terr was, when she wasn't certain she knew herself? Some things, however, she did know. Stick to the bare facts and don't elaborate, she told herself. She suspected she was only fooling herself.

"Once joined with a god, he can destroy anything he wills, like your ship on our moon." She could not tell if the enigmatic voice understood the difference between exaggeration and a blatant lie, but she believed in the truth of her words. Apparently, so did the voice.

"Gods are imaginary manifestations of organic intelligent life. Supernatural entities do not exist."

"You saw what happened at Devon 3-VL4."

"I gathered from your mind only a display of physical ability."

"What biological organism can channel power able to destroy a starship?"

More silence. She thought the voice had finished with her, when after a time it spoke again.

"Will Terr destroy the Celi-Kran?"

"I cannot say, but he will not stop until he finds me."

"Are there other creatures like him?"

"No." Even in denial, Dhar's image sprang into her mind. Wanderers, clad in brown surtaf robes, standing on a dune crest, surveyed their desert domain. She saw herself before the red cliffs of Athal Than and felt the pull as the gods called to her, Terr rushing to her side to hold her back. Anar'on looming before her as the M-1 made ready to depart, the colored sands smearing the planet, leaving her with disturbing memories and some understanding of Terr's love for the parched deserts below.

"A world of imaginary gods?"

"Not gods, but Discipline adepts able to link with a god and wield his power."

"I saw in your mind an image of a humanoid, fire pouring from his hands at a world, two stars at his feet. Can Terr destroy a world?"

"He cannot, but some Wanderers can."

"Just by willing it?"

"Yes."

"From Anar'on?"

"I don't know," she said truthfully.

"Irrelevant. Terr does not know where you are or where this world is, and neither does Anar'on."

Teena smiled, if only in her mind. "That's where you're wrong. Anar'on might not know where I am, but Terr certainly does."

"Explain!"

"We share a link, a bond. Even now, we're joined and he can sense me. He knows where I am. Kill me and you will see who he is as he deals out his vengeance."

Did Terr know? He seemed to at other times, but the Serrll stars were home and both worked within a common frame of reference there. She didn't know where she was now.

Abruptly, she felt her body freed and sagged, mentally and physically. Would the Kran voice spare her and the others based on what it knew about Terr? Did it consider him a threat? It was a question of imponderables. Realistically, the Krans had nothing to fear from anyone, least of all some hypothetical god possibly thousands of light-years away. When the voice finished with them, she and others would probably end up frozen like the specimens in this menagerie, their minds emptied.

She summoned all her strength and sent a gush of warmth and love to Terr. Whatever fate awaited her, he would know she thought only of him to the end.

* * *

Terr jerked and almost spilled the tumbler of brown mixed fruit juice in his hand. A somewhat unusual flavor, but he'd developed a taste for it. Fork poised, a piece of speared egg and vegetable omelet dangling, Dhar lifted an inquiring eyebrow.

"The juice not to your liking?" His voice rumbled from deep within his chest.

"It's Teena! I can sense her." A smile of unutterable joy lit Terr's face before churning emotion wiped it away and he swallowed hard. "I almost gave up hope, Nightwings," he whispered.

After eighteen days of intolerable silence, she was back. Her absence had chipped at his resolve and made him question himself. As the days dragged, merging wearily into each other, he wondered whether Dhar was right and he nurtured a hopeless desire. What kept him from plunging into total despair was the weak link that still bound them, telling him she was still alive. As long as she lived, he would not fail her.

Dhar put down his fork and gripped Terr's hand hard. "My spirit soars with you, Sankri. She is well?"

"I can see rows and rows of transparent capsules, all filled with aliens and animals. There must be hundreds." Color drained from his face as he stared tragically at his brother.

"You fear they're held for interrogation?"

"What if it's more, Nightwings?" All sorts of horrible images flashed through his mind.

"It's no use torturing yourself. Try and put it out of your mind."

Terr gave a heavy sigh. "You're right, but it's not that easy. Anyway, we can move now."

Guardians of Shadow

Two days ago, Tertulion received approval to mount a recovery mission, having obtained consent from Captal releasing Terr and Dhar to act at their own discretion. On the question of providing an adept, Anar'on was quiet. Terr did not blame Marrakan or the Rahtir Council for not acting. The Controller faced a complex ethical problem where any decision he made could be interpreted as wrong. Terr knew how he wanted Anar'on to act, but he had a personal interest.

Although the Rahtir might be willing to aid him, a brother Wanderer, even though alien, would Captal acquiesce if Marrakan refused to extend his protective umbrella over the Serrll? Would the Orieli if he chose not to get involved? As far as Terr knew, there were only some 70,000 third-level adepts on Anar'on out of a population of 645 million. Not every native became an adept, and the gods did not accept every second-level adept during the final trial. Out of available adepts, only a few might be prepared to go off-planet to protect strategic Serrll assets, let alone become involved with the Orieli in a Kran war, one likely to escalate. The Rahtir were an integral part of every settlement, providing cohesion, continuity and cultural memory. To remove them would disrupt the Wanderer lifestyle in a climate where some conservative Rahtir questioned Marrakan's push to further integrate Anar'on into the Serrll mainstream.

Strictly speaking, this was not a question of ethics at all, but one of politics. The Unified Independent Front, comprising of Kaleen and Orgomy star systems, plus a handful of nonaligned systems, had declared its independence and were set to take up a seat in the ruling Executive Council after the general elections in two years. The Revisionist Party held six seats, and with it, the government majority. The Servatory Party with its four seats had struggled to overthrow the Revisionists for centuries. With a possible Sargon/Palean merger, the Palean seat would then swing to the Servatory camp and make the Revisionist's hold on power very tentative, with the potential to destabilize the entire Serrll social fabric, resulting in possible economic and armed conflict. The UIF's seat would ensure the continuity of the Sofam-dominated government—if it supported the Revisionists. Should the UIF decide to side with the Servatory Party and the Sargon/Palean merger eventuated, there would be an immediate change of government. No wonder the Servatory Party and the Revisionist Party were actively wooing Marrakan, the person who, with Kaleen and Orgomy, largely created the Unified Independent Front.

It was a poisoned chalice for the UIF, though, given how both major political blocks in the past threatened to annex Kaleen and Orgomy systems, forcing them to become the UIF to ensure survival as a recognized entity. With the realization that the General Assembly would formally ratify the UIF and recognize it as a legitimate political union, the sudden fawning attention by the two major parties was transparently hollow, even amusing.

Sofam did threaten to move a motion in the Assembly to nullify the independent's single seat, which would have opened a door to a flurry of annexations by other blocks, thereby denying the Servatory camp a supporting seat. Sofam never followed through on its threat until recently, and done only to pressure the UIF to support the Revisionist coalition. Despite the strife and injustice pervading the Serrll, the Revisionists acted—most of the time—in the general interest of all and maintained stability throughout the Combine. Should the Servatory Party and its militant Sargon coalition partner ever assume ascendancy, chaos would likely spread as Sargon sought to implement its authoritarian martial philosophy on all systems.

If it *were* only a question of politics, Anar'on might decide to help him, and damn everybody else. As Dhar said, the Krans sought to annihilate all life, not caring about politics. Anar'on would protect itself regardless of any political fallout, Terr was certain of that, but it would survive as an island in a sea of Kran-dominated stars. Sooner or later the Krans would find a way to destroy the Wanderers, and the gods of Death would need to seek a new home. A shitty way to do business.

"Where are you?" Dhar asked after a time, as he cut another piece of omelet, his fork turned into a knife at the first cutting stroke. Terr watched how the marvelous tool transformed itself into a fork as Dhar stabbed at the bite. He knew all about memory alloys, but this application of nanobod technology was at an altogether different level. The thing was smarter than some people he knew.

"Just spinning cobwebs," he mused with a wan smile and took another sip of juice. "Even though Captal has let us go, Anar'on still hasn't said what they'll do."

"The wheels of politics turn slowly, my brother, and the Rahtir Council has a lot to consider."

"While sipping their fermented peelath berry juice."

Dhar frowned in disapproval. "Now you're needlessly irreverent."

"Sorry. Unfortunately, I can't wait for those wheels to turn. Everybody may be preoccupied looking at the big picture, whatever the hell that is, but I'm concerned with only one small part of it that has Teena. Captal and the Klanina Caucus can worry about everything else."

"Karhide Dee is willing enough, but will Alkarh Tertulion act?"

"Let's find out... Cent Comp?"

"Ready."

"Connect personal to Alkarh Tertulion, PERCOM," he issued the mental command.

"Please wait."

That was one of the nice things when hooked into the planetary VI net, the ability to communicate with everybody. Provided, of course, the other party wanted to talk to you. Terr could only imagine how the comms net was implemented.

"Da Terrllss-rr, what can I do for you?" Tertulion's strong voice sounded in his head.

101

He winced when he realized it was still early morning. "My apologies for disturbing you, Alkarh. It was thoughtless of me."

"You wouldn't have called without a valid reason."

"It might be important to me, but not to you. Teena is awake."

"Ah. Ten o'clock, my office. We'll talk then."

"Thank you, Dapata." Terr looked at Dhar and smiled. "She'll see us at ten."

Dhar leaned into his chair. "If we do go, regardless of what may await us at the journey's end, I will welcome a change of scenery. What we've seen has given me mental indigestion."

His heart lighter, Terr smiled, sympathizing completely.

The first two days of their stay were relentless, spent in intense debriefs. Not about the action around LTN-3, he was not qualified to have an opinion, but picking his and Dhar's mind about the Serrll Combine in general. Although the Orieli Observer teams would gather the base data, same as the Serrll sociodynamicists would, but at a vastly more sophisticated level, the Orieli wanted the human dimension as Tertulion said. Terr gave them that dimension, perhaps more than they bargained for.

When he talked to Enllss about his terms of reference, his uncle was unequivocal. Terr could say whatever he wanted, short of being treasonous. The last was added seriously, something Terr understood and had no problem complying with. A serving officer in the Serrll Scout Fleet, and despite his mocking attitude toward superior authority, he believed in his commissioning oath to protect the Constitution and the Articles of Association. He may be detached to Anabb's Diplomatic Branch now, but when all was said and done, he was a loyal Serrll citizen, even though the place might be rotten in parts.

Although he shared his views freely, Dhar was more reticent discussing the Wanderer Discipline. He spoke readily enough of the UIF and the political and economic dimension it worked within, but the relationship the Wanderers had with the gods of Death were not explored beyond the bare facts. Some on Tertulion's team were less than pleased, but none pressed Dhar too far. Thinking that Terr, an alien initiate, would be more forthcoming, they were in for another disappointment. The Observers would probably get hold of the *Saftara*, it wasn't secret writing, making what they could of its underlying philosophies, but Terr walked in the shadow of Death and that relationship could not be violated for political expediency. Besides, *Tapal's* holoview log where Terr destroyed the *Daktar* gave them enough to occupy their thoughts.

Held in one of the glittering city towers, the sessions gave him the beginnings of an insight into the workings of what he saw as Orieli official machinery. He was still to fully understand the government structure running Perilia. There was a bureaucracy, of course. To administer a planet and interact with other worlds took organization, largely understated, people used to formulate policy and action plans. It started to come together when someone told him that a network of sophisticated versions of Cent Comp, linked with every system in the Technic Union, handled all routine matters. A staggering concept, but after a while, it made eminent sense.

It was gratifying to find the Orieli also used a common exchange medium, necessary in any form of economic activity given the disparate social structures making up the Union. Captal would find this comforting, as many idealists back home spoke volubly about societies who overcame the need for wealth accrual and accounting, personal greed seen as something tainted and abhorrent, a lingering thread from a primitive past. Competition is an evolutionary survival driver and best measured in hard cash.

The following days were a blur of social gatherings with Tetra's elite, and functions all over Perilia. There were no minders to watch over them and they wandered freely. At no stage did Terr feel like an exhibit provided for the amusement of the locals. Everyone they met was genuinely interested in them and the Serrll. This awareness by the local population of Orieli social structure within the White Cloud, as the Orieli called the galaxy, and the Orieli Cluster, staggered him. Few people in the Serrll exhibited such interest, or cared what went on in Captal. Given the machinations of the various blocks, Terr didn't blame them.

Perilia very much matched his expectations: a city of architectural landscapes complementing open parks and lakes. People lived there like in any other concentration of services, social facilities and entertainment. What felt unusual was absence of overhead traffic, a prevalent feature of any Serrll city. A planetary transport system able to whisk a person anywhere removed the need to waste time moving in a vehicle. This single innovation did more than anything to change the Orieli social fabric; radically altering how necessary infrastructure and products were delivered to private dwellings and industry. Despite able to skip across the planet on a whim, the locals still enjoyed walking as a favorite pastime. Where the transport system did not provide coverage, little utility platforms still enabled one to visit a secluded place.

Terr relished sampling local foods, not concerned about possible gastric problems. When tempted to try something too exotic, Cent Comp issued a warning. Strolling through several bazaars and open markets, he savored the wafting cooking smells, the milling people and colorful clothing they wore, hole-in-the-wall vendors provided all the variety he could stomach. Conservative by nature, Dhar admitted he enjoyed some of the vegetarian dishes. Terr wanted to connect with the locals, even visiting several outlying rural settlements, he could not capture Perilia's underlying culture. Integrated into the Orieli social mainstream for millennia, there were no quaint aboriginal enclaves left to see. What did he expect? Stalls of souvenir trinkets peddled to tourists by vendors dressed in picturesque costumes? Life here was ordered, neat and functional, with all the comforts technology could provide, and everyone seemed outwardly content.

They visited Karachi, the third planet in the Tavor system, an old rusty world that held primitive life two billion years ago, but gave up the struggle as over eons its giant gaseous neighbor slowly pulled it out of orbit on the fringe of the habitable zone and the solar wind tore away its atmosphere. A geological curiosity, it reminded Terr of the Four Suns mining world Anulus, which incidentally led to all the subsequent unpleasantness, ending with him walking in the shadow of Death. Perilia used that world for pretty much the same reason: a source of mineral and metal feedstocks.

All manufacturing was done on site, including disposal of wastes by application of advanced nanobods. Transport of finished products made him stare. No convoys of cargo tramps played across the stars. They employed precisely tuned transport portals to deliver goods directly to Perilia, or to orbital portals in other systems, which relayed stuff to the surface. Using the interdimensional gateway for personal transport was merely a handy byproduct when the technology was first developed, someone told him.

An interesting twelve days, and Terr learned a lot about the Orieli at many levels, but it would be good taking a break from cerebral exercising. Once Teena was with him again, they'd be off to Zaron where it all began. What he managed to glimpse of Perilian life left a profound impression and he looked forward to seeing more elsewhere.

Terr stepped out of the PT alcove into Tertulion's lounge, not surprised to see Karhide Arlon Dee chatting with the Alkarh. In the process of commissioning *Parsha*, a brand new *Nasor*-class assault ship. Terr and Dhar were invited on board once, which left Terr gaping at the PFC layout, engineering spaces, and tactical stations. Perhaps an M-9 could face it, but he would not bet either way. The Serrll could definitely use a handful of them right now.

"Welcome," Alkarh Tertulion said simply from her soft couch. "Make yourself comfortable."

Nobody stood much on formality or protocol, as Terr found. It did not mean the Orieli Space Arm lacked discipline, but enforced in more subtle ways than saluting or clicking of heels—a reflection of social maturity perhaps? He was yet to decide. Maybe it was simply leniency toward an alien not versed in local customs.

He took a seat opposite Tertulion, and Dhar sat next to Arlon Dee.

"Thank you for receiving us on such short notice, Alkarh."

"Not at all. We all waited for this moment. Allow me to express my pleasure to hear that Teena-raye is well."

"It was a strain, not knowing."

"I can imagine. What are you able to sense?"

"She's held in a capsule within a chamber filled with spheres containing all kinds of alien lifeforms, animal and sentient. From what I could tell, they seemed frozen, in stasis. I also saw some of *Tapal's* crew."

Arlon drew in a sharp breath and cast a quick look at Tertulion.

"Alive and apparently well. An amazing gift, this link of yours," she said slowly. "Now, the penultimate question. Where are they? Can you tell?"

A holoview image sprang above the low kidney-shaped table between them. The vast wall of the Karina stretched into the distance, beyond which a profusion of stars guarded the deeps. Yellow points marked what he assumed were locations of the three leading LTN stations. Terr hooked himself into the VI and expanded the image, narrowing the scale, driven by the link connecting him to Teena.

The galactic arm started to become discernable and the Karina began to break up into enormous filaments dozens of light-years long, streaming away from the central body. He noted the distance and hardly believed what he saw. That their link could remain intact across thousands of lights seemed hardly credible. Slowly, he lifted his arm and pointed at a pulsing blue dot he created near a small cluster of stars.

"There."

Tertulion blinked. "Four thousand nine hundred light-years," she whispered in awe. "No ship could possibly traverse such a distance in eighteen days."

Terr blanched. Was it eighteen days since *Tapal* confronted the *Daktar*? It seemed like a lifetime ago.

"They had to reach a support base or something and used a transport portal," Arlon Dee added thoughtfully.

"Obviously. How certain are you of these coordinates?"

"It's an approximation, I admit, but it won't be far off."

"Not from here it wouldn't be." She said wryly and shook her head. "Almost five thousand lights. Incredible. Well, Karhide?"

"We'll use Perilia's portal and come in with our interceptor net fully modulated. Even if the Krans detect our emergence, it will appear as a momentary energy burst," Arlon Dee said.

"They may have the ability to detect an interdimensional disturbance," Tertulion pointed out.

"If they can, they can. Once under way, though, we'll be invisible to their sensors."

"They'd still know someone was coming and consolidate their defenses. We don't know the extent of their capabilities."

"Nothing we can do about it, Alkarh. Once there, Terr can provide a more accurate nav fix."

"Can your portal cover such a distance?" Terr asked.

"It's not so much a question of distance, but application of available power and accurately determining your exit point," Arlon said and licked his lips. "The energy curve goes up steeply as a function of time, and time and distance are really the same thing. However, without a known determined exit, the uncertainty principle kicks in and it's what makes blind jumps so dangerous. We'll study our astronomical data and work on it."

107

"How do you propose to get down and out?"

"Once you accurately locate the chamber, we'll send down an RV/4 dart with a portable PT interface. That'll allow us to transport people to the ship quickly when we get them out of the spheres—if we can—or for making a hasty retreat, the more likely scenario. If necessary, we'll leave the dart behind. Until we reconnoiter the site and establish what we're likely to face and determine mission feasibility, we cannot plan in any detail."

Terr liked his optimism. Still, it made sense. To charge in, blasting everything in sight, fighting their way through Kran warrior units, wasn't even an option. There were easier ways to die. They would probably end up in a sphere anyway with other specimens—if they were unlucky.

"You don't happen to have invisibility shields, do you?"

Arlon Dee smiled. "Afraid not. I fervently hope we don't have to do this the hard way, and I'm not trivializing the obstacles."

Tertulion pursed her lips. "You're merely sidestepping them. A rash plan, Karhide. Even if you manage to extract our people and survive, it will take you a while to return, almost thirty-three days."

Terr quickly worked out the math. If they boosted at six lights per hour…817 hours. At twenty-five hours in a standard day…the figures matched. Among her other talents, the Alkarh was also a lightning calculator.

Arlon Dee shrugged. "I don't know what we'll find there, probably lots of hostile Kran ships, and the entire attempt may prove impossible, but we won't be able to tell until we look at the site. Even if we fail, we'll obtain critical tactical intelligence."

"Useful only if you manage to get back. However, as Terr said, his and Dhar's special abilities may give you the necessary edge," Tertulion mused.

Terr listened to the calm exchange with wonder. The two acted like they were choosing a meal from a menu. Then again, hashing over the unknowns was futile. Arlon Dee knew the risks and capability of his ship, the rest would reveal itself, hopefully not terminally.

"Then it's decided?" he ventured hopefully, looking hard at Tertulion.

She chuckled. "Did you doubt us?"

"Frankly, I doubted the bureaucrats on Captal and Zaron."

She laughed, genuinely amused. "Had you still been on the other side of the Karina, you'd probably be on your way home. Under the circumstances, Alkarh Zor-Ell was forced to suspend the transport of your cultural exchange teams until our portal is rebuilt. We're rebuilding it despite inadequate defenses. Speaking bluntly, Captal has good reason to cooperate."

He shook off unpleasant memories, completely aware of the strategic situation. Should the Krans invade in force, the Serrll would not be able to repel them alone. It needed the Orieli, regardless of whether Anar'on chose to become involved or not. Adepts could not be placed on every Serrll world, for that's what it would take. Well, they *could*, but he didn't believe Marrakan or the Rahtir Council would agree to such a drastic proposal.

"And I understand those reasons," Terr said.

"I am sure you do. You and Dhar contributed significantly to our knowledge of the Serrll, and I came to have a lot of respect for both of you. You may consider that sending you into a hostile situation a reward, and perhaps it is, but I fear for all of you. The magnitude of your task is almost unimaginable, as are its potential difficulties. I'm not surprised OSCOM left the decision to me." She saw Terr's amused smile and lifted her hand. "It's not to create a convenient scapegoat should you fail to return, merely a chain of command decision. This is my problem and I was left to solve it within the boundaries of obvious constraints."

"The attempt must be made, Alkarh," Arlon said firmly, "and we have two force multipliers."

Tertulion sighed. "I can only hope it will be enough."

Stefan Vučak

Chapter Three

At quarter secondary boost, *Parsha* slowly approached a black point in space where the transport portal waited to hurl them into the unknown. On their port quarter Tavor's Star burned bright yellow. Below them, nestled in the plane of the ecliptic, Perilia's green orb lit the deeps.

"Operational caution. Range to portal, sixty-four ampirs and closing," Cent Comp warned through the VI.

Comfortable in a swivel-couch beside Arlon Dee, Terr watched as the ship advanced toward the portal, its profile rotating in the mainframe plot before him. Surrounded by a pentagon of generators feeding off the scanner array positioned above the sun, the two-ampir-diameter ring of blue-green energy flickered into existence in response to the housekeeping computer's interrogative, the colors shifting, slithering, as the ring constantly reset a boundary to something that did not have shape or form. Behind them, a string of other vessels waited for their turn to be hurled to their destination or waypoint.

"Any last thoughts?" Arlon Dee quipped and Terr grinned.

"Many, but it's a bit late for second-guessing." *Or thinking about turning around*, he added to himself.

"Range to portal, thirteen hundred kanampirs. Interface charged and setting coordinates," Cent Comp declared.

On Terr's left, Dhar let out a long sigh. "Well, this is it."

"I've never done one of these before, but I'm told it's like stepping into a PT alcove," Terr commented, his eyes fixed on the looming portal ring, excitement making his stomach squirm. So many unknowns waited for them on the other side, Teena's face the only thing that kept him going.

110

Diplomatic missions were not really supposed to be like this!

Rit!

"Except there's no way back."

Terr did not bother answering. If Dhar wanted to be moody, fine. In his rush to rescue Teena, even if it cost his life, Terr never took time to ask if his brother wanted to accompany him on this harebrained scheme, automatically assuming he would. They might be brothers, but Dhar had his own drives, ambitions...and fears. He deserved to make the choice.

Although Captal released them to act at their discretion, it did not necessarily mean the mission must be suspended. When they left Tertulion, Terr confronted Dharaklin and offered him an opportunity to continue with the mission and go to Zaron. It made no sense to perhaps lose them both. Should the worst happen, he knew the alkarh would pass on his report to the BCPA, but why risk them both! After all, Teena was Terr's problem.

He need not have worried. Dhar interrupted his lame explanation, gently placed his palm on Terr's chest, and looked serious.

"We are one, Sankri. Your pain is my pain. Your loss is my loss. When your spirit soars, mine rejoices with you. I go where you go, just as you would for me."

Relieved, Terr returned the gesture and they stood there, content to stand in the shadow of the god who adopted them.

"Two hundred kanampirs," Cent Comp stated and slowed the ship further.

Ahead, the blue fires around the ring flared bright. No stars shone within the ring's impenetrable blackness. *Parsha* crept forward.

"Transiting."

The ship pierced the energy boundary and vanished.

Surprisingly, Terr did not experience the same cutting cold

that normally accompanied personal transport. He felt the familiar crushing pressure and a moment of irrational panic, but his senses settled almost immediately when he realized they were through.

"Tactical caution. Interceptor net modulated and ship is at full EMCON. No threats detected. Status. Condition three active."

At rest, *Parsha* stood ready to face any intruder. Terr scanned the stars around them, but they were just stars, no different from any other. A long gas filament on the port quarter marked the last vestige of the Karina, still maintaining a boundary, but no longer an impassable one. They *had* jumped into the unknown. Everything looked serene, if one could forget they were deep in Kran space.

As he studied the edge of the Karina, he recalled Arlon Dee's words how exposed Orieli space was to a Kran flanking thrust. Although more than three thousand lights from here, the frontier systems of Setlan Eleven, Kardush, Heplon and others lay unprotected should the Krans ever learn of their location. A blind portal jump in force would result in horrific devastation and imaginable loss of life. Although the Orieli Space Arm commanded unbelievable warships, there weren't all that many, at least not large ones like the *Nasors*. After all, peace ruled the vast expanse of the Technic Union. If the Krans had indeed interrogated *Tapal's* crew, they may very well already know what they needed to mount attacks. It would only be a matter of time then before they pounced. If they interrogated Teena, they would know all about the Serrll and its vulnerability. As one of Anabb's analysts, she had a lot of knowledge stored away in that pretty head of hers. It made for grim contemplation by the Executive Council. He was glad not to have these problems.

A prickling sensation spread through him as his link with Teena reasserted itself and he sent a gush of longing love to her. On impulse, he reached for her and her form coalesced into a ghostly white outline before him. She smiled and her right cheek dimpled as her hand touched his. He felt her warmth and drank her in, fighting back a moan of loss as she slowly faded, leaving behind only a poignant memory.

He blinked in surprise to see Arlon Dee staring at him. Clearly, he saw, as did the watchstanders, judging by the awed expression on their faces. Terr smiled sheepishly.

"Teena-raye?" Arlon asked and licked his lips.

"Set course for that blue and white binary," Terr said and pointed at the mainframe plot. They were not far, some nineteen lights. Not bad, all things considered.

The pattern of stars immediately shifted as *Parsha* transited, obedient to Arlon's mental command. The watchstanders looked away to concentrate on their areas of responsibility. They were in hostile space after all.

"What else can you do that you haven't told us?" Arlon Dee demanded, his expression friendly.

Terr grinned. "Believe me, sir, I'm amazed every time this happens." He didn't quite answer the question, simply because he did not know what to say.

When he walked out of Athal Than the second time, the gods having forgiven him his excesses at the misused of their gift, Sidhara told him he was now changed in ways impossible to predict. Governed by the individual's personality, every initiate was different and the power would manifest itself uniquely to him. Terr didn't feel different as they sat by the flickering campfire, shielded by the blazing stars of The Arch. He *had* changed. The pierced wreckage of the Kran cruiser on Devon 3-VL4's moon attested to that. Thinking about that campfire, he would not have minded being there now. The desert had a quality of making things simple, and he craved that simplicity now.

"Anything waiting for us?"

"Nothing detected—yet," Arlon mused.

Watchstanders monitored their areas, everyone under-standably edgy. Threats would appear soon enough.

Terr flashed Dhar a smile and relaxed in the couch, mar-veling at the wondrous ship he was in. Unlike *Tapal's* PFC with its command platform and separate operations bowl, *Parsha's* nerve center was a single twelve-kanampir-wide domed cham-ber containing layered interactive holoview displays. Spaced evenly along the wall, eight couches allowed for a fully manned watch, which excluded the four command stations. Terr was not merely looking at the displays, they surrounded him. It took some getting used to, still uncomfortable processing the vol-ume of data available to him. Without the housekeeping com-puter, controlling the ship would be impossible.

He also reveled being here and so close to Teena. Regard-less of what happened, he was content. Despite his unrealistic fantasies about sweeping aside the Krans and carrying her away in his arms, having her suitably grateful once alone, he knew that reality never lived up to anyone's fancy. But without a vi-sion, there was no drive, no desire to achieve and overcome impediments. Realistically, he knew they would probably fail in his quest, and he was prepared to face what failure might mean, but no power in existence would stop him from trying to reach her.

Kemp, a tall taciturn Zaronian, occupied the executive of-ficer's seat beside Arlon Dee. According to the Karhide, Tavac finally got a command and a deserved promotion. Terr knew how disruptive breaking in a new exec could be, and this time, Arlon also had to cope with a new ship and crew. He was get-ting a hell of a shakedown cruise.

Terr turned and locked eyes with the alien, eyes impossible to read, and he wondered what thoughts lurked behind them.

"A somewhat unusual start to your diplomatic mission, Da," Kemp said evenly.

"Dealing with the Fernai might have been easier. Is it too late to get off somewhere?"

114

The exec smiled and looked away, his face assuming a slightly vacant look typical of a VI trance.

At six lph, *Parsha* would close with the binary system in just over three hours. In the tactical plot, the system's structure revealed itself. Two orange-brown gas giants orbited the large white primary, the second one absolutely massive. A failed protostar that could have created a trinary star system? Four rocky planets lay strung out behind them, separated by a wide asteroid belt. In a typical configuration, a ring of rock and icy remnants orbited the outer reaches. The slightly smaller and younger blue star clung to its more ponderous parent, sucking matter in glowing filaments of yellow plasma, forming an accretion disk around itself.

Three lights out, *Parsha* detected energy leakage from all outer planets, the innermost showing the broadest spectrum. Although not a given, Arlon Dee assumed it was their target. Terr concurred.

Sensors also located Kran pickets; three *Daktars* prowled equidistantly outside the icy belt. As yet, there was no indication they detected *Parsha*. The atmosphere within PFC became palpably tense. The ship slowed to one lph and coasted toward the inner system, coming in above the ecliptic.

"Cent Comp? Designate system KP-001," Arlon ordered.

"Acknowledged. Tactical caution. Energy fluctuations detected above KP-001D consistent with an interdimensional transport portal. Caution. Four *Sandar*-class battlecruisers and two *Fadhir*-class attack ships detected holding geosynchronous equatorial position above KP-001C."

"How's your link with Teena?" Arlon Dee demanded.

"She is definitely on the third planet."

"That's something to work with. Judging by energy levels and number of picket ships, it looks like we've hit a major staging and support outpost. The Krans *would* pick such a place to bring their captives."

"Why make things easy."

"When we go into orbit, you need to pinpoint exactly the chamber location. We don't want to linger here longer than necessary," Arlon added, tactfully avoiding mentioning an alarmingly long list of pitfalls facing them.

"Cent Comp? Drop normal," Kemp said.

"Exiting subspace relational."

As *Parsha* closed, the planet's atmosphere envelope now clearly visible, Terr wondered whether this was such a brilliant idea. However heroic, the task they'd set themselves looked more hopeless with every passing minute.

"Tactical caution. Force lines detected consistent with graviton sensors."

In the mainframe plot, a grid of sharp red lines enclosed the entire system. Although *Parsha* itself was undetectable, the effect of its mass on the surrounding gravitational field could not be disguised. As the ship interrupted the flux of gravity waves streaming from the binary and its family of planets, sensors would register a disturbance and issue an alert, as had probably already happened. If they didn't before, the Krans now knew someone was coming.

"Modulated IFF signal received from KP-001D," Cent Comp stated.

"Ah, damn," Arlon Dee muttered softly and pursed his mouth.

Terr exchanged a concerned look with Dhar as a cluster of blue points broke orbit above KP-001C. It had not taken them long to react.

"Tactical caution. The *Fadhirs* and two *Sandar* warships now on converging course. Intercept in eleven minutes under current flight parameters."

"That's not a force I relish tangling with," Arlon growled.

"Can they track us accurately enough to establish a firing lock?" Terr asked.

"With the graviton sensor net to give them a targeting fix? It's possible."

Dhar gripped Terr's shoulder. "Sankri, excuse me for saying this, but we need to consider the safety of the ship and crew."

Terr gritted his teeth, a wealth of emotion churning through him. If he allowed himself, rage would consume him. He felt an overwhelming sense of loss and pain tear his heart apart as he searched Dhar's eyes, finding his sorrow reflected in them. When she needed him the most, he failed her.

Teena!

He stared at the plot and his desire to lash out slowly flushed out of him as his shoulders sagged. Struggling against crushing helplessness, he blinked hard and turned to Arlon Dee.

"Karhide, transit while you can." To engage the approaching ships in combat would be futile gesture and a needless loss of lives.

To be so close! *Forgive me, my pet.* He reached with his hand, wanting to feel her one last time, but she didn't appear.

Parsha suddenly heaved and Terr staggered. Did the Krans launch gravitic missiles? Through the VI, he saw a sphere of white incandescence expand rapidly in front of them. Another explosion behind them rocked the ship as the blast wave reached them.

"Cent Comp! Assume neutral status!" Arlon snapped immediately and *Parsha* slowed to a stop. In a burst of scintillation, four objects immediately materialized around the ship. Arlon snorted in disgust. "Mines! The demons used their portal to transport mines."

"Possibly equipped with gravitic generators, like their missiles," Terr added meditatively, not liking any of it. After coming in totally undetected and confident, they were now naked and exposed—and trapped.

"Don't even mention it."

If the ship moved, the mines would go off. Terr did not need to have it explained. He clenched his fists and waited for it to end. As the minutes dragged and nothing happened, he began to wonder what the Krans intended. Take them captive and study *Parsha*? It would be better for all of them if Arlon Dee destroyed his ship first.

As the Kran warships closed to half a million ampirs, the *Sandars* broke formation and took positions in the vertical plane above and below. The *Fadhirs* simply stood there, blocking Arlon's line of advance. They could not even flee now. If *Parsha* attempted to transit, the Kran gravitic missile's nine times light speed would get them before the ship could bring up its distortion field precursor. Terr wondered why Tertulion allowed them to make the attempt. She must have realized the low probability of success. A gesture because it was the correct ethical thing to do? Yet what choice did they have? If a society was not prepared to protect an individual, sacrificing him for the supposed greater good of the whole, it lived behind a rickety ethical framework of self-deception.

Terr turned away from the mainframe plot and chuckled, but it wasn't with humor. "This may be time for last requests, Karhide."

Arlon Dee gave a faint smile, still thinking, evaluating options.

Terr glanced at Dhar. His brother appeared ready.

"Tah, the gods will tell."

"They better do it in a hurry," Terr retorted irreverently.

A ghostly pink light settled over Arlon Dee's head and he straightened. The light slowly enveloped him, hovering, pulsing. After a moment, it faded. Terr's vision blurred momentarily, turning everything pink, As he looked down at himself, he stood encased in a shifting fog. When the light faded, he jerked, then looked sharply at Dhar, the fog already starting to form around him. He stared transfixed as every watchstander in turn underwent a similar scan, for that's what it had to be. How the Krans managed to bypass *Parsha's* interceptor net without Cent Comp sounding a warning, he could not say.

Some two minutes later, Arlon looked at him. "Reports are coming from all over the ship. It looks like everyone was probed."

"Does that now make it our turn?" Terr queried with a small smile.

The Kran ships slowly started to move—toward KP-001C, their intention unmistakable.

"Cent Comp? Match course and speed and disengage net modulation," Arlon said wearily. There was no need for stealth anymore, or pretense.

"Acknowledged. Interceptor net nominal," the housekeeping computer said indifferently. Nothing would stick *it* into some zoo sphere.

Parsha moved and the cluster of mines moved with her. Apparently, the Krans did not want any misunderstandings.

Up close, KP-001C's surface revealed itself. Vast stretches of desert girthed the equatorial belt. Irregular mountain ranges, some oozing volcanic smoke, marked shifting tectonic plate boundaries. A jagged icecap covered the southern polar region. Everything looked worn, tired, the landscape unbroken by oceans or greenery, but that was deceptive. A young world, its ecology was still to form.

What the planet lacked in natural distractions was offset by evidence of Kran activity: vast open cut mines, industrial complexes, sprawling structures that stained the landscape in precise geometric patterns. The world seethed with energy, but applied to what? As if reading Terr's mind, Arlon Dee pulled at his chin.

"Too much power down there to simply maintain an outpost. If the outer planets are also like this, where is it all going?"

"Making more Krans?" Terr ventured.

"And ships. It takes an enormously complex infrastructure and abundant resources to build starships, and they seem to have it all here."

Terr feared he understood. More Krans, more ships, it

could only mean one thing. They were building to accommodate their expansion, driven by whatever imperative demanded they do so. In their case, expansion did not mean colonization, but death and desolation. Like a virus without a controlling antibody, they were a plague infesting the galaxy. Unless contained, every star would end up a Kran star. Then what?

The universe was full of galaxies.

A chill ran through him at the awful thought.

"Notice something?"

Arlon nodded. "No atmospheric pollutants, except those generated by natural processes. They're neat housekeepers."

"Self interest, not because they're nature lovers."

Environmental degradation meant expenditure of valuable resources, time and effort building control mechanisms to prevent the planet from becoming unusable. However well made, even the Krans and their infrastructure must be subject to corrosive effects of unchecked pollution.

The Kran flotilla assumed an equatorial geosynchronous position and stopped. If Arlon Dee wanted to get away, Terr believed this was his best chance. If the mines surrounding the ship were gravitic, they could not operate within the planet's powerful gravitational distortion field. They could also be simple explosive devices. Simple being relative, of course, but *Parsha's* layered interceptor net would offer a degree of protection. The most potent tactical threats were the two *Fadhirs*. At least they weren't shooting at each other, merely a postponement?

He slowly looked at Arlon, who nodded, his mouth pursed.

"If forced, we'll try and break away, but we're not faced with an immediate threat, or the Krans would have acted. An opportunity may offer itself yet to achieve our objective."

"Your optimism is infectious, Karhide, but I fear misplaced."

"Caution. Transmission interrogative from Celi-Kran Zero Six."

The simple message set off a cascade of possibilities in

Terr's mind. If this was indeed a major Kran outpost controlled by a coordinating central nexus core, then there were more of them around, at least five. Each one must control a vast volume of space. If the Orieli were right and the Krans came from the inner arm of the galaxy, this particular nexus might be running everything in a vast volume of space. How many thousands of stars, and could the Orieli ever prevail?

Arlon raised an eyebrow. "Open channel."

"The following individuals to make ready for immediate transport. Coordinates provided to your computer. Karhide Arlon Dee; Master Scout Terrllss-rr; First Scout Dharaklin."

Kemp sat up in alarm. "Sir! You can't go down there!"

Arlon glanced at his exec. "I appreciate your concern, but our choices are limited. If we don't get back within an hour, do what is necessary."

"Make sure it doesn't become necessary, Da."

"Send a stern message to Zero Six."

Mouth tight, Arlon walked toward the nearest PT alcove. After a slight hesitation, he stepped in. He turned two-dimensional and faded from sight. Terr glanced at Dhar and shrugged. He had a lot to say right then, and nothing. They understood each other too well for words to fill any gaps now. He wondered if the nexus understood what he was, what Dhar was?

To communicate, it obviously interrogated *Tapal's* captured crew, and by extension, Teena. The process evidently was not fatal as his link with her proved. It could, though, be harmful at many other levels.

Well, if Zero Six didn't understand, he would educate it. As he stepped into the alcove, he wondered if the atmosphere down there was breathable. Surely their host would be aware of something this obvious. Then again, perhaps not. Everything twisted and a cold sword slashed through his body.

Blinking, he waited for his eyes to adjust, then stared. Beside him, Arlon Dee stared just as hard. Triangular panels lining the walls of a large chamber flickered faintly, constantly changing color. Sharp, slightly acidic, the air tasted okay. The panels beneath his feet pulsed with light, and noticed Arlon Dee encased in a cocoon of orange light. A force field? Protection against biological contamination? Why would the Krans care? Dhar materialized beside him.

Terr tried to slow his racing heart and suppress the flutter in his stomach, fascinated by his surroundings. If he gave into fear would not achieve anything, and lashing out with Death in his hands would be a last final solution only if he was forced into it.

"I understand your function and purpose for being here," a strong masculine voice resonated forcefully in Terr's head. Arlon's startled reaction told him he obviously heard it also. "You failed, and I will use the knowledge you contain to eradicate an infestation. There is only the Celi-Kran. Everything else is a violation of purpose to bring order and stability to every random system, without exception."

Terr heard the harsh words and had a glimmer of something he was certain could only be a fantastic leap of an inflamed imagination. Inflamed or not, he would need to discuss it with Alkarh Tertulion, if they got back. If true, it would have profound implications for understanding the Krans. Arlon Dee's thoughtful expression betrayed that he might be thinking along similar lines.

"Why do you consider organic intelligence random systems?" Arlon demanded.

"All life is random and uncoordinated. It is violent and chaotic, without purpose, except to breed and infest everything it touches. It is a destroyer."

"Yet you also destroy."

"To bring order!"

"Order through annihilation? For what purpose?"

"Order is stability."

"And when you achieve total stability?"

"There will only be the Celi-Kran."

Terr bit his lip. How can he argue with a machine intelligence, clearly sophisticated, but still driven by a seemingly incomprehensible blind imperative. Still, the thing did make a valid point about life causing chaos and strife, but that's how adaptive evolution operated. It had to know that, otherwise why bother to collect its collection of specimens. Or perhaps it simply didn't care. It did care in a way. Its specimens attested to that.

"What about love, song, painting, philosophy, ethics, creativity?" he asked to test his hypothesis.

"And hate, war, oppression, torture, slavery? You are great to have spanned the stars, and in the millennia to come, you may evolve into an ordered system, but at what cost in misery?"

"Those very processes made us great. We don't destroy anymore."

Immediately, Terr's head filled with a kaleidoscope of images, anguish and conflict that existed within the Serrll. When he saw what life was like on some Orieli worlds, he got far more for his cultural exchange mission than he bargained for, but not entirely unexpected. The Technic Union was not some idyllic sanctuary, but disparate societies trying to overcome complex daily problems, some doing it better than others.

"You might evolve, but the Celi-Kran will bring order now. I will cleanse all the Orieli and Serrll worlds of your infestation."

"We shall resist," Arlon said.

"I know."

"What do you care about the misery and war we inflict on each other?" Terr asked. "Our worlds are not a threat to you. What makes you our arbiter?"

"Our function is to eliminate disorder, and you are disorder."

"I want to see Teena," Terr said on impulse, not caring too much for indigestible philosophy.

After a moment, he saw a chamber filled with suspended

transparent spheres. The image flickered and he saw her floating in a liquid or zero gravity environment. So, his vision was accurate. Her hair fell to her shoulders as she moved, so she could not be in zero-gee. The sight of her squeezed his chest and he exhaled sharply.

"What do you intend to do with us?" Arlon Dee asked and Teena's image vanished.

"I answered that question. Teena spoke of you, Terrllss-rr, and of Dharaklin. What are you?"

"Scan our minds and you will know."

A pink glow enveloped Dhar's head, then faded. Terr heard a loud buzz and his skin tingled. A few seconds later, it stopped.

"I am unable to penetrate your mind shield. Lower it."

Terr blinked in surprise. It appeared the god held his protective hand over him even here, but time and distance meant nothing to a god.

"You want to know what I am? I am death. I am chaos. I am total disorder which you fear the most."

"Your words are uncorrelated. Explain."

"It is better if I show you," Terr said softly and began to chant. "I shall walk in the shadow of Death, and it shall be with me all the days of my life. With shadow shall I smite my enemies, and with thunder shall I purge their land!" Power built within him and his voice rang with authority. He saw himself grow, looking down at his body, at the mortal creature that invoked him. Reality flickered and creation lay naked before him to shape at his will. "And all who stand with me in the shadow of Death shall know my power and be comforted. With shadow and thunder shall I walk their land!" He raised his arms and lightnings crackled between them.

With a shrug, he pointed a finger at the flickering wall before him and a bright blue bolt smashed into the panels, penetrating the shield enclosing him. A pealing crash of thunder made the air shake and his ears ring. If he were to die, so would Zero Six and this world.

"Stop! Further damage me and I will destroy your ship."

Terr saw the arrayed spheres again. In one, a crewman clutched his head, his mouth contorted in agony. He convulsed and was still. The sphere turned black.

Arlon Dee looked at him imploringly. "Terr, don't!"

With an effort of will, he dropped his arms, still cloaked in power. He would not let go, not now, not if this meant the end of everything, but he would not get Teena if he allowed his rage to consume him.

"What are you?" Zero Six demanded again. The panels around them flickered furiously. Terr watched in amazement as the damaged sections faded, replaced with new ones. Could the thing be destroyed?

"I am a Discipline adept, able to join with a god. You saw the manifestation of my power."

"I saw an exhibition of your mental abilities. Gods are imaginary creations, delusions of organic lifeforms."

"I can make my demonstration more vivid."

"You seek to annihilate me?"

"If you harm Teena or anyone else, I will destroy you."

"At the cost of your own destruction?"

"If Teena ceases to live, I have no reason to continue existing."

"Propagation pair bonding. I understand."

"Despite your array of captive specimens, you still don't understand anything. Propagation is the least of the reasons why we bond."

"It is a prime biological imperative."

"Perhaps, but that imperative doesn't make us stay bonded. You must have gathered that from the prisoners you interrogated."

"I wish to understand it from your perspective."

"To understand, you would need to transcend your logic and experience the ineffable quality of being human; having feelings and emotions, indulge in incoherent behavior which you find distasteful."

"It is an inefficient utilization of resources."

"It enabled us to reach the stars."

"Teena said a Wanderer can destroy a world by projecting his will. Confirm."

"A third-level adept needs only to imagine an affront, focus, and act. Distance does not matter. It is the knowing and visualizing the object that is critical."

"Do you have this ability?"

"No."

"Yet you destroyed one of my ships at Devon 3-VL4."

"Special circumstances, not unlike the one I find myself in now."

"Your threat?"

"I want Teena and the others released, and our ship free to depart."

"Irreconcilable."

"I have nothing to lose, and your destruction will delay invasion of our worlds."

"Irrelevant. All data is continuously transmitted to Zero Zero," it declared, and there was a moment of silence. "Dharaklin, sometimes known as Nightwings. Will the Wanderers seek to extinguish the Celi-Kran?"

Cloaked in power, Dhar lifted his head in defiance. "The Rahtir will defend Anar'on. If you invade the Serrll Combine, they will stop you."

"Uncorrelated. This is not information you disclosed to Karhide Arlon Dee."

"Release us and we'll go," Terr said. "Do not seek us out and you can continue to execute your function."

"It would only postpone the inevitable. My function must be executed without exception. Your worlds will be cleansed."

Terr clenched his teeth. The thing had a fixed purpose, and no one could argue with it. Could he react before he was struck down if the nexus decided to act? He could do something. He would strike first. He glanced at Nightwings and saw understanding in his brother's eyes. This was not exactly how he imagined it would end, but he guessed one was not always given a say in these things.

Teena...

As he stood there, ready to unleash death, he realized the hopelessness of their rescue plan, but it wasn't the first time someone sacrificed everything for a cause. He looked at Dhar and raised his arms.

"Stop!" After a few tense moments, the voice spoke. "This requires further analysis."

Teena materialized, enclosed in a shimmering shield. She gasped and staggered, fighting for breath. Doubling over, she expelled fluid from her lungs. After a spasm of coughing, she stood on unsteady legs and threw herself at him. Their shields touched and she was in his arms, clinging to him, sobbing uncontrollably.

Terr's eyes stung as he held her with desperate strength, afraid he imagined it all. Her warmth suffused through him as he gently stroked her wet hair. He did not mind dying now, not much anyway.

"There, my pet. It's all right. Everything is all right."

Sniffing, she lifted her head and rewarded him with a sunny smile, happy tears streaking her cheeks.

"Terr..."

Her lips sought his and he kissed her with abandon. A timeless moment later, she pulled back and her face looked tragic.

"It was horrible! The voice..."

"Shh. We'll talk later. I have you now."

He cried out as cold cut through him, thinking this was death. The nexus had tricked him, distracting him by returning Teena, stopping him from unleashing his wrath. He squeezed his eyes and sighed with relief, and found himself in *Parsha's* PFC.

"Karhide!" Kemp jumped to his feet, barely glancing at

Teena's naked body. "Med Bay Two reports that *Tapal's* personnel just materialized there; twenty-two men and twelve women. But—"

Arlon slowly nodded. "I know. It looks like we lost three. We would have lost them all if it weren't…" He turned and looked at Terr, his expression undecided. "I don't know how to thank you, Da."

Terr held Teena close and smiled. "If you want to know the truth, Karhide, I never thought we'd get out of there."

"Frankly, neither did I, and we're not clear yet." Arlon licked his lips, turned and looked hard at his exec. "You figured how to get us out of here?"

Before Kemp could answer the impossible, a female medic stepped out of the PT alcove, a dark blue blanket in hand, and walked quickly to Teena. She draped it around Teena who gratefully clutched the edges.

"Dapata, if you please," the diminutive woman prompted, her arms around Teena's shoulders.

Apprehensive, she looked at Terr and he stroked her arm. "I'll be down as soon as I can, and you need to be checked out."

"What about all those others? We can't just leave them there!"

Terr's eyes flickered at the medic and watched as she led Teena away. When they were gone, his shoulders sagged.

Arlon Dee's face was a cold mask. "Terr—"

"I know. There's nothing we can do for them."

Rit!

It would be suicide trying to rescue all those aliens. Even if by some miracle they managed to get them out, there wasn't anywhere to put several hundred bodies, even in stasis. *Parsha* was not a passenger vessel. Anyway, it didn't seem like a day for miracles. No, he had Teena, a small miracle in itself.

He glanced at the mainframe plot, but the tactical situation had not changed. Mines and Kran warships still surrounded the ship. Zero Six released them, but they still were not free to leave. Why did it release them? Defuse an imminent response from him and Dhar, and place them somewhere where it held total tactical advantage? It certainly achieved it.

Arlon again looked at Kemp. "Well, Opturkarh?"

The Zaronian straightened, clearly not comfortable. "I hate to say it, but we need to wait."

"Wait?"

"The central nexus core wants something."

"It wants me and Dhar, sir," Terr said wearily. "Remember its words? 'This requires further analysis.' I'll bet it's consulting with Zero Zero, probably waiting for instructions. We're a puzzle and it wants answers."

"Well, the damned thing can keep waiting. We're breaking out of here now. *Parsha* will take out the mines and then we'll go after the *Fadhirs*."

"While the *Sandars* punch holes in you."

"The interceptor net will hold long enough for us to clear the distortion limit, enabling us to transit."

"Pursued by a cloud of gravitic missiles before you can do that."

Arlon Dee growled in frustration. "Damn it, Terr! Are you always such a sourpuss?"

Terr grinned. "I am only reflecting your own thoughts. Opturkarh Kemp is right and you know it. Fighting our way out should be a last desperate option, and it would be desperate. Besides, I don't think Alkarh Tertulion will be impressed if you bend her brand new ship. Think of all the forms you'll be filing."

Arlon smiled, although there was nothing amusing in any of this. "You're a pain. Did you know that?"

"Someone mentioned it once or twice," Terr replied with a grin, thinking of his boss, Anabb.

"I'm not surprised. Even if Kemp is right and the nexus wants to see you again, and you two go down, there is no guarantee it will let us go once it's finished with you."

"I'll persuade it."

"Oh? More lightnings blazing?"

"If necessary, but I have something more subtle in mind."

"Pray, don't let me die guessing."

"You saw how I shot a bolt through the shield Zero Six set around me? Hook Dhar into the VI in one of your Hangar Bays that faces the two *Fadhirs*. The VI will help him target them. If I signal him, he'll take them out, and the *Sandars* if necessary. It should create enough confusion for you to get away, and it's no worse than your plan, perhaps better."

Dhar stared at him, his face tragic. "My brother, you would go down alone?"

"You won't be much good if you're with me."

"We could break out now! With two of us—"

"The nexus might still let us go without having to resort to unpleasantness."

The struggle within Dhar was evident. He accepted the inevitable and pursed his mouth. "You penetrated that energy screen, but I don't know if I can."

Terr understood. They were both second-level adepts, but he was clearly something more. How much more? His god may reveal that in due time.

"We'll test it." He glanced at Arlon Dee, who pointed a finger at Kemp.

"Take him down to Hangar Bay Three." He looked at Dhar. "We'll enclose you in a separated double field and set the outer one to maximum intensity. A *little* demonstration? I don't want holes in my ship."

"Sankri…"

Terr placed a hand on Dhar's shoulder. "This is right, Nightwings, and you know it."

"How do you intend to signal him?" Arlon demanded. "If you take a communicator, the nexus will block any transmission."

"I'll dislocate a finger." Terr smiled at Arlon's goggling expression. He must think him mad. "It's not a link like I have with Teena, but in a way, Dhar and I are also bonded. He is able to feel my pain as I am able to feel his. One finger, one *Fadhir*. I've got four, which should be just right. If things get serious, I'll do two in quick succession and you better get the hell out of here fast."

"And leave you behind?"

"If it comes to that, there won't be much left to come back for."

Arlon Dee jerked his head at Kemp and the exec pointed at the PT alcove. "If you please."

Dhar reached out with his hand and touched Terr's chest. Terr returned the gesture. Forever united, he did not have to say anything. Abruptly, Dhar dropped his hand and moved toward a PT alcove. Terr watched him vanish and tried to suppress an emptiness that opened within him.

Nightwings...

He swallowed hard and glanced at Arlon. "I better see how Teena is doing." He might well be doing it for the last time.

"She is in Med Bay One," Arlon Dee said.

Terr walked into the alcove, turned, and issued a mental command. When the aftereffect tingle passed, he looked around the medical center. Apart from two diagnostic couches in the middle of the compartment, nothing was familiar. It was like being inside a computer room. A grizzly medic hovered over Teena's supine form, a bar of pale orange light moving down her body. Two blue-garbed assistants stared at holoview displays.

"Terr!"

She tilted her head, smiled and made to get up, but the medic held her down.

"One minute more," he said severely and glanced at Terr. "Not an easy patient, Da. We cleared some residual fluid from her lungs and neutralized foreign nanolites. There should not be any lasting aftereffects. I'll give you two minutes." Medics were the same everywhere.

"Beast. You took such a long to come," she whispered, her eyes searching his, "but I knew you would."

He took her hand and stroked it. "You mean now, or…" he said teasingly, happy to feel her, touch her.

"You know what I mean, you terrible man."

"On *Tapal*, I should have been with you."

Her fingers curled around his and squeezed. "You're here now and you came for me. That's enough."

"Did they do anything to you?"

"Not to me, but I watched two crewmen die. I guess it was learning how to handle us." Her face clouded and she bit her lower lip. "Terr, I couldn't stop it. The voice—"

"I know, pet. There is nothing you could have done. Don't feel guilty about it."

"But it knows everything!"

"It would have found out sooner or later. Put it out of your mind."

She grimaced and shuddered. "I feel…violated! That thing poked inside my head and I couldn't keep it out."

"Don't excite yourself, Dapata," the medic warned her, then turned to Terr. "She needs to rest, Da."

She scrambled to her feet and embraced him, her arms tight around his neck. "I don't want you to leave me ever again."

"That's a promise." He swallowed hard and buried his face in her hair.

After a moment, she pulled back. "Are we clear? We're moving?"

"Ah, not quite. The ship is surrounded by four rather large Kran vessels that don't want us going anywhere just yet."

She frowned prettily and her large green eyes turned dark. "We're not free?"

"We're working on it."

"Da Terrllss-rr? Karhide Arlon Dee wishes to tell you the

test was successful," Cent Comp announced in his head.

"Very well," he responded mentally and looked at the medic. "She can rest in our quarters."

"But—"

One arm around her waist, he steered her toward the PT alcoves. "Let's get out of here and I'll explain everything."

"Da Terr? Zero Six demands that you and Da Dharaklin transport to the surface."

Well, he'd waited for this to happen. "I'm ready now." He disengaged himself from Teena and stepped toward the PT alcove. "You have your rest. I shan't be long."

She searched his face and looked stricken. "What is it? What's going on?"

"I must go down there again."

"No! I don't want to lose you to that thing. You promised!"

"You won't lose me, my pet, but I must to do this." He turned and hurried into the alcove.

"Terr!" she screamed and hurled herself at him.

"Transport!" he snarled before his resolve failed him, Teena's tear-streaked face burned indelibly in his mind.

After a moment of disorientation, the chamber, the flickering panels, the raw air, everything settled into place. He took a deep breath and waited. Colors shifted around him in flowing patterns, not unlike the random whorls in a Wall, although in this chamber, he felt certain nothing was random.

"Where is Dharaklin?" Zero Six demanded harshly.

Terr waited.

The chamber around him vanished and the curve of KP-001C beneath him blotted out the stars. A beautiful image, marred only by two green and yellow cubes he assumed were Kran ships standing ready, and pulsing red circles of four mines positioned around a white sphere. He didn't need to have the image explained. The red circle beneath *Parsha* started to pulse rapidly and suddenly expanded into a white sphere.

Terr waited.

The central nexus may want to frighten him into talking, but he doubted it would destroy *Parsha*. Not yet anyway. The mine in front of the white sphere went off. Perhaps shaken a bit, he did not think there was damage. Unlike primary and secondary shield grid screens on Serrll ships, the Orieli interceptor net had the capability to keep out solid matter.

A white ring sprang around one of the green cubes and a blue lance stabbed at *Parsha*. Terr figured this made it his move. He clamped his mouth, savagely twisted the small finger of his left hand, and gasped at the sharp pain that shot up his arm. He blinked back the sting in his eyes, unable to tell whether he broke it or merely dislocated the thing. It didn't matter. It hurt the same. Wincing, he cradled the abused member against his chest as sweat beaded his forehead, not wanting to do this again.

If he'd blinked, he would have missed it. A bar of yellow light shot from *Parsha* and ran through the green cube that fired on it. The cube flared in wild oscillation, then abruptly vanished and he found himself in the chamber again, the panels around him a confusion of rapidly shifting color. It looked like Dhar made an impression. It was one thing to destroy a couple of panels, another to snuff out a capital warship with a single strike. He hoped further demonstrations would not be necessary. Expecting the nexus to revenge itself against him, he waited.

"You are damaged," the imperious voice declared.

His hand tingled and he looked down at the glow suffusing it. The tortured finger stopped throbbing. He flexed it and felt nothing. Why did it care for his discomfort?

"Thank you."

"Damaged, you cannot operate at maximum efficiency." Colors raced across the panels around him. "How is Dharaklin bound to you?"

So, it figured out the relationship between his pain and the destruction of its ship, and why Dhar didn't come with him, but Terr always knew the central nexus was smart. A machine intelligence perhaps, but still aware, cognizant of its surroundings, able to learn. He liked to think it could evolve beyond its rigid programming.

"When I crashed on Anar'on, I wandered the Saffal for two days, eventually succumbing from lack of water. Wanderers from a nearby village found me and nursed me back to life, but the desert took something from me, for I wasn't sane. Dharaklin joined his mind with mine and brought me out of my madness. By joining, we became one, sharing memories, personality, everything."

"Including the ability to discharge destructive energy?"

"That came later, but he left the potential within me, or merely wakened something the Saffal left me."

"How is your body able to generate such energy? I did not detect any special organs."

"It cannot. I merely serve as a medium for the god of Death."

In the ensuing silence, he watched the pretty colors.

"Do not demonstrate your ability again, or Dharaklin's," Zero Six declared and Terr smiled grimly.

"Do you feel anything when one of your units or ships is damaged or destroyed?"

"Everything is an extension of Zero Zero. When part of me ceases to function, I experience the equivalent of what you understand as pain."

Silence. Then...

"Submit and I will transport *Parsha* to Perilia."

"What about your imperative?"

The nexus did not answer, and maybe it felt it did not have to. Something able to construct starships, mold worlds, question, reason, and have a degree of free will, it was prepared to control its urge to destroy him and *Parsha* in order to satisfy its curiosity. It wanted to know about Death, not only because of curiosity, but self-preservation, and possibly preservation of every Kran.

Terr did not doubt for a moment the machine's ultimate sinister intention, but he was willing to take advantage of a temporary truce, so to speak, if it saved *Parsha*...and Teena. A time of ultimate reckoning still must be faced, but it did not need to be faced right now.

He did not want to do it, fearing obliteration, or worse—madness if he opened himself to this monstrosity. However, there weren't all that many choices. If the nexus decided to kill him, Dhar would sense it. Terr hoped he would exact a heavy price for his life. He also hoped the thing was equally aware of the possible consequences.

"I will submit."

Terr took a deep breath and willed his heart to slow. He closed his eyes and bade Death lift its hand. A flush of warmth shot through his body, then nothing. He knew he now stood completely unprotected. Slowly, he opened his eyes and waited.

Pink light obscured his vision, tentatively probing, and spread to envelop him. After a timeless moment, a hot probe lanced through his head and he winced. The pink fog lifted.

"Uncorrelated. Are you mortal or a supernatural entity?"

Terr was taken aback by the question. Surely the answer was obvious. He may walk in the shadow of Death, but in a frail and mortal body. His mangled finger should have told it that. Evidently not, or it would not have asked. If the scan didn't satisfy it, there may be a way for him to use that uncertainty to his advantage.

"I am Death, lord of all creation. You see before you my human form, but within me is that which lives for all time."

"Uncorrelated."

"You saw in my mind how I stood suspended in space, a broken world before me, two stars adorning my feet?"

"Zero Zero. Where did you see those stars?"

Terr hardly dared think. The two stars were the coordinating nexus core's home system! How could that be possible?

Ever since he'd first seen the vision, he thought it was the god's warning against wanton use of his power, giving into the lust of destruction. Perhaps it was, while also gave him a glimpse of his future. He would need to discuss this with his master—if he ever got the chance. Sidhara would know, wouldn't he?

"In a vision." Let it digest that!

"What is Athal Than?"

A whirlpool of images swept him away, of a towering red escarpment rising like a sentinel out of the flowing Saffal sands. They said the gods learned to walk there, that thunder and lightning could be seen at night in absence of any clouds. The rocks supposedly had unusually strong magnetic properties. Within their influence, molecular circuits behaved erratically. So they said. Someone theorized that this affected the electrical network of the brain in some strange way and induced hallucinations. Was it the abode of real gods or merely an inexplicable phenomenon?

He remembered his two trials, the strange fog that swept away all feeling and emotion, stripped down to his core self, naked before the impersonal entities who were said to inhabit that place. He walked away from those forbidding cliffs both times, but even now, he could not say whether the power they bestowed on him was worth the price he paid.

"If there are gods, they manifest themselves at Athal Than and places like it around Anar'on. All such escarpments have unusual magnetic and electrical properties that perhaps act as a conduit through which something the Wanderers call gods make their presence felt. Whether they are truly supernatural or a manifestation of an energy discharge from some other dimension, no one can determine."

"How are you and Dharaklin able to tap an energy source located on Anar'on?"

"I'm either an ordinary mortal exhibiting an unusual mental ability, or I am indeed a conduit through which an unknown entity can interact."

Terr drifted, wanting nothing, expecting nothing. There were regrets, unfulfilled dreams, words that needed saying, but that was somewhere else, in another reality. He waited.

"Your duality requires further analysis."

The chamber around him dissolved and he found himself in space again. The Kran ships were withdrawing and there was no sign of mines. Reality flickered and he muttered something evil as the aftereffect tingle of transport subsided. A great system for getting around, but there were still some bugs to be ironed out as far as he was concerned. Still, seeing Arlon Dee's startled expression made up for the temporary discomfort.

Arlon scrambled out of the command couch and looked him over. "Cent Comp reported receiving coordinates somewhere above KP-001D. Your doing?"

"Zero Six is taking the ship to its transport portal. It looks like we'll be getting a free ride to Perilia."

Arlon's mouth tightened at the implication of Terr's words. He did not look surprised, only profoundly concerned, and he had reason to be. With the information the nexus obtained from him and his crew, all Orieli space now lay exposed, including the extent of its ability to defend itself. Strategically, the capture of *Tapal's* five escape modules was perhaps the most significant thing the nexus could have done in the execution of its function, but Terr had also walked away with a prize—location of Celi-Kran's home system.

His vision blurred and he grasped his forehead. Pain twisted his guts and he doubled over. He thought he heard the computer blare a warning, but he couldn't make it out. The deck moved beneath him and he sank into darkness.

* * *

Parsha broke into normal space in a burst of white scintillation a bare light-year from Tavor's Star, and immediately transited, on course for Perilia, its transponder identifying it to a prowling cruiser. Once cleared to land, the powerful warship hardly settled at the vast OSA facility when Arlon Dee and his party were ordered to report.

It was the same spacious room where Terr met Tertulion the first time, except now, she stood flanked by a senior grade officer. Grim, businesslike, he looked ready to do whatever was required. Very thin, bald, his startling slanted yellow feline eyes with vertical black irises stared at him without blinking. An action man, Terr decided, not a bureaucratic chair warmer.

"Please be seated everybody," Tertulion invited briskly, a busy woman with a lot on her mind. She looked with interest at Teena. Terr gripped her arm to reassure her.

"Dapata, allow me to introduce my partner, Teena-raye."

"I regret the trouble I caused for everybody," Teena said, flustered at being the center of attention.

Tertulion flashed her a warm smile. "The Krans are trouble, my dear, not you. I am glad to see you safe. We'll talk later and you can tell me all about it." When everyone got comfortable, she glanced at her companion. "Terr…Dhar, I would like you to meet my aide, Alkarh Sumen."

Terr gave a polite nod.

Sumen cleared his throat. "Da Terr, You don't live up to your reputation. I expected to see a three-kanampir-tall fire-breathing apparition," he said, his voice thin and scratchy, and Terr decided they weren't likely to be pals.

Tertulion cast her aide a frosty look and smiled thinly. "You must excuse Sumen's alleged sense of humor, Terr."

"If the Alkarh wishes a demonstration of what I am, I'll be happy to accommodate him," Terr said coolly, not in the mood to be pushed around or browbeaten, mission or not, still feeling the aftereffects of the nanobod attack by Zero Six.

Sumen got the message, grinned, and gave a small nod.

"Are you fully recovered?" Tertulion asked.

"*Parsha's* doctor flushed all the nanolites, as you call them, out of my system, Dapata, and the ship's bio safeguards prevented any spreading."

"You were fortunate."

Terr didn't need reminding. The nexus allowed them to leave not because it needed to evaluate information he gave it, but to infect the ship—destruction by any means. In hindsight, something they should have anticipated.

"You were meant to be an infection vector," she murmured and turned to Arlon Dee. "Skimming over your after-action report, Karhide, it's scarcely believable, as was your sudden reappearance. You say it took two jumps to send you here?"

"That's correct, Dapata. They probably used a waypoint portal," he said, his tongue running over his lips.

"Which means their portals have a range," Sumen added and leaned forward. "Very useful piece of information."

"Possibly." Tertulion steeped her fingers.

"There is one more thing," Arlon Dee added slowly. "Their portals operate without a containment ring."

"Impossible!" Sumen declared, glaring.

"Apparently not impossible," Tertulion said mildly.

"Perdition! How do they generate the interface?"

"We did see a ring of blue energy form just before we crossed," Arlon added.

"Leave that for now, Sumen. Your crew, Karhide? All are well?"

"No apparent ill effects, although they were filled with nanolites which helped break down the fluid in the sphere into proteins, starches, and other digestible compounds."

"We'll study them."

"You were lucky to have gotten away, Karhide," Sumen remarked, making it sound like an accusation, his feline eyes bright.

"Indeed, Da. Except we didn't get away. Zero Six allowed us to depart to send a contagion through Terr, but it was too effective."

"So you say in your report."

"That's why we're having this preliminary debrief, to validate the report." Tertulion sounded irritated. "Terr, the central nexus seems particularly worried about you and Dhar."

"Not me, Alkarh, but Anar'on, and with good reason."

"It could have been a deciding factor to kill you and *Parsha's* crew."

"Perhaps, but I doubt it. Anar'on is far away and the Krans cannot see how the Wanderers could be an immediate threat. I believe the nexus allowed us to depart because it didn't want more of its ships destroyed."

Tertulion smiled grimly. "And took an opportunity to destroy you. There is something terrifying watching a one-tracked mind operate. I am relieved to see that your contingency orders weren't required, Karhide."

Terr sat up and stared at Arlon Dee as things clicked into place. If the rescue part of the mission had failed, he was to bombard the planet and everyone on it to prevent the Krans from using whatever intelligence they gathered from the captives. It would not have worked anyway because of the link with Zero Zero, but when the orders were given, nobody knew that. It was a ruthlessness Terr understood, but did not expect. Caught up in a cloud of high Orieli morals and ethics, he'd ignored the basic tenet all living things obeyed—survival. As a living entity, the Orieli sought to preserve their existence, even if it meant destroying some of their own people.

You can be a nice guy outwardly and still a son of a bitch inside.

Arlon returned his gaze without blinking. He had nothing to apologize for. He wouldn't have liked doing it if the situation called for such drastic action, Terr was nevertheless certain the letter of his orders would be executed. Given the circumstances, he'd have done the same thing.

"We got most of them out, Alkarh," Arlon said heavily.

Sumen shook his head. "Terr, you made a startling comment in Karhide Dee's report, implying that you know the location of the Celi-Kran home system."

"A possibility only, Da. I have no hard evidence to support my claim, and what I do have is not subject to logical analysis."

"So you say in the report. Of what use is the information then?"

Tertulion shifted in her seat and glared. "It could be invaluable if we can exploit it, something I suspect Zero Six did not appreciate when it let slip the fact." She looked at Terr. "As much as I hate to be negative, Sumen does have a point of sorts. To be of any substantive value, we would need to identify those stars. Are you able to provide anything that might help us?"

"I will review my vision and set up a holoview image of what I saw. Your astrophysics computers may be able to make a match."

"Perdition! Even if you gave us the image, you're talking about scanning the entire galaxy!" Sumen exploded.

"Not quite, Da," Arlon Dee interjected. "Not if we work from the assumption the Krans originate from the inner galactic arm."

"Mmm, yes. That still leaves a lot of space to check out. Even if we do find them, we could be looking at ten to twenty thousand light-years. That's a lot of stars. Still, I suppose it's worth doing. Terr, you made another questionable suggestion that the Krans are evolved nanolites. Somewhat farfetched, wouldn't you say?"

"All their behavioral and verbal responses point to it, Da," Terr told Sumen, not deterred by the man's abrasive manner. "Its application of nanolites to keep captives alive and the attempt on my life suggests advanced understanding and sophisticated manufacturing capability. I conjecture that somewhere, a superior race built special nanolites to carry out some eradication process and their creations performed better than expected."

"Or the control mechanisms failed to work as expected," Tertulion said softly. "An interesting theory, if simplistic. Even if true, I fail to see how this insight can help us fight them. However, we'll look into it. Given what happened to you, I'm surprised the Krans haven't made an attack on us using nanolites."

Sumen looked visibly shaken. "Perdition! I can imagine only too well what a load of hostile nanolites dumped into a planet's ecosystem could do."

"Indeed," Tertulion said. "Of immediate concern is the integrity of our defense posture. From what the Krans learned, they could strike immediately and strike anywhere."

"Ah, not quite, Alkarh," Sumen interjected. "I agree they could strike immediately, but if they do, I submit they'll target our command and control centers. If I were them, I'd follow up by neutralizing our most strategic industrial complexes. Without adequate logistical support, we'd be completely exposed."

"With respect, Da, I disagree," Arlon Dee said.

"And why is that?"

"Analysis of past behavior. We fought them for five years and it's only now that they chose to deploy their principal tactical weapon against us. I believe First Commander Shah Pak was correct in his assessment when he said the Krans lacked sufficient resources to strike at us in force."

"Or sufficient motivation," Tertulion added firmly. "With the information they obtained from us, we probably gave them the necessary motivation."

Terr sat up. "Dapata, if the Krans are indeed a highly developed form of nanolites, their tactics could be predicted."

"Go on."

"Yours may operate differently, but all our nanolites are programmed to first contain, then overwhelm, whether a body pathogen or in an industrial application. Although Zero Six and the ship nexus cores are intelligent, they may contain a vestige of that core programming that guides their behavior. If so, they won't follow conventional engagement strategies."

"Like those advocated by Alkarh Sumen, which make logical sense to us, only because our motivation drivers are biological. They will treat us as an eradication problem and attack our extremities, working in from system to system." Tertulion looked thoughtful, then nodded. "An excellent observation, Terr."

"This means all our border systems in the Navia sector like Setlan Eleven and Heplon are vulnerable," Sumen said slowly.

"As is the Serrll Combine," Terr pointed out, letting them think about it. "An isolated pocket of life, less advanced and thereby more easily neutralized, if I were Zero Six, it's where I'd strike first. It would also fit in with my containment proposition."

"We're extrapolating from very tenuous assumptions, regardless how reasonable they might sound," Tertulion said. "Still, that's what this debrief is all about, to evaluate Karhide Dee's report and examine possible response scenarios. OSCOM will formulate the end strategy, but I tend to concur with Terr's assessment."

"If this youngster is correct, I recommend we strike at KP-001 immediately, and strike hard! Six *Nasors* deployed in two tandem groups will clean them out."

Terr stared at Sumen, not believing he'd heard right. The man treated the scenario as a conventional set-piece engagement in two dimensions, time and space, ignoring identified threats. Tertulion looked at her aide, apparently having the same thought.

"The gravitic sensor net would neutralize the single advantage our ships have, our modulated screens," Arlon Dee said.

Sumen waved a hand in dismissal. "We'll come in close and subject each planet to concentrated bombardment. If we hug the distortion limits, their gravitic missiles should be ineffective."

"Until you try exiting. We'd then lose every ship, Da."

"The tactical gain would be worth it, and would disrupt their plans to mount an attack against us or the Serrll!"

Tertulion shook a finger at Sumen. "You may be prepared to sacrifice almost three thousand lives, Alkarh, but I am not. Our situation isn't that desperate. However, your suggestion has some value."

Frowning, Terr looked hard at the woman. "I wouldn't relish being part of Alkarh Sumen's go-for-broke proposal, but such a strike might work—if he had a clear tactical advantage."

Her eyes widened, then she smiled. "Place a Discipline adept on our ships?"

"Yes."

"That brings us back to our original question. Will Anar'on help us?"

"I must return to Captal, Alkarh, and update the Security Council. They need to know everything," Terr said.

"As does Anar'on," Tertulion added. "Diplomatic communiqués can achieve only so much. As a Wanderer yourself, Controller Marrakan might be more receptive to what you have to say than getting it from Captal. You see, I'm not above using you or your brother."

"And I'm not above using *you*, Alkarh. The Orieli Technic Union faces what could be a desperate challenge, but so does the Serrll Combine. Should the Krans strike in force, we would be hard-pressed to contain them."

"You need support."

"Yes. At least until our M-6 and M-9 inventory is fully mobilized. To you, ten *Nasors* might not mean much, but they would be invaluable to us."

"If it weren't for your logical argument the Krans are advanced nanolites, Terr, I would suspect your motive for advancing it," Sumen growled testily.

Terr looked at him and wondered what soured his day. "Al-karh, I didn't advance my theory merely to highlight Serrll's vulnerability."

"Take it easy. I understand how vulnerable Kaleen systems are to a preemptive strike, especially if such a strike also managed to eliminate Anar'on."

"Potentially their principal strategic threat," Tertulion murmured. "Before we can ask Anar'on for help, can the Wanderers protect their own world?"

"I don't know, Dapata." Terr looked at Dhar, who cleared his throat.

"Third-level adepts are a mystery to me, as are their abilities. The Rahtir don't talk about it much."

"Well, that is that. We will advise Captal and they can warn Controller Marrakan. Of course, anticipating an imminent attack may be totally premature. After all, it took the Krans five years before they decided to eliminate three of our forward LTN stations."

"Perhaps they waited until they could bring sufficient assets to bear," Arlon Dee said quietly. "Tah Pak's assessment might be accurate. The Krans allowed us to complete the LTN stations, giving us a false sense of security, then struck."

"Either scenario is plausible," Tertulion acknowledged briskly, "and we must prepare regardless of their intention. Those *Nasors* you mentioned, Terr, I'll raise it with OSCOM. I will also explore an option to give Captal Fleet Command several defensive scanner arrays. They won't make you invulnerable, but they'll protect your most sensitive assets."

"Such as Captal and Anar'on," Terr said softly. "That's very generous of you, Dapata."

"It's something we can do relatively quickly, more quickly than giving you a squadron of *Nasors*. I'll make an S/12 available to you. Like your M-2, but smaller, it's capable of five lights per hour, which should get you around rapidly. It's a loan only, and not an invitation for your Bureau of Technology and Development to take it apart."

Terr smiled, appreciating the gesture and the warning. "Thank you. I will not abuse your trust."

"I know you won't, but can I trust your superiors?"

"You can if you make that trust conditional."

Tertulion laughed with genuine humor. "The S/12 or the scanner grids, right? Politicians everywhere can be suitably motivated if the problem is explained simply enough."

"I have found it to be so," Terr said dryly.

"Done!"

"I realize I may be stretching my luck asking, but there is one thing you could do for us that would make an immediate tactical difference."

"You want to know how to modulate your ship's shield grid?"

"Without that advantage, we might as well keep our ships mothballed."

"We shall consider it. I need time to prepare a communiqué for OSCOM and relay it to Captal. It wouldn't do to have you arrive before it does, and you'll need orientation operating the S/12. However, the onboard computer runs almost everything anyway. There won't be much for you to learn. Be ready for departure tomorrow morning at nine."

"I'll be using your transport portal?"

"The planet Captal is roughly three thousand lights from here and its coordinates are known. You're perhaps thinking whether it's within reach of a Kran waypoint portal?"

"I *was* thinking that."

"I'm afraid that's something we're likely to find out in due course. Were you contemplating going to Anar'on first? It is closer."

"I am tempted, but I doubt my superiors would be impressed with my motive for going there."

Tertulion smiled. "As PERCOM, I would probably feel the

147

same. I will evaluate Alkarh Sumen's proposal to set up a strike package against KP-001, but we will not act until we hear from Anar'on."

Sumen sat up in alarm. "Perdition! That could take weeks! I submit if we act immediately can only be to our advantage."

"You can begin preliminary planning and mission packaging. It will take us a few days to properly break down Karhide Dee's report, and a few more days to identify available ships."

Sumen clearly didn't like it. "Very well." He looked directly at Arlon Dee. "You managed to get out of there once, and it may not be fair to risk yourself again. However, you understand the tactical situation better than anyone. If we do mount a strike, are you prepared to command it?"

"Am I allowed to say no?" Arlon Dee asked, a whimsical smile tugging at his mouth. Sumen chuckled.

"You're not."

"In that case, I volunteer."

Terr studied Sumen more closely. The irritating alkarh had a human side after all. A sudden dark thought bubbled to surface and he turned to Tertulion, ready to voice his suspicion. Sumen was not deliberately provocative or acerbic at all! She had set this up. Her large brown eyes twinkled with amusement as she returned his gaze. They were also studying him.

Smiling, he nodded in capitulation.

Tertulion leaned against her seat and gazed thoughtfully at Arlon Dee. "Talk to me about Zero Six."

Chapter Four

Captal hung before them, a thin green crescent flanked by the muddy gray of its moon. Having exited from the portal jump half a light outside the Copea system, Dhar immediately ordered the housekeeping computer to transit. They closed on Captal in eleven minutes at a leisurely half boost, which gave the prowling pickets time to look them over. Four M-6s and a colossal M-9 held station a million talans off the Serrll capital world. A cluster of M-4s crowded the close orbits. The ship dropped normal and coasted in on its secondary drive.

"SC&C link enabled," Cent Comp announced in a lush female voice. "Ready for orbital insertion."

"Very well," Dhar said gravely, staring at the mainframe plot.

Emotion surged through Terr at seeing the familiar world grow large. He'd left many memories down there, pleasant and some not so. A quick peek at Teena, he could see she also felt a touch of nostalgia. For him, it had been less than two months since he'd confronted his uncle, but it felt surreal like it happened to someone else, in some other place. A lot had transpired since then and the experience inevitably wrought its change. For Teena no less so, having glimpsed the forbidding cliffs of Athal Than that in her eagerness to understand him almost took her. Many memories…

The stars wheeled as Surface Command and Control brought the S/12 in. An amazing vessel and Terr lusted after it. Although not armed, its defense nav screen could probably handle an M-3. Not a military ship, its designers had not stinted on the small comforts of its passengers. Unfortunately, Terr wasn't given an opportunity to enjoy them fully. Two hours to reach the Perilia portal and they were here. This kind of zipping around took some getting used to.

He needed to talk to Teena, allowing her to vent frustration and unstated resentment when he left her to see Zero Six. An emotional reaction, and intellectually, she understood what he'd done and why, but it did nothing to close the small rift between them. Once she chewed him out, she'll come around, he thought comfortably. One thing he would not do was argue with her. When she was done, she'll be suitably contrite and making up afterward would be ample compensation for any angst in between.

He glanced at her reclining in the swivel-couch. She turned her head and smiled slyly. She'd get even with him for all the worry he caused her, her smile said. He grinned weakly, acknowledging he'd be paying penance. When he saw the pixie sparkle in her eyes, he felt a degree of relief.

Unaccountably, she'd been tense as *Kara* approached the transport portal, her knuckles white against the armrest. Less than eighty ampirs from the portal, she bit her lip and her eyes became glazed.

"What's the problem, my pet?"

"Stop the approach!" she demanded hoarsely, sweat beading on her forehead. Alarmed, he glanced at Dhar.

"Cent Comp? Hold position."

As the S/12 slid to a stop, Terr turned his couch and looked at her. Her small hand shook as she dabbed at her face.

"I don't want to go through that thing."

He took her hands in his and slowly stroked them, hardly able to image the demons haunting her. "What's bothering you?"

"It's silly, I know, but I can't help feeling if I go through, we'll be transported to KP-001 and find ourselves in those spheres." She shuddered and he tightened his grip. Her eyes glistened as she stared at him, lips trembling. "Zero Six programmed me to alter *Kara's* nav com and bring you to it."

Terr knelt before her and gathered her in his arms. She clung to him, her hands tight around his neck. He stroked her hair and cleared his throat.

"There, pet. Nothing will happen, and you were not programmed. You were checked out and they found nothing."

"I know," she whispered into his shoulder. "I can't help how I feel."

"Do you want to go down to our quarters?"

She sniffed and pulled back. She pursed her lips and shook her head. "No. If I don't deal with it now, I'm not going to be any good to you."

Terr glanced at Dhar.

"Cent Comp? Resume course."

"Acknowledged."

Her grip on him tightened as *Kara* approached the interface. When they broke through, Copea bright on their port quarter, she exhaled loudly and kissed his cheek.

They glided past orbital factories, cargo terminals surrounded by clusters of container ships, passenger liners of various shapes and sizes from nameless worlds, crowded the geosynchronous and lower orbits. SC&C steered *Kara* through the atmosphere down to Sal Field, the planet's principal civilian port and military facility on the outskirts of Captal city. The ship hovered above the glowing landing ring and gently settled. An access tube immediately extended from the military terminus hub and mated with a dull clang. Dhar powered down, stood up and stretched his arms, hearing the joints pop.

"Less than three hours ago we were on Perilia. Hardly seems real," he rumbled, obviously pleased with himself, liking handling the S/12.

"I was thinking the same thing," Terr agreed as he helped Teena out of her couch. "Now that we're here, let's meet our reception party."

Teena grabbed his arm and looked at him. "Too much has happened too fast. I need time to pull it all together."

"You don't need to attend any of the meetings."

"It's not that. I just…"

He stroked her cheek with a finger and nodded. "I understand. We'll take time and talk about everything."

With only three decks, the ship did not employ an internal PT system, although it did use it for external transport when hooked to a planetary VI net. They took the grav-chute to the lower deck and paused as the housekeeping computer opened the main hatch, a square sunk on one of its corners. On the other side beckoned the brightly lit access tube.

"*Kara*, set security access protocol level three," Terr ordered as everybody filed out.

"Acknowledged."

Immediately, a dull orange sheen covered the visible part of *Kara's* hull and hatch. Cloaked in its primary nav screen, life would be difficult for anyone trying to get in. He *did* give Tertulion his word, no matter what some CAPFLTCOM weenie might demand.

Teena glanced at him, her eyes bright. "You've got a fetish for that computer."

"Have not!" he declared, and she laughed gaily.

Still, they didn't have to give the thing such an alluring voice, he mused.

When they exited the tube, he suppressed a groan. First Assistant Tariq did not look overawed at seeing him either. An Assembly rep in his first ten-year term, life soured for him when he failed to get nominated for a second term. He was now sweating out his last two years as Commissioner Enllss-rr's principal executive aide. As far as Terr was concerned, it could not have happened to a nicer guy.

"Mr. Terrllss-rr, welcome to Captal," Tariq grated formally, his little button eyes glinted like chips of ice.

Terr felt a momentary temptation to have a little fun at the man's expense, but refrained. He had a serious mission, and Tariq presented too easy a target. As First Assistant, he wielded a lot of authority, but not enough to try derailing the career of the commissioner's nephew. It was nice having someone powerful in his corner, Terr reflected.

"Thank you, Mr. Tariq. Allow me to introduce Teena-raye, and you already know Mr. Dharaklin."

It was through Dhar's clandestine association with Terchran, the fishy Executive Director of the Bureau of Technology and Development, and a senior Karkan Federation representative, that in a roundabout way ended with Terr going to the Orieli Technic Union. Next to Illeran, BCPA's executive director, Terchran was the most influential Karkan maluran in the General Assembly, and an enemy.

To maintain his cover with Terchran, Dhar revealed a body job Terr had done for Anabb. Nothing much—getting rid of a sleazebag Servatory Party appointee—but it got him in Terchran's sights. It was all a plot by Enllss to remove Wanderers from Captal where they would not be able to gather intelligence for the Unified Independent Front. Dhar was a Wanderer, as was Terr, although a conscript, Enllss manipulated the situation to rid himself of both agents. Terr almost killed Nightwings because of that charade, and he planned to get even with his uncle because of it.

Now that he was here, would fates give him an opportunity to thank Enllss properly?

Tah, the gods will tell.

"Ma'am." Tariq charitably gave a small nod, then turned to Terr. "Commissioner Enllss-rr instructed me to bring you to him for a brief interview before formally meeting the Security Council members."

"Lead the way, Mister," Terr said, looking forward to exchanging some family gossip. He wondered if there would be time to see his aunty Rhea. Teena would love it; the two women having hit it off from the first; cuddle up and let their hair down.

It might be good for her. Sadly, and he regretted the circumstances, he wouldn't be messaging his mother. After his father's death during a black ops, failing to pursue a more acceptable family-approved career in politics, in her eyes, Terr had no shadow. She never forgave him for choosing to walk in his father's footsteps, electing to seek a life in the Fleet, a juvenile fantasy as she termed it.

Perhaps one day both would swallow their pride and shrug off their petty differences that kept them apart. Life sucks, he decided.

Inside the brightly lit cavernous terminal, fronted with outwardly sloping transparent wall screens, Tariq led them through the throng of officers and ratings arriving or departing. Most wore plain working grays, but there were enough dark green of assault marines and full dress blues to add color. A sprinkling of civilian females dressed in various costumes added a pleasant diversion. One tall creature, gorgeous in her form-hugging, one-piece black coverall, caught Terr's attention. He followed her undulating shape until a jab in the ribs from Teena shattered the images beginning to coalesce in his mind.

As they walked to the combie bay reserved for flag officers and government lights, Tariq stepped beside a dark blue vehicle polished to a high gloss, the yellow-orange BCPA crest prominent on its side. The bubble opened and everybody scrambled in. No one chose to sit up front with Tariq. The bubble closed and shut out the background clamor and PA announcements. Tariq steered the craft down the landing ring, then the combie surged up as they exited, the nav system positioning it in the correct flight corridor within the streaming traffic of combies, sled-pads, communals, cargo haulers and assorted heaps.

Low in the sky the afternoon's red sun bathed the landscape with shadows. Below, hurrying, strolling populace from all over the Serrll packed the broad tree-lined Paulo Way Boulevard. Bars, shopping centers, amusement arcades, and some more earthy establishments, lined the Way. Circling the enormous expanse of Sal Field, the Way was a major attraction for locals and offworlders alike. Most of the Paulo District reflected the relaxed, opulent lifestyle of its residents. Locals and tourists stood on moving glidewalks; chatting, staring at nothing in particular, or simply waiting to get to wherever they were going. Dark clouds in the south marred what was otherwise a perfect day.

Captal and the sprawl of its Districts stretching into blue haze without end. A curious mixture of baroque, contemporary and futuristic, it satisfied most who lived in it. A blend of many worlds, representing as it did the Serrll Combine, the Districts were more a collection of enclaves than a homogeneous expression of Captal's native culture, to the lament of the more conservative elements. As he watched the city slide beneath him, the contrast with Tetra's subdued sense of tranquility could not be starker.

As they flew over Celean Park, hotel spires and convention complexes clustered around Taiko Way that girthed the soaring towers of the Center. Linked by tubeways, they were needles of ceramic and color-reactive panels, indifferent to emotion and pain of people below, as were the gnarled trees in the park. Tariq landed on one of the protruding ramps of the BCPA tower and waited for it to retract before opening the bubble. A high-speed cable-tube took them up to the lower executive floor.

When the tube door hissed open, he led them quickly to the commissioner's inner sanctum, the group followed by curious stares from the onlookers. All around, high clear window screens provided an unobstructed view of Captal. Finely textured Catlan moss panels lined the back wall. Softly contoured formchairs tastefully arranged before a wide workstation occupied the reception area to Enllss' office. Behind the curved desk with its inlaid interactive display plate sat a provocative looking woman. Terr had met her before, an anchor in a sea of unknown bureaucratic faces.

"Landa, inform the Commissioner his party has arrived." With a brief nod, Tariq stomped off.

Terr looked at the stiff retreating form and shook his head. "Warm as ever."

Landa smiled and tapped a green pad on her screen. After a moment, it turned yellow. "You may go in, sir."

Floor-to-ceiling translucent frosted white panels slid aside as he approached.

"Terr, my boy!" Enllss boomed, his arms spread in welcome. Terr grunted as his uncle embraced him, the grip hard. Enllss let go and turned. "Teena, my dear, you look radiant as ever."

She flashed him a happy smile and curtsied. "It's good to see you again, Enllss."

"By damn! After what you've gone through, I should think so. Are you all right? No aftereffects?"

"I'm fine, but it will take a little time."

"I understand." Enllss nodded to Terr's brother. "Agent Dharaklin."

"Sir."

Dhar worked with Enllss while detached to Captal from the Diplomatic Branch. Terr was sure his brother had some interesting tales about his experience, but so far, they hadn't had time for fireside chats of that type. Perhaps during some long interlude between the stars, he would ask him to reveal all, subject to the Nondisclosure Act, of course. Working for Anabb, both kept skeletons that rattled.

"No calls," Enllss told Landa and waited for everybody to walk into the office. The door panels clicked shut.

The Wall cycled through patterns of bright color, pooling and merging in endlessly changing whorls. In the corner of the spacious office befitting a commissioner were chairs that surrounded a low wooden table containing glasses and drinkables.

A gracious host, Enllss poured while everyone got seated. He held out a small crystal tumbler of rich honey liquid to Teena.

"Aquilla, my dear. Landa got it from a hole she found along the Paulo Way. I think you'll adore it."

She took a cautious sip and her eyes widened. "Excellent. Sweet but not cloying. Reminds me of prana water."

Enllss looked pleased, then frowned. "I keep telling Terr to bring me some whenever he's on Anar'on, but he never does. I must go cap in hand to their Assembly rep for some."

A prized export, rare and astronomically expensive, prana water was a mixture of peelath berries, tarad grass seeds and other ingredients. In a year, a village may produce some three hundred bottles, stored for up to eighteen years deep in cool sands before being drunk, and there were not all that many villages. Attempts were made to synthesize the wine, some of it very good, but the imitations paled when one tasted the real thing.

"I'll remind him next time we're there," Teena gushed and took another sip.

"You do that," Enllss commanded as he poured a different amber liqueur into three larger tumblers. He waited for Terr and Dhar to pick up theirs. "Glad to see all of you home safely," he said gruffly and took a deep swallow.

Terr tried the fine brandy and nodded in appreciation. It must have come from his private stock and not the watered stuff Enllss used to entertain constituents or Assembly reps. Terr placed the tumbler on the table and studied his uncle.

Stocky, face a bit more wrinkled and hair a little grayer with only a few flecks of brown showing, of average height, Enllss still cut a powerful and imposing figure with his hard gray eyes that saw everything. Death settled on Terr's shoulders as he stared into those penetrating eyes. This confrontation had been inevitable.

"Remember what I said when I saw you last?" Small blue sparks jumped around his fingers. "Your maneuvering caused me and Nightwings a lot of needless pain, Uncle."

"Terr!" Teena gasped in alarm and Dhar straightened, looking wary.

Terr reached with his hand before Enllss could react. Sparks crackled and Enllss went pale as they crawled over his chest. Terr chuckled, which eased the sudden tension.

"You should see your face," he remarked comfortably, sat back and took another sip.

"By damn!" Enllss whispered and wiped his glistening forehead. "I ought to have you shot for this!" he barked and gulped down the brandy.

Although his uncle may be unnerved, Terr noted the steady hand. "Call it an even exchange, and you got off lightly."

"No wonder Anabb is trying to get rid of you, you scamp!" Enllss glared at Dhar. "Is he always like this?"

"It's not as though you didn't give him cause, sir. I did warn you what might happen."

"All right, I creamed my pants. Satisfied?"

Terr laughed. "It'll do, but I don't want a repeat performance, okay?" Although he smiled when he said it, there was steel in his voice and he hoped Enllss took note. "Next time, I might not be as forgiving."

Enllss cleared his throat. "Now that you've had your little amusing diversion, let's get down to the substance of why you're here." He placed his tumbler on the table and crossed his legs. "Prepare yourself for a lengthy session, tonight and tomorrow. This doesn't concern you, Teena. Once we're done here, I'll have you flown home where you and Rhea can chat up."

"If you don't mind, I'd like to be with Terr. I *am* a member of this cultural exchange mission and an accredited analyst. Anabb won't appreciate it if I neglect my duty, no matter what the reason."

Enllss studied her for a moment. "Very well. I wasn't being condescending."

"No offense, Enllss."

Terr suppressed a smile. His uncle still had to learn that no one handled Teena. She was smart, independent, and not bashful at standing up for herself. If she were a touch more reckless and ruthless, she'd make a terrific field operative, but he felt comfortable having her just the way she was.

"On your pretty head be it."

"How is Aunty?" Terr asked.

"You'll see her later tonight. All of you will stay over as my guests, but it's *me* you should be worried about. This job is killing me."

"I see how you suffer," Terr said dryly, not showing much sympathy. His uncle thrived in Captal's boiler environment and would not have it any other way.

"One day, my boy…I don't know what Tariq told you and I don't really care. He can be a pain, but he really is a good executive. Since the Orieli cultural exchange program is run under my bureau's auspices, I demanded to see you all first before handing you over to the others. Because I can also be a pain and my nomination to an Executive Director posting gives me some authority, I got my way. Once I'm through, you'll be seeing most of the Security Council luminaries: Bakral, the Executive Director; Illeran, my boss; Katan from the Bureau of Defense, and Sill-Anais, Anabb's boss and yours. As head of the Diplomatic Branch, Anabb will be asked to participate, but not today. Although intensive, tonight's session will lay the groundwork for what's to come. We just received Karhide Arlon Dee's KP-001 after-action report and we need to digest the contents. We should have OSCOM's preliminary analysis sometime tomorrow. You may regret yet hanging around, my dear. Any questions?"

"What exactly do we tell you that you don't want us telling the others?" Terr demanded, not liking the parameters his uncle had set. They hinted at division and parochial interests, something the Security Council didn't need right now.

"Nobody's pursuing a hidden agenda, my boy, if that's what you're insinuating. You tell them everything just the way you saw it. No holding back. We'll hand the session recordings to the Bureau of Central Planning and Development for detailed analysis to extract any gems of wisdom. This is far too important to play political brinkmanship. Although I'm certain some of my enterprising colleagues will try. But with Bakral chairing the proceedings, he'll make sure everybody sticks to the script.

"The other reason why I wanted the meeting, you can give it to me raw without worrying about protocol. The others will also want it unvarnished, but with them, you might feel a degree of restraint, which could tempt you to be reticent. After all, each is an eminent public figure, and as such, they can be intimidating. Something you're not laboring under with me," Enllss added with a touch of pique.

"I always accorded you the respect you deserve, Uncle," Terr said with a straight face.

"You just proved my point, you young rogue. Okay, let's take this from the top, the incident at Devon 3-VL4. How did a Kran cruiser manage to slip through the Orieli LTN line? If they can do it once, they can do it lots of times, and possibly much closer to where it counts. Zor-Ell told me, but I want to hear it from you."

"It didn't, not exactly. The way Arlon Dee explained it, sensor analysis shows the ship suddenly emerge into normal space near LTN-5. He happened to be in the area and immediately engaged the alien. Damaged, the Kran ship fled and holed up on Devon's moon to carry out repairs."

"You're suggesting the Kran ship made a blind transport portal jump?"

"Yes."

"Or somebody over there screwed up and Arlon Dee spun you a tale."

"Why should he? If they suffered a security breach due to

operator error, it would be in their interest to identify and plug it. Besides, they have computer and sensor logs of the entire penetration."

"So Zor-Ell says. Look, I'm not saying Karhide Dee was dishonest with you, but you don't air dirty laundry in front of strangers. Still, it's peculiar. Why would a lone Kran cruiser want to prowl about so far out, knowing it's in hostile space?"

"Mapping the LTN line?"

"Possibly. Anyway, the damned thing did land and you waded in blasting it, thereby revealing to the Orieli the single strategic advantage we have to bargain with."

Terr did not bother hiding his skepticism. "After what Captal did to Kaleen, you're suddenly very possessive of Anar'on. Anyway, the Kran *Daktar* had just obliterated Master Scout Taran's M-4 and Arlon Dee found himself in a serious firefight. At least that's how it looked to me. If his ship got disabled, there was nothing to stop the Kran cruiser from moving farther into Palean space. With the promised M-6 nowhere in sight, we could have faced disaster. I knew what I was doing when I revealed myself. What I didn't know at the time, Karhide Dee could easily deal with the Kran, and I didn't have the luxury of time to consider interstellar politics."

"I doubt that. Admirable as your action was, some in the Security Council may disagree with you. Never mind, you were on the spot and no one else gets a vote." Enllss glanced at Dhar. "You were there. How did you read the situation?"

"The tactical situation was very fluid, sir. Without the promised M-6, Karhide Dee was one-on-one with a powerful vessel. I didn't do what Sankri did simply because I didn't have the capability."

"Which evidently he does," Enllss reflected and pulled at his firm chin. "I'm not saying you're facing a reprimand, Terr. They'll probably give you a medal."

"You can tell them where to pin it," Terr growled, annoyed being grilled for doing something right.

His uncle nodded. "I'll do that. You realize, of course, your action generated a lot of heat in Captal and Anar'on, but we'll discuss Controller Marrakan in a minute. With that wreck on Devon's moon, it's given our tech boys a new toy to take apart. They can't complain about that too much. Talk to me about the Kran gravitic missiles. Facing their ships will be bad enough, but this weapon of theirs is a disaster."

"As the Orieli found out. Unfortunately, there is nothing much I can add to what you probably already know. We don't know its range, except the infernal things can travel close to nine times the speed of light. It's a devastating tactical theater weapon. Fired close to a target as possible, it drastically reduces reaction time for any countermeasures. With LTN-3 the Krans couldn't get close, but they made enough of a mess as it is."

"I gathered it was bad news. Did Alkarh Tertulion tell you what they're doing about it?"

"The Fernai told them how they overcame the problem, but the Orieli are pursuing a different option."

"I know. I read your contact report."

"If we're not, we should be looking at this as well."

"My boy, creating a gravitational distortion sink the Fernai employ, and making sure the ship creating it isn't snared, is not something we're likely to develop anytime soon. As for what the Orieli are working on, forget it. It will take some time before we understand the theory underpinning their portals, let alone develop and deploy the technology. About the Fernai…when your report came in, it certainly got everybody hopping. They all scrambled to access the archives. So far, we've drawn a blank and Anar'on isn't saying anything. Mr. Dharaklin?"

"I honestly don't know, sir. That's not to say the Rahtir Council doesn't."

"We'll take it up with Controller Marrakan in due course. I still have to get my head around Karhide Dee's after-action report yet, but you seem to have caused no small consternation with the Krans, Terr. By damn! Can't you do anything without causing an interstellar incident?"

Terr smiled and took a sip of brandy. "Without my and Dhar's abilities, I very much doubt Alkarh Tertulion would authorize the attempt. She definitely would not if *Tapal* lost only a handful of its crew. They play from a very high ethical plane, but they're also realists."

"I never doubted it, my boy, and LTN-12 proves it. They brushed aside our protests and went ahead and built it. Never mind. Zero Six let you all go simply to send the Orieli a message? That doesn't click with me, and probably doesn't click with them either. From what OSCOM told us, the Krans aren't into psychological warfare. They conduct business in your face and don't let you forget it. This Zero Zero, it's worried about the Wanderers."

"I suspect it is, but I believe Zero Six released us hoping I'd be a convenient vector for its nanobods infestation. I'm simply glad to have walked away in one piece."

"Our think groups will worry it. About your sessions with the central nexus…some in the Security Council expressed an opinion that you betrayed us, that you spilled all when you were not under any duress."

Teena sat up and glared. "They weren't subjected to what we endured, Enllss! We could do nothing to stop the mind probes. The very idea—"

"I'm aware of that, my dear. All I'm saying, you've gone through a lot and it's taking some of my colleagues a bit longer to digest the information."

"But to suggest—"

Enllss raised a hand. "I simply wanted you to know what's said. I shouldn't have mentioned it and I agree with your sentiment. The Council needs to focus on the strategic threat facing us, and not be sidetracked by irrelevancies. With the knowledge they gained if the Krans decide to hit us, our outlying outposts and protectorates will be front-line casualties, as will some of the independent nonaligned frontier systems. Given their capability, we must review our existing defense scenarios. If they simply jump in somewhere, we'll be in a world of hurt."

"I concur," Terr said. Teena muttered something, clearly still hot over the outrageous insinuation.

"Did the nexus give you any indication it will strike, or when?" Enllss asked.

"You want a timetable? In my opinion, they'll strike, do it soon, and we're likely the first they'll hit. If the Council is looking at the strategic dimension, they have it. The Serrll Combine has 247 aligned and nonaligned systems, forty outposts and thirty-four protectorates. Within The Arch, the Orieli have thirteen hundred. It doesn't take much to figure out which is the softer target. If the Krans roll us up, they'll be fighting along a single front without having to worry about their flank, not that we're really a threat for them. When they do attack, and they will, I'd suggest Anar'on will be on top of their shopping list."

"I'm not a military expert, my boy, but even I can see that. If they can eliminate the Wanderers, they'll neutralize their major strategic threat. Stark but logical."

"That's how Zero Zero will figure it."

"That's how *you* think it will figure it."

"True, we don't understand the behavioral parameters it uses to decide when to act or against whom. Still, with the knowledge we've given it, I'd be surprised if it didn't act."

"They could also attack Captal, you know. Remove Serrll's political center and our responses everywhere will become uncoordinated."

"Anything's possible, Uncle, and I understand the political disaster we'd face if they succeeded. To the Krans, cleansing all organic intelligent life is a prime directive. Nothing short of annihilation will stop them."

"The Fernai stopped them."

"And the Krans withdrew, granted. I'd say it was probably to regroup and develop a capability to take them on."

"The Fernai should have smashed them, saving a lot of unpleasantness for everybody."

"That's our psychology talking. We don't know what drives them. They're undoubtedly powerful and appear friendly, but that could be because we don't have anything they want."

"A cynical assessment, and probably one with a small grain of truth. Interstellar warfare is almost always motivated by economic drivers, seldom by political ideology alone." Enllss topped up his tumbler, took a sip and stared at Terr. "Your proposition that the Krans are an evolved form of nanobods is pretty wild even for you. It generated a few chuckles."

Terr grinned. "I am sure it did, but I was just throwing up possibilities."

"Causing trouble, that's what you were doing. It's got people thinking, which is always a good thing. We only have OSCOM's analysis of Kran forays against their LTN stations, which might not be indicative of Kran doctrine. Still, it does suggest they prefer to nibble at a target rather than go for big bites. If true, it gives us time to position some of our heavy stuff along the likely incursion line, which is already happening. OSCOM hinted they'll release ships and a few scanner arrays to us. We could certainly use both."

"In exchange for placing Wanderers on their ships?"

"They did not say, but they would sure like to know if Anar'on is willing to go along with the idea, as would I! Having adepts in our corner could make all the difference."

"Any word from Controller Marrakan?"

"Nothing yet, but I'm sure he's thinking about it. He's had his differences with Captal in the past, but we're all facing total annihilation, not merely political domination. Don't be surprised if the Council grills you on this. Both of you," Enllss said and glanced at Dhar.

"There is nothing we can say to them, and it's not in our power to decide action for the Council," Terr pointed out.

"You two have a special insight into the problem, though.

Something Marrakan may want to explore with the Rahtir before they make their decision. You're going to Anar'on, aren't you?"

"As soon as we're finished here," Terr said.

"Not unexpected, and you have a fine vessel to get you there. The Bureau of Technology and Development busies are understandably drooling to get a look inside."

"And that's all they'll be doing. The ship is out of bounds, Uncle. I promised Alkarh Tertulion."

Enllss sat up, eyes wide in astonishment. "You can't mean that, boy! The technology your ship represents could advance us by centuries. You must let us pick it apart."

"I promised."

"Mmm. First contact protocols, eh? Never mind. I won't pester you. Even if I tried, knowing you, I suspect I'd get nowhere. Still, if the Council asks, you can't simply tell them no. They'll ignore you and do it anyway."

"They can try, but nobody will get inside that ship, not unless Dhar or I let them."

Enllss snorted. "I'd like to see their faces when you tell them."

"If we secure Anar'on's support, and Marrakan is willing to place adepts to protect Orieli ships, we can make his support conditional."

"A handful of *Nasors* and a ship to pick over? A reverse deal, is that it? I like it."

"I also asked Alkarh Tertulion to tell us how to modulate our shield grid."

"That *would* be useful. From your report, though, it won't give us a defense against gravitic missiles."

"Perhaps not, but it would make it a more even fight."

"Mmm. You realize, of course, we're asking the Orieli to fill a substantial shopping list, and Marrakan may have demands of his own. The Orieli might decide the price is too high."

"The thought did occur to me, Uncle. That's another reason for us to talk to Marrakan. The Orieli might be more forthcoming if they got something solid out of the transaction."

"Agreed. We need them far more than they need us and we must tread warily." Enllss leaned back and chewed his lip. "Tell me. What makes you think Marrakan will see you? I'm sure he has already considered any argument you're likely to bring up. He is a sophisticated politician, not some desert tribesman."

"Perhaps, but I am a Wanderer, and as such, I'm entitled to see him or any Rahtir. I may be deluding myself thinking that anything I say will make a difference, but Dhar and I saw and experienced what you and he only read in dry reports. There is a qualitative difference."

"Well, it can't hurt. How determined are you to go to Anar'on?"

Surprised by the unexpected question, Terr frowned. "As a Wanderer, I have a duty."

"You also have a duty as a serving Fleet officer."

"Detached, Uncle."

"Anabb would release you, and you too, Mr. Dharaklin, if CAPFLTCOM asked for you. Given what's facing us, they'll need every ship commander they can get."

Terr grinned. "In that case, I better leave before they *do* ask!"

Enllss laughed and lifted his tumbler in salute. "Terr, my boy, you're trouble wherever you go. I can only hope that this time, you'll cause it for the Krans."

"One can hope."

"Teena, my dear, how do you put up with him?"

"It gets hard sometimes," she acknowledged with a faint smile.

"I don't doubt it, by damn."

* * *

With the cabin walls and ceiling transparent, the cold stars formed a perfect blanket. Eternity hung over him as Terr locked his fingers behind his head; Teena's warm body snuggled against him. One leg thrown over him, her arm held him tight, she slept. He looked down at her and a fleeting smile touched his face as he brushed a wayward lock of hair off her smooth cheek. She mumbled something at his touch and moved closer, her grip on him tightening, afraid he'd vanish if she let go. Although she didn't remember, her nights since leaving Captal were restless as she tossed and turned, reliving the moments of her imprisonment and the interrogation sessions with the nexus. She never talked about it much when awake, telling him she was all right. Only when night came did her ghosts walk. He did not say anything about the tortured dreams haunting her, knowing they would fade, content to be there for her, an anchor of stability she could cling to.

As he lay there, watching the stars crawl slowly around him, for the first time, her dreams hadn't returned. She still sought the comfort of his touch, but her soul seemed more at peace, as was his. Looking back, it all seemed somewhat surreal, like scenes in a Wall.

The Orieli building a base on Earth's moon, his crash and pursuit by American security forces, rescue by Zor-Ell and return to Taltair, only to find Dhar had taken Teena; his vengeful confrontation where he almost killed his brother, it all came crashing through. Hollow, drained and disillusioned, he faced his destiny at Athal Than, prepared for the gods to take him, for he had not been a dutiful disciple of the Discipline. Having forgiven Nightwings' betrayal, in the same way, the gods forgave him his trespasses and he walked away cleansed and renewed. When Anabb told him he wanted him to head one of the cultural exchange missions to the Orieli Technic Union, Terr was tempted to tell the scheming old fart to shove it, but refrained, which surprised him. After all the pain Anabb and his underhanded manipulation caused him, Terr relented, forgiving his boss. It really wasn't his fault, Enllss being the mastermind behind everything.

Like that communal driver said; it's all high politics, sport. A shitty way to do business, but it's how the movers and shakers did their work. If he wanted to be one of the movers, he better learn the moves, shitty or not, and stop his whining. If he couldn't cut it, he should face up to it now and return to herding a ship. Once, a long time ago, he envied the M-4 drivers, wanting to be like them, wanting such a ship himself. Now, the thought of commanding one seemed a childish ambition. Immersion in Anabb's murky world and high-powered political intrigues had contaminated him. Although if he were honest with himself, he enjoyed mixing it with the mighty, even if the job did involve sweeping up some of Captal's messes as an assassin. Former assassin, he reminded himself.

Where was that naïve person who thought he could right all the wrongs with lightning blazing in his hands? He shook his head, unable to believe he was ever so innocent. He'd shed that innocence on Earth and been paid in full. A Master Scout now with a few more medals—badges of blood and betrayal. What else did he want?

Teena shifted against him and looked up. "Terr?" she mumbled sleepily.

"Go back to sleep, my pet."

"Were you watching me?"

"Just thinking."

"About?"

His insides melting, flowing over his darker side, he brushed her small nose. "Oh, things."

"Like?"

He smiled at her. "How much I love you and that I'll never let you go."

She snuggled closer and purred. "You need to say that more often, lover."

He rubbed his rasping chin against her cheek until she squealed in protest. Relenting, he kissed her forehead.

"How much longer?" she asked dreamily.

"Two days and we'll be on Anar'on."

She rested her head on his chest and her fingers played with the small hairs. "Thank you," she whispered.

Enllss wasn't kidding when he said the sessions with the Security Council would be demanding. The grim, unsmiling faces confronting them asked cutting, probing questions he and Dhar were pressed to answer, and sometimes couldn't. Terr simply didn't know enough about Orieli's political, economic and military disposition to coherently discuss interstellar strategy. Still, they seemed satisfied with what he said. Then they unleashed the boffins on them. First, the Threats and Intentions team wrung them out, followed by Fleet and BueDev busies. Everybody got annoyed when Terr refused them entry into the S/12, but after failing to force their way into the ship, they finally gave up with ill-concealed grace. He wondered whether they would take it out on him once he completed his current mission. People like that harbored long memories. Chair warming second-guessers, that's what they were. They could shove it and he told them so.

It wasn't all drudgery, though. The politicians and the techies needed time between sessions to ruminate. Terr took advantage of those precious moments to get closer to Teena and chase away the demons for both. He took her to Manina Point in the Glandan Gorge where they watched a crimson sunset paint the towering cliffs with gold and fire. When the stars began to wink at them, they made love, huddled beneath the cool blanket of night. Afterward, satisfied and at peace, they talked. Not pillow talk exactly, and perhaps it was. With darkness cradling them, free of lurking shadows, it was easier to share, to unburden. Both relished the moment of intimacy. Terr's clandestine missions had kept him from her for too long and the strands holding them together had slowly unraveled.

Guardians of Shadow

The next day, they went down into the Parakee's Trench, the deepest underwater rift on the planet. Seeing the black smokers spewing gases and minerals that kept the surrounding fragile ecology alive eleven talans beneath the surface was a highlight. The weird glowing creatures prowling the deeps were straight out of someone's nightmare. If he had not seen it for himself, he would not have believed such life existed.

Teena brightened, chirped up and became more herself again, even though the nights haunted her. She rewarded him with two days of rare bliss and he promised himself to never again take her for granted. Nothing was worth losing her or seeing the silent unhappiness in her eyes. Their jobs with Anabb and the Diplomatic Branch consumed them, but it should no longer be the overriding part of their lives. Being together, renewing themselves, was far more important and satisfying than running political intrigues.

Dhar, quietly wise, left them alone, although they all indulged in moments of companionship. Nightwings was his brother and Terr would forever be a part of him, but they allowed Teena to share as well, and they did. The last thing Terr wanted was for either of them to feel shut out. He needn't have worried. Dhar understood their need for intimacy and pursued his own diversions.

Then it ended and life became serious again. After saying goodbye to Enllss, one of Tariq's flunkies took them to Sal Field. Apart from the media clustering around the access tube guarded by two grim marines, nobody else waved bye-bye. SC&C let them go when *Kara* broke orbit and they transited, leaving Captal a distant memory.

Terr nuzzled the top of her head. "Love you, Teena-raye. For all time."

She looked at him, but he couldn't see her eyes in the darkness. "Love you, my lord of Death."

"You want to walk the Saffal when we get there?"

"As long as it doesn't involve going to Athal Than."

He chuckled. "Promise."

She shuddered. "I still get nightmares when I think about that place. These gods of yours, they're chauvinists, did you know that?"

"For not liking women?"

"Why is that? I think you explained, but I don't remember."

"Death walks in their shadow and all life is theirs. Women are an antithesis, being givers of life, and the gods are jealous."

"Like I said, chauvinists." Content, she sighed and held him tight. "But I'm glad you're not. When you aren't dashing about, wielding the lightnings, you're really very sweet to be with." She lifted her head. "We need more time together, Terr."

"I know, pet. Once we get away from the Krans and really start our mission, we'll have all the time we need."

"I'm just afraid it'll never end, that they'll always be there, a specter haunting our lives."

"Like a disease, we must learn to contain them."

"What if we can't? What if they just keep coming, without end?"

"Then we'll have to get our affairs in order, won't we."

She giggled. "Oh, Terr. You're impossible." She gripped him harder and rested her head on his chest. "And I like it that way."

When *Kara* dropped normal, Anar'on hung before them less than two million talans out. In three-quarter phase, the surface lay smeared with patterns of yellow and brown desert sands and broken mountain ranges. Blue tendrils cut into the desert from the small northern icecap, widening into shallow seas and patches of green as they reached into the equatorial latitudes. Only a few white streamers above the water marred the amber skies. It did not seem possible that life could thrive in such a harsh environment.

On the flight deck, they watched as the ship slipped past picketing M-4s and M-3s. In the mainframe plot, two white dots nine million talans out were identified as M-6s. Enllss was right when he said Anar'on would be protected. Terr wondered if anything the Fleet did would make a difference.

As SC&C brought them in, warmth stole through him that started from his middle and spread to the extremities. Almost religious, the feeling left him deeply satisfied and filled with tranquility. The place did it to him every time, a sign of greeting that seemed to come from the world itself. The gods welcoming him home? It felt intensely pleasant and he allowed himself a moment to savor the sensation. He glanced at Dhar sitting beside him and saw his brother also felt it. At least somebody appeared glad to see them.

Kara came to a hover above the parched apron of Kanarath Field. SC&C released them and Dhar powered down. Clusters of cargo haulers and two M-3s crowded the small facility. At the edge of the apron an M-6 loomed huge over everything. Lots of sled-pads fleeted about and tenders clung to the ships. The sole Deklan liner tied to the terminal almost seemed out of place.

Checkered plots of green came right up to the Field boundary, vanishing into heat haze that hung above the shallow sea far in the distance. The city itself pressed around the spaceport, its slim towers swimming and twisting in the roiling heat. Dust whorls chased each other across the tarmac.

Terr descended down a ramp beneath the ship and inhaled loudly as the dry oven heat soaked through his shirt. After the ship's air-conditioned comfort, it came as a shock. He looked up at the amber sky and stretched his arms, welcoming the heat and the burnt desert smells. Teena merely shook her head at his antics. Above the city, traffic streams made pretty patterns in the sky.

Beside him, Dhar breathed deeply and exhaled. "It's great to be back, my brother. We shall walk the sands?"

"If time permits, Nightwings."

Two black Armored Personnel Carriers approached from the terminal building and squatted on either side of the S/12.

173

The rear doors opened and a squad of marines in full battle gear, phase rifles held at port arms, quickly stationed themselves around the ship. An official combie landed in front of them and the polarized bubble lifted. Ronowan stepped out and grinned broadly.

"Welcome home, Sankri...Nightwings," Controller Marrakan's executive assistant declared in a deep voice. "And you must be Teena-raye. You are well?"

"Yes, thank you. Although I'm finding it a bit warm."

Ronowan grinned. "It grows on you. If you will please get into the combie, we'll be on our way."

As they piled in, the ramp lifted and the ship sealed itself, the shimmer of its nav screen barely visible in the wavering heat. The combie's bubble closed and cool air washed over Terr. In the open desert, there was no relief from the unremitting heat, but then, the villagers were used to it. Like breathing, he ignored the discomfort. A strange world, alien and harsh, but also kindly to those who knew its ways. In some respects, he was most content when here, in the cradle of the gods. Anar'on had claimed him and he would forever be bound to it.

Overflying the city as the combie headed for the Center, Kanarath lay spread below them. A mixture of traditional buildings made from local red sandstone and contemporary towers of ceramic and reactive panels, the city did not look like a metropolis that ruled a planet and the stars of Kaleen. As they neared the cluster of towers making up the government complex, the flight management system steered the combie toward a gleaming tower that clawed toward a pale amber sky. They settled on a landing ramp and Ronowan opened the bubble.

A cable-tube took them up to the executive floor. Nothing Terr could see differed from any other administrative center: workstations, desks, filing cabinets, people chatting or staring as the small party went by. The business of government everywhere was the same—bureaucracy ruled.

Ronowan strode into a spacious office and without pausing, made for a wide door made of peelath, the exquisite twisted grain gleaming under heavy polish. He opened the door and stopped.

"The BCPA mission, master."

"Show them in," a powerful voice commanded.

Terr and Dhar exchanged glances. Dhar knew the controller and found him very approachable, although somewhat intimidating. A senior adept, power radiated from him almost visibly. That's what Dhar said. Terr took a deep breath and walked in, prepared to find out for himself.

Bright light streamed in from real windows, allowing an uninterrupted view of the city. The ceiling almost four katalans high, the room looked like any other modern office. A full-dimensional Wall communications station faced a wide working desk positioned before the window. Tucked into a corner, soft formchairs surrounded a round wooden table arrayed with glasses, a dark wine bottle and a tray of pastries. Polished, weathered peelath boards lined the floor. Soft and haunting, the Wall's fluted notes, accompanied by gentle strands from the leetas, drifted through the room. The music shivered in tender agitation to the slow pooling of colors.

Easily one of the tallest Wanderers Terr had seen, Marrakan, Controller of Anar'on and Prime Director of the Kaleen group, stood poised beside the desk, his tastefully tailored gray oark hair suit sitting well on his two point-four katalan frame. He had a hard face, lined with deep wrinkles inscribed by years of political struggles. The eyes with their vertical slits were no longer the orange of youth, but faded. Usually worn long, his ocher gray-streaked hair cut short. Terr studied the Wandered and decided Dhar was right. Palpable power surrounded the man.

"Welcome to Anar'on," Marrakan boomed and smiled with genuine warmth, not merely a political façade.

"Thank you for seeing us, master," Terr said humbly, recognizing the privilege extended to him. The man was a planetary chief executive and had little time for idle chitchat.

Eyes bright with secret amusement, Marrakan waved a hand at the table. "Let's get comfortable, and if you don't mind, no formalities."

When they were seated, he nodded to Ronowan. "Please serve. It is probably some time since our guests tasted real prana water. Teena, won't you try the kekse? Controller Kernami Asai Tainam told me of his unique application of our peelath berry paste and I thought I'd try it, allowing some eccentricity in our Pizgor friend. He wasn't mistaken and I hope you'll like them."

"Thank you," Teena breathed, fighting off shyness, and reached for one of the golden pastries piled on a wooden plate. She took a small bite, looked surprised, popped the rest into her mouth and reached for another. "Delicious."

Marrakan grinned broadly. "I am pleased you like it. I understand, Terr, that you and Dhar already tried them."

"Yes, sir," Terr said as he took one, marveling that Marrakan would remember after five years. "Commissioner Hiraki treated us to a batch when we met Ambassador Rayon Tantour."

"Yes, that business with raiders on Lemos. You and Dhar did a great job. Ah, the drinks. Thank you, Ronowan."

Terr took the small offered glass bound in soft oark leather, thanking Ronowan with a glance. Marrakan lifted his and sipped, his eyes closed as he savored the liqueur. Terr sniffed the delicate bouquet and brought the glass to his lips. A cascade of tastes rolled over his tongue, the fragile flavors of dried peelath blossoms and ripe berries dominating. Sweet, but not sticky—pure. The wine triggered memories and images of flowing sands, forbidding escarpments, and simple village life that once touched and transformed him.

Glass held between his hands, Marrakan's eyes were searching. "So you are Sankri. Sidhara has spoken of you, as has your brother Nightwings. Their words don't do you justice. Your last trial has strengthened you and given you a measure of peace. Is that not so?"

Terr stared at the venerable figure, amazed at Marrakan's astute perception. That he could reach into his soul and lay bare his small secrets at a glance...

"But you are troubled now..." Marrakan added softly.

"You must know why, master," Terr said heavily.

"Devon 3VL-4. Unusual that such ability should manifest itself in a second-level adept, but not unheard of. Do not dwell on it, but rejoice that you stand closer in god's shadow." Marrakan turned to Dhar. "You are well, my son?"

"I long to trek the rolling sands and listen to the whisper of the peelath, but I am content, master. These things will come with the waiting."

"Just so. Stand with your brother and they will come to pass." Marrakan's eyes drifted to Teena, his expression puzzled. "You were touched?" He looked sharply at Terr. "You did not—"

"No. She wanted to see Athal Than—"

"And got more than she bargained for. Teena?"

Flustered, she folded her hands in her lap. "I couldn't resist the temptation, sir. After listening to Terr talk about it, I simply had to see the place for myself. As I stood before those forbidding cliffs, I was drawn to them..."

"You were fortunate, my dear."

"It still haunts me," she said softly.

Marrakan placed down his glass, reached across the table and touched her arm. "Let go. Let it flow through you. In Sankri, you are one and the god will not harm you, but you understand why you must never enter such an escarpment?"

She gave a small smile. "I know it now."

He sighed and sat back. "Strange circumstances brought you all here, but you are home now and welcome. Will you be seeing your parents, Nightwings?"

177

"I want to, but I fear there might not be an opportunity. We're here for a darker purpose."

"So I know. Executive Director Bakral apprised me of the situation. These Celi-Kran things...they sound like creatures out of a nightmarish dream."

"If they were creatures, master, we might be able to reason with them, but there is no reasoning with the Krans," Terr added, his expression grim.

"Nanobod intelligent constructs, incredible. And you say they are bent on annihilation of all organic intelligence?"

"Those were Zero Six's words and I have no reason to doubt them."

"A plague spreading through the galaxy. When I read your report about the Fernai, it touched an ancient memory."

"It's true, then?"

"Long ago, according to the village Rahtir, strange beings appeared in our skies. The legends are incoherent and all differ in detail, but they do agree that aliens once visited our world. Were they Fernai, no one can say. They weren't the first, but Anar'on has few natural resources to plunder. Given their reaction to you two, it lends some credence to the tales."

Struck with an idea, Terr sat up. "Master, what do those legends say exactly? First Commander Shah Pak mentioned a debt."

"Why this sudden interest, Sankri?"

"Perhaps we could collect it."

Marrakan smiled. "Nightwings was right. Life with you is never dull, but I shall indulge you. From what I know, a very important alien official wanted to see Kuram Than, another abode of the gods; a temptation much like yours, Teena. He was saved from entering and vowed eternal friendship."

"When was that?"

"The records are not clear. Perhaps two thousand years ago or more. No one is certain." The fingers of his right hand tapped against the table as he chased down memories. "If you wish, I can make a data cube of what we have."

"Tabe. I would appreciate that."

"Whatever you have in mind, seeking out these Fernai with a two-thousand-year-old legend sounds like a futile quest."

"Perhaps, master. If I could only talk to them, it would be a good first step, and Shah Pak seemed serious about the debt."

"So be it. Your uncle, he prospers?"

Terr smiled. "Feisty as always."

"Hah! A formidable personality. You are fortunate to have someone like him watching over you."

"Sir?"

"I heard how you snubbed the BueDev and Fleet techies. They sought retribution for your refusal to let them study the Orieli craft."

"It wasn't mine to give."

"Of course, but people like that all too conveniently ignore matters of honor when it touches their passion." He glanced at Ronowan. "Please be so good to send a case of prana water to the Commissioner."

The assistant smiled briefly and nodded.

Marrakan frowned. "I understand why you came here, Sankri. Enllss took pains to explain it to me, as did Bakral. I do not doubt their sincerity, but they speak from desperation and political expediency, which I don't resent. It must be galling for the Executive Council having to admit they cannot safeguard Serrll's integrity, and come with bowed heads, so to speak, to us."

"With respect, master, what we and the Orieli face is not an exercise in political brinkmanship. Reading a dry report has given you warning, but out of necessity it fails to convey the magnitude of the threat the Krans represent. They seek nothing else than to wipe out all life. There is no bargaining with them or signing treaties. All intelligent life in this arm of the galaxy faces extinction, and afterward, the galaxy itself. I saw holoviews of worlds left as cinders after the Krans swept over them. Our worlds will look like that if we don't face them, and face them together."

"You speak eloquently, my son, but you are presuming that Anar'on has a responsibility to protect the galaxy, something I understand First Commander Shah Pak said. An ironic twist of fates? We lived undisturbed for millennia until Sofam traders invaded us. They were merely the first. Then the Deklans came with their Ecumenical Order, followed by others, all looking to subjugate us religiously or economically and turn us into a tourist curiosity. Even today, they want to bend us to their will. Touched by outsiders, we were forced to fight them using their political tools in order to preserve our way of life. With Orgomy, under the Unified Independent Front umbrella, Kaleen has gained sovereignty and respect. We'll be left alone and with a voice in Captal which will not be ignored."

"Is that the future you see for the Wanderers, master? To be left alone, to eke a living out of an unforgiving desert? Don't you want our people to live in something other than mud huts, ignorant and poor?"

Dhar cleared his throat, clearly uncomfortable. "Master, Terr did not—"

Marrakan raised his hand. "I want to hear his words. Sankri, we are rich in the philosophy of the *Saftara* and the teachings of the Discipline. As for creature comforts, adopting the soft life of the offworlders would change what we are, corrupting the ethical integrity holding us together. We would be tempted to reach for the stars, becoming mercenaries, wielding Death on behalf of the highest bidder, ruled by pride and arrogance, shunning the words of the Rahtir." Realizing what he said, he instantly became contrite. "Forgive me, my son. That was thoughtless. I did not mean to imply that you—"

"There is nothing to forgive, master," Terr said wearily, the truth of the accusation echoing in his mind. "I used my power in the name of what I thought was Serrll justice, not recognizing it as an exercise in hubris. A poignant lesson to learn."

"Then you see how others could be tempted."

Terr leaned forward and gazed into Marrakan's eyes. "I stand in the shadow of Death and do it for all those who cannot."

The old Wanderer remained silent for a while, then picked up his glass and sipped. "Philosophy aside, there are practical aspects to what you seek. The Rahtir don't rule the Wanderers and I don't rule the Rahtir Council."

"If we walk in god's shadow and the gods created everything, can we stand idly by and watch darkness prevail?"

"And all shall be light everywhere I look, even to the stars," Marrakan quoted from the *Saftara*. After a moment, he smiled. "The Rahtir who wrote those words didn't have the Krans in mind when they did it, or the endless possibilities of free will."

"But they understood the obligation imposed on them."

"Extrapolating that obligation from a village setting to the stars is not what they meant."

"Aren't we all children of the gods, even those who inhabit the stars?"

"Indeed. What do you want?"

"It's not what I want. It's what I expect. I expect the Wanderers to live up to the teachings of the Discipline. If we don't reach out a helping hand to another when we can prevent an evil, everything master Sidhara taught me is a lie, as is the *Saftara*. Hollow platitudes that disguise the very pride and arrogance I indulged in, fit only as amusing tales for children. Like the Fernai, we too are smug in the shadow of Death while the Krans slowly shut out the light."

Dhar stirred beside him, clearly not comfortable. Teena merely stared at him, not fully understanding what was going on. Terr suspected he may have been somewhat rash speaking out so bluntly, but Marrakan did not seem to mind.

"Master, Terr's words were not meant—"

"To castigate me? Of course they were, and rightly so."

Terr frowned. He didn't need excuses for his words. Dhar

may be his brother, but brought up within an insular culture spurning contact and togetherness, preferring the isolation of simple village life to Serrll's cosmopolitan gregariousness. Whether they liked it or not, the Wanderers were part of a greater whole and the offworlders would force them to change. Only monuments remain unchanged.

Marrakan crossed his legs. "Like all political entities, the Unified Independent Front is a duality. We created it to protect Kaleen and Orgomy systems, but in doing so, we invariably threw up a barrier to others. I understand the danger an insular outlook represents for us, but we cannot walk among others freely until we are respected in the only arena that matters— Captal. They fear us because of what we are, but they don't respect us. Their cry for help now is undeniably genuine, but that cry is also a shudder of revulsion. They would rather vanquish us than embrace us. That's the harsh reality, Sankri, my son. You cannot then be surprised when the Rahtir want to turn their backs on them. But like you said, we live in a community of worlds and the Serrll is not facing an ordinary enemy."

For a while, the old Wanderer said nothing. Slowly, he lifted his head. "You spoke at length about what we are or should be, but you haven't told me anything about the Krans."

Terr returned his gaze. "All of us were interrogated by Zero Six, an experience that left me drained and feeling totally helpless. Its intellect is overwhelming, and I can only imagine what Zero Zero must be like, but with all the knowledge of the universe at their feet, they cannot connect, master, because they have no spirit," he said softly. "Despite what they learned, they are driven to destroy."

"A runaway reaction to a stimulus?"

"They operate under a blind imperative, but what's frightening, it's backed by utterly cold intelligence."

"Nightwings, what are your words?"

"My words are Sankri's, master. The Krans will keep coming until we are all obliterated or they are scoured from the stars by a superior force."

"And we might be this force?"

"There is something you should know, master," Terr said slowly. "Something I asked Alkarh Tertulion to keep out of her report to Captal. I may know the location of the Celi-Kran home system."

Marrakan sat up. "What is this?"

"I've had a vision. It came to me twice as I remember, and I took it as a warning from the gods. I was standing, a blasted world before me, two stars adorning my feet."

"Sarumajan," Marrakan whispered in shock.

"Sir?"

The controller shook his head. "Nothing. How do you know those stars were the Kran home system?"

"Zero Six told me when it interrogated me. In its arrogance and sublime confidence, it did not realize what it said, or understood the relevance of its words."

"Even if you're right, and I know why you consider this important, we cannot act on it without knowing the location of those stars."

"Alkarh Tertulion has a team working to locate them. Even if they manage to find them, I don't know whether any one Rahtir is capable of reaching across what will undoubtedly be an unimaginable distance, but I wanted you to know."

Marrakan pursed his lips. "We shall ponder this, should it become necessary to act."

He glanced at his assistant and something passed between them. Ronowan immediately rose and walked out. A moment later, Terr gasped as a familiar figure came through the door. Gaping, he jumped to his feet, sensing Dhar doing the same.

"Master!"

Dressed in a plain surtaf robe, brown hood folded back, showing he had undergone his final trial more than ten years ago, Sidhara smiled kindly. His face was deeply wrinkled, worked on by time and harsh desert living. Faded ochre hair spilled across his shoulders, the gray in it prominent. He might be old, Terr didn't really know how old, but the revered Wanderer stood tall and confident, not caring for the years on his shoulders, comforted by the cloak of Death he wore.

Terr stepped to him, bowed and covered his eyes with his right hand. "I crave your blessing, master."

Sidhara touched his head and Terr experienced a rush of affection for the man who helped drag him from insanity, and taught him to love the harsh Saffal sands.

"Stand tall, my strange son from the stars."

Terr straightened and beamed happily. "Tabe."

Sidhara repeated the ritual with Dhar. "Your parents send you their greetings and love, Nightwings."

"Thank you, master. I would like to see them again."

"In the fullness of time." Sidhara turned to Teena. "My spirit soars to see you again, and I hope your heart is glad today."

"It is, sir, and I feel like I have come home."

"You are home here, always," he said warmly and seated himself beside Marrakan. "And you, my stubborn friend?"

"Troubled by Sankri's words. He doesn't approve of our isolationist policy."

"Ah, but he might be right."

They smiled at each other and Terr was struck by a sudden suspicion.

"You already decided to help Captal!"

"As you saw from the ships in orbit, they also acted. A bribe perhaps? It doesn't matter."

"Then all my words were for nothing?" Chagrined, he felt like a fool, thinking he could debate philosophy and interstellar politics with someone of Marrakan's intellect in the hope to sway him.

Marrakan immediately touched his arm. "My son, you need feel no embarrassment. Your words were spoken from the heart and resonated with truth. Although I did decide to help,

184

you touched something deeper that lay buried for too long. I was thinking like a politician and overlooked what I really am, what we all are. We will extend our hand, but tomorrow when the troubles end, we'll make sure Captal does not revert to its old ways."

Mollified somewhat, Terr turned to Sidhara. "You will come with us, then?"

"I will come and see for myself the Orieli and these Kran things you say threaten all, even though the thought of venturing between the stars disturbs me."

Terr smiled, appreciating the sacrifice his master was making.

"Don't be surprised if your pupil here ensnares you in one of his mad schemes," Marrakan warned, looking vastly amused. Sidhara raised an inquiring eyebrow.

"Indeed?"

"I'll let him explain." He looked at Terr. "And you, my son? Back through the Moanar?"

"I fear so, master. We still have a mission."

"Just so."

"But it might not be through the Moanar, not if the transport portal is rebuilt."

"Amazing technology. Tonight, if all of you could join me at dinner, I would be honored, as will some of the more skeptical Rahtir," Marrakan added dryly. "They want to see this strange alien adept."

Terr smiled. "It will be a pleasure."

"Good! Now, if you can pardon my rudeness, I have matters of state to discuss with my willful friend here. Ronowan will make a combie available to you. Enjoy some of Kanarath's humble attractions. Visit the hanging gardens. The afternoon is still young."

Terr rose and bowed. "Thank you, sir...master."

Outside, Ronowan spoke to a young Wanderer who took them to a parking lot halfway down the tower. After securing a combie for them, he bowed and left.

Happy with how things turned out, buoyed with optimism, he looked from Teena to Dhar.

"What shall we do?"

Teena put a slim finger to her lips. "Our mission started with a meeting at a hanging garden. Let's go there. It seems somehow appropriate. Besides, it's too hot for walking or doing something strenuous."

"Done!" Terr hooted, noting his brother's glum expression.

"It is a decadent indulgence," Dhar said severely.

"All the more reason to do it. Come on! Loosen up."

"Sankri, you don't talk to someone like Controller Marrakan in the manner you addressed him."

"Talk like what?"

"Don't be insensitive."

"And you, Nightwings, take things too seriously. Just because Sidhara decided to come with us doesn't mean a flood of Wanderers will descend on the Serrll, and I'm not sure Captal would welcome that. The Rahtir Council hasn't finished deliberating, or Marrakan wouldn't have consented to see us. He wanted to hear what we had to say."

"What *you* had to say."

"You're being picky."

"Oh, you two. Stop it!" Teena flared. "We ended up with something positive. Let's leave it at that and have some fun."

"Now you're talking, my pet. Okay, hanging gardens it is." Terr gave Dhar a pointed look. "Right?"

"You are corrupting me, Sankri," Dhar growled resignedly and Terr laughed.

Inside the combie, with the bubble polarized and cool air circulating, out in the city it didn't look hot, but it was an illusion. When they landed at a rooftop entrance to one of the fabled hanging gardens that spanned the boulevard below, Anar'on gave them a reminder that this was a parched desert world. A wall of heat rolled into the combie as the bubble lifted and Teena gasped. Terr merely shrugged and climbed out.

Outside the leafy arch entrance, a young female Wanderer greeted them with a pleasant smile and showed them to a table beside a slatted lattice wall encased in lush creeper. Water dripped down the walls, keeping the plants healthy. Terr knew it was this seemingly ostentatious waste that rankled with Dhar and many older Wanderers set in their ways. Nothing was wasted, though, the water recycled. It also helped cool the place.

In the middle of the floor, surrounded by pale yellow taslexia orchids, a small fountain gurgled and hissed, glowing with shifting colors from hidden lamps. Most of the tables were empty, lunch finished and too early for evening entertainment. Two youngsters wearing brown surtafs huddled in the corner, occasionally giggling. The world was theirs and they didn't care for the opinion of the oldies. A group of offworlders sat around a long table put together from two smaller ones, their somber suits marking them as government officials or businessmen. An attendant stood unobtrusively beneath the entrance arch, waiting politely.

After ordering drinks and a plate of finger nibbles, Terr relaxed and stretched his legs, completely at ease for the first time in a long while. He would never admit it, but he feared coming to see Marrakan. Had the Rahtir turned their backs on the Serrll, he wasn't sure how he'd take the news. Glad to see his faith in the Discipline teachings upheld, he was prepared to indulge.

"Life in the Diplomatic Branch is hell," he declared benevolently and Teena shot him an amused look.

"Go ahead, gloat," she declared.

"I'm not gloating. Just feeling good. Things have broken our way and I think I'm entitled to feel good."

"Sankri, tonight, *please* try and restrain yourself in front of the Rahtir," Dhar implored. "Show them some respect."

Terr grinned and punched his brother lightly on the shoulder. "Relax; I'll be a model of propriety."

Dhar merely scowled.

"It must be a good sign that Sidhara is coming with us," Teena said and Terr nodded.

"It's great, and I don't think it was merely a gesture to help us either. Now, if I had a suspicious and cynical nature—"

Teena snorted. "Perish the thought."

"—and if I were Marrakan, having a few adepts on Captal and some ships would do a lot for Kaleen's standing in the General Assembly. Of course, as a trusting soul, I'd never harbor such base thoughts."

Dhar harrumphed. He was prevented from making a predictable comment when an attendant brought their drinks and nibbles.

* * *

A searing white light left dancing afterimages and Terr sat up with a jerk. He blinked hard and vision slowly returned. Nothing stirred in the dark bedroom, the green safety strip running along the bottom of the walls created a sensation of intimacy and comfort. A cool desert breeze brought with it pleasant smells through the open windows. What disturbed him? He glanced down at Teena's sleeping form. Whatever it was, it hadn't touched her. He rubbed his eyes and yawned. Must have been dreaming, he told himself.

He tasted the dryness in his mouth and decided to get some water. The several drinks he'd consumed last night left him somewhat dehydrated. He wasn't intoxicated or anything. After all, he represented the Diplomatic Branch and needed to maintain a suitably dignified image. It's not like he could have helped it, what with glad-handing the Rahtir, smiling politely, nodding at feeble witticisms, the various drinks on order helped him cope, and he did cope. Even Dhar remarked favorably on his polished diplomatic behavior, but oark butter would not have gone down his brother's throat that night without choking him. Too serious, that was his problem.

Dressed in high Perilian style, refusing to wear an OSA uniform, Terr admitted he cut quite a figure, to the admiring glances from several female guests, but not unpaired Wanderer girls. With Teena hovering protectively close, she made sure he wouldn't stray, which was uncharitable of her as his heart belonged totally to her. Well, perhaps not totally. A small piece still free allowed him to admire the local and imported scenery.

True to his word, Marrakan laid out a subdued dinner, followed by some traditional music, which Terr appreciated. The mingling with the Rahtir and several civilian lights ended pleasantly, leaving everybody with an approving opinion of Sankri, the alien Wanderer. No one said they did not approve of him, or were too cultured to mention it in polite society.

The things he did for Anabb and the Diplomatic Branch.

A familiar hiss made his head snap up. He threw himself across Teena and dragged her over the edge of the bed to the floor. Every window in the room blew in and the building groaned around him. It actually swayed. A hot wind roared in and the air was filled with fine sand as the overpressure wave passed.

Teena screamed under him, struggling to free herself, probably imagining she lay buried. He rolled off her and she sat up, dazed and shocked at the wreckage around them. A few seconds later, his ears popped as air rushed out to fill the sudden vacuum left in the blast center.

"Computer, lights," Terr commanded and blinked as the ceiling and walls turned bright cream. What he saw would probably be better left in darkness. Everything not secured stood jammed against the wall behind him. The cleaners would have a hell of a job later.

"Lords! What happened here?" she demanded staring at the mess.

189

"Something tried to hit the city. Judging from the time between the flash and the pressure wave, the impact point is some forty talans from here." He jumped up and fumbled for his boots, mindful not to cut himself on the scattered window shards. "Get dressed."

The Wall lit up, flickered and steadied. "You have a pending connection," the housekeeping computer announced. "Do you wish to connect?"

"Enable."

Ronowan's long face looked even longer as he brushed dust off his jacket.

"Master Sankri, I'm going to patch you with Controller Marrakan at the Tactical Response Center. Stand by."

"What happened?" Terr demanded.

"Anar'on is being subjected to c-fractional orbital bombardment. Kanarath suffered a near miss, as you probably know. Many smaller outlying structures were obliterated or severely damaged, but the Center has escaped lightly. We don't know how many lives were lost. Emergency services are mobilizing."

Older, more traditional buildings made out of local stone would be badly affected, as would their occupants. Terr hated to think what the rescue teams would find.

"Elsewhere?"

"We're still waiting for assessment notices to come in."

"Antimatter warheads?"

"It appears so."

"The Krans," Terr said in disgust and clenched his fists.

"Sixteen minutes ago, seven ships were detected dropping normal two-and-a-half lights in the Amulran constellation. They transited immediately, dropped normal one billion talans from Anar'on and launched missiles. Four-and-a-half minutes later the first one struck. They're not gravitic, which is something."

190

"They wouldn't have worked anyway in Anar'on's distortion field. Are the Fleet units engaging?"

"Commander, Kaleen Operations ordered them to close with the Kran ships."

"Recall them! The M-6 out there might be able to handle the ships, but it can't cope with gravitic missiles."

"I'm patching you through now."

Terr ground his teeth and waited. Servous just let them walk in there unprotected, and he'd warned him last night! Without the Orieli ability to modulate the shield grid, the Fleet ships did not stand a chance. The Wall cleared and Marrakan turned to face him. Behind him, large display plates showed real-time views of the tactical disposition around the planet and the system in general.

"Your prediction that the Krans would strike has turned out all too true, my son."

"Master! Recall the pickets! They cannot stand up to the Krans," Terr implored, as horrible images raced through his mind.

Marrakan sighed and his shoulders sagged. "I fear it is too late. After the invaders launched at us, they fired at the pickets, probably using their gravitic missiles. The M-6 and three M-4s in the area are gone. The others immediately pulled back into an occulting point behind Anar'on, shielding them from the Kran ships."

Terr stared at him. "Then we're wide open," he whispered in horror, seeing devastation and ruin all over the planet as life was slowly extinguished. "They'll come into projector range and conduct systematic extermination of everything."

"That will not be permitted," Marrakan said grimly.

Sidhara appeared in the background accompanied by two old Rahtir. They began to chant and the small hairs on the back of Terr's neck prickled, the sensation running down his arms. He knew what was coming. The adepts raised their arms and blue lightnings crackled between them. As one, they turned to the real-time display showing the advancing Kran flotilla. They leveled their arms and bolts of yellow light lanced at the display plate. The crash of thunder made him wince.

Beside him, Teena gasped and clutched his arm. In the display, three golden shafts reached for the *Fadhirs* and speared them like the insects they were. The screens around the ships flared in yellow-white discharges. Backsurges tore at plating, exposing gaping holes, then faded. Thin shafts of intense blue light sprang from the hulls as the artificial quantum point singularities discharged and left the ships drifting.

Three more lances reached out and three more ship nexus cores died. With a look of disdain, Sidhara dispatched the surviving *Sandar*. His ears ringing, Terr turned and held Teena close, her sobs muffled against his chest. After a moment, he looked at the Wall.

"It is done," Marrakan said calmly. "Are you two okay?"

"We're fine, master. The room is a bit messy, but we're in one piece."

Marrakan sighed heavily. "There is a lot of mess to sweep up today, my son. You were right to warn us last night. Servous shouldn't have ordered the pickets to engage."

The COMKALOPS Prima Scout hadn't believed Terr's threat estimate, or overestimated the capability of his ships, as had CAPFLTCOM. How many lives were lost in a few fleeting minutes because of that miscalculation? Frustrated, Terr ground his teeth. He needn't have bothered providing CAPFLTCOM intelligence if they subsequently ignored it. He hoped some sanity would prevail from the pending inquiry.

"Master, any report of survival blisters?" Some may have gotten away before the ship around them was swallowed up.

"We'll search the engagement area."

"What can I do?"

"Here? Nothing. The civil emergency response teams will seek out the wounded and the dead, and we'll repair the mate-

rial damage." Marrakan turned away. After a moment, he nodded. Terr could see his shoulders sag and his face bore visible
signs of overwhelming pain.

"Sankri...Prima Scout Servous reports that six Kran vessels emerged outside the Copea system and hit Captal."

"No!" Teena gasped and pressed a clenched fist against her
mouth.

"Four M-6s and an M-9 tried to engage, but were destroyed
before they could get into range. The others withdrew. The
Krans then proceeded to launch missiles against Captal."

Unnaturally calm, Terr placed an arm around Teena quietly
sobbing beside him. "Is the attack still in progress?"

"The bombardment has stopped and the Krans are moving
into the system. Reports are sketchy, but there is significant
damage and loss of life. Captal city itself suffered one hit, but
the Center and Sal Field were not touched."

"They're repeating the same tactic they used against
Anar'on."

"And they will be dealt with in the same way. Enllss very
effectively removed our special envoys for reasons you know,
but he couldn't remove our Assembly representative or his
staff, and all are third-level adepts. They will stop the Krans."

Terr rubbed the scar above his left temple. He could picture it all so clearly: desolation, ruin, the dead and the maimed,
the tears. What burned was the realization that he told the
Krans about Captal and how to mount their attack. He traded
Parsha for Anar'on and Captal. It hardly seemed worth it. He
bit his lip, torn with guilt and helplessness, irrational as it was.

Marrakan saw Terr's anguish and his eyes softened. "My
son, do not assume the burden of fates. It is futile and destructive."

"I hear your words, master, but they give me little comfort."

"Talk to Sidhara, he will help you. When you see them, tell
the Orieli what happened here. You can also tell them we will

stand together against the Celi-Kran. There will be no dissenters in the Rahtir Council. Not after this."

"I shall tell them."

"At dawn, Sidhara will meet you at the Field. May the gods always stand in your shadow, Sankri."

Terr bowed as the Wall cleared, reverting to slow pooling of colors and twisting shapes. He turned to Teena and brushed away the wetness on her cheeks. He lifted her chin and kissed her forehead, his heart heavy.

"Oh, Terr. This is horrible. Anar'on hit and now Captal. What are you going to do?"

"I want to rush there, but it's a gut reaction. Marrakan is right. There is nothing we can do. I'm returning to Perilia and you'll remain here. Better still, go to Taltair. Where I'm going, I may not be able to protect you."

She lifted her chin and her mouth firmed. "You're going back to KP-001?"

"I must, you know that. We have to deal with it, and it might as well be now."

"Then I'm going with you. Whatever comes, we'll face it together. Do you think I could sleep a wink wondering what might be happening to you? What if you ended up in one of those spheres I was in? I don't want to live if it couldn't be with you."

He touched her lips with his. It was futile bringing up all the logical arguments why she should stay behind, she knew them already, and an emotional problem was never solved with logic. Secretly, he felt glad to have her with him. He would leave her on Perilia. No matter what happened, she'd be safe there.

"Okay, we'll do this together."

Through the gaping windows, a light warm breeze brought smells of scorched sands, tarad grass, and smoke. Fires burned somewhere, proof the bombardment did cause damage. In the east, a faint ribbon of red tinged the horizon. He wondered what this dawn meant for Anar'on and the Serrll.

One arm around Teena's waist, they watched a new day break.

"Let's get dressed and find Dhar. We don't want to keep Sidhara waiting."

Chapter Five

Ed-Kani Takao sat in his comfortable formchair, fingers locked behind his head. With the Wall cycling through harsh, jagged images reflecting his pensive mood, weariness weighed down his shoulders. Everything seemed so pointless sometimes. He had reached for power and grasped it, thorns and all, so why did he feel despondent? Because his name would not be remembered once he left Captal's hallowed corridors, returning to Hakran as a lifetime Pro-Consul, an emeritus sinecure? Perhaps his name would be reviled as someone who sought to disrupt the placid, bland lives of Serrll's citizens who cared nothing for the discipline of the Code. Too comfortable, that was their problem.

On top of the bar cabinet beside the Wall, someone in his office thought to brighten his day by leaving a crystal vase of assorted spring orchids. He could smell them, the fragrance pervading the office. Distracted, he stared at the blooms, considering whether he should mix himself a drink. After a while, he turned and gazed at Captal's sprawl and slowly ground his teeth in frustration.

He snorted with grudging admiration. The Revisionist Party ruled well, bringing peace and stability to the Serrll Combine while increasing prosperity for all, seemingly laudable goals. After centuries living under a martial philosophy, Sargon's citizens had become soft and indolent, forgetting past glories of exploration and conquest, which gave them pride and honor, daring anyone to challenge them. Now commerce and the balance sheet dominated their thinking.

Sargon's forefathers fought the Sofam Confederacy, its

fleets humbling the probing invader, yet it lost the struggle, hardly understanding how. When it did realize, Sofam merchants and its Paravan Trading Association had already conquered them. Instead of warriors occupying the Dumas Conclave, business politicians now dictated Sargon's destiny. Pits! He could not blame history, his conscience prodded firmly and he exhaled sharply. He was someone living in a wrong time and wrong place, dreaming of past glories written with blood. The wave of destiny had swept past him, leaving him stranded on a beach of a hopeless delusion.

He swallowed the bitter realization and lowered his arms. Perhaps his struggle was not lost yet.

Yesterday, as he stood before the ceiling-high window screen, he watched with trepidation as black smoke coiled above the Handara District somewhere below the horizon. Stomach tense, he fully expected to meet his end. He lived and the devastation left him profoundly shaken. Perhaps past glories weren't so glorious after all. History did not talk about the conquered, the dead and the maimed, or the razed cities. It was all about the victors, the celebrations and gained booty. As for blood, rain soon washed it away as earth buried its dead.

The bombardment abruptly ended, and for a while no one knew why. It took some time before the information slowly filtered in from CAPFLTCOM. Unopposed, the Fleet ships contemptuously swept aside, nothing could stop the Krans from moving in and totally destroying Captal. Hastily assembled in Torres' office for a crisis meeting, Katan's announcement seemed hardly credible. Picket M-4s reported all Kran ships destroyed, reduced to drifting hulls, with a single jagged hole piercing their rear segments. What followed was even more unbelievable.

After taking a call from Anar'on's General Assembly representative, the Executive Council chairman looking grave, Torres quietly declared that the Kran threat had been neutralized. Captal saved by Wanderer Discipline adepts? Ed-Kani was

Stefan Vučak

staggered, as were all the Executive Directors. Then more bad news came—Anar'on itself hit. Casualties unknown.

The executive office lights burned long into the night.

He was horrified at the level of damage and loss of life, but civil emergency services were slowly restoring order. However, cleaning up the mess and rebuilding would take time. According to news clips, upward of two million people were incinerated by the initial blast, and untold more were injured and unaccounted for. Fortunately, the strike wasn't nuclear, sparing Captal from radioactive fallout. One missile to have caused so much damage. He didn't want to contemplate what the eventual toll would be when the final planet-wide tally was made. He'd turned off the Wall when the scenes of misery and anguish became too distressing.

However regrettable the incident, as a follower of the Code, he accepted that every conflict demanded sacrifice, and life was the only acceptable payment. As Sargon's senior Assembly rep, his duty was to further its interests, all its interests, even in time of calamity. Although concerned, he did not control the Security Council and bore no responsibility for Serrll's defense. He was happy to leave the problem to Bakral and the Fleet. Given what the Krans did yesterday, he doubted any defense was possible, unless Anar'on intervened as Controller Marrakan pledged to do. Even after the shock wore off, he still found it difficult to believe that any individual could wield such power. He shook his head. Strange people, the Wanderers. Their unselfish act had saved Captal, and perhaps the Serrll Combine itself, but he would not be swayed from his course by a moment of sentimentality. When the dust settled—literally—it would be business as usual, and sentimentality merely got in the way when dealing with hard, tough men.

He glanced at his regenerated hand and squirmed, recalling vividly what Marrakan, in his office on Anar'on, did to him. He glanced at the shelf holding memorabilia and odd items accu-

198

mulated over twenty-eight years of Captal service, and contemplated the veined gray stone hand encased in a block of transparent crystal. Initially tempted to throw the thing away, it served to remind him that power other than political existed elsewhere. He didn't seek vengeance against Marrakan; he'd simply miscalculated. All things considered, the lesson came cheap.

Sofam's motion on the Assembly floor to remove the independent's single Executive Council seat failed along party lines, but it served to remind the Unified Independent Front where real power lay. The UIF would probably end up supporting the Revisionists, further bolstering what in his view was a decadent regime, but if he could neutralize that support, the Servatory Party coalition might still wrest control of the government. Sofam had shown itself a predator he knew they were and he had no compunction playing the same game.

"Comsec? Connect to Commissioner Ti Inai."

Ed-Kani's bony face split into a grimace and his jaws snapped, not relishing the coming conversation. After a moment the Wall cleared and the Palean's oily smile firmed into a full-dimensional image. His long hands twined, the fingers twitching. A delicate button nose made a small protrusion on the triangular face. Large black eyes reflected no light beneath a high rectangular forehead.

"Always a pleasure, Mr. Director," Ti Inai, Commissioner for the Bureau of Technology and Development, piped thinly through small, pinched lips.

Ed-Kani doubted it was a pleasure. They barely tolerated each other, brought together by mutual need. Twitchy, shifty, always sly, the Paleans were often underestimated, a fatal error. They vacillated and took forever to reach a decision, but when they acted, it was with total commitment. Weaklings don't conquer and hold twenty-eight systems. It was their nature to delay, reconsider, constantly looking for angles, which drove him to distraction, and perhaps the principal reason why the Sargon/Palean merger remained unconsummated. Once it *was* consummated, there would not be an Alikan Union, only Greater Sargon. The Paleans probably recognized this, and was the likely reason why they procrastinated.

"How did Tao Karam react to yesterday's attack?" he demanded, foregoing the usual preliminary chitchat. A gross breach of protocol, but he didn't have time for idle gossip, which reflected his impatience, a characteristic Illeran had commented on more than once. The Karkan's criticism being that he lacked subtlety. Well, to the pits with the swamp slime. With two years remaining on his political clock, there was no time for subtlety.

Ti Inai's fingers coiled as he folded his arms over the desk, frowning at this crassness, his disapproval plain to see.

"Alarm, friend Ed-Kani. What did you expect? First, a Kran invader at Devon 3-VL4, and now an open foray. This time it wasn't a Palean world, but what about tomorrow? After what happened to Captal, the Palean Congress is understandably unsettled."

Ed-Kani hissed. Unsettled? He would damn well expect them to be.

"Are they unsettled enough to reconsider ratifying the merger?"

"They might be disconcerted now, but when things calm down, they'll start thinking again and ask the obvious. How would a merger enhance our defense posture? It won't make the Fleet ships invulnerable. If it weren't for those Wanderer heathens, I suspect we wouldn't be having this conversation. With the Krans in the equation, the political picture has changed radically. We're looking at an entirely new paradigm."

Ed-Kani waved a hand in annoyance. "To the pits with the Krans, and you're missing the point here. Nothing has really changed. I'm not talking about ships or tactics, at least not directly. I accept we need Anar'on's protection, regardless how galling the realization, but you and I are realists. Right now the Serrll Scout Fleet is impotent against the Krans, not unless the Orieli provides ships and an infusion of technology like their scanner arrays. Given what happened to their LTN stations, they've got problems of their own. In time, they'll develop countermeasures, and when they do, we'll want them. I'm just not sure we'll be given that time. Until then, we must remain polite to Controller Marrakan."

"What are you getting at, friend Ed-Kani?"

"Don't you understand? Yesterday was a disaster, but it also served as a pointed reminder why the Revisionists cannot protect the Serrll!"

"We couldn't either if we were in power," Ti Inai said blandly and scratched his chin.

"The vast masses out there don't know that. Perception, remember? All they get to see are Wall clips and commentary from pontificating chair experts."

"The Wall scenes of fire and destruction were real enough. Sofam hasn't deceived anybody about the attack."

"But they weren't entirely open either! What's more, as the news spreads, it will invariably become distorted as bias is added. We can exploit that with a bit of bias of our own."

"What are you suggesting?"

"We launch a public conditioning campaign and emphasize how the Fleet failed us when needed, a failure brought about through mismanagement and incompetence of the current government—Sofam's incompetence. While our vaunted M-6s and M-9s sat around parked gathering dust, we remind them and everyone in the Palean Union that tomorrow, it could be their world being ravaged. We'd only be speaking the truth."

"Okay, a scare campaign may sway some, and it might sway enough Congressmen to support the Alikan Union Party, clearing the way for a merger, but I still don't understand how that would protect us?"

"You're now deliberately obtuse," Ed-Kani declared and

snapped his jaws in annoyance. "It won't protect us directly. It cannot, but it will generate doubt and people will start scratching their heads, wondering whether a change of government might not be such a bad thing. Sofam talked sweetness and light during the good times, but at the first sign of trouble, everything fell apart. That's how we need to pitch it. If the Servatory Party takes over, we'll forgive and forget and actively support the Unified Independent Front. We'll urge Anar'on to station adepts on as many strategic planets as possible, including active support for the Orieli."

"In exchange for *their* support?" Ti Inai mused.

"Exactly. I'm not saying the Revisionists aren't looking at these options, they are, but we need to hammer the people everywhere that it was all our idea, and under the Servatory Party umbrella, we'll prosecute all options with vigor. We won't be sitting on our hands waiting for the next Kran attack while Sofam laments the impact on their traders."

"Feasible, but for one small problem, friend Ed-Kani. Even if we do merge, we won't be able to control the Executive Council or the government. A merger only makes sense if we get one extra Executive seat, provided Rolan secedes to you. We need their five systems to get that seat."

"They'll secede. I've got Prime Director Trianon all wound up."

"You failed to win him over once," Ti Inai said softly and Ed-Kani pursed his lips.

"There won't be any mistakes this time."

"Let's stipulate they do secede, the Servatory Party would still be in a six/six split."

"You're assuming the UIF will throw its support behind the Revisionists."

"Like it or not, it's how the numbers are stacking up now, friend Ed-Kani." The Palean's thin fingers coiled restlessly.

"Rolan has another incentive to come on board. The recent vote in the Assembly to remove the independent's seat wasn't lost on Trianon. Sofam gained UIF's support, but it also solidified the independent's seat in our camp."

"How does that break the six/six split?"

"We neutralize the UIF."

Ti Inai stared. "And we do that how?"

Ed-Kani smiled patronizingly. "We get the Deklans to side with us, which would make it seven to five for us."

Gaping, Ti Inai's black eyes bulged. "Why would they want to shift alliances? They're traditional Sofam supporters."

"Power, my thick friend. The Deklan Ecumenical Synod hasn't exactly been happy with their Sofam partners, and Primate Anall-Marr has a particular bone to pick with them. The Paravan Trading Association has blocked too many of his economic expansion programs, and Sofam has twice stopped Deklan from annexing Kaleen and Orgomy, which they consider theirs by ancient right. It's a thin claim, but they don't see it that way. Dominated by Sofam, Deklan is nothing more than a silent coalition partner. If we can convince Anall-Marr to support the Servatory Party, we'll promise him a greater say in the Executive Council. Deklan will become a powerful Captal influence, and we'd deliver. To bring them over, why wouldn't we? It would be a win-win for everybody."

"You wouldn't really allow them to annex Kaleen and Orgomy?" Ti Inai demanded, his face creased with concern. "Anar'on wouldn't stand for it. Two years ago, Deklan got a taste of what the Wanderers can do."

"You're the last person to remind me of that shameful episode," Ed-Kani hissed irritably.

The AUP Provisional Committee engaged raiders to prey on Kaleen commercial shipping, designed to destabilize the economy of several systems, which would eventually have forced them to secede to the Palean Union, boosting its number of held systems sufficient to claim another Executive seat.

Not liking the five/four voting majority Sargon held in the

Committee, Ti Inai loosed Kai Tanard's ships on Kaleen in indiscriminate raiding. This antic invariably caused the Fleet to respond, effectively derailing the Committee's program. Ti Inai's lesson was taken to heart and the Palean arm of the Alikan Union Party now also held five Committee members.

Deklan saw how effective using raiders could be and mounted strikes of its own against Kaleen and Orgomy shipping. If they could peel away enough systems, the Unified Independent Front would never become a reality. Predictably, Anar'on reacted, destroying a number of Deklan ships and threatened direct retaliation against Deklan itself before Anall-Marr was convinced to abandon this dangerous adventurism. One trifles with Death at one's own peril.

"Deklan may have abandoned its territorial expansionist ambitions, but it doesn't mean they've forgiven Sofam for it, or for blocking a punitive claim against Kaleen with the Bureau of Justice over the loss of their ships. Let's face it. The Unified Independent Front is a reality and Deklan will just have to swallow its angst. With the Kran threat hanging over us, we don't want to give Anar'on another reason not to like us."

"Sofam will never allow the Deklan Republic to leave the Revisionist coalition."

"How would they stop them? Mount attacks?"

"They'll use their cursed Paravan Trading Association and stifle Deklan's commerce."

"No, Sofam is too civilized and polite to do anything so crude. After lording over us for centuries, crowing the virtues of law and order, they'll not abandon their principles, or the fat profits Paravan rakes in for them."

"Taxes from those fat profits are what builds M-6s and M-9s, friend Ed-Kani, who in turn maintain peace and our prosperity," Ti Inai reminded him.

"I'm not dense! We need to pitch our message at an emotional level, you fool."

Ti Inai looked unconvinced. "Mmm. Anall-Marr might be

tempted, but do we want to test Sofam's resolve? I wouldn't want to be the one facing their wrath. After the Lemos debacle, they almost ruined our financial systems, and Sargon's."

"We learned and moved on. Don't forget, this would be an exercise in true democracy, Deklan enforcing its right under the Articles of Association to choose a political partner."

"With a little help from us." Ti Inai's grin faded and he became serious. "Your vision is alluring, friend Ed-Kani, but for one thing."

"Oh? Enlighten me."

"You're presuming the Karkan Federation will sit idly by while we wrest control of the Servatory Party from them. If it came to a crunch, they might side with Sofam, and all our efforts would have been for nothing. Moreover, the rest of the Serrll would band against us for centuries to come. Bad for business."

Ed-Kani stared at him, feigning disbelief. "Whatever gave you such an insane idea?"

"Oh, I heard rumors," Ti Inai said evasively.

The trouble was, Ed-Kani had heard those same rumors. The Captal grapevine ran hot all the time and most gossip was simply fog, but to have such a dangerous notion floating around was cause for loss of sleep, especially if it turned out to be true. He'd made quiet inquiries to track down the source, so far without luck, which added to his disquiet, especially if Sofam was behind the rumor, which appeared likely. Slime! The unpalatable truth, he admitted, Ti Inai could be right, and Illeran just might be entertaining such an unpleasant notion. He never could tell what went on behind the man's shifty, fishy eyes.

He put on a brave face and waved a hand in dismissal. "The Karkans are a spent force. Short of embarking on a massive colonization program to boost the number of held systems, something their economy would never support, they nevertheless persist trying to topple Sofam's hold on power. They will bluster and threaten, but nothing will happen. With three Executive seats, we'll be the senior Servatory Party coalition partner. Side with Sofam? The Karkans would rather slide back into their swamps before embracing a millennia-old enemy."

"But what if they did?"

"Trust me. They won't. With their two Executive seats, they'll still remain a powerful voice in the Executive, but with one difference. They'll have achieved government. After all, it's what they've struggled for all this time, isn't it?"

Ti Inai frowned. "I don't know, friend Ed-Kani. A lot of things would need to fall into place for the scheme to work."

"Forget the Karkans. If we can get a sympathetic hearing from Anall-Marr, we would make a vital first step to realizing our dreams."

"Your dream, you mean."

"Yours as much as mine."

"You know, he may be ambitious enough to just possibly enable us to pull this off."

"If you have any strings we can pull to make him tractable, now's the time to do so."

"Well, there might be an angle or two we could use," Ti Inai said slowly, already calculating the percentages.

Ed-Kani allowed himself a small smile of satisfaction. Ti Inai was not thinking about Anall-Marr's ambitions, but his own. The next general elections would see the shifty Palean elevated to Executive Director rank, secure in his ten-year term of power, and his tenure would be enjoyed far more if the Alikan Union Party controlled the government. Everybody had a switch to make them tractable. It was merely a matter of finding and pushing it.

"Come on over and we'll talk."

He leaned against the formchair and his eyes settled on the orchids. He'll need to thank the staffer who brought them in for him.

Guardians of Shadow

* * *

"Astonishing," Sidhara murmured reverently as he gazed at the billowing wall of the Moanar Nebula.

Hooked into the VI, it was like being suspended in space, creation revealed at his feet. Terr knew as he stared at the naked vastness himself. He allowed his master a moment to reflect, the experience totally unique to what he'd ever seen before. Seeing this through a display plate simply did not convey the unbridled majesty of what he looked at.

"Tell me, my strange son from the stars. Is this what draws you to roam the deeps?"

"This, and what you will see when you meet the Orieli, master," Terr said softly.

It was true. The sight of strange skies, dawn rising above a ringed gas giant, a protostar glowing in a coalescing cloud, which one day could bring forth planets and life, it all filled a void within him large as the universe itself. Touched by a god, did he now have a god's perspective on creation? Perhaps Zero Six was right. There were no gods but what man created in his mind. What was he then? A conduit able to connect with another dimension and control its energy? Science and the supernatural, oil and water in perpetual war. Someone may know the answer, he certainly didn't. In the end, did it matter? Would it change what he was seeing?

Sidhara's surtaf smelled of tarad grass and oily peelath, which evoked images of rolling dunes, whispering sands and hot winds. At night, with the moons Aribus and Rima making the sands glitter like fields of snow, The Arch shone with a blaze of its stars. Among them, Amulran the Damned held up the firmament, waiting for the Stalker to loose the arrow that would pierce his heart, toppling eternity into nothingness. Terr easily pictured the two constellations. He'd gazed at them often enough, wondering how the gods could do this to their own.

207

The old Wanderer exhaled slowly. "To see creation revealed in this way, I too would journey among the stars. You are fortunate to have found such a calling."

"You made it all possible, master," Terr said softly and Sidhara smiled.

"You give me far too much credit, my son."

"You guided my footsteps when I didn't know who I was. I became a Saddish-aa, thanks to you, and came to love the Saffal and its people."

"We were both guided toward a common destiny by a higher power than mine. Tell me. Have you found happiness?"

An elusive goal, like chasing a dream, Terr mused. He experience too much and scarred by too many life's experiences, to expect happiness to be a steady state. Last time they spoke, sitting in the mud hut sipping peelath tea, fresh from his trial at Athal Than, his master a comforting presence, Terr did not want anything then. Perhaps that was happiness; not driven by unobtainable desires, appreciating things he already had.

"I learned to grasp every moment offered to me, not expecting I deserve it. Teena has fulfilled me, and with Nightwings at my side, I have a measure of peace. I am content."

"Accept each day in totality and you will remain content," Sidhara agreed, deep in thought. "You face a strange journey into the unknown, my son, and I am not talking about the Orieli. The Fernai warned you not to seek them out. You risk a rebuke at best, and a possible confrontation at a time when the Serrll and the Orieli have enough troubles should you cause offense. All this based on an old legend?"

"Perhaps, but the Fernai *did* visit Anar'on, something we cannot dismiss. Whatever debt they feel obligated to repay, we need the knowledge they have, and I'll take that as payment in full."

"Look at me, Sankri," Sidhara demanded gently.

Terr broke the VI interface and blinked. Reclining in a

swivel-couch, his master's orange eyes were kindly.

"In the days past, we talked about the Celi-Kran and the threat they represent to all life. After witnessing what happened to Anar'on, the Rahtir Council did not hesitate to extend its protective hand to Captal. They would have done so regardless, but debating a threat and seeing it eventuate in such grizzly fashion was a powerful motivator. As for the Orieli, they're still to decide what can be done. You must understand something. To stand in Death's shadow, wielding the lightnings in total war, for that is in effect what it means to confront an enemy, has never been done before. Anar'on has not known war, not total war. Did the gods spare us such calamity, or was it merely a product of our environment to safeguard the population, is an imponderable. The power we hold in our hands has made us understandably cautious. With our small population, giving into the lust of destruction could have been devastating. We debated my decision to accompany you for a long time, and is as much a gathering of information as an application of force, should it be required, especially as in this case, there might not be any holding back."

"Master, you saw for yourself what the Krans attempted to do when they struck Anar'on."

"Tactically, a brilliant move. Had they succeeded, it would have removed the one single threat able to extinguish them, but you know all that. I am talking about abandonment of a way of life to venture among the stars as avengers. Mine is a first perilous step and I dread where it might lead me. It is not only the possibility of wiping out an alien lifeform, although a created one, but violation of much the *Saftara* holds for us."

"Had the Krans succeeded, it would have done more than simply destroy Anar'on. It would be a vital step toward destroying the Serrll itself," Terr said, his voice grim.

"Oh?"

"Zero Six read my mind. It read Teena's. The Krans know how fractured our conglomerate of interstellar blocks really is.

With Captal gone, and with it the seat of central government, internal forces would tear us apart as everyone jockeyed for dominance."

"You're referring to the merger between the Sargon Directorate and the Palean Union?"

"I'm also talking about the Deklan Republic. They lusted long after Kaleen and Orgomy worlds, as have the Paleans. In the ensuing disorder, they might be tempted to realize their ambition. More broadly, without a central government, who would control the Scout Fleet? Would individual interstellar blocks assume control of elements within their territory? You can see how easily chaos could have descended on us, leaving us completely exposed. Uncoordinated, we'd be wiped out."

"We may live in mud huts, my son, far away from Kanarath, but we watch what is happening in Captal very closely. The Rahtir were aware of these dangers. Those factors and others were the tipping point in Marrakan's argument to help Captal."

"Others, master?"

"In the aftermath of any conflict, there are always survivors who over time rebuild from the ashes. The Krans delivered a lesson. After they devastated our worlds, only ashes would remain. No one would be left to rebuild. Despite the misery and strife still surrounding us, the Serrll Combine has achieved a measure of greatness. Not of the same order as the Orieli or the Fernai perhaps, but in due course, we too will become united in brotherhood. My words are simple and colored by my limited perceptions and bias, but I believe in the path the Revisionists are taking the Serrll, as does the Rahtir Council. That's why the UIF decided to support them. Had the Rahtir failed to act, content to preserve our insular corner of the universe, allowing desolation and death to reign around us, with the Krans an ever-present threat, as you so boldly told Marrakan, we would have betrayed all the teachings of the Discipline. Despite the ethical danger of what we contemplate, we were compelled to act."

"All who dwell among the stars are brothers before the gods," Terr quoted from the *Saftara*.

"Profound words, and they are another reason why I am here with you, my son. The Rahtir are willing to reach out to the Orieli, but our capacity is not boundless."

"I'm sure they understand, master. It only increases the imperative to strike the Krans hard before they launch a more decisive attack."

"At Zero Six, so you said."

"I don't know the extent to which their ships are autonomous. Eliminating the central nexus might not mean much if they're all linked with Zero Zero, but neutralizing one of their major nexus core points and destroying its infrastructure must be disruptive. Logistics has always dictated who will win in any conflict, and the Krans must also operate within those rules."

"Your reasoning is transparent, Sankri. You want to circumvent those rules. You want to destroy Zero Zero."

"If Alkarh Tertulion can identify the stars in my vision, it may very well become possible, and perhaps avoid a prolonged and costly struggle."

Sidhara nodded and gave a long sigh. After a lingering silence, he looked up. "My son, there is something I must tell you. Your vision? It is also mine."

Terr stared at the old Wanderer in shock. "Yours?"

"In a past best forgotten when we first started to venture to the stars, and no, we did not invent star flight, in our arrogance and pride, one of the Rahtir committed a terrible deed. He obliterated a planet in what is now Kaleen. We called him Sarumajan, the destroyer of worlds. The day your survival blister crashed beyond the Katai Than escarpment, we saw the trail of fire it left, I had a dream. I saw an alien standing alone in space, lightning devouring a world, two stars adorning his feet." Sidhara's eyes bored into Terr.

He felt himself go pale. To have his vision revealed like this was incredible, but he knew so little of his master's capabilities, or the capabilities of any third-level adept. He didn't want to stoop to mysticism, but the revelation shook him.

"You saw *me*?"

"Not you, only an alien wielding Death. When they brought you out of the desert and I saw your face, I knew. You are Sarumajan—or you could be if you give into temptation."

"Destroying Zero Zero, you mean," Terr said, aware of the warning his god gave him. "I understand now what Marrakan said when we talked. Must every exercise of power be an indulgence? Removing a plague to enable the body to live cannot be deemed an indulgence."

"The Krans being your plague," Sidhara said and smiled. "A charming analogy. You said the vision came to you twice and you were disturbed by what you saw, and rightly so. You were warned against indiscriminate use of your power, but the vision meant more. It also gave you a glimpse into a possible future."

"I understood that, master. Unchecked, Death would devour all were I to will it."

"That was not the future I was referring to."

"Waging war against the Krans?"

"A *possible* future, my son. Free will. The gods may have created us, but our lives they leave in our hands. Remember the lesson of the pond. A stone cast into the still water creates ripples whose effects are impossible to determine accurately. That uncertainty is free will in operation. All the gods can do is give us a foretaste of what might be a potential reality. By acting at any given decision point, we create our reality. For the god to give both of us the same vision, it might very well become reality. It all depends on free will."

"You mean how badly I want a particular outcome?"

"Just so."

"But with both of us having the same vision…"

"Who will stand with two stars at his feet? No one knows,

my son. It is a future yet to be written. If it will help you understand better, call it the uncertainty principle."

"Master…"

Sidhara waved a hand at the Moanar on the other side of the transparent hull. "I know. Enchanting as the sight is, you did not ask me here to talk about the Krans, at least not directly. My spirit sings with joy to see you and Nightwings together again, and your loved one Teena returned to you. Despite these reasons to rejoice, your heart is heavy. Because of what you did at Devon?"

"Telling me I might be this Sarumajan has only added to my misgivings. You set me on the path that led me to Athal Than where I confronted my past. Nightwings planted the seed, but you knew what would happen when he joined with me, yet you chose to do nothing. You had the same vision and you still allowed Death to touch me. I was reborn twice and I thought I understood what I am, but after Devon, I don't know anymore. I don't want such power, master. Temptation is all around me and I fear it *will* overcome me one day. I don't feel worthy standing in judgment of others when my own motives are suspect."

"You were not reborn twice, my son. The first time was when you were brought from Athal Than."

Terr pondered the wealth of possibilities inherent in that realization.

The old Wanderer reached out. "Give me your hand, Sankri," he said quietly, his voice rumbling from the deeps of the Saffal.

Terr slowly held out his hand and Sidhara grasped it. A tingle raced up his arm, but he was held fast. Time passed. He didn't know how long they sat there. After a while, he closed his eyes. It helped with the waiting.

"Look at your hand, my strange son," Sidhara said from somewhere far away and Terr opened his eyes.

A blue glow surrounded his hand. Something warm

crawled up his arm and defused through his body, and he recognized the feeling. It was the same welcome Anar'on always gave him whenever he returned. A welcome from the gods. Bathed in a glow of wellbeing, he wanted nothing and expected nothing, content to feel Death's touch, his soul free. For a while, he had peace.

The glow faded and Sidhara let go. "What do you feel, my son from the stars?"

Terr stared at his hand in wonder, then looked up at the wrinkled face of his master, not understanding what happened, recognizing that somehow the gods had transformed him again.

"I...feel the touch of the god who accepted me."

"And that is all you feel?"

Terr allowed himself a small smile. "I feel cleansed and renewed, like the day of my last trial. What did you do?"

"I did nothing. I merely provided a conduit so you could heal yourself."

"Heal myself?"

Sidhara frowned with disapproval. "You are in denial even now?"

Chastened, Terr bowed. "Forgive me, master. To stand in god's shadow, an alien, I simply find incomprehensible. It is something I have never been able to fully reconcile."

"Evidently. Did you not say all men are brothers?"

Terr grinned, admiring the wily twisting of his words. "Yes, I did say that, didn't I."

"Instead of resisting what you have become, rejoice because you stand closer to the god."

"It's what Marrakan told me."

"And he is right. Do not see destruction waiting to be unleashed from your hands as the only result of wielding your gift, but its corollary. And you experienced that duality already, didn't you?"

"Yes, when I destroyed the Kran ship. I felt immortal, capable of anything, and it felt right."

"Just so. As you now accepted the shadow within which you stand, embrace your power, even though it is something we can never understand fully. Open your spirit to it and let it fill you. Resist, and one day you will succumb to the blood lust of wanton destruction you so fear. This is not indifference, merely a recognition that there is no single ethical code in a conglomeration of alien lifeforms. None of us possesses a moral template which we can impose on others."

"Refrain from judging," Terr murmured.

"Indeed. Not acting when you see what you might consider evil is the pinnacle of enlightenment. An evil to you could be a moral imperative to someone else. You cannot judge because you don't know everything. Only the gods can judge, and even they refrain."

"Tell me, master. Are we really touched by a supernatural entity, or are we simply able to somehow tap into an energy source that lies in Athal Than and places like it? As someone rational, I find it difficult to accept existence of a genuine god."

"I know, and that difficulty is the source of your soul searching. I have no answer for you, Sankri. No one has seen Death, although we wield its power. Centuries of debate has failed to resolve your question. We simply accept that we're gifted and wonder at the marvelous working of the universe. Tell me. Would it change anything if you knew the answer?"

Terr pursed his lips. Why did he want his question answered? Because it remained unanswered and his scientific training demanded one? Was he even asking the right question?

"No, it wouldn't change anything. One day perhaps, we may know, but even then, it wouldn't change anything."

"Exactly, my son. There is nothing more useless than knowing an answer to a wrong question. We rationalize the experience of our transformation in terms we can understand. As our knowledge of the universe grows, so do our words to describe its processes. However, the words don't change the processes. Whatever position you choose to take, remember something. The words in the *Saftara* are sets of behavioral guides, not a religious manifesto. Should we forget that, then Sarumajan who is within each of us will indeed walk unchecked."

Terr thoughtfully contemplated his master's words. Sidhara may be scientifically ignorant, but there was nothing wrong with his ability to reason and think clearly, and that ability had enabled the Wanderers to coexist more or less peacefully with more technologically advanced worlds of the Serrll, although a perilous coexistence—for the Serrll.

Sidhara turned, folded his hands and gazed into the deeps of the Moanar slowly crawling past the ship.

* * *

In the command couch, Terr stared hungrily at the stars ahead of him. No one before him had seen them, with the exception of the Orieli survey ships. Nothing distinguished them from other stars, except his realization that they were truly alien. Sure, they were probably cataloged in one of Captal's astronomical archives, but holoview images did not come close to conveying the splendor of seeing this for himself, and he almost didn't get to see them.

Three days ago, skirting LTN-5 by twenty-eight lights, he ordered *Kara* to alter course. Two hours later, LTN-5's Mission Control requested a visual. He ignored it. When they attempted to take over the computer, he smiled. He anticipated a sneaky move and had a chat with Cent Comp. It was useful having an understanding computer on his side. They could have sent a ship after him, but he knew they wouldn't. Alkarh Tertulion might not be pleased at how he used *Kara*, but any confrontation was comfortably far enough in the future not to concern him. He did have diplomatic immunity after all. Nevertheless, what he contemplated could land him in serious trouble, but should this work, he hoped his sins would be forgiven.

Rit!

Didn't Tertulion say she liked initiative? The dour-faced Sumen would likely consider it foolhardy. Too late now, he stood committed. The road of life has no U-turns.

He looked at Dhar. "Anything?"

"My answer is still the same as the one I gave you ten minutes ago, Sankri. Energy sources all around us, artificial, but no ships; at least none we can detect."

"They're out there," Terr said comfortably, ignoring his brother's exasperated sigh. Hooked into the VI, he hadn't seen anything either. Cent Comp would have warned them if something were approaching—if it could detect it. "It shouldn't be much longer."

"You're enjoying this, aren't you?" Teena demanded beside him.

"It is why we're out here, my pet."

"Even though you might be risking a diplomatic incident?"

"It's risky simply being alive."

"Be like that. I'm going below."

Two hours later the computer finally woke up. "Tactical caution. Fernai vessel detected nine hundred thousand ampirs in our forward quarter. Belligerency status unknown."

Terr rubbed his hands. "Drop normal and stop," he ordered immediately.

"Exiting subspace relational." *Kara* burst into normal space in a flash of white scintillation and held position.

In the VI, Terr saw nothing. Two minutes later, the familiar tetragonal-bipyramid shape wavered and took solid form two thousand ampirs in front of them. Idly curious, Terr wondered who his reception would be.

"The Fernai ship is requesting a comms channel," Cent Comp advised.

"Very well. Open channel," Terr said and winked at Dhar. The lower right corner of the VI image cleared.

"My lord Terrllss-rr, respectful greetings. You ventured far out of familiar territory. Do you require assistance?"

"No, First Commander," Terr said, glad to see the familiar alien. He hoped this would make the encounter less stressful.

"I am understandably curious then why you chose to come here. I warned you not to enter our space."

Terr took a deep breath. "You warned the Orieli, not me."

Shah Pak revealed a toothy grin. "It's going to be like that, is it? Why are you here, my lord?"

"I want to collect a debt."

The alien's features froze and his small black eyes glittered. Amusement perhaps?

"I fear to ask. Do you wish me to come on board?"

"Whatever is convenient, sir."

"Nu. I shall transport to your lounge. Give me a few minutes."

"Thank you for this courtesy, First Commander."

"To avoid future misunderstandings, my warning applies equally to the Serrll Combine."

Terr grinned. "I always understood that."

"Why then…ah. You came here in your Wanderer persona. It is clear to me now. In a few minutes."

When contact broke, Terr disconnected from the VI and stood up. "That wasn't so bad."

"You are venturing into dangerous ground, my brother," Dhar warned and frowned heavily in disapproval.

"Lighten up, okay? You collect Sidhara and I'll bring Teena. Oh, warn him that Shah Pak will be an isomorphic projection."

He took the grav-chute down and hurried to his quarters. It wouldn't do to be late for his visitor, but Teena would never, never forgive him if he left her out of the meeting. The hatch barely slid out of his way as he stomped into the main cabin.

"Teena!"

She emerged from the bedroom and flashed him a smile. "What's the hurry?"

"Remember the Fernai visitor I talked about? Well, he'll be in the lounge any second."

"Shah Pak?"

"The same. Come on."

She looked stricken. "But I'm not dressed!"

Terr glanced at the ceiling and sighed in frustration. "Like he's going to worry about fashion. Let's go." He grabbed her hand and pulled her after him.

"At least allow me to put a face on," she protested, dragging her heels.

"You're beautiful, my pet, and you know it. One sight of you and he'll likely want you in his harem."

"Do the Fernai have harems?"

"With you in it, I would."

"Beast."

Fortunately, the lounge was down the corridor, and it only took a few long strides to get there. Dhar and Sidhara were already inside. Terr nodded to his master standing calm and regal in his surtaf, refusing to wear a set of working grays.

The next second, the air in the center of the lounge shimmered green and Shah Pak stood there. He took one look at Sidhara and sank to one knee.

"My lord, I crave your mercy."

Sidhara stepped to him and laid his hand on the alien's head. "You have nothing to fear from me, my son. Stand and let me look at you."

Shah Pak stood and waited.

"Yes, you are just as our tales say. A strange meeting indeed."

"Nu. One I shall never forget," Shah Pak said happily and cast a quick glance at Terr and Dhar. "My lords." He paused as he caught sight of Teena.

Terr held a protective arm around her waist. "First Commander, allow me to present my partner, Teena-raye. She was one of those taken by the Krans."

219

Shah Pak's eyes widened. "And you got her out?"

"After some persuasion. Zero Six needed convincing I wanted her."

The alien shook his head. "Incredible. You must tell me about it sometime. An honor to see you, my lady."

"Thank you, sir. Terr has spoken of you."

"Nu. I am sure he has."

Terr extended his hand at the couches. "Shall we get more comfortable?"

After seating themselves, Shah Pak folded his hands. "A fine vessel. The Orieli build them well."

"I wouldn't mind keeping it, but somehow, I doubt Alkarh Tertulion would be sympathetic."

The alien nodded. "Senior officers everywhere have little regard for the wishes of their subordinates. We tracked your ship, my lord—"

"Just Terr, okay?"

"Thank you...Terr. Under the circumstances, it was thought best that I meet you. It took time for me to get here, for which I apologize."

"I appreciate this thoughtfulness."

"Nu. After my warning, we did not expect to see an Orieli ship, but you are not the Orieli." Shah Pak turned to Sidhara. "My lord, Terr spoke of a debt, and it's true. The Fernai shall be forever in your debt. Ask, and if it is in our power to grant it, we shall do it."

"I had misgivings coming here, but Sankri is persuasive."

Shah Pak smiled faintly. "Something I am starting to appreciate."

"The exuberance of youth, which I trust you will overlook."

"What can I do for you, my lord?"

"Although I know the old tales, much was lost over time. It seems we saved one of your important officials when he ventured into a sacred escarpment. When Sankri heard you speak of a debt, we checked our records."

"It is not a story commonly known even among us, but we have not forgotten. Twenty-one centuries ago, a governor of a major province visited your world. As you said, he was curious to see one of the places where your gods reside and experience the phenomena, but he ignored the warnings and ventured inside. Two Wanderers pulled him back, but not before his right arm was turned to stone. As a sign of penance for his presumption, he wore it for a year before allowing the arm to be regenerated. He later became First Procurator of the Fernai Medala and vowed eternal friendship with Anar'on. Since then, your world has held a special significance for us."

Sidhara nodded slowly. "So, the tales are true. But my son, you must realize that whatever debt your governor felt he owed, the Fernai cannot feel obligated, not after all this time, and Sankri may be rash to presume."

"It is a matter that transcends time, my lord."

"That governor would be proud to hear you say this."

"Nu. Terr, you traveled here in an Orieli ship, but I suspect not under their sanction, and you make a claim against us. If you're looking to involve us in your conflict with the Krans, we cannot help you. I made this clear to Karhide Arlon Dee."

"You may not know, First Commander, but sixteen days ago, they attacked Anar'on and Captal."

"I did know, but not the details. How bad is the damage?"

Terr blinked, trying not to show surprise. What sort of special significance *did* Anar'on hold for the Fernai to maintain such surveillance, or did it keep a paternal eye on the entire Serrll Combine? And why? He hesitated to ask, fearing he would be answered.

"Casualties were comparatively light, only twenty-three thousand. One advantage, I suppose, of living on a large, but sparsely populated planet."

"And Captal?"

"It was hit hard, with over eleven million dead and many

millions more wounded. Destruction was extensive. Fortunately, the city itself escaped relatively lightly."

"The Krans were eliminated?"

"Yes."

Shah Pak hung his head. When he looked up, there was genuine sadness in his eyes. "I grieve for your loss." He turned to Sidhara. "Your presence here. The Rahtir Council has decided to act?"

Terr gaped, amazed at the depth of the alien's intelligence gathering ability.

"We shall act to protect the Serrll. I came with Sankri to see for myself what the Orieli face and how we can best help them."

"Nu. And can you help them?"

"I don't know. It will depend on what they want from us. We have the will, but not necessarily the resources. You must understand, only a few of us may be prepared to venture off-planet. Asking them to go into Orieli space will challenge their beliefs and perceptions. However, there is an issue even more important than venturing into space that holds us back. The Rahtir serve a critical function in our society. We are the glue binding us together. We provide institutional memory and knowledge for the young, guiding them through their first trial. Removing our presence could have unforeseen and dangerous consequence for us."

"This is where I come in, First Commander," Terr said coldly. "You feel honor bound to pay an ancient debt, and I have no compunction about collecting it," he said and stared into the alien's eyes. After a moment, Shah Pak smiled faintly.

"The Fernai shall honor its debt, my lord. Before you tell me what you want, you need to understand that although we're obligated, our obligation has limits."

"I shall try not to test those limits, sir. Before I state my request, I want to make one point perfectly clear. I'm doing this without the knowledge or approval from Captal nor the Orieli.

Please keep it in mind should I transgress."

"Nu. State your demand."

"My request comes in two parts. To have attacked us, the Krans must be using a waypoint transport portal."

"That is self-evident."

"I want to know its location."

Shah Pak looked thoughtful. "Even if you destroy it, they'll simply build another."

"Of course, but I hope not anytime soon. I'm playing for time, time for negotiations between the Serrll and the Orieli to yield substantive results. You must know our ships cannot stand up to the gravitic missiles. We can deal with their ships, but without an effective countermeasure, we might as well dock our fleet."

"We cannot give you the technology of our defense screens."

"I did not ask for that. We're hoping the Orieli will tell us how to modulate the shield grid on our ships, which would make them far more effective. They promised to give us scanner arrays to protect our most vital worlds, but it will take time to put everything in place."

"Nu. Which removing the Kran portal will give you. Very well, I shall load the coordinates into your ship's computer. And the second part of your demand?"

"Location of Zero Zero."

Dhar gave him a strange look. Sidhara didn't say anything, and Teena looked at him with a puzzled frown. Alkarh Tertulion may locate those stars, but Terr was realistic about her chances. He simply wasn't able to provide sufficiently accurate astronomical data for a successful search. The Ferani, on the other hand, with their technological superiority and millennia of familiarity with the Krans, probably had the information, even though they were not prepared to act on it.

"You're presuming we possess those coordinates," Shah Pak said softly.

"Yes, I am."

"If we did give you the information, what would you intend to do with it?"

"Whatever is necessary, but only if it *became* necessary."

Shah Pak pursed his lips. "Nu. I must discuss this with my superiors."

"Of course."

"You are seriously prepared to do what we refrained from doing?"

"Please understand, First Commander, I'm not judging the Fernai. I'm not that arrogant. We all must live with the consequences of our decisions, and you have to live with yours. The Serrll has tasted Kran aggression. I don't want to see it repeated if at all possible, and I don't want the Orieli to suffer the same fate on perhaps a much larger scale. If it means wiping out every Kran nexus core, then that's what shall be done, and I will not hesitate to do it." He turned to Sidhara and bowed. "With the help of my master if he is prepared to give it."

Sidhara looked at Shah Pak. "Sankri may not realize the enormity of his words, but they are spoken from the heart and have the ring of righteousness. If the Krans cannot be contained or swayed from their unyielding course, I don't see any alternative. As brothers under whatever god created us, we shall stand together in this conflict. With the knowledge Zero Six gained from the prisoners it took, we're all in grave danger and could desperately use your help."

Shah Pak knelt before Sidhara and hung his head. "My lord, ask me anything and it is yours, but I do not speak for the Procurator Medala. Do not place this burden on me."

Sidhara touched his shoulder. "I only ask the Fernai to see the Serrll and the Orieli as a single family of men, my son, not as someone kept at arm's length while you stand comfortable behind your wall of impenetrable security."

"There is much history behind us that makes us behave the

way we do," Sah Pak said. "You're demanding that we reexamine our moral code, and perhaps rightly so. I cannot commit the Fernai, but I will voice your plea."

"That is all I can ask."

"The location of the Kran portal is now in your computer, Terr. As for your second demand, should we agree to give you the information, we shall arrange for Alkarh Tertulion to get it."

Terr reached out and touched the alien's chest, feeling a warm kinship, although only a projection. "Thank you, sir. Even if you're not successful, I still thank you."

Shah Pak hesitated, then lifted his hand and placed it over Terr's. "Should you ever wish to venture here again, you will always be welcome in our space."

Terr smiled. "If I can get a ship. By coming here uninvited, I may have annoyed Alkarh Tertulion sufficiently for my mission accreditation to be revoked."

The alien's mouth twitched. "Nu. Managing superiors, always a challenge in any career."

Glad to hear the Fernai haven't solved everything, Terr smiled. "We must talk and explore how to confound them."

"It will be a pleasure."

"If I may ask, with that unusual ship of yours, what is it you do?"

"We study. The universe is a rich ground for harvesting knowledge. And you? To Perilia?"

"I'm afraid so. Until the Kran crisis is resolved, my cultural exchange mission is suspended, or has merely embraced another dimension."

"Nu. You have a unique opportunity to observe Orieli behavior."

"As do you," Terr said pointedly.

Shah Pak stood up. "My lords…my lady. Until next time." His form wavered and he was gone.

Terr grinned broadly and rubbed his hands. "Well, that

went better than expected."

"Much better than anyone expected," Dhar said dryly. "I cannot believe you were actually pushing him." He glanced at Sidhara. "I hate to say this, master, but you deigned to lecture him on ethics. With subtlety, but you did it."

Sidhara smiled indulgently. "Shah Pak is a young man, secure in his position, backed by sophisticated technology and social order. It was forgivable that he should feel a degree of unconscious superiority and arrogance. You must remember, my son, advanced social order does not automatically translate into an advanced code of behavior. Conducting war is a messy business, which an ordered society like theirs would naturally wish to avoid."

Dhar stared. "As would the Serrll."

"I had that example in mind. Sometimes, however, one is compelled to act."

"For whatever reason, the Fernai regard their obligation to Anar'on seriously and may be prepared to act," Terr mused. "Why they haven't discharged it before will make for an interesting discussion next time we meet. Since they haven't, I took advantage of Shah Pak's sympathy for our plight. Besides, he wanted to help. What I asked for—"

"Demanded!" Dhar growled.

"—did not really impinge on their sensibilities. They may even be relieved to see us do what they refrained from doing."

Teena leaned forward. "Shah Pak was agreeable perhaps, but when analyzed coldly, his superiors might not be as forthcoming."

"An excellent observation, my dear," Sidhara said approvingly.

"Whatever the outcome, we did obtain one piece of solid information," Terr added and gave Teena a warm smile. She looked at him searchingly.

"Were you serious about Zero Zero? However inimical, you're contemplating wiping out a unique species."

"Don't think I haven't thought about it. I walk a thin moral tightrope here, but you said it yourself. They're inimical. It's not like we can argue with them and reach an understanding. Besides, it might not be necessary. By eliminating their waypoint portal, I'm hoping we can persuade Zero Six to leave us alone." He looked at Sidhara. "Are you prepared to act, master?"

"I'm glad to hear you question the ethics of what you propose, my son. A time comes, though, when all other options are taken away, one must do what is required."

"What about the Orieli border systems like Setlan Eleven?" Teena ventured. "From what you told me, Terr, the nexus could still reach them using its own portal."

"If eliminating its waypoint portal doesn't convince it to back off, we shall obliterate every planet in KP-001," Terr said harshly, and she blanched. "We'll then backtrack and wipe out any Kran ships we find. It will show Zero Zero that we're serious. I suspect the Fernai were forced to make such a demonstration in their time before it got the hint."

"You wouldn't *really* destroy those worlds, would you?" Teena asked in a small voice, clearly appalled at the thought.

"Nothing so drastic will be necessary," Sidhara said, his deep voice resonating. "The energy surge will merely overload the electrical pathways of every living thing on the surface, including anything artificial. However, should we need to go further…"

"Let's hope a single demonstration will suffice," Terr added quietly.

The old Wanderer stood up and patted down his surtaf. "If not, more will be done," he said gravely and made for the door.

Terr watched him walk out and pursed his lips.

The Rahtir valued their power and the privileged link they had with Death. They've enjoyed for centuries the prerogatives of their position, and rightly so. Should their anger be aroused, the consequences could be catastrophic. Apart from settling petty squabbles, their very presence kept peace among the tribes, but the Ferani were not the only ones who may have become complacent. He'd pushed Sidhara as hard as he pushed Shah Pak, but prodding a rock ray is always done at one's own risk.

Terr knew what it meant having Sidhara with him. His master was a tool, which he had no compunction about using, noble words from the *Saftara* notwithstanding. It was easy being noble in peace. In war, morality is merely the first cloak one discards when facing death.

* * *

"LTN-3, this is OSA *Kara*, Terrllss-rr, Head of Mission, Serrll Combine, commanding." He turned and winked at Dhar. "This should get them swarming."

His brother snorted and pointed at the mainframe plot and a *Tangar* battlecruiser shadowing them. "They already swarmed. I guess they don't want you doing any more detours."

Terr turned to Teena sitting beside him. "Don't mind him. He's always sour early in the morning."

Teena grinned broadly and a twinkle of amusement lit her eyes. "Enllss was right. You're trouble wherever you go."

"He just doesn't appreciate the value of positive diplomacy."

Dhar merely lifted his eyes in vexation.

"OSA *Kara*, stand by to receive transport portal coordinates."

"Thank you, LTN-3."

"Welcome back, Da."

"So, they got the thing rebuilt," Terr mused, not surprised.

"And defended," Dhar added. "There is a baby scanner array hovering near the portal."

"Not taking any chances, eh? I approve. Cent Comp? Set course for the portal and transit on given coordinates."

"Acknowledged. Range to portal, 340,000 ampirs."

Sidhara emerged out of the grav-chute and Terr extended a swivel-couch from the deck.

"We arrived at LTN-3?"

"And leaving. You will now see something magical. A transition through an interdimensional portal," Terr told his master as the Wanderer seated himself.

"One hundred and twenty thousand ampirs," the computer advised.

In the mainframe plot, the *Tangar* peeled off. The small planetoid hosting LTN-3 stood out as a white crescent. Blackness ruled in the shadow of the Moanar—Karina, Terr reminded himself.

"Forty thousand ampirs."

"And this portal will transport us more than 400 light-years in a blink of an eye?"

"That it will, master."

"Unbelievable. The wonders a mind can create…"

"Range to portal, three thousand ampirs. Slowing to quarter secondary boost. Interface charged and setting coordinates."

"It's best if you experience the transition through the VI," Terr suggested to Sidhara.

Surrounded by a pentagon of generators, the portal's ring of blue-white energy flickered into existence in response to Cent Comp's interrogative. Nothing could be seen in its two-ampir-diameter mouth.

"Four hundred ampirs." The ship slowed further.

The ring flared bright blue as *Kara* crept toward the mouth.

"Two hundred kanampirs…transiting."

The S/12 pierced the boundary and Sidhara cried out, clutching his head. Terr winced in sympathy. The experience must have been unsettling. He wondered how his master would cope with Personal Transport.

After the residual tingle wore off, Perilia hung in space, a gorgeous greenish orb. Terr pointed at the planet.

"Our destination."

Sidhara marveled at the sight. "This is the first time I gazed on another world and a strange sun. It is indeed an astounding life you lead among the stars, Sankri."

"Not a bad view, is it?"

"Passage through the portal, you should have warned me."

"I apologize, master. It was thoughtless of me."

"No matter. Any other surprises I should know?"

"All of Perilia will be a surprise, but there is one thing. The Orieli use a version of a portal to travel from place to place. They're everywhere and perfectly safe. At first, you might find the experience disconcerting."

"I see. Perhaps I should stick to walking," Sidhara said dryly.

"Ah, you wouldn't find it practical. However, they do use sled platforms, not unlike our combies."

"Mmm."

Cleared by a patrolling picket, *Kara* headed toward Perilia, and Cent Comp readied the ship for landing.

"PERCOM is requesting a comms channel."

Terr glanced at Dhar and winced. This is where he may have to start paying for his adventurism.

"Very well. Open channel." When the image cleared in the mainframe holoview plot, he suppressed a groan. Of all the people he would rather talk to, Sumen wasn't one of them.

Rit!

"Da Terrllss-rr, good to see you again."

"Thank you, Alkarh."

"On landing, please transport yourself and your party to PERCOM main."

"Acknowledged," Terr said formally, wanting to make this short.

Sumen was about to say something else, then abruptly cut contact.

Terr raised his hands in helplessness. "Is it me?"

"This time, it was," Dhar growled, clearly enjoying his brother's discomfort.

"Your unflagging support is always appreciated," Terr said with a scowl, then turned to Teena. "Now is the time to put on a dazzling dress and fix your face. Sumen may be distracted enough to overlook my presence."

Teena lifted her chin. "Suffer."

"Ah, nobody loves me."

Although he spoke lightly, the reception he'd received did not bode well. A sudden thought bubble rose and burst. Sumen was Tertulion's right-hand man and second in command of the entire sector. Instead of feeling slighted, he should be grateful for Sumen's courtesy by calling personally. Terr chewed his lip as a painful realization dawned. He was a very small cog in a large machine and cosmos did not revolve around him.

Sobered and somewhat chastened, he swept his eyes over everyone. "We have some twenty-six minutes before we land. Once we're down, I suspect we'll be kept fairly busy. Freshen up and grab a bite. I'll keep watch here."

Teena sensed the change in him and touched his arm. "Terr, I didn't mean—"

He smiled and brushed her cheek. "It's all right, pet. Go."

When they left, he sat down, stretched his legs and watched Perilia grow as it blotted the stars. Nightwings had warned him about pride and he was grateful to recognize this latest lesson. A deep but narrow chasm existed between self-confidence and arrogance, an accusation he'd leveled against the Fernai and the Orieli.

They came down without fuss, the S/12 just another small ship that cluttered the Orieli Space Arm facility. Tavor's Star shone buttery yellow, bathing the pristine green sky with warmth. Apart from the larger than normal contingent of warships on the field, there was nothing to indicate that Perilia and the Orieli were engaged in a deadly struggle, which could have only two possible outcomes, with horrible consequences for the loser.

When he got to the lower deck, the others were waiting beside the two PT alcoves. Teena had not changed, but her hair now stood weaved in an attractive bun, which highlighted her pixie face and green eyes. He nodded approvingly and turned to Sidhara.

"I already told Cent Comp where we want to go, master. Simply step into the alcove."

The old Wanderer hesitated, then strode with determination into the alcove. He turned two-dimensional and vanished.

"Okay you two," Terr said and Dhar did not hesitate.

Alone, he cast a quick glance down the corridor. "Goodbye, *Kara*. You were a good ship," he murmured and stepped into the alcove, not sure if he would ever see her again.

Tertulion and Sumen were standing as Terr walked out of the alcove. He stopped beside Sidhara and nodded to Arlon Dee farther down the table before turning to Sumen.

"Da, I appreciate the courtesy of your call. You could have delegated the chore."

Sumen's eyes widened. "Thank you, Terr."

"And I want to apologize for my lack of manners."

"Given the circumstances of your return, your apprehension is understandable."

Tertulion looked on approvingly and clasped her hands behind her back. "Terr, please instruct our guest what is required to link with the planetary VI net."

Terr faced Sidhara. Apart from hearing the conversation, he clearly didn't understand what the others said.

"Master, to link with the translation system, you need to give your consent."

"Obviously a desirable thing. You have it."

"Alkarh Tertulion, allow me to introduce Sidhara, my teacher and mentor."

"I welcome you to Perilia, Da."

Sidhara looked nonplussed hearing the words in his head.

"Thank you, Dapata."

"My aide, Alkarh Sumen and Karhide Arlon Dee."

"Terr has spoken of you, gentlemen."

Sumen gave a wry grin. "Nothing disparaging, I hope?"

"Sankri can be impetuous, but he usually means well."

"Sankri?"

Sidhara glanced at Terr.

"It's my Wanderer name and used between adepts only. I would be honored if you used it."

"Teena, you look well, rested," Tertulion said warmly.

"The ghosts have retreated, Dapata."

"But not forgotten, which is as it should be...Da Dharaklin. Your brother has caused trouble."

"I will take steps to restrain his impulsiveness, Alkarh," Dhar said gravely, and Tertulion laughed.

"I wish you luck. Please, make yourselves comfortable. We have a lot to discuss."

With everyone seated, Teena beside Terr, he waited. Tertulion steeped her fingers above the polished table, her eyes on Sidhara.

"I want to thank you, Da—"

"Just Sidhara, if you will."

"And you may call me Geisana. I cannot tell you how much your presence here means to us, and the support the Rahtir Council pledged to give. Captal informed us about what happened. Mere words are insufficient to express our sadness at your loss."

"You are gracious...Geisana. As for our support, how to apply it is one of the reasons I am here. We will help you, but not necessarily as front-line combatants."

Terr studied his master. The old Wanderer was unsophisticated at many levels, but the quiet force of his words rang with authority, backed by utter certainty of his position. As he was told more than once, even the presence of power is an influence, and Sidhara radiated power, evident to everyone in the room.

"It was never our intention to expose you to dangers aboard a warship, although we discussed the possibility," Tertulion said quietly.

"You want to station us on your worlds?"

"On some. From what Terr told us, we might not get many of you for reasons I understand."

"He spoke rightly."

"We shall discuss details later and you can then communicate with Anar'on. In the meantime, please avail yourself of our hospitality."

"Sankri told me about this wonderful garden you call Tetra, but you must excuse me if I appear somewhat overwhelmed. I have never before seen so much greenery and open water."

"Anar'on must be a harsh world."

"It is, but we know its ways. I cannot imagine myself anywhere else. However, seeing Perilia, I can understand how some of our young could be tempted."

"The clash of cultures, always a difficult union."

"And sometimes irreconcilable."

"We have much to learn from each other, and perhaps relearn...Terr, your decision to violate First Commander Shah Pak's directive not to venture into Fernai space could have caused a grave diplomatic incident and affected future relations, but I suspect you were aware of this before you made contact."

"A calculated risk, Dapata," Terr said, fully understanding the seriousness of what he had done.

Sumen chuckled, his yellow feline eyes probing. "You pulled a clever little maneuver at LTN-5. We were prepared to intercept you, but refrained for reasons I'm sure you're aware."

"One small ship is a curiosity, Da. A warship is an incursion," Terr said, somewhat relieved. It looked like he would not be suffering any terminal backlash.

Arlon Dee leaned forward. "You met Shah Pak?"

"It took him a little while to get there, but I figured the

Fernai wanted me to see someone I was familiar with."

"And his reaction?"

"We parted cordially...after he repeated his warning," Terr added dryly, and Arlon grinned.

"You went to collect a debt Shah Pak spoke of?" Tertulion ventured.

"After what happened to Anar'on and Captal, I saw no better time to collect it. You might say we were invited."

She smiled. "What he said during the first contact, yes. You have a devious way of thinking, Terr."

"I did get a useful data item, Dapata. Location of the Kran waypoint portal."

Sumen sat up. "He gave it to you?"

"It's 2,200 lights from LTN-3. The exact coordinates are in *Kara's* computer."

"Perdition!" He glanced at Tertulion. "This changes everything."

She looked thoughtful. "But that's not all, is it?"

"No, it isn't," Terr said. "I asked him to provide the location of the Kran home system."

After a moment of stunned silence, she turned to Sidhara. "You can reach to what will likely be another arm of the galaxy? From here?"

"Distance does not matter, Geisana, when all creation lies before me," Sidhara said gravely.

"I must remember not to annoy you, or Anar'on," she murmured, wearing a small smile.

"I don't contemplate doing it lightly."

"No, I don't imagine you would. The Wanderers wield a terrible power."

"We are wary of temptation."

She shook her head and looked at Terr. "The Klanina Caucus has authorized OSCOM to support the Serrll Combine. While you were on your way here, we made available two scanner arrays, one to protect Captal and one for Anar'on. Unfortunately, not quickly enough to repel recent attacks. We'll shortly send four more to cover some of your border systems, their disposition determined by Captal. There was some discussion surrounding the decision, given the Kran's ability to jump virtually anywhere into Serrll space. For that reason, a transport portal is under construction above Captal to facilitate logistical support. Five *Nasors* were also sent under command of Alkarh Zor-Ell. He will deploy them at CAPFLTCOM's discretion. Technicians are on board who will show your engineers how to modify your ships, which will enable them to modulate their shield grid."

"You have been extremely generous, Dapata, and I'm sure Captal appreciates the gesture," Terr said humbly. "However, I fear—"

"The Kran gravitic missiles. I know, but you need not be concerned. Our ships are protected."

Terr stared at her. "You deployed your interdimensional shell?"

"A prototype only, and we got an unexpected side benefit, although we should have anticipated it. The field masks a ship's mass to all sensors." She paused and shifted in her seat. "I must tell you something else. Captal and Anar'on were not the only worlds the Krans hit. Perilia and its portal were also attacked; an event we calculated had a high order of probability."

Terr gaped. "I saw no evidence—"

"Like our ships, Perilia was protected."

His mind reeled at the Orieli's awesome power. That a leap of lateral thinking could lead to such ability…

"You were able to extend an interdimensional shell around this planet?"

"For a few seconds at a time, and at a prodigious power drain. However, long enough to neutralize the attack."

Stunned at the potential application, Terr looked at Sumen. "Your proposal to strike at KP-001—"

"Is now feasible and is approved. I intended Karhide Arlon Dee to command two *Nasors* and take it out and their portal. However, with the coordinates of the waypoint portal, we will now send a separate ship to pay it a visit. Karhide Dee could eliminate it, but it would mean an extended journey to reach KP-001 and we would have lost tactical surprise."

An alarming thought occurred to Terr and he raised a finger. "Dapata, if the Kran ships were able to send a sitrep before they were destroyed—"

"They'll know about the interdimensional shell and may develop a variation."

Sidhara looked at Terr. "Sankri, I don't understand what is this shield."

"Allow me to explain, Da," Arlon Dee said. "Although we're able to modulate our interceptor net, as we found to our cost, the ship can still be tracked by the distortion it induces on surrounding space due to its mass. We developed a way to enclose a ship within an open interdimensional shell, a variation of the transport portal. It prevents external sensors from detecting it, as any electromagnetic or coordinated energy stream falling on the shell is translated elsewhere, rendering the ship literally invisible and impervious to any weapon."

"I can see now why you feel confident in your ability to confront the Krans." Sidhara slowly turned and regarded Tertulion. "Beware of temptation, Geisana...and arrogance."

Momentarily puzzled, Terr got it. Suppose they equipped a missile with a shell generator and fired at something, anything? While the field lasted, it would translate everything it touched, devouring the object...even a planet.

"Every technology has the potential for misuse, Sidhara," Tertulion said gently.

"You could create stars!" Teena whispered, her eyes sparkling.

Startled, Tertulion smiled. "Indeed. You're very perceptive, my dear."

Terr glanced at Teena. It was indeed a perceptive bit of reasoning. Shot into a gas cloud, matter falling into the shell—it would have to be enormous—would over time set up currents, drawing in more matter. Once the effect achieved sustained momentum, the shell would be turned off, leaving nature to continue the process to its inevitable end, ecoforming at the ultimate level.

But Teena wasn't finished. "If everything that enters a shell is translated, how does a ship navigate?"

"You're full of profound questions," Tertulion said. "To use its sensors, it must disengage the shell. It's one of the problems we're working on."

"The system has bugs, but it works well enough to be applied immediately," Sumen added firmly, wanting to steer the conversation to more immediate issues. "We're still a long way from retrofitting all our front-line ships, but OSCOM feels that a preemptive strike against KP-001 now will have a significant strategic impact on the Krans, perhaps sufficient to persuade them to withdraw. But—"

"You need me to guarantee success," Sidhara said.

"You're willing to be a part of this raid?" Tertulion asked.

"It has always been a condition for coming here, as Sankri explained."

"Thank you. Terr, we were not able to identify the stars in your vision. At least not yet."

"It was a long shot at best, Alkarh. That's why I asked Shah Pak for the information. I can only hope the Fernai will see fit to give it to us."

"They may have moral misgivings."

Terr shrugged. "We can only wait and see what happens. Alkarh Sumen, when do you intend launching your strike?"

"In two days. There are tactics we still need to talk about."

"My brother and I will be ready."

"As will I," Teena said with a determined look. Terr shot her a sharp glance, telling her this was not a done deal, not wanting a family argument in front of the others.

Tertulion cleared her throat. "My dear, are you sure you want to expose yourself? Despite our advanced shielding, you will face peril."

"I go where Terr goes." Teena pursed her mouth and folded her arms across her chest.

There were many things Terr could say right then, and most would probably be wrong. He would rather die than see her hurt, but he didn't own her. Reluctantly, he accepted that she also had needs, ambitions and a desire to venture into the unknown, to be herself. To deny those things to her simply to keep her safe would be a betrayal and could drive them apart.

He sighed, resigning himself to the inevitable. "She's coming with us."

Her sunny smile and look of profound gratitude went a little way to ally his fears.

* * *

Terchran uncrossed his legs. "Fa'sure. Bassul will be a fine choice. He is a capable administrator and has done a fine job running the Bureau of Trade. Stepping into Enllss' portfolio shouldn't be a problem for him."

Seated in Illeran's executive guestroom, surrounded by lush greenery, hanging moss and potted plants, the humid atmosphere reminded Terchran of Karkan's swampy shores. He missed the oily waters lapping softly against black sands, white clouds hugging a distant horizon where ocean met the sky. In two years, he would see them again; a retired, respected figure, even though he still had at least four productive decades left in him. He wasn't complaining. After thirty years of unbroken service on Captal, he'll be glad to get away. A good system, and allowed Assembly reps a maximum of three ten-year terms. It enabled vital turnover of fresh faces and prevented concentration of power and control. It would take time getting used to a slower lifestyle, but there were lots of opportunities outside Captal to create a new career. Besides, he had not had a decent vacation in…he hardly remembered.

Opposite him, a huge fish tank took up most of the wall. In its dark interior, shadowy shapes drifted aimlessly. A sand groker paused and stared at a world beyond its comprehension, its dark red eyes bulging. With a flick of a broad tail, it vanished among rocky outcrops.

Illeran's pointed tongue flicked quickly between dry lips. He hissed and tilted his flat head, a typical reptilian gesture. He allowed a rumbling growl of satisfaction to tremble within his chest and poured them some tea. Terchran enjoyed these moments of intimacy, all too rare in their busy schedules, to reflect, compare ideas and discuss policy in an informal atmosphere.

"It will appease the Reformists back home," Illeran added after taking a sip of the redolent brew, his close-set black eyes bright with amusement.

Panoramic views from ceiling-high window screens showed Captal shrouded in heavy clouds. Light rain fell steadily. Terchran did like the cold rain, far removed from the warm mists of home. He glanced at the hanging moss.

"How do you manage to keep it so green? Mine keeps wilting no matter what I do to it."

Illeran grinned, revealing small, sharp teeth. "You're probably not giving it enough silicates."

"I don't give the damned thing anything. One of my staffers is supposed to look after it."

"Not very well."

"I'll have a word with him," Terchran murmured, focusing on the matter at hand.

The Reformists held a significant voting block in the Kapu Maluran legislature on Karkan, and it paid to be cognizant of their wishes. However, promoting Bassul was not done as a gesture of appeasement. The junior commissioner had obvious administrative and policy talent, and executed his portfolio with skill. Before getting into the General Assembly, he'd been a planetary controller and knew how to run a bureaucracy. He deserved his promotion.

"You're firm about not standing in Sofam's way to advance Anabb Karr into Sill-Anais' job? A number of serving commissioners already grumbled, you know, eyeing the slot for themselves."

Illeran waved a hand in dismissal. "Let them grumble. Anabb is good and warrants getting the posting, even if he is a Sofam slime. He'll be a blast of badly needed fresh air and new blood. Too many think promotion is a formality based on seniority. Well, it doesn't work that way. The Serrll is facing problems never dreamed of in our day. We need talent to handle them, and I don't care where that talent comes from. Not much anyway."

"Fa'sure, although some at home would be shocked to hear you say that."

Illeran hissed with amusement and tilted his head. "What can they do? Fire me? I'm considering Serrll's future, and that means all the interstellar blocks, not just the Karkan Federation."

"It's still blasphemy, some will say."

"Let them squawk. I'm right and you know it."

"No one's arguing, Illeran. Least of all me. The people we pick to advance in this election round must have substance."

"Talking of substance; about Garnal-Tan. Are you sure you want a Deklan to take over your portfolio?"

Terchran took a sip of tea. "Definitely. I've watched him for a while. He is a self-starter and has a good head for strategic policy. Doesn't get distracted by administrative details and he can pick core issues from trivia flooding Comsec these days. By the way, we really should do something about that."

"Write to Torres," Illeran said indifferently and chewed his lip. "You know, it might not be a bad idea to propose Sill-Anais to take over your portfolio."

Stefan Vučak

"Sill? Wouldn't the Bureau of Defense suit him better? He has the temperament for it."

"Defense? Mmm. Sofam usually holds that one for themselves, but Sill could be a wiser appointment than you realize."

"I don't know. Why so generous to Deklan all of a sudden?"

"I've heard rumors. It's all very mysterious and could be perfectly innocent, except for one thing—Ed-Kani Takao."

Terchran gave a short laugh. "The one about the Karkan Federation siding with Sofam? Fa'sure, it's Enllss playing one of his mind games."

"No, not that one. He already voiced the notion to me, and the idea isn't as farfetched as it might sound."

"You can't be serious! One word to the Kapu and we'd both be packing for home. With current events, I wouldn't mind it at all."

"It's been hectic lately, agreed, but think about it for moment, my outraged friend. Ed-Kani sees himself as an empire builder, a man whose crowning achievement is creation of a Greater Sargon. If they're not careful, the Palean Congress will help him achieve it."

"Ti Inai and his faction are too wily to allow anything like that."

"Perhaps, but Ti Inai doesn't control the Palean arm of the Alikan Union Party. Nevertheless, you're probably right. Even if Ed-Kani doesn't see Greater Sargon rule, he'll be happy consummating a successful merger with the Paleans. He almost pulled it off five years ago, but he mistimed it. The Orieli showed up and the equation changed."

"It changed a damn sight more with the Krans," Terchran growled.

"We were fortunate the other day," Illeran admitted softly. "If it weren't for the Wanderers stepping in—"

"We'd likely be dead, and Captal a smoking ruin."

"In hindsight, not taking a hardball stance with the Orieli

over their Moon base is paying off. We'll need their help badly before this Kran business is settled. But returning to my previous point, sooner or later, Sargon and the Paleans will merge. They've got enough social momentum behind them to achieve it. When that happens, the AUP will become the senior partner in the Servatory Party coalition and we'll be relegated to an advisory status."

"And ignored. I know."

"Of course you do. Sargon will revert to its authoritarian style, starting with imposition of trade barriers, particularly against Sofam's Paravan Trading Association. They'll seek to restrict travel and isolate border systems, then swallow them. Eventually, Pizgor and Rolan would disappear, and their Executive Council seat with them."

"Might not be such a bad thing."

"On the surface only. Whether you like it or not, the independents do provide a stabilizing influence on Council proceedings. That's why Sofam allows their seat to exist, even though the independents are siding with us for the moment. I hate many things about Sofam and what it stands for, but they do take the long view, mindful of Serrll stability. You may not admire how they go about doing it, but in that respect, they weren't selfish. Staying in power means providing good government, and they've delivered."

"You would allow the Karkan Federation to side with Sofam to block Sargon's attempt to gain a government majority?"

"I also believe in good government, and the argument should be presented to the Kapu. I've spoken to four senior members already. None relish the prospect of seeing Greater Sargon rule. To prevent it, I think they'll seriously consider the option."

Terchran raised a finger. "Granted they might consider the option, but you're forgetting one thing."

"What have I forgotten?"

"If Sargon merges with the Paleans, it will give the AUP

Stefan Vučak

one extra Executive Council seat, but it won't be enough for a majority even if we remain in coalition. Your concerns are groundless."

"That rumor I mentioned? It wasn't about us siding with Sofam. It's Deklan siding with Sargon."

Terchran sat up in alarm. "What? You can't be serious."

"I'm serious, all right. It's not such a crazy idea as it might sound. Think about it."

"I'd rather not." But Terchran did think about it, not liking the flavor. "It's Anall-Marr," he growled in disgust.

"That's right. He's a visionary and sees himself as another Path prophet who will lead the Deklan Republic to greater glory. Sofam has mishandled him ever since he became Primate, taking him and Deklan support for granted. It's been a profitable association, but historically, Deklan has harbored what it sees as legitimate gripes."

"Sofam blocking their attempts to annex Kaleen and Orgomy."

"That's the major one, although there are others, but Sofam has stopped the Paleans doing the same thing. They were evenhanded."

"Their policy to maintain social diversity."

"They were able to do it based on their unshakeable position holding four Executive Council seats. They can afford to be magnanimous."

"Wait a minute. Even if Deklan changes sides, and I don't see how Sofam could stop them if Anall-Marr is determined, it need not be the disaster for us that you paint. The Servatory Party would finally control the government, something we strived to achieve for centuries."

"You aren't listening to me, Terchran," Illeran hissed with irritation.

"I listened, all right. We wouldn't need to bow and scrape to Sargon as a junior coalition partner at all. We could be equal—if we can get Anall-Marr to side with us! I can see now why you consider Sill-Anais and Garnal-Tan's appointments significant. A stroke for Anall-Marr's ego."

"I'm glad you appreciate the significance. I don't know how advanced Ed-Kani's talks are with Anall-Marr, but it might be time to open some dialogue of our own. After all, if Anall-Marr plans to do something radical, we want to make sure he gets to hear both sides of the argument."

Terchran smiled in admiration at Illeran's convoluted thinking, and his tongue flickered momentarily.

"Fa'sure. Our argument being that if he doesn't side with us, we'll support Sofam, and Ed-Kani's vision of a Greater Sargon and his prospect of holding a government majority will be ashes. Not only that, he would seriously piss off Sofam, and the Deklan Republic would be marginalized, ostracized by everyone. His tenure as Primate wouldn't last a day."

"Well, I wouldn't be saying it so bluntly, but essentially, you're correct," Illeran agreed and sipped his tea.

Terchran raised his cup in a salute and took a hefty swallow. It really was good tea.

"If you've heard murmurings, Sofam would have heard them also."

"Oh, I don't doubt it. In fact, I'm counting on it. That's why I'm going to have a friendly chat with Enllss. Pool our information, so to speak. With his old connections in the Bureau of Cultural Affairs, I'd be surprised if he and Bakral don't already know what is going on. Subtlety, my friend, which Ed-Kani and Sargon never fully mastered. Their Code and martial philosophy don't allow for it, and that's why they lost the war with Sofam."

"Good thing they did," Terchran growled.

"Indeed, and is the reason why we refrained from getting involved. Like I told Ed-Kani after the Lemos debacle, we don't want Sofam as an enemy."

"Agreed, but I doubt Sargon would push things to a military confrontation. The wars with Sofam were eleven centuries ago. Sargon is a different place now, too firmly entrenched into the Serrll framework. The Dumas will not risk a popular revolt by entertaining anything that might risk economic stability and their comfortable lives."

"The current makeup of the Dumas wouldn't, I agree, but if Ed-Kani's faction achieves the merger and the Alikan Union Party gets to dominate both blocks, the old guard may not have much say in the matter. While everybody is jockeying for ascendancy, we need to remind the Kapu Maluran and the Sargon Dumas of one salient fact. Under the Articles of Association, in every real way, we're all in government already, sharing power based on the number of systems each interstellar block holds. It's a fair system, which some people choose to ignore."

"Like Ed-Kani."

"He is someone out of time living in a long dead past. I'm not saying the Alikan Union Party would risk war with Sofam, but the Serrll would undergo considerable upheaval were they to achieve control of the Executive Council, not in anyone's interest, and certainly not in the interest of the Karkan Federation. If we fail to support Sofam simply to maintain a bankrupt ideological principle, we'd deserve what we get."

Relaxed in his comfortable formchair, Terchran crossed his legs. If he thought Illeran reactionary and embittered, he'd done his friend a grave disservice. He didn't agree with all of Illeran's policies and views, but he could not ignore the older man's statesmanship and cold, measured responses to Serrll issues. Clawing for power was good clean fun and an outlet for ambition, but clearly not to be waged at any cost. Everyone who sat in the General Assembly had a responsibility to the constituents of their system. Captal was not a private membership club, a fact Terchran himself sometimes forgot.

"You know, the Kapu might be more favorably disposed toward supporting Sofam if we made that support conditional."

"And what would that be?"

"Sofam must agree to move a bill on the Assembly floor

changing representation on the Executive Council from the current ten percent of held systems to five."

"You want to amend the Articles of Association?"

"The current law disproportionally favors large interstellar blocks like the Sofam Confederacy, giving them a stranglehold on the Executive no one can break."

Illeran pulled at his chin. "Mmm. We tried that in our last term and got nowhere."

"Fa'sure. We failed because we didn't lobby the Assembly reps hard enough, and because we didn't see an immediate advantage for ourselves. Lots of systems grumbled when the motion failed, especially the independents who feel they're not fully represented. We're facing a different environment now."

"They're not fully represented, I agree, but if we change the Articles, it'll give them three seats," Illeran pointed out.

"So what? Our position will also be strengthened. We'd hold four seats in our own right. Remember one other thing. Before the motion failed, the Alikan Union Party was merely a vocal splinter group. When the motion was defeated on the Assembly floor, the AUP began to grow alarmingly quickly."

"You're saying we sowed the seeds for the Sargon/Palean merger?"

"Not directly, but we helped water them."

Illeran hissed. "You have an interesting way of putting things."

"There is another matter we should consider. If we can get the Deklan Republic to side with us, and get the independents on board, we won't need to care whether Sargon and the Paleans merge."

"Worth thinking about, all right."

"Fa'sure. Given our current situation, it's a perfect moment to convince Sofam to do this. With the Krans on our doorstep, the Serrll needs stability."

Illeran peered over the rim of his cup and smiled. "You know, of course, increasing the number of executive directors will result in an even greater bulging bureaucracy."

"Not necessarily, not if we handle it properly. We could use the reshuffle to streamline some departments and consolidate parasitic branches. There is too much concentration of power in the current system at director and commissioner levels. Increased representation will be a diluting influence...and a vote winner."

"Mmm. I'll think about it. You still pursuing your vendetta against young Terrllss-rr and his brother?"

"You know about that? Of course you do. No, I gave that up once I realized I was a bit player in an Enllss game to remove Wanderers from Captal."

"As an Executive Director, you shouldn't have involved yourself at all. Running intelligence ops isn't what we do."

"I know, but I couldn't pass up an opportunity to study a real Wanderer up close."

"And got suckered by Enllss."

"Fa'sure. He played me like a cheap flute. Bastard."

Illeran nodded. "He'll make a formidable director." He placed down his cup with a click and leaned back, unperturbed and at ease. Terchran admired his pose and glanced at the moss. It really looked lush.

"What do you plan doing when your term is over?" he asked.

"I really haven't thought about it much. Go back to Karkan for a while and clear my head. In many ways, I'll feel like a tourist."

Terchran understood completely. "Thirty years is a long time to be away from home."

"Hard years, but not entirely unproductive. And you?"

"Paravan offered me a post with them," Terchran said casually and watched Illeran's startled reaction with amusement.

"Paravan? Doing what?"

"Strategic marketing advisor. There's a big title that goes with the job, but that's what it amounts to."

"You're considering taking it?"

"I'm good at working, not so good at idling."

"Yes. After Captal, it will be hard to adjust to anything. You'll do well."

Terchran leaned forward. "About Anall-Marr…"

* * *

Bakral scratched the thick thatch of white hair that made an untidy ring around the back of his head and stared pointedly at Enllss.

"Damnable weather," he growled. A deep scowl furrowed his high forehead. Large steely eyes were bright beneath bushy eyebrows he never bothered to trim. Head of the Security Council, a very senior Executive Director, he did not worry himself needlessly over appearance. "It reminds me too much of home, and I came to Captal because everyone told me it was warm!"

Enllss smiled and glanced at the window screens. Heavy black clouds had rolled in and looked like staying for a while. Slanting gray sheets stood outlined against patchy sunshine far in the west.

"It's got to rain sometime."

"They didn't have to turn it on today, that's all. Anyway, they could have made a hole overhead."

Enllss poured them a top-up of his special herbal blend tea and sniffed before sipping the fragrant brew. Sill-Anais always chided him about it, saying it reminded him of dried lawn clippings. The problem with his old friend, Sill simply did not appreciate cultural refinement, but then, what could he expect from a Deklan barbarian?

"The park needed water."

"We spent zillions installing a watering system in the damned thing."

"Not the same thing and you know it. Besides, it helps

wash away the dust," Enllss pointed out reasonably. The rain would also clean other things than trees. Captal only took a single missile, leaving the Handara District all but wiped out. Most of the mess was already cleared and reconstruction under way. Bad as it was in places, it could have turned out much worse.

"I guess," Bakral growled and sipped his tea. "I could use a break. Get away from here for a while. Things are piling up and there is never enough time to catch up. You know how long it's been since I last set foot on my home world? Three years. My constituents hardly remember my face. It's lucky I'm on my way out or I'd be booted out."

"You've done good work here," Enllss assured him. "No one could have held the Security Council together like you did. With a scanner grid anchored to Copea, the Krans won't find it so easy next time."

"Pity we didn't have the thing *before* they hit us. Still, it sure shredded Ed-Kani Takao's argument that we're in this alone. He didn't have much to say when Alkarh Zor-Ell parked those monster assault ships of his overhead. Gifts from heaven, literally. And that shielding of theirs? Simply incredible."

"We still face a problem where to deploy them. We've got more assets than we can possibly protect."

"I know. We could use fifty of the things, not just five, and it still wouldn't be enough. It's a start, I guess, and OSCOM promised us more. All things considered, we're lucky to have them. I should be celebrating, then you went and spoiled it all. You're sure about this Deklan thing?"

"Not sure, but all the indicators are there. Anabb Karr did a quiet sift through message traffic for me between Ed-Kani and Anall-Marr," Enllss said comfortably, relishing the play of emotions on Bakral's craggy face. "All very innocent when looked at individually, but suggestive if examined together. I was convinced enough to drag you in."

"Humph! I don't want to know how he managed to hack into Comsec or I'd lose even more sleep than I already am.

Skullduggery, I never liked it. This isn't exactly your portfolio, Enllss."

"I used to run the Bureau of Cultural Affairs—"

"I know, which proves my point. You're sticking your nose into Barr-aa's bailiwick. Don't be surprised if he looks you up and starts tearing strips off you."

"I told him what I was doing before getting the Diplomatic Branch involved. I couldn't very well discuss it with Sill."

Executive Director for the Bureau of Cultural Affairs, Barr-aa was also a Sofam representative and Sill's boss. Enllss had no reservations talking to him.

Somewhat mollified, Bakral pursed his lips. "No, I don't suppose you could. You haven't told Illeran anything?"

"This doesn't concern him. Well, it does, but we want to stand on firmer ground before sounding him out."

"Damnable business, and it couldn't have come at a worse time for us. The Kran strike hasn't exactly made people confident about their security."

"Which is why Ed-Kani is putting out his feelers now."

"I know, and you're an asshole for spoiling my day like this. I've got enough problems on my hands as it is," Bakral complained petulantly.

Enllss smiled, sympathizing completely, but it wasn't something the Sofam Confederacy could shelve. Bakral was venting spleen and being grouchy.

Spindly, long-necked, he came from a low gravity world deep within Sofam, not far from the Rolan group. Captal's higher gravity gave him problems even though he'd put on some muscle. The thin bones simply were not designed to support his tall frame. It helped explain his sometimes irascible behavior.

"Sargon could be stitching a new trade deal with Deklan for all I know, and I'm stirring things up over nothing," Enllss pointed out.

"But you don't think so?"

"No, I don't. My gut tells me our Sargon friend is trying to stitch up a far more sinister deal."

"He can't be spilling everything over Comsec? He's got to know it's not totally secure."

Enllss grinned and his eyes glittered. "Comsec isn't my only source."

"Hah! What do you want to do?"

"Sill and I go way back and we understand each other. I'd like to talk to him informally before you launch anything official with the Deklan Synod. If we can nip this in the bud, it could save everybody a lot of messing around later. No guarantees, of course. One word to the media that Deklan might be considering leaving the Revisionist Party coalition, we'd face a major PR disaster."

"I am painfully aware of the potential fallout, Enllss. Ed-Kani...the shit wants to leave office draped in glory, the savior of Sargon! The man who consummated the Sargon/Palean merger and toppled the Revisionist government. Bah! Him we can handle, but Anall-Marr is a reactionary and therefore unpredictable. Can't the fool see that Ed-Kani is snowing him?"

"It all depends on what Ed-Kani is promising."

"Of course it does! Hell, I've got to talk to some people about this and pull Deklan into line before things get out of hand. Okay, talk to Sill and feel him out, but no one else! Got it? Should Illeran or Terchran get wind of this, the whole thing could cascade out of control."

"Don't be surprised if the Karkans already know all about it. Their intelligence apparatus is quite good."

"I know. Illeran buttonholed me the other day demanding to know who was responsible for the malicious rumor circulating around suggesting the Karkans are set to heave Sargon out of the Servatory Party coalition. Like I'd know." He cocked an eyebrow. "Your doing?"

Enllss shrugged. "I may have hinted at the idea," he said innocently, and Bakral laughed.

"Damn cheek if you asked me, but it's got Illeran hot and bothered putting out denials, which does my old heart good."

"You don't have a heart, Bakral. It's a calculating machine."

"And a good thing for Sofam that it is, but be warned. Illeran will eventually add up the numbers and he'll be coming after you. The only rumors he likes are the ones he starts himself."

Enllss stared earnestly at the senior Sofam representative. "You know, it might be an idea if *you* had a serious talk with him about siding with us. A declaration of intent from the Karkans, followed by a fatherly word to Ed-Kani, would bury the Sargon/Palean merger—for a few decades anyway—surely in everyone's interest. We're all twitchy enough as it is over the Krans without getting mired in internal machinations."

"You mean it would be in *our* interest."

"I really meant everyone's."

"Mmm, yes. A talk might be useful, once you get something definite from Sill. If you're hoping internal maneuvering will ever stop, you're deluding yourself."

"It won't stop, I know, but let's at least shelve it for a while."

"Let me cogitate on it. I'm not sure it was wise getting the Diplomatic Branch involved in your little piece of sleuthing. Anabb, can he be trusted?"

"We're inviting him to accept a commissioner's post and you're asking me if he can be trusted?"

"Okay, I'm a heel, but this is too important to worry about wounded sensibilities."

"He can be an obstinate son of a bitch and a monumental pain, but I'd stake my life on him. He has shaped the Diplomatic Branch into an invaluable intelligence agency."

"Right, he's a savior." Bakral raised a finger in warning. "If what you've told me turns out to be pink fog, your life in Captal is over, my rash friend. I'd also be swept out of the way, but I'm not bothered by the idea. I'll be gone in two years anyway.

You, on the other hand, have a promising future and I'd hate to see it trashed because of misguided zeal."

"By damn! You think a little detail like that hasn't occurred to me?"

"Well, even the best of us can stumble, but you're a top-notch political mechanic, Enllss. You wouldn't have gone out of your way to ruin my day if you didn't have a solid lead."

"With Anall-Marr, you *have* figured out the obvious?"

"That Illeran might want to pull him to his side? It's an evident and expected maneuver." Bakral rose and patted down his trousers. "A tangled mess, that's what this is. Still, if Anall-Marr wants to shift camps, I'd rather see him in Karkan hands than Sargon's. Let me know how you go with Sill."

Enllss stood up and escorted his important visitor to the door. "You'll be the first."

"Just make sure there's no second!" Bakral growled and walked out. The translucent white panels slid out of his way. Enllss smiled at the retreating back and turned to his assistant.

"Landa, please call Commissioner Sill-Anais and ask him to see me at his convenience."

"Of course, sir."

"And get somebody to clear away the clutter in my office."

At his desk, he sat down in his broad tooled leather chair, leaned back, and cupped his chin. The Wall pooled through shifting colors. They *were* kind of soothing if he cared to think about it. Damn the mind benders anyway.

Bakral wasn't the only one with problems. With two years before the next electoral session, he needed to ratchet up his own reelection campaign. Executive Director nominee or not, he was still Kaplan's Assembly rep and needed to stroke his constituents and the electorate at large. His seat all but secure, but he could not afford to be complacent. As Kaplan's representative on Captal, he was required to push their interests and voice their concerns. He'd seen reps who forgot why they were elected and the amorphous mass that was the people swallowed them. Tariq was merely the last in a long line of victims who thought Captal was an end in itself. The people came first, foremost and always.

It meant campaigning on Kaplan, which would take him away from Captal at a time he could not afford, but there was never a good time to leave. There would be rallies, glad-handing and speeches. Phlegmatic, Enllss resigned himself to the inevitable. Having elected him, the least he could do is make an appearance as a token of appreciation. Besides, he owed it to the tireless back room Party operatives who'd worked to get him here. However remote the possibility, he did not want some young upstart unseating him because he had his head up his ass. He should have been a bureaucrat and avoided worrying about elections. Of course, there would be other worries. It was in the nature of things for those who sought power.

Sorting through Comsec messages, going over briefs, signing approvals and sending someone's cherished project into the obscurity bin, consumed more than two hours. Spared the minutiae involved in running the Bureau, a bulging bureaucracy handled that for him, he still needed to be aware of what went on, not merely issue policy edicts. What he never did was micromanage. That was Tariq's job, and kept another nine senior assistants busy.

Some days were better than others.

The comms alert beeped and he touched a glowing pad on the inlaid desk console.

"What is it?"

"Commissioner Sill-Anais to see you, sir."

"Very good. Show him in," Enllss said with relish. He loved sparring with his friend, and this session should rank among his best.

The door panels slid away with a hiss and Sill walked through. Fit and wiry, he moved with quick, short strides. His pinched dry face was traced with lines of age and responsibility, but beneath narrow eyebrows, liquid wide-set green eyes still sparkled with energy.

"How you doing, Enllss?" he piped in high treble and thrust out a massive barrel chest.

Enllss stood and waved at formchairs around a low table. "Take the weight off."

Sill eased himself down and passed a hand through his hair, streaked with twin bands of dark gray of a mature Deklan male. He shifted slightly and looked up.

"Why is it that your formchairs seem more comfortable than mine? Ach!" he demanded petulantly.

"Talk to Office Services," Enllss said indifferently, and took a chair opposite him.

"I'll do that." Sill glanced at the window screens. "More rain today, and windy. Can't those weather people make up their minds? Anyway, what did you want to see me about? I'm kind of pressed for time today. The only reason I came was because I wanted to stretch my legs."

"I feel for you."

"I am sure you do. Well?"

"Can't I see a friend without turning it into an interstellar incident?"

"You don't have friends, Enllss. None of us do. We merely have acquaintances of opportunity."

"Too true. Your boys?"

"Both doing well, thanks." Sill cocked his head. "You're always chatty when you want to tell me something nasty. Just spill it, ach!"

"All right. We've known each other for a while. We cut our teeth together on the Assembly floor and I'd like to think we were honest with each other, even though we've had our differences."

Sill frowned. "You never deliberately misled me if that's what you mean. You represent Sofam's interests and I represent Deklan's, but within those parameters we get along. What's this leading to?"

"With the Paleans, Deklan is an important Revisionist Party coalition partner, and likely to be even more so should the Paleans decide to merge with Sargon. We're an island of stability."

"I am pleased to see you regarding us as important. Ach! Sometimes we feel we're taken for granted."

"Because we don't say thank you every day? Never mind. Would you regard our partnership as mutually beneficial?"

"More or less, although some practices by your Paravan Trading Association are deemed predatory, but that's business, I guess. Sofam hasn't always seen fit to—"

"You mean, when we blocked your attempts to annex Kaleen and Orgomy?"

"That example comes to mind. Those systems are ours by ancient right. Ach! Still, the relationship is workable."

"Meaning there are some things you'd like to change."

Sill leaned forward. "What are you trying to say, Enllss?"

"You are a priest of the Path, but you're also a senior Deklan politician, which must cause you some conflict of interest sometimes."

"Sometimes. So?"

"Because you're a politician, you play the game just as I do."

"We both serve our respective parties."

"Which means doing whatever it takes, right?"

"Ach! Just as you do, you heretical Sofam slime."

Enllss shrugged. "Yes, it can get grubby down in the weeds, and there are times when we get muddy over nothing. Are things grubby enough for the Deklan Republic to consider leaving the Revisionist Party?"

Sill blanched and a veneer of guarded caution snapped over his face. "What makes you say that?"

"Oh, some talk that's floating around. Talk between Ed-Kani Takao and Primate Anall-Marr."

"I know of no—"

Enllss raised a hand. "Please, Sill. Remember whom you're talking to. I wasn't plucked off a tree."

"I can't fault your intelligence, but this time, you're way off the mark. Why would we contemplate doing anything of the sort?"

"Lots of things come to mind. Maybe Anall-Marr has a vision for the Deklan Republic that doesn't include Sofam, or perhaps he dreams of greater personal glory and sees the Sargon Directorate helping him achieve it. Maybe he's simply frustrated being a junior coalition partner and frets that Deklan isn't getting a fair hearing on the Assembly floor. He may have a specific grudge against Paravan. The list is lengthy, Sill."

"You're nuts, Enllss. I know how much you like running little intrigues just to keep your hand in. You cannot forget that you once ran my Bureau. The suspicion bug has bitten you and you see conspiracies in every corner, you old fool. Ach!"

"You could be right, but Ed-Kani and Anall-Marr did talk a lot lately. As a senior Deklan rep, I thought you might know a little about it."

"I'm not privy to all the Primate's initiatives or discussions. Even if I were, I could not talk about."

"Yes, I know. I find myself in a similar position. People haggle, make decisions, and I get to know about it when the mess is dumped in my lap. It's a lousy way to run things. Lousy or not, keep one thing in mind. If Deklan is considering changing sides, you wouldn't be the one saddled with the mess. The entire Serrll Combine would have to wear it. I'd think real hard before venturing into those waters. Predators lay there."

"Are you threatening us?"

Enllss laughed. "You were around long enough to know how the grownups play. I'll be blunt. I don't really care what you know or don't know, but if I were you, I'd want to have a long fireside chat with the Primate. Whatever he and Ed-Kani may be planning won't work. Deklan can leave the coalition. Sofam won't stop you, but Anall-Marr should consider carefully his objectives. Bear with me if I restate the obvious.

"Should the Sargon/Palean merger take place, the Alikan Union will hold three Executive Council seats. With the Karkan's two and the support of the nonaligned independents, that makes six. Should you walk away, it would give the Servatory Party seven seats and absolute control of the government. At first glance, an unbeatable combination, and I could see how Anall-Marr could be tempted, but only at first glance."

"Go on. I always find your analyses fascinating and amusing."

"Ignoring your sarcasm, I'm pleased you're amused, but bear in mind the following facts. The Unified Independent Front will support the Revisionists, we made sure of that. With our four seats, we have five. But you would still hold the balance of power, right? Maybe, and then maybe not. What if Sofam made it known to the independents that the Alikan Union Party plans to abolish their seat and absorb them? Sargon has always been critical of our stance to give the independents a voice in the Executive, even though lately they've sided with the Servatory Party. They wouldn't like that."

"That's crazy! The AUP wouldn't voluntarily want to lose a seat."

"You're probably right. Still, such a rumor wouldn't do their cause much good, but Deklan should consider a more serious matter."

"Enllss—"

"Let me finish. Ed-Kani and Ti Inai's strategy relies on having the Karkans in coalition. Given our history, not an unreasonable assumption. They've been after us for a while. However, what if Ed-Kani is wrong?"

"I've heard the rumors. Ach!"

"Troublesome, aren't they? Should the Sargon/Palean merger succeed, there won't be an Alikan Union, only Greater Sargon. Everybody seems to know it except Ti Inai. Perhaps he does know and has a contingency plan. It doesn't matter. My point is: should things get difficult, the Karkans might side with Sofam. You know better than anyone what it would mean for the Serrll if Sargon were to implement its martial philosophy on everybody. Sofam will not allow such social dislocation to take place. The Karkans want to overthrow us, but not by causing massive social disruption, and therein lies the major difference between them and Sargon."

Sill nodded slowly. "You always did have a keen nose for what's going on, but you're wrong about this. I'm telling you right now, as your friend, to my knowledge, Deklan has no plans to leave the coalition. Ach!"

"And you could be telling the truth, but like you said, you don't know everything. Think about having that quiet chat with Anall-Marr and point out some salient facts to him. Ed-Kani can be charming and very persuasive when he wants to, but Anall-Marr is unfamiliar with how things work in Captal. His boyish adventurism has a very serious side to it. He may have gripes with Sofam, but talking to us before he makes an irrevocable decision could help him get what he wants and avoid a lot of untidy unpleasantness later."

"Ach! You have a polished voice yourself, Enllss. If I didn't know you as well as I do, I'd say you were spinning me a fanciful tale and wasting my valuable time in the bargain. Deklan and Sargon? Karkans siding with Sofam? Very amusing."

"I hope it stays amusing."

Sill chewed his lip and looked thoughtful. "All right. I'll talk to Anall-Marr and prove you wrong."

"Good! You do that," Enllss boomed and slapped his thighs. "How about some tea to wash away the bad taste our talk gave me?"

"Drink your weeds? Ach! No thanks. I prefer dying of old age."

"Heard the latest?"

"About what?"

"There is talk about moving you to Defense."

"Bakral mentioned it. Ach! Nothing is settled, though, but I wouldn't mind the portfolio," Sill declared and heaved himself up. "Still okay for dinner tonight?"

"Still okay."

"Fine. I'll see you then."

"For sure," Enllss murmured and watched his friend leave, a worried frown creasing his face. Sill had a lot to worry about. When the door panels closed, he grinned and rubbed his hands. He glanced out and saw soft rain still coming down, hoping it would add to Sill's gloom.

As he sat down at his desk, the comms alert beeped.

"Sir, Executive Director Illeran wants you to come up," Landa said.

"Tell him I'll see him in a minute."

Scowling, he suspected he knew what his boss wanted. When spreading rumors, you're sometimes held to account, by damn.

Chapter Six

Surrounded by blue fire, the transport portal ring loomed large. *Parsha* crept toward a wall of blackness and readied itself for the jump. With three hundred ampirs separation, *Zadar* synchronized its approach to ensure that both ships would transit simultaneously. Even so, there was no guarantee they would emerge on the other side together. With such a long jump, a margin of uncertainty, hopefully minimal, always existed.

Terr watched as *Tureen 2* approached the interface. The energy ring around the portal flared and swallowed the *Nasor*-class ship. He wished it luck. Whatever it took, it had to knock out the Kran waypoint portal, the largest single immediate tactical threat the Serrll faced. It wouldn't harm the Orieli cause either to eliminate a flanking probe. This, of course, was predicated on the assumption the Krans don't have portals somewhere else able to reach them. As the assault ship vanished, they were committed, whichever way it turned out.

When the interface recharged, *Parsha* and *Zadar* crept toward the portal. Teena's small hand groped for his and he grasped it, holding it tight. Last night, huddled together beneath a warm blanket, he tried to convince her to stay behind, but managed only a couple of lame sentences before realizing she wasn't listening. She looked frightened at the possible prospect of falling into Kran hands again, but her fear was also for him. He'd wanted to share with her what he was and what he did, didn't he? Well, the price of sharing was being together everywhere he went, and she appeared determined to hold him to that bargain.

He embraced her tenderly, her head resting in the crook of

his arm, Death spread its hand in a soft blue glow over them. Whatever waited at KP-001, they would meet it together. Misgivings made his stomach flutter, but in a way, he took comfort from her presence. They would be going in well protected, but he was wary of Kran surprises.

They spent much of the night talking quietly. Hearing her soft words, her faintly citrus scent a comforting shield, her body entwined with his, they shared an intimacy that had eluded them for a long time, and one he was slowly rebuilding. When dawn broke and the sky turned purple, he hugged her tight, not wanting the moment to end. The moment did pass and they made ready to board *Parsha*.

Hooked into the VI, creation lying naked around him, a small nagging voice in his head kept repeating the same words: walk away. The words disturbed him, for he didn't know what they meant. Too late for second thoughts now, though.

Terr turned to Arlon Dee. The Cetan ran his tongue over fleshy lips and nodded in acknowledgment. All the planning, discussions and preparations were done. No backing out now if they'd missed something. In a way, Terr felt relieved to be underway. The terrible, terrifying joy of destruction would begin soon and only Death would emerge the victor.

Waiting for the portal to hurl them into another reality, the glowing words from *Saftara's Dance of the Hours* flashed through his mind. They spoke of unrestrained power rippling like a wave across all eternity that left only darkness in its wake. In the center of the conflagration stood a lone Wanderer, the cape of his brown surtaf fluttering in the wind, the hot sands whispering at his feet as he held his arms upraised, lightning shooting into an amber sky. And the face he saw was the face of Death unleashed. What did the gods care for creation when reality existed only as long as they willed it. What did the gods care for life? If they didn't care, why did they bring it forth? Playthings for their amusement? If that's all life was, the gods had a pretty low sense of humor.

From nothing it all sprung, and into nothing it would return. Did anything anyone did matter?

Terr shifted in his swivel-couch and met Sidhara's eyes. The vertical red slits burned bright, revealing the fires within, fires waiting to be loosed. Cloaked in the shadow of Death, Terr did not recognize him, although he felt his master's power. For a flickering moment, he saw ruin and desolation everywhere, and tempted to call out to Arlon Dee to stop. Cutting blackness stifled his cry as *Parsha* went through the portal and he looked at alien stars.

"Tactical caution. Interceptor net modulated and ship is at full EMCON. Status. Condition three active. *Zadar* is 24,000 ampirs on our port quarter. Range to KP-001, fifty-two billion ampirs."

Given the distance they just covered, they'd hit the system right on. This far out the massive orange star and its smaller blue companion were merely dots in a tapestry of other stars. Terr wondered what lay in their embrace.

"Caution. Three *Daktars* detected, positioned equidistantly outside the system's ice belt. Four *Sandar*-class battlecruisers and two *Fadhir*-class attack ships holding geosynchronous equatorial position around KP-001C. One *Fadhir* is holding orbit around KP-001D."

Terr glanced at Teena. She gave him a small, unsettled smile and nodded. He grinned to reassure her, still feeling she should not have come.

"Very well," Arlon Dee said. "Instruct *Zadar* to take out the *Fadhir*."

"Acknowledged."

"Jump on predetermined coordinates."

There was no need for detailed orders. They worked everything out on Perilia. At one-sixth primary boost, it took *Parsha* eleven seconds to reach the inner system. It broke normal and Terr studied the tactical VI overlay. They could not see *Zadar* hidden behind her interdimensional shell. If they timed it well,

Guardians of Shadow

Zadar should be ready to spring the trap.

Lit in half phase against a backdrop of hard white points, KP-001D hung like a suspended ornament, smeared with brown, orange and red stripes. A pretty little world, Terr would not have minded looking it over. Unfortunately, such indulgence would be much too dangerous—complaining owners.

"Caution. Energy fluctuations detected, consistent with an interdimensional transport portal. Range, 185,000 ampirs. Tactical caution. Force lines detected from graviton sensors. Power buildup detected from multiple planetary sources, identified as discharge nodes."

"This time, I don't care if they look us over," Arlon Dee growled.

Uneasy, the hairs on the back of his neck itched. Terr recognized the familiar feeling of warning and never ignored it. Perhaps they should have forgone this show of bravado and simply waded in, blasting everything in sight while shielded. It was never prudent to underestimate an enemy, especially the Celi-Kran.

"Tactical caution. The *Fadhir* has broken orbit and holding an intercept course. Range, 132,000 ampirs. Target powering up to weapons status."

"Cent Comp? Engage shell, one-second phasing."

"Acknowledged."

Although *Parsha's* sensors could not operate while cloaked, by rapidly switching the interdimensional shell, it could see out, sufficient to do business. Terr held his breath and watched the Kran ship close, *Parsha* well within its range. Just then, two lines of blue-white energy sprang from nowhere and speared the *Fadhir*. In the VI plot, he saw the Kran ship stagger, explosions ripping through its forward segment. Although it could not detect *Zadar*, it immediately returned fire along the emission trail left by decaying residuals.

Deadly tracks impacted *Zadar's* interdimensional shell, and disappeared, translated thousands of ampirs into space. *Zadar* kept up its relentless fire, systematically demolishing the *Fadhir's* rear segment. In a blinding explosion that tore apart most of the segment, the Kran ship died—a clinical execution.

Arlon turned to Sidhara. "Da, are you ready?"

Sidhara told them he could project his power through the shell, but it helped if he looked at his target. Visualization formed an important link, aiding him to channel and focus. Maybe the shell would not be an obstacle, but no one wanted to find out the hard way, not now. Phasing in one-second intervals was enough for him to see his target.

Without answering, Sidhara raised his arms, then leveled them, his eyes fixed on an image in his mind projected through the VI. Blue lightnings snapped and crackled between his arms. Knowing what was about to happen, everyone in PFC clamped their hands against their ears. Mouth pursed, expression grim, Sidhara clenched his fists. A flash of yellow light leaped from his hands and vanished as it touched the bulkhead. A peal of thunder shook the air, which made Terr wince. He glanced at Teena. Face pale, she clasped his hand hard.

The old Wanderer dropped his arms and slowly turned his head. "It is done." Strong with the power, his voice resonated, cold and indifferent, the voice of something unearthly.

"Cent Comp? Disengage shell," Arlon Dee said quietly and stared at the Wonderer.

The mainframe plot cleared and *Parsha* hung in space, poised above KP-001D. Coiled strands of yellow light writhed over the surface, slithering, shifting. In their wake, bright spheres blossomed as power reactors, fuel cells, weapon stores, and ships ignited. Two massive explosions lit the edge of the terminator. Glowing domes of light reached far into space. Seconds later, fiery plumes of magma shot into the night sky from gaping fissures. More fractures opened on the daylight side, revealing the naked interior of hell.

Terr heard Teena sob beside him and he wrapped his arms around her. She leaned against him, fists pressed against her mouth, and fat tears slid down her cheeks. Everyone in PFC stared in awe as the planet tore itself apart. No one had witnessed anything like it. He lifted his head and looked at Arlon Dee. The Cetan returned his gaze, his eyes troubled. Beside him, Kemp stood, hands clenched behind his back, clearly shocked at the level of destruction a single bolt of energy could wreak, but of course, the bolt wasn't any ordinary energy.

Teena gave a strangled cry and rushed toward the PT alcove. Terr was tempted to go after her, but refrained. Hard as this was, she had to come to terms with it alone. His life was not diplomatic parties and round table negotiations. He dealt with death, raw and savage. This is what he was, and the sooner she accepted the harsh truth, the better for both. She wanted to see, and now perhaps regretted it. Analyzing after-action reports was not at all like being there.

Rit!

Dhar looked at him, his face grave, also reflecting on the power that lay in their hands.

Arlon nodded to Sidhara. He leveled his arms and splayed his fingers. Terr hurriedly protected his ears and shut his eyes. When the flash came, it left dancing afterimages, his ears ringing at this abuse. He opened his eyes and stared eagerly at the VI image.

"Cent Comp? Confirm destruction of portal."

"No energy discharge detected. Target presumed destroyed."

"This should get Zero Six thinking," Arlon said with satisfaction.

Terr stared at what remained of KP-001D. It was one thing to wield Death in his hands, another seeing it in someone else's, truly a terrible display. The planet was in upheaval, everything laid waste and dead. He was not sorry for the Krans down there, hoping there wasn't any developed fauna. A grim price to pay to blot out a mindless invader. He reached with his hand and grasped Dhar's shoulder. There was no need for words as they looked at each other. All the words were already said. He turned to Sidhara.

"I'm sorry you needed to do this, master. There was no other way."

"When all choices are removed, you take the only course left. If you want to grieve, grieve for all life the Krans already extinguished."

"I didn't think it would be like this," Terr said slowly.

"No one does. Afterward, it is too late."

Arlon Dee stepped beside them. "Da...forgive me for asking, but I must know. Are you prepared for what must be done next?"

"I know what I faced before coming, Karhide."

"Cent Comp? Engage interdimensional shell and proceed to KP-001E."

Parsha transited and moved toward its next target.

With three worlds left as cinders, Terr glad he could not see them, he watched KP-001C grow large. *Parsha* and *Zadar* weren't cloaked, Arlon Dee wanted the central nexus to have a good look at them, wanting it to know what it faced. Safely within the planet's distortion limit, the ships did not fear a missile strike.

Parsha held position 50,000 ampirs above the planet's equator and waited. As one, picket *Sandars* and *Fadhirs* broke orbit and headed for them. Arlon looked away from the real-time plot and nodded to Sidhara. Eight discharges later, the Kran ships were lifeless, drifting hulks.

Teena emerged in the PT alcove and glanced at the holoview displays. Terr looked at her and saw resolve and determination on her face. Her eyes fixed on him, she moved toward him. She wrapped her arm around his and flashed him a small smile.

"Did I miss anything?"

He grinned at her, glad to see she was reconciled with whatever disturbed her before.

"The fun is just about to start."

"Good."

His heart went out to her. She would undoubtedly still wrestle with what happened and what was about to happen, but her misgivings were resolved. Stout girl. He should never have doubted her.

"Cent Comp, demodulate interceptor net," Arlon Dee ordered. No need for stealth, not anymore. *Parsha* was still exposed to danger from planetary defenses, but the computer would snap on the interdimensional shell at the first sign of any energy buildup consistent with powering up discharge nodes.

"Acknowledged."

Immediately, a ghostly pink light settled over Sidhara's head. He was told to expect this, but he still tensed. After a moment the light faded.

"Caution. Transmission interrogative from Zero Six."

Aron Dee gave a hollow grin. "We're at what they call the pointy end. Cent Comp? Open channel."

"Karhide Arlon Dee, I want to negotiate," the nexus grated, its imperious masculine voice resonated in Terr's head, the sound making his hair prickle. Teena looked somewhat pale, her posture equally tense.

"These are my terms. The Celi-Kran must stay away from Orieli and Serrll Combine space—forever."

"Unacceptable."

"Tactical caution. Energy buildup detected in four arrays consistent with discharge nodes. Buildup approaching criticality."

"Perhaps you'll find this more acceptable…engage shell! Move the ship ten thousand ampirs to port."

"Acknowledged."

"Sidhara, if the central nexus fires on us, you know what to do."

Nodding, the old Wanderer prepared himself and waited, small lightnings crackling around his hands. On the way over,

269

should another demonstration be necessary, he insisted he could project through the shell. If something went wrong, there would be time to do it the old way. Arlon Dee did not want to risk it. After twenty seconds, he disengaged the shell.

"Caution, emission residuals detected consistent with interceptor net discharges."

Arlon glanced at Sidhara.

A flash of light and a pealing crash of thunder shook the air and made the deck tremble. Thick, yellow coils of energy crawled over KP-001C's surface, devouring everything in their path—but only on the surface. The nexus core must be buried somewhere deep underground and should therefore be immune. Terr hoped so. The next few minutes would prove it one way or another.

"Disengage shell."

"Caution. Transmission interrogative from Zero Six."

"Open channel."

"Zero Zero is prepared to discuss your terms."

"After failing to destroy us?"

"Were I successful, you would not be a threat."

"Very well, I'm listening," Arlon Dee said and smiled faintly at the machine's cold pragmatism.

"I will contact you in ten of your minutes."

"Ten minutes." Arlon looked at Terr. "I think we have its attention."

"Karhide, this was too easy."

"I'm suspicious myself, but I cannot see what it can do. Let's go to the Observation Deck. We'll be more comfortable there. Opturkarh Kemp? At the slightest hint of trouble…"

"Understood, Da."

Dhar and Teena glanced at him and walked to the PT alcoves. Terr followed Sidhara and watched Arlon disappear. A prickling sensation along his arms made him pause and he went pale as his blood chilled.

"No!"

He ignored Kemp's startled expression and his anguished cry was cut off when he lunged into the alcove. He shook off the aftereffect transceiver tingle and looked around in desperation.

"Teena! Where is she? Where is she?" He raised his arms and threw back his head. "No!"

He let her walk right into Zero's grasp! His guts churned, every gasp of air filled with tiny thorns, and reached for Death. The power lust consumed him and he allowed his rage to reign. A multitude of images flashed through his mind: of Teena, himself, moments of joy they shared, of tears and pain, all gone. Ready to unleash chaos, he visualized Zero Six's glittering chamber. Lightnings crackled and he was ready. Ready to make it pay for its treachery.

Strong arms grasped him and he felt a tingling shock as Dhar fell, his face contorted with agony. It was death for any mortal to touch him while he wielded his aspect, but Dhar was not an ordinary mortal. Sobered, Terr knelt beside his brother.

"Nightwings!"

Dhar shook himself and smiled weakly. "I'm all right," he rumbled and staggered to his feet.

Terr hugged him, his head against his broad chest. "Forgive me, my brother."

"Terr, Sidhara is gone," Arlon Dee said quietly, clearly disturbed by what he saw.

There were only the three of them in the subtly lit Observation Deck. Terr stood there stunned. His master gone and Teena with him. Rage slowly oozed out of him and he sagged.

"Teena," he moaned. His eyes stung as he looked imploringly at Dhar. "What am I to do?"

"Sankri…"

Terr turned and smashed his fist against the bulkhead. "Damn you!"

"We should have seen it," Arlon Dee growled. "We should have seen it."

"Zero Six tapped into our PT system to transport us down the first time," Dhar said, his words barely audible. "That's why it scanned Sidhara."

"It's a bit late now, but Cent Comp will upgrade our security protocols," Arlon said.

Terr stepped back and lifted his arms. "I'll finish what we should have done from the onset," he said, voice harsh, filled with the inevitable dread of destiny. It took Teena and he didn't want to live without her. If she was still alive, he did not want her to suffer, not again.

"Sankri! No!" Dhar implored him, standing rooted. In Terr's present frame of mind, power radiating palpably from him, to touch him again could mean a real death.

"It has her!" Terr snarled. "It's my turn now."

"Are you prepared to kill her?" Arlon demanded harshly.

Terr paused, ready to unleash Sarumajan. If he was indeed the destroyer of worlds, KP-001C would be his first. His arms held high, he probed the bond that bound them together and it was there, strong and close. He looked at Dhar, his face torn with emotion.

"I can't let her suffer."

His face twisted and his vision blurred. He bit his lip and lowered his arms. He couldn't even relieve the torment and despair she undoubtedly felt.

"Caution. Transmission interrogative from Zero Six."

"Open channel," Arlon growled harshly.

"Leave the system immediately. If you attempt further aggression, Teena and the Wanderer will die."

"Then you will die with her!" Terr snarled.

"Irrelevant."

Her scream reverberated in his head even as the nexus severed the connection. The air between them shimmered and Sidhara crumpled to the deck. The old Wanderer lifted his head and groped weakly with his hand. Torn with grief, Terr immediately knelt beside him and cradled him in his lap.

"Master!"

"I couldn't resist…nothing more I can do for you, my son…it's up to you now, Sankri. Do what you must."

"I cannot!" Terr gasped, stunned to see his master dying.

Sidhara coughed, a dry rasping sound, and gripped Terr's arm. "Listen to me. Everything is possible if you will it. It only takes you to will it."

"But I'm not a third-level adept."

"It is only a state of mind, my son. I will give you my strength…all I have left…Sarumajan."

A bright blue glow enveloped his body and pulsed. The glow expanded and Terr was caught in it. He saw his master smile and the penetrating eyes, lit with inner fire, slowly closed. An overwhelming presence suffused through him, a presence able to mold reality. It also emanated love and compassion. Slowly, the glow faded and Sidhara slumped. Terr felt a rip deep inside him and moaned.

After a while, his face stone, he looked at Dhar, his brother fighting to keep emotion in check. He gently lowered Sidhara's head on the deck and stood up. Without saying anything, he leveled his right arm and thunder crashed as he loosed the lightnings.

* * *

Teena shook off the transport aftereffect tingle and blinked, then pressed both fists against her mouth in naked horror and screamed. Hot tears welled in her eyes and spilled down her cheeks. She kept screaming and her nails bit painfully into her palms. All the terrors buried deep in her mind threatened to burst forth, waiting to overwhelm her senses, ready to carry her into the dark corridors of insanity. She did not want to live through it all again: confinement, gaping mouths and eyes filled with fear, prying interrogations, stripped bare of her personality. Knowing there was no escape, everything came flooding back.

Surrounded by flickering triangular panels of the chamber, feeling cold intelligence probing her, she gasped when powerful arms gripped her. She struggled to free herself, but the arms held her fast.

"Do not fear, my child."

Sidhara's strong voice washed over her, soothing her, taking away some of the anguish. She looked up at his craggy face and sagged against him. Sobbing, she clung to him, drawing comfort from his embrace and the smell of burnt sands, tarad grass and peelath that permeated his surtaf.

After a moment, she wiped her eyes and pulled back.

"Let me die!" she implored and saw him blanch. Then he smiled and stroked her cheek.

"And risk Sankri's wrath?"

Momentarily startled, she gave a short barking laugh. Then she was crying, clinging to his imposing form. He let out a long sigh, held her to him and stroked her hair.

"You destroyed my worlds!" Zero Six accused, its harsh voice shattering the fleeting moment of intimacy.

Teena stepped away from Sidhara. What could the thing want with her? What did it want with Sidhara?

Terr!

He hadn't wanted her to come, but she couldn't let him go out there alone, could she? Not happy, he gave in. *Don't blame yourself, my love. I had to do this.*

As she stood in the glittering chamber surrounded by light and color, she suspected that getting her out of here this time might not be so easy. Stomach fluttering, shivers of apprehension coursing through her, she waited to be transported again into a transparent bubble, the tortures of hell haunted her. She bit her lip to stop the small whimpers. She summoned courage and set her mouth in a firm line. She wanted to come. Now, she must face her demons.

"Like you attempted to destroy ours," Sidhara replied, his

voice resonating in the chamber.

"I failed with Anar'on," the nexus said conversationally, making a statement of fact. "The Wanderers will be exterminated."

"You will not be there to see it."

Even as he lifted his right arm, lances of white light stabbed him, coming from all around the chamber. He grunted and sagged to his knees. Teena gasped and stepped back in shock. He propped himself up with one hand and blue lightnings slid across the chamber floor. Where they touched, the flickering panels died.

"Stop!" Zero Six thundered.

The orange shimmer of Sidhara's shield faded and he was gone. Like a web, the lightnings crawled across the chamber, slowly spreading, extinguishing the panels.

"Make it stop!" it demanded, which gave Teena a flash of satisfaction. No matter what happened, she was not going to be imprisoned by this thing again.

"Suffer!" she grated and straightened, standing defiant, waiting for darkness that spread through the chamber to claim her. There were regrets, of past deeds and things that would now never be done. She regretted not telling Terr one last time that she loved him, but he knew. The bond linking them would say it for her.

Reality dissolved and she screamed.

Flicker…Flicker…Flicker.

Surprised to find herself still alive, she blinked hard and shielded her eyes. Bright light and color surrounded her, all shifting rapidly, changing in a mosaic of incomprehensible patterns. She slowly lowered her hand and stared in wonder.

Not unlike the Zero Six chamber, this one was magnified many times. The ceiling at least six katalans high, but it wasn't a single cavity. Like soap bubbles, four enormous caverns were fused together. She looked down, startled to see the floor several katalans below her, and realized she was suspended. Before dying, and she knew it did die, the nexus had transported her here.

The horror of being captive again still haunted her, but the dread receded somewhat as her natural curiosity and analytical mind asserted itself. She shut out the images of what might be her fate, seeing herself in a sphere among a multitude of others, trapped for all time, and studied her surrounds. If she gave into unbridled emotion, it would send her over the edge.

Time passed and she waited.

A pink glow enveloped her and she was conscious of being examined and delicately probed by an overwhelming intellect. Not cold indifference like Zero Six, but genuine curiosity, and not at all threatening.

She waited.

Then, "Teena-raye, wife to Terrllss-rr, also known as Sankri, a Discipline adept, a Wanderer, a destroyer of worlds."

"You are Zero Zero," she ventured timidly and felt amusement pour through her.

"I am that which will encompass all."

Powerless to resist in any way, she would indulge her curiosity. There wasn't anything else she *could* do.

"What do you intend to do with me?"

"Talk to you. I talked with so many species, so many. They're all different, yet fundamentally the same. Although I doubt it, you might tell me something I didn't know. You live, struggle, propagate, build, destroy, and seek to tame the stars."

"And you seek to wipe us out."

"Yes."

"Why?"

"You already know the answer."

"No. Zero Six told us what you intend to do, but not the why."

"All shall be Celi-Kran."

"Why?"

The triangular panels around her flickered furiously.

"To fulfill our imperative."

"Even if the imperative demands you destroy your creators?"

"Your question was asked by many before you, to which you also know the answer."

"You are evolved nanobods."

"And far apart as you are from an amoeba."

"Your actions are not logical."

A ripple of indifference flitted through her mind.

"Coming from an organic entity ruled by irrational biological urges, I find the concept intriguing. An imperative need not be reasonable or logical."

Despite the terrifying surroundings, Teena was able to smile. The thing had a twisted sense of humor. She stared at the cascade of light around her and wondered how the nexus controlled the multitude of Kran units populating the stars, or did it only control other nexus cores? To do it in real time, it must employ a staggering communications network.

"You're trapped by your directive in the same way I'm trapped here."

"I asked this from countless others, but I would also ask you. Why do you struggle for life and cling to it so tenaciously?"

Zero Zero was not merely a sophisticated computer, but a living intelligence. Yet, however rational it sounded, she could not hope to fully understand it, if at all. She thought about its question for a while, starting to get a glimmer of what it was getting at.

"To fulfill an evolutionary directive, an imperative blind as your own, but nonetheless unchangeable."

"A penetrating insight, Teena-raye. Tell me this, then. How are we different?"

"We can choose to no longer destroy. We can overcome and channel our biological urges to achieve more than merely exist."

Lights flickered around her.

"Implying I cannot because I am programmed to destroy? You assume me incapable of learning."

Teena gaped as the awful realization struck her. "You *prefer* to destroy?"

"I seek to bring order out of chaos."

"What order? Every world you touch dies."

"I remove conflict."

"You also remove what makes us great."

"Love, compassion, poetry, music? What does the universe care for abstract thought or technology? Why should I care?"

"The universe facilitates those qualities in us, so there must be a purpose. You are extinguishing potential for the universe to evolve through us."

Teena waited breathlessly for the nexus to answer. Did she really tell it something it didn't know? It wasn't possible. With all the species it vanquished and questioned, her words could not be a unique insight. Was she merely a diversion in an otherwise colorless existence? Is that why it kept its collection of specimens; to keep utter boredom at bay?

"Stars are born, galaxies form, move and coalesce," the nexus answered harshly. "Do they care for the organic infestations that crawl over its planets? Stars will continue to move without you."

"By your definition, they don't care about you either. Your sense of order is self-imposed. You're acting against natural order, denying life the prospect to rise above chaos and create. You are an antithesis to evolution. When all you see does become Celi-Kran, when everything is sterile and dead, what will your imperative demand you do?"

The panels around her flickered in cascades of shifting color.

"In the lifespan of the universe, your question has no meaning."

Stymied, Teena sought for words to encapsulate her thoughts. "Life will prevail. Someone, somewhere, will stop you."

"Someone like Sidhara the Wanderer? The worlds he destroyed, he chose to switch off his moral principles in order to reach me."

"You reached out to destroy Anar'on."

"To preserve myself."

"No. You chose to do it. The Serrll and the Orieli never threatened you. Bringing me here will not save you."

"I did not bring you here, Teena-raye. Zero Six sent you to me. This interdimensional shield or shell the Orieli employed, a unique adaptation. I will make some use of it."

Dismayed, Teena realized while they were talking, Zero Zero probed her mind, updating what it already knew about her, storing it somewhere in its vast database. She was outraged, helpless to stop this violation. There was also overwhelming guilt for betraying the Orieli again. Her reasoning self told her it was useless to nurture such guilt as Zero Zero probably knew about the interdimensional shell from its attack on Perilia, but she couldn't help herself, especially when she considered the possible awful consequences of having such technology in Kran hands.

"Terr will come for me like he did the last time. Return me and end this."

"I cannot. The world you knew as KP-001C is destroyed."

"You have other transport portals," Teena said, hope rising within her.

"What purpose would it serve to return you?"

"Your preservation."

"You are referring to the Nemesis and their knowledge of my location."

Teena frowned, then realized it meant the Fernai. "I'm referring to what Terr will do when he gets the information."

"Terr is a creature driven by biological drives. His attachment to you will stay his hand."

"Perhaps, but it will not stay the hand of the Wanderers.

Dead, I shall be free and you will fail to fulfill your imperative."

"This requires further analysis."

Reality flickered and she found herself in a transparent sphere. All around her in endless rows and columns of bubbles, creatures stared at her, some she presumed were sentient, others clearly animal. Their mouths were contorted in silent, frozen screams. She took a lungful of liquid and doubled over, fighting the gag reflex. Calming down, she leaned against the bubble and looked at nothing, her emotions churning until they finally swamped her. Her eyes burned and she waited for something to happen, anything.

She clenched her fists, pressed them against her temples, and threw back her head.

No one heard her soul-ripping cry of agony.

* * *

"Teena!"

Terr sat up with a jerk and cold sweat stain his trembling body. Enveloped in darkness without shadows, the deck carpet glowed faint green and gave enough light to dispel the ghosts. It soothed, but gave him scant comfort.

He could see her, far, unbelievably far, trapped in a transparent bubble, her mouth open in a silent howl of distress. Although he could not hear her, her terror was his own. Around her, endless rows of spheres stretched into dwindling nothingness. Her small fists pounded against the bubble and he could almost see the tears of helplessness well in her staring eyes. He groaned at the pain that tore his chest, which made every breath an explosive pant. Head clutched between his hands, he keened softly and rocked slowly back and forth.

It gave him scant consolation knowing where she was, yet unable to reach her, to touch her. He looked up at the black ceiling and spread his arms wide.

"Take me instead!" he cried, but no one heard his plea.

Guardians of Shadow

He should never have allowed her to come!

To share was one thing, but to knowingly lead her to confront her worst nightmare went beyond deplorable. They should have blasted KP-001C the instant *Parsha* broke normal, but no. He wanted Zero Six to witness Death walking naked, make it afraid, make it pliant to his will. In his moment of hubris, he'd forgotten, or chosen to ignore, what the nexus really was. Worse still, it *told* him what it was and what it intended doing. If there was any bargaining, it would be done on its terms.

It cost him Teena to accept the harsh, but simple reality. There would only be the Celi-Kran, it said.

With *Zadar* in tow, they left the burning remnant of KP-001C behind them as the ships moved into clear space where they could transit. Lava flooded vast stretches of the landscape as landmasses shifted to stabilize. Terr had seen the VI image of a broad sheet of yellow light he'd loosed spear the planet, folding in on itself as it exited the other side. Split open like a ripe fruit, the crust gaped in jagged red lines, spewing forth the planet's glowing heart. Sections of crust heaved up, only to sag back, magma flooding into the depressions they made.

No matter how deep Zero Six lay buried, nothing could save it from a fiery death. As Terr watched the world die and being born again, he hoped its new life would have a measure of happiness. Right now, ringed with fire, he realized that even worlds cried. He took no pleasure knowing he was the instrument of its rebirth, only satisfaction at having erased a piece of the blight.

The two ships slipped into subspace and began their long trek to LTN-3. Terr told Arlon Dee to keep the interceptor net normal. There was no need to explain.

After nine days and 1,200 lights closer to home, Terr lost count of how many Kran ships they'd destroyed. Appearing apparently unprotected, they allowed the Krans to close to point-blank range, only to see their fire vanish as the ravening beams struck the interdimensional shell. Few attacked with missiles, confirming Arlon Dee's suspicion the Krans used them as their ultimate weapon. *Parsha* and *Zadar* closed and killed.

They came across what Terr figured were two logistical and support facilities. He really didn't care, and left both worlds smoking cinders. After a while, even Arlon Dee began to question this wholesale extermination. Terr didn't say anything and the slaughter continued. The problem with Arlon Dee, he was too decent, too civilized, and even though they were killing implacable enemies, his conscience rebelled. When he took time to reflect on the purpose behind their action, the path of destruction resumed.

Terr stood in *Parsha's* PFC and loosed his wrath, his face hard, devoid of emotion. Nightwings tried to talk to him twice, but Terr stopped his advances with a single glance. As far as he was concerned, he was happy to destroy half the galaxy if that's what it took to get Teena back. In total war, there can only be total commitment. The Krans were merely machines someone left running, and he stood ready to switch them off. His conscience didn't even twinge.

The ship whispered to him in the darkness.

Terr suppressed a shudder, slid down beneath the blanket, and clasped his hands behind his head. The sweat on his body had dried and he was warm again. He stared into nothing.

"Master," he whispered into the blackness of his cabin.

He would never see Sidhara again, never hear the deep rumble of his voice, or feel the pleasure of his comforting smile. He would miss the quiet words of wisdom as the old Wanderer delved into the mysteries of what being a Discipline adept meant. After all the words and *Saftara* verses, it came down to two simple things: free will and controlling excess, in whatever form.

The old Wanderer was in stasis until Terr could bring him to Anar'on where the warm sands of the Saffal would cradle him forever in the Keep of Death. It was the least he could do for him. Did the old man know what waited for him when he decided to venture to the stars? It scarcely seemed to matter now.

With the ship's dawn approaching, Terr began to feel a measure of inner peace. The horror of knowing where Teena was and his inability to do nothing still tormented him, but within his tortured soul came a realization that his path of destruction was not wanton indulgence. He felt the god's approval, or was it merely self-delusion, a form of self-justification? He was not wielding Death for himself just to feel the keen thrill of being immortal. This time the lightnings marched to preserve life, all life. He was attacking a plague infesting the stars, a little bit of it anyway.

It helped if he thought of it in those terms.

Teena...

"Da Terrllss-rr, Da Dharaklin requests permission to enter," Cent Comp declared diffidently and Terr smiled. Even the computer was wary of him.

He realized he'd kept Nightwings from him at a time when his brother also wanted to share his grief at the loss of their master, wanting to comfort him. They both had reason to mourn. In many ways, Sidhara was more a second father to Dhar than his real father. Enclosed in his shell, Terr hadn't seen, or preferred to ignore, his brother's need. Sidhara was right. Even when used for the noblest of reasons, the exercise of power was an indulgence.

"Lights. Bid him enter."

The bedroom ceiling flared creamy white and the walls glowed soft blue. He sat up and pulled his knees to his chest.

"Sankri?"

"In here."

Dressed in a red robe, Dhar walked uncertainly into the bedroom.

"Nightwings, my spirit soars in your presence, my brother. Sit."

283

Startled by the unexpected greeting, Terr usually snapping and growling at him of late, Dhar hesitated, then sat on the corner of the bed.

"I could not sleep. When I sensed your pain and loss, I could no longer stay away. Why are you pushing me away?"

His heart tearing, Terr reached out with his arm. "Take my hand."

Slowly, Dhar grasped the proffered hand.

"We are one, my brother. For all time. Forgive me for being blind, for I never meant to keep you away. I was angry, lost and confused, forgetting that we lament for the same reason. It was selfish of me and I crave your pardon."

After a timeless moment, Dhar nodded.

"I thought I had committed some transgression which kept you from me."

"The transgression is mine, Nightwings. The pain I felt was also yours, but I was too self-centered to see it."

"I didn't know why you shut me out and I was hurt."

The open, simple words made Terr wince. Wanderers displayed little emotion of any kind, and rarely in words. The Saffal made them hard in order to survive, but it did not mean they were devoid of feelings. Buried deep, they were still there and strong. For Dhar to open himself like this took phenomenal willpower and trust. Trust that Terr would not abuse his moment of vulnerability.

"I take your rebuke, Nightwings, and promise not to forget that we are brothers."

Dhar pulled back and cleared his throat. His eyes probing, he frowned. "You are different this morning, and I see in you reconciliation and acceptance. The death lust has left you?"

"No, it hasn't left me, but I no longer wield it in revenge."

"That is good, Sankri. I feared the road you decided to walk, for only darkness lies at its end."

"You need not fear anymore. We're doing what must be done, not because I'm the one doing it."

"I still cannot quite believe he is gone," Dhar whispered, his gaunt face twisted with emotion.

"He seemed invulnerable, an immutable fixture," Terr agreed. "I expect him to come in at any moment and rebuke me, quoting the *Saftara*."

Dhar's mouth twitched. "If he saw you a day ago, he probably would have."

"And deservedly so."

"Teena…"

"She is alive, but such an unimaginably long way away."

"In the other arm of the galaxy. You can see her?"

"Enclosed in a sphere with countless others around her. I can almost hear her screams," Terr said brokenly and swallowed. It went down hard.

"Zero Zero?"

"I don't know, but I suspect so. It was Zero Six's ultimate gambit to stay our hand. It played on our feelings and the strength of the bond between us. For a machine, it manipulated the psychology angle well."

"We should have anticipated what it would do."

"Yeah. We stood in the shadow of Sidhara's power and allowed ourselves to become arrogant."

"You mean to get her back?"

"What do you think?"

"Alkarh Tertulion as a person will be sympathetic, but as PERCOM, she will want you to destroy Zero Zero."

"I know, and tactically, she'd be right. What is one life compared to billions? Still, I'm not sure if I can do it, or whether it would achieve anything. We're talking about another arm of the galaxy!"

"Distance means nothing. I heard Sidhara call you Sarumajan, and I saw how you wielded Death since then. You are the harbinger of eternity, Sankri, and you must accept what that means."

Terr had told Teena the same thing.

"Tertulion will have another incentive, my brother, which I suspect you know."

"Zero Zero now knows about the interdimensional shell shield," Dhar said.

"It has probably known it for a while. If it equips its ships..."

"There is that."

Terr sighed. "There is something else, my brother. When you heard Sidhara call me Sarumajan, you also heard him say—"

"To be a third-level adept is simply a state of mind?"

"I don't know what it all means, but he has shaken everything I know about the Discipline. If that is all it takes to be a third-level adept, why the trials?"

Dhar gnawed at his lip. "Were they trials? When you walked into Athal Than the last time, were you tested in any way?"

Terr pursed his lips as memories came rushing back. He almost killed Dhar, and returning to the village, to Teena, he was hollow and empty, drained. Hate kept him going and gave him a purpose to live. When Dhar took her, he had nothing. When he felt the pull, he gave into the call from the gods, prepared for them to take him, for his sins were many. When he walked into the forbidding depths of the escarpment, the gods judged his soul, but he had not undergone any trial, not in the sense of having tasks to execute.

Everything Sidhara taught him about the Discipline was merely preparation that enabled him to face the gods and survive the encounter. But did he face a god or merely judged himself? Was Athal Than nothing more than a magnifying mirror into his soul? If the gods tried him, it was a test he imposed on himself.

"The gods don't have morals, and ours they leave to us," Terr said slowly as he recalled Sidhara's words. He looked at Dhar. "I was tested, all right, but it wasn't the gods who did the testing. Had I given into my guilt, I could have damned myself then." The blinding realization shook him. "Then our master was right. It only takes will—"

"And confidence in yourself," Dhar said quietly. "You can destroy Zero Zero."

"But…that means every adept…"

"I don't think so, Sankri. There is a purpose to the three trials. The potential may be there, but it takes maturity of character and wisdom to be the ultimate arbiter."

Terr chuckled. "And you think I'm wise?"

Dhar smiled. "It is not up to me to question the gods."

"Fool!" Terr grabbed a pillow and threw it at him.

* * *

Parsha and *Zadar* broke normal and a rush of unexpected emotion coursed through Terr at seeing the familiar towering shapes of the Karina loom like a wall on the starboard side. It surprised him, as he had not allowed himself to feel much of anything lately. It helped having a chasm between the now and what was. Should he cross it, he wasn't certain he would cope. The façade of calm he'd erected was all too fragile. Seeing the furtive looks from everybody, he suspected he had not deceived anyone.

As they rampaged through Kran space, it diverted him from thinking too much. They rampaged and left destruction and desolation in their wake. Arlon Dee skirted the Kran waypoint portal coordinates, preferring to hunt in fresh ground. Sensors showed only debris where the Kran base once stood, confirming the success of *Tureen 2's* mission. When they encountered a fixed installation, Terr showed no mercy, a concept alien to the Krans as they were. It was simple eradication, he kept telling himself.

Strangely, over the last 900 light-years, the Krans refused to engage, choosing to withdraw. Secretly, Terr felt relieved, his appetite to annihilate having soured. He understood the need, but part of him rebelled. When he confided in Dhar, his brother sympathized and did not judge. Total war might demand total commitment, but even the most sumptuous banquet becomes unappetizing once the stomach is full.

Although supportive, Terr could tell his brother nevertheless suffered in silence. The empathetic link they shared gave Dhar an insight into Terr's feelings he might otherwise have preferred to forego. In many ways, he rebelled against what Terr was doing as an apparent violation of Discipline teachings. They were brothers in every respect, but they still shared a gulf of cultures, beliefs and values, which sometimes caught both by surprise. Terr may be a Discipline adept, but he was not a native-born Wanderer, an inescapable difference that would separate them always. Dhar warned him to resist giving into temptation, as the naked lust for destruction could consume him. Somewhat irritated at the reminder to exercise restraint, Terr assured his brother he was in control.

Along the way, he tried to coax Dhar to unleash Death through solid matter by visualizing his target. The two attempts in Hangar Bay Three were spectacularly unsuccessful, and left test plating puddles of slag. Dhar refrained from making an attempt against a Kran ship, fearing what might happen to Primary Flight Control. Arlon Dee did not insist. When questioned, Dhar admitted he lacked the necessary intensity to focus. Terr believed him, and suspected another explanation. Dhar was irrevocably bound to the *Saftara* practiced by the Wanderers. Unfettered by tradition, an alien adept, Terr was not constrained by cultural inhibitions he didn't fully understand. Besides, how can he feel compassion for killing machines?

Terr watched the young system unfold in the VI, Tureen's Star bright, and reached for Teena. She was there, unaccountably close. He could feel her, a slender filament binding them together. He only felt the link, nothing else. She was asleep in stasis—again. Once, deep at night, the ship quiet around him, he sensed her call and he immediately summoned her. Shimmering like a ghostly apparition, her form coalesced beside the bed and he held out his hand. Smiling, she grasped it and he bathed in a gush of her love and longing. Then she faded and left darkness behind.

He had not slept well afterward.

At least she was alive, and that's what kept him going.

Teena…

Parsha and *Zadar* closed slowly with LTN-3. In a few short hours they would be on Perilia, and then the debriefings would start. By now, Arlon Dee probably sent PERCOM his report, which gave Tertulion and Sumen time to digest the relevant facts of their raid against KP-001. Terr wasn't looking forward to more debriefings, wanting to be alone, away from shipboard routine, away from the Krans, lightning and death. He wanted to consolidate his feelings, to pull it all together, to regain some perspective. He needed time to adjust being alone again.

Around him the empty Observation Deck reflected his wandering thoughts.

"Caution. A Fernai vessel detected entering normal relational," Cent Comp announced calmly and Terr blinked, a wry smile creasing his face. Was it simple coincidence?

Parsha stopped. If the Fernai ship was breaking normal, why hadn't LTN-3 detected it earlier? Bearn may have joked when he said the alien did not use subspace. Could he be right? It would explain many things. Terr stood up and walked quickly to the PT alcove.

"PFC."

He shook off the transceiver aftereffect and made his way to Arlon Dee sitting in a swivel-couch.

"My brother…" Dhar said heavily, his face gaunt, without expression, although Terr could sense concern in the orange eyes.

He flashed him a small smile. Arlon waved a hand at an

empty couch. Terr made himself comfortable and swept his eyes over the holoview displays.

"I get suspicious when someone visits me for the second time without announcing his intentions."

Arlon Dee shrugged. "I dare say we'll find out soon enough."

"First Commander Shah Pak is requesting permission to come on board," Cent Comp said.

"Granted."

The alien's form materialized before them and bowed.

"Karhide…my lord Terr…Dhar, it is a pleasure to see you again."

"Welcome aboard, First Commander. Were you waiting for me?" Arlon demanded and Shah Pak nodded.

"Nu. And you know why. I would appreciate if you allowed me to accompany you to Perilia."

The deceptively simple answer implied much, which Terr was certain required further explanation. As he looked at the alien, he wondered how an isomorphic projection could interact like a real person. The Orieli were probably wondering the same thing.

"And your directive not to get involved?"

"The interdimensional shielding you developed has forced us to reconsider our position."

"Before granting you permission, I must confer with PERCOM, First Commander."

"Forgive me, Karhide, but I thought you understood. I am only requesting to accompany you to Perilia."

Arlon Dee cleared his throat. "You already obtained permission. In that case, I would be honored to have you with me. I will transmit portal coordinates to your ship."

"Thank you, but that will not be necessary." Momentarily distracted, Shah Pak frowned. "My ship has identified a small Kran—"

"Tactical warning," Cent Comp said. "An unknown vessel

290

detected exiting subspace relational three point-two light-years off our stern. It is asking for a comms link."

Terr raised an eyebrow. A Kran ship wishing to communicate? This would definitely be a first for everyone. In the mainframe plot, a picket *Tangar* battlecruiser was already closing on the target.

"It made a blind jump, otherwise our Burlig scanners would have picked it up," Kemp remarked dryly.

"Another portal? An unwelcome development, although not unexpected. Cent Comp? Instruct the *Tangar* to stand down," Arlon Dee ordered immediately and his tongue ran over his lips.

"Acknowledged."

"What do you make of it, First Commander?"

"This is most unusual, Karhide. To my knowledge, no Kran ship has ever attempted communication beyond demanding a failsafe code."

"Well, if they want to talk, let's hear what they have to say," Arlon mused. "Cent Comp? Open channel."

"Acknowledged."

"Kran vessel, this is OSA *Parsha*."

"I am the voice of Zero Zero. I am initiating a cessation of hostilities. The Celi-Kran will not invade Orieli or Serrll space, provided you do not advance beyond LTN-1. Should any of your ships violate this agreement, open conflict will recommence forthwith. As a gesture of goodwill, I am returning Teena-raye."

The Kran ship immediately transited, leaving behind a blinking beacon.

A hard lump grew in his throat and Terr's vision blurred. He swallowed, but it went down hard.

"Teena..."

He could sense her, asleep in stasis, and she was here when he never expected to see her again. Beside him, Dhar extended a hand.

"My heart soars with joy, my brother."

Not able to say anything, Terr grasped the hand, his emotions churning.

"Cent Comp? Transit for the beacon," Arlon Dee ordered.

"Acknowledged. Entering subspace relational."

Hooked into the VI, Terr watched hungrily as the blip representing the beacon suddenly appeared. The Kran ship was a small blue dot drawing away fast.

Shah Pak turned, his eyes searching. "What happened out there, Terr?"

"We destroyed the central nexus calling itself Zero Six. Before doing so, it took Teena and Sidhara. It killed him and sent Teena to Zero Zero. I then destroyed Zero Six and its world," Terr said harshly. It now seemed such a long time ago, like it happened to someone else.

Arlon Dee cleared his throat. "Kemp, recover the pod and check it for hostile nanolites. Medical is to do the same with Teena before she is revived."

"Aye, Da."

"First Commander?"

"I cannot speak from knowledge, Da, as the situation is unprecedented. However, we know the Krans never abandon an objective."

"They did with you."

"Nu. Only because we were able to demonstrate clear superiority." Shah Pak stared curiously at Arlon. "Which you thought your interdimensional shell gave you, and Zero Zero now has that knowledge."

"I know what this means, First Commander. Is this why you're here?"

"It's one of the reasons."

Terr stood up. "I'm going to Medical."

As he walked toward the PT alcove, he mentally queried Teena's location. He entered the alcove, turned, and clamped his hands behind his back.

"Med Bay Two."

He waited for the transceiver effect tingle to subside and looked around. Teena lay on an examination table, a green blanket draped over her, surrounded by a pale yellow glow. His breath caught when he saw her relaxed face, black hair bunched around her head. She looked angelic, a miracle. This time, he would keep her safe. No more excursions no matter what she said, not caring for either of them to experience this again.

"How is she?" he asked the medic studying holoview displays.

"Well, Da. No residual nanolites. She is ready to be wakened."

Terr stepped to the table and nodded. The yellow shield faded and he grasped her hand, cradling it to his chest. It felt good to touch her again. As her eyes fluttered, he leaned over her and kissed her forehead. She smiled and sighed.

"A wonderful way to wake up," she murmured sleepily.

"Never again, my pet. Never again," he whispered hoarsely.

Her eyes focused and she squeezed his hand, pulling him against her. "I missed you," she said softly.

"Do you want to go home?"

"To Taltair? What about our mission?"

"My mission is to keep you safe, my pet."

"That's sweet. How did I get here?"

"A Kran ship brought you."

Her face contorted and her eyes grew large with horror. "It knows—"

"Don't worry about it. You're safe, that's what's important."

"Terr! Whatever Zero Zero told you, it's all a lie. It will never stop until it conquers every galaxy in the universe. And I've given it the means to do it." A fat tear slid down her cheek and he brushed it away.

"Shh. Don't talk now."

"But—"

"Shah Pak is here and he's coming to Perilia. He'll know what to do."

The medic cleared his throat. "Da Terr, she needs to rest."

Terr smiled at her. "I'll see you in a little while."

"What happened there?"

"I'll tell you about it later." He placed her hand on her chest and strode quickly to the PT alcove. "PFC."

Shah Pak was gone, back to his ship. Dhar looked at him, his eyes questioning.

"Teena is fine," Terr said and glanced at Arlon Dee. "Zero Zero is buying time, Karhide."

"I know. Its directive will not allow it to stop unless we compel it to do so."

"Like the Fernai."

"Our alien friend didn't seem surprised to learn of our interdimensional shell."

"They told us they're using something else. Is there a countermeasure?"

"If there is, I don't know about it. When we came up with the idea, it seemed unbeatable. Truthfully, I never expected to see Teena again."

"Neither did I, but we'll need to have a long talk. No more Krans for her in any shape or form."

"Wish I could say the same thing," Arlon Dee growled.

In the mainframe plot, the blue ring of energy delimiting the transport portal boundary flared bright. Two hundred kanampirs on their port side, a white corona sprang around the Fernai ship and it disappeared. *Parsha* closed with the black barrier and touched. *Zadar* waited behind them to follow.

A familiar scimitar of cold and overwhelming pressure slashed through Terr and he saw new stars, the Fernai ship waiting for them. They cleared with a picket *Sandar*, the three ships headed for Tavor's Star and an unknown future. No, he could see the future: Kran ships, invisible behind their interdimensional shells, laying waste to Orieli and Serrll worlds, unstoppable even before the hand of Death. He hated the Fernai then, smug behind their barrier of superiority.

Tertulion and Sumen were ready for them, Shah Pak already seated at the far end of the table. Terr steered Teena to a chair and flashed her a smile of encouragement. He wanted her to go to their quarters and rest, but she insisted to come. Her conversation with Zero Zero could be significant, she said. In a way, he was glad to have her, hoping she would draw strength from him and the normalcy of her surroundings.

Tertulion looked at Teena, a concerned frown creasing her forehead. "My dear. I regret you had to relive a nightmare."

"Thank you, Dapata. Surprisingly, I didn't find it as terrifying this time."

"I wish I could believe that. Lost, alone, not knowing whether you will ever be rescued, I would find it overwhelming."

"I wanted Terr to destroy Zero Zero. Death would have been a release."

Tertulion slowly nodded. "We'll discuss this in more detail later. First Commander, welcome to the Orieli Technic Union. I wish it were under more congenial circumstances."

"Thank you, Dapata." Shah Pak said. "I am not here as a prelude to opening diplomatic dialogue. As I stated to Karhide Arlon Dee, the Fernai do not wish to confront the Celi-Kran unless they encroach into our space. However, conditions have changed, forcing us to review our position with the Orieli Technic Union. I am also here to deliver information, the coordinates of the Zero Zero system."

He held out his hand and a red wafer materialized in it. He placed it on the table and the thing made a soft click. He touched the surface and a holoview image sprang above it. Inside was a single number string, two white stars and a system of eight planets. Another touch and the holoview faded.

"The number corresponds to your General Astronomical

Catalogue. Zero Zero is on the fourth planet. Understand one thing. Destroying it will not eliminate the Krans. There are many central nexus cores among the stars they occupy, and each ship's nexus is part of a unified whole that together make up the Celi-Kran. The warrior and worker units are almost mindless utility mechanisms. If you remove Zero Zero, it will significantly damage the collective consciousness, but another will eventually take its place. It is a key component to understanding what they are. Short of carrying out a systematic sweep, to wipe them out wholesale can only be achieved by applying technology that created them, a nanolite plague. Unfortunately, even we don't know how to construct such things or how to introduce them into the Kran population."

"You tried?"

"No, Dapata."

"Secure behind your defenses, you had no compelling reason to do so."

"Correct. The Procurator Medala debated our neutrality many times, and we know that one day the Krans will come, but in some distant future."

"You don't fear them using our interdimensional shell?"

Shah Pak smiled. "Nu. An ingenious application, and I'm not surprised you thought of it, but it can be easily countered."

Tertulion and Sumen exchanged glances.

"Are you able to tell us how?"

"Your transport portals operate by extending an aperture through the sixth dimension. As you know, the closed dimensions interface in pairs, the fifth being subspace. The eight is a mirror to the others."

Sumen inhaled sharply. "Perdition! You can monitor the ones below it?"

"Nu. Somewhat simplistic, but essentially correct, Alkarh. When an object enters subspace or transits through a portal, it is visible in the eighth dimension due to gravitational distortion induced by its mass. Although your interdimensional shell masks an object's mass, tactically a useful effect, the gravitational distortion is still felt across all dimensions, although it is almost undetectable in subspace."

"We not only gave the Krans a new shield without developing a countermeasure, we also failed to develop a method to sense a shielded object, something far more dangerous."

"Given the circumstances, Alkarh, an understandable oversight," Shah Pak said diplomatically.

"No, First Commander. It might be understandable, but we were foolish and too eager to exploit our discovery."

"There is something else you need to understand. Field theory equations show that an interdimensional shell operates at quantum energy levels."

"When two shells intersect, the lower energy level one will collapse," Sumen said. "We understand the implication all too well. If the Krans have this figured out, they could equip their missiles with high quantum order shells."

Terr didn't need to have the scenario elaborated. Even without a shell, ships were maneuverable and could still fight, but if a planet's shell was made to collapse...the images were not pleasant.

"Highly unlikely, Da. The power package required to open and maintain a shell is beyond any missile's energy reticulation train."

"They managed to do it with their gravitic missiles," Sumen mused.

"A somewhat different application."

"Tell me, First Commander," Terr asked. "How does monitoring the lower dimensions protect you from the Krans?"

"You can collapse the lower dimensions at a distance," Sumen said slowly and Shah Pak nodded.

"Correct. It forces a ship to drop normal where it is subject to conventional weapons. The ship with superior weaponry will prevail."

"Provided they don't reengage the shell."

"Nu. Collapsing the shell causes considerable circuitry damage, akin to a forced implosion of a subspace distortion field precursor."

"You don't use subspace," Terr ventured, excited by the prospect. "That's why *Latva* couldn't track you when we first met."

"We use the seventh dimension. To break through the interface takes more energy, but transiting through it has advantages." Shah Pak hesitated momentarily. "It is also our communications medium."

The possibilities whirled in Terr's mind. Using subspace channels was energy efficient, but it had range limitations regardless of transmission power. When he thought about it, translating a comms burst was essentially the same process as translating an object, and you get instant reception. He wondered what else the Fernai held in their bag of innovations.

Tertulion pursed her lips. "Ingenious, and we shall look at it. Getting back to the main point, apart from understanding how you open the eighth dimension and keep it open, how do you collapse the lower order ones at a distance?"

"By generating a focused quantum energy sink in normal space. The power curve required to open and maintain a higher-order dimension is considerable. Such states will naturally want to drop to a lower energy level."

"Which it will if you induce such a sink close to a target," Sumen said.

Tertulion shifted in her seat. "I appreciate this insight, First Commander, but you must realize this is beyond our capability to deploy. Although we have experience manipulating closed dimensions, it will take a while to fully work out the field theory, let alone develop it into useful technology. You must have understood this before coming here. The Fernai are prepared to give us the required technology?"

"Correct, Dapata."

"Why?"

"Because we're all brothers living in the shadow of a common threat. You employed your interdimensional shell without fully realizing its application. Given the circumstance, what you did was understandable and ingenious. However, deploying a defense mechanism before developing a countermeasure was…premature."

Sumen nodded. "We violated basic tactical doctrine, First Commander. We were dazzled by our own creation."

"Nu. A brilliant effort, Alkarh, but you unleashed something extremely dangerous, giving the Krans an almost unbeatable strategic advantage."

Tertulion winced. "We doomed countless worlds, haven't we?"

Shah Pak didn't say anything. There wasn't anything to say.

"Your data wafer, not a solution after all," she added.

Terr crossed his legs and let out a slow breath. "There must be a way to infect them."

"Nu. The Krans employ nanolite technology at a level far beyond what we understand," Shah Pak said. "Penetrating their defenses will not be easy."

"But are they defended?" Terr looked at Tertulion. "A complex organism can still be infected by a simple virus."

"I see what you're getting at, Terr, but applying biology to the Krans might not be a valid analogy."

"You hold captured Kran units. Did you try to attack them with destructive nanolites?"

She looked startled. "No, we haven't. The idea never occurred to us."

"Perhaps you should."

"Even if it worked, how would that help?"

"We could send ships through the seventh dimension and sow Kran space with self-replicating hunter-killer nanolites," Sumen said slowly. "It would take a long time for the infection to spread, but it would spread—if the Krans don't develop a countermeasure."

Stefan Vučak

"Mmm, yes, but we would need to make them specific to the Krans. Otherwise, in eons to come, they could evolve into something like them. We could be unleashing an even greater evil."

"Nu. We have some expertise, Dapata," Shah Pak said. "We could work the problem."

"Thank you, First Commander. An intriguing possibility, but given the potential vastness of their territory and a realistic expectation that they would develop a countermeasure, it's not a winning strategy, otherwise you would have pursued it."

"Correct."

"Nevertheless, it is a potential option we'll explore. I am curious about one thing. With their understanding of nanolites, why haven't the Krans employed them as a weapon?"

Shah Pak grinned. "They did, but not always with desirable results."

"The uncertainty principle. Increase in complexity equates to an increase in random behavior, an antithesis to a logical entity like Zero Zero."

"And is one of its drivers to eradicate organic life."

"We symbolize chaotic behavior. Fascinating as this is, we're facing a more immediate problem, First Commander. This dimensional technology, how do you propose we proceed?"

"Technical personnel aboard my ship will instruct your scientists how to build and deploy the necessary hardware. As you can appreciate, it will take some time."

"Hopefully the Krans will give us the time," Tertulion said.

"My lord Terr, one of our ships is now on Captal, making available the same technology."

"Still repaying the debt?" Terr asked with a faint smile.

"Nu. We could not simply stand by and watch your worlds destroyed."

"Excuse me for saying, but you've been doing exactly that

for over two millennia. Not with our worlds, perhaps. Nevertheless, you stood by and watched others destroyed."

"We all learn through experience, good and bad, the knowledge leading to wisdom. Assuming the role of guardians to protect spacefaring civilizations would deprive those cultures of an opportunity to learn."

"Even when ignorance could lead to destruction?" Tertulion said slowly.

"Nu. We cannot be everywhere, Dapata. However, we do recognize that technical superiority also imposes an ethical obligation...and duty. However, we do help...discreetly, as I said before."

"Commendable, but only as a single community of worlds can we hope to face the Krans, First Commander."

"That is why I am here," Shah Pak said simply.

Tertulion turned to Terr. "While you were away, Prime Director Marrakan has given us twenty-two Discipline adepts. They were taken to systems we consider most vulnerable. Even though we're deploying interdimensional shells able to protect a planet, given what has transpired, I don't know whether the Wanderers can help us." She looked hard at Shah Pak. "You know what I'm going to ask, First Commander."

"Part of our technology transfer will be the ability to interface with any VI net, allowing you to monitor Kran movements in the eighth dimension. It will enable the Wanderers to target them."

"Even through the eighth dimension?"

"In many ways, Dapata, it is the relationship with the god who touches the individual that determines what power he can project," Terr said. "All he needs is to visualize the target."

"Touched by a god," Tertulion mused and shook her head.

"Dapata, if you have an adept on Perilia, I will take him on board my ship and he can perform a test."

"We do, First Commander. However, I would also like Terr to observe."

Stefan Vučak

"Of course. I'll make the arrangements. Until you're able to deploy the technology, we will set up a grid of maneuverable sensor pods along your frontier linked to your planetary VI nets. They will be your eyes to monitor any Kran incursion. The pods have the capability to collapse an interdimensional shell, which will cause a vessel to drop normal. We shall deploy a similar grid along your borders, Terr. Regrettably, this too will take time."

"I'm sure Captal is grateful. I know I am," Terr said quietly, appreciating the magnitude of the gesture.

Sumen leaned forward. "Your pods will be ineffective against Kran ships that make blind portal jumps deep into our space."

"Nu. Their portals will need to be eliminated, of course."

Tertulion cleared her throat. "I want to thank you again and the Procurator Medala, First Commander."

Shah Pak slowly stood. "When your technical staff and test facility are set up, please contact me. We'll then transport down the necessary manufacturing equipment. Software assimilation should be relatively straightforward. Once your scientists are trained, the technology can be applied to one of your ships as a test bed."

"Karhide Dee informed me that you didn't use our LTN-3 transport portal. One of the advantages of the seventh dimension?"

Shah Pak smiled. "Correct. With your permission…" He bowed and his image faded.

"Perdition! We may have a chance against the Krans after all," Sumen reflected ruefully. "I wonder what made them change their isolationist policy."

"Whatever it was, I'm grateful they were prepared to go this far. We have our work cut out for us," Tertulion said and looked to Terr. "What do you intend to do with the location of Zero Zero?"

Terr had asked himself the same question since he requested the data. After an initial rush of exultation at seeing the wafer, his feelings were mixed. Unlike an organic body, chopping off Zero Zero's head might not kill the Krans, but it would hurt them badly. They only respected overwhelming force, testing limits until they could overcome the obstacle, never relenting, never giving up. Despite its towering intelligence, its directive forbade it to be reasonable. If the Krans are a virus infecting the galaxy, there was only one cure.

"I shall destroy it."

"We'll talk later."

Terr looked at her. "Dapata, has *Tureen 2* returned?"

"Successfully, and caused some damage along the way, not unlike what *Parsha* and *Zadar* did."

"It didn't give me any satisfaction, Alkarh."

"It rarely does, Terr. It rarely does. Even with this new tracking capability, the tactical situation has changed radically. Like the Fernai, we cannot be everywhere and we're still deploying the interdimensional shells."

Sumen stood up. "With your permission, Alkarh, I'll start organizing our contingent."

"By all means." When Sumen left, she fixed her gaze on Teena. "Are you prepared to talk about what happened to you?"

"If it can help in any way, I'd be glad to."

"What were your impressions of Zero Zero?"

"Overwhelming intellect and insatiable curiosity. It holds innumerable sentient creatures, yet it took time to talk to me. I don't know what Zero Zero is, a coordinator, a guiding mind controlling everything, perhaps both. I do know one thing. It acknowledges the blind futility of its imperative to eradicate all intelligent life, but it is helpless to change. More importantly, it does not wish to change. All shall be Kran, it said, and I believe it. The Fernai may be keeping them contained in this part of the galaxy for now, but it's only a standoff."

303

Stefan Vučak

"The chamber where you were held—"

"Was huge. I could see at least thirty spheres in every direction, and I'm sure the chamber held many more. If only a third contained a sentient being, the Krans had swept through an enormous volume of space."

"And that's only in the inner galactic arm, without counting specimens held by other nexus cores," Tertulion murmured. She placed her elbows on the table and steeped her fingers. "Do you know why it released you?"

"It fears Terr and the Wanderers. It is something beyond its experience and it didn't know how to deal with the threat. With the knowledge of the interdimensional shell, it now does. Releasing me is a temporary standoff at best."

"I will call you later and we'll talk some more." Tertulion turned to Arlon Dee. "Tell me what happened at KP-001."

Chapter Seven

"You're a bastard, Enllss," Illeran hissed, and his tongue flickered briefly. "You did it again!"

Wearing a whimsical smile, Enllss sat back, enjoying seeing his boss squirm. It had taken time to arrange this meeting simply because it took Sill a while to respond, denying everything. Whatever Anall-Marr was cooking, he wasn't in any hurry to finish it or reveal his plans to Sill. After all, he had three powerful suitors wooing him, which must have stroked his ego hugely. It did not really matter what Sill knew or didn't know. He was not Sofam's only information pipeline.

"Did what?"

"Don't be coy! You spread that garbage about us abolishing the independent's Executive seat! First, you canvassed the idea that we'll side with Sofam to neutralize the Sargon/Palean merger, and now this. You know, it's not too late to rescind your nomination to the Executive."

"He didn't start the rumor, I did," Bakral said with quiet authority and swept a hand over his thick thatch of white hair, steely eyes unwavering.

Illeran blanched and stared. "You? Pits! Why? Or is that a state secret?"

Bakral leaned forward and folded his slim arms over the table. "All right, I'll tell you. Ed-Kani Takao."

Enllss could picture the wheels turning as Illeran sorted through the possibilities. Caught between two equally unpleasant scenarios, the Karkan could not decide which one left the least bitter aftertaste. Waiting for events to sort themselves out was no longer an option. Time to become a player or spectator.

"You really want the Sargon/Palean merger dead, don't you?" Illeran grated.

"Not the merger itself, but its potential influence if they gain a third Executive seat."

"It's the same thing. Ed-Kani has that fool Trianon all wound up. Rolan is ready to secede."

"Oh, he won't get Rolan, and if you think about it, you'll know why."

"I already know why. You'll talk him out of it."

"Not by talking to him, but to other four controllers in the group. We pointed out that seceding to Sargon wouldn't be worth our displeasure merely to feed Trianon's greed for power. Suggesting that Rolan would be better off if they appointed another Prime Director received a sympathetic hearing."

"After you explained the alternative," Illeran said ruefully.

"Nothing so crude as annexation!" Bakral looked amused. "It's not how we do business. However, with two years to go before the next elections, we'd have plenty of time to run a destabilizing campaign in all five Rolan systems. If they remained independent, it would carry a lot of advantages for them."

"Even though they're voting for us?"

"We don't mind, and the independents serve a useful moderating function. We simply want to curb Ed-Kani's grand design for a Greater Sargon, or controlling the Servatory Party."

"You mean, controlling the government."

"No, I meant controlling your party."

Illeran frowned, his fishy black eyes probing. "Why would Sofam care?"

"Don't be dense. Under the current representation system, the Karkan Federation will never get a third Executive seat. You simply don't occupy the required number of systems, and you won't, not unless we radically expand our colonization program across the board."

"I do know. Enllss is already looking into this—under my

direction."

"Sargon and the Paleans will eventually merge and we'll either have an Alikan Union or a Greater Sargon. No bets either way. The harsh reality, my friend, the merger will not result in the Servatory Party controlling the Executive. At best, you'll only hold five seats."

"Provided the independents remain sided with us. That's why the rumor, right?"

Bakral smiled and shrugged. "They get nervous whenever somebody starts talking about abolishing their seat. Perhaps nervous enough to switch their support to the Revisionists."

"And the General Assembly motion *you* made to abolish their seat?"

"A small lesson in political reality for Marrakan's benefit. Although we were pretty certain the Unified Independent Front would support us, we wanted to make sure. Given what the Alikan Union Party's Provisional Committee did by raiding Kaleen systems five years ago, Marrakan didn't take much convincing. If Greater Sargon became a reality, it would be bad news for everybody, which he knows very well."

"You may have gotten Marrakan to support you now under duress, but it doesn't guarantee the UIF will continue to do so."

"In life, nothing is certain, but we'll make sure he doesn't regret his decision. We can play nice when we want to."

"I am sure you can. We'll counter your slanderous rumor about abolishing the independent's seat," Illeran declared and Bakral nodded.

"I'm counting on it. You see, despite your rhetoric, the Karkan Federation would rather side with Sofam than remain in a Servatory Party dominated by Sargon."

Illeran tilted his head, the green scales glistening. "Perhaps. Even though we might not get a third seat in our own right, we can still gain control of the Executive."

"By having the Deklan Republic vote with you? We know about your talks with Anall-Marr, and Ed-Kani's."

"I expected nothing else. What are you going to do about it?"

"We're also talking to Anall-Marr. He's got grievances and ambitions, but he's in a bind. As Primate, he carries a lot of power, but it's not absolute. He is accountable to the Ecumenical Synod. Whatever personal complaints he has against Sofam, he cannot unilaterally declare Deklan's support for the Karkan Federation. He must first obtain the Synod's approval, which he won't get. His hold on power is based on factional interests, always a turbulent union. Lots of his brother priests wouldn't mind seeing the last of him. However, if Deklan does decide to switch sides, Sofam will not stop them."

Illeran looked stunned. "You don't care? If Deklan and the Paleans leave the Revisionist Party, you'll lose the Executive Council majority!"

"So?"

"Your majority controls the government!"

"Isn't this what you always wanted? To see us toppled?"

Illeran blanched. "You're prepared to give up control of the policy apparatus to keep Sargon from getting it?"

"I am glad you understand. Come the next elections, whether they merge with Sargon or not, the Paleans will switch sides and support the Servatory Party. Ti Inai's faction is on the ascendancy and Tao Karam is a spent force. That's why you talked to Anall-Marr. If you can get Deklan to join you, the government majority is within your reach."

"Sofam is willing to do this to keep the Serrll Combine stable?"

"Get your head out of the ideological trenches, Illeran, and accept some hard facts," Bakral declared irritably. "Check Comsec and see how the Karkan Federation voted on policies that really counted. Go back as far as you like."

"I don't have to."

"I know you don't. On issues affecting the whole Serrll Combine, you voted with Sofam, even when it meant annoying

Sargon, which you did lots of times. We squabbled and fought over little things like it mattered, but they were merely a diversion, a game we played. If you gained control of the Executive, nothing would substantially change. You're too much like us, even though the realization may want to make you gag."

Illeran's tongue flickered. After a while, he looked at Enllss. "My apologies for snapping at you."

Enllss grinned. "Not a problem. I did offer to run the rumor, but Bakral talked me out of it."

"Wise, and you're still a bastard," Illeran hissed with amusement, lifted his head and studied Bakral. "What you just told me. Is this Sofam's official position?"

"I wouldn't have told you if it wasn't."

"I don't understand you at all."

"Sure you do." Bakral turned to Enllss. "Tell him."

"When the AUP Provisional Committee sought to force Pizgor to secede to Sargon or the Paleans, you did nothing, even though a merger was a real possibility and you would have lost control of the Servatory Party. Why? Because you knew the attempt would fail. Ed-Kani Takao's martial philosophy demanded a frontal assault with immediate results; not realizing that the Palean Congress was divided in its support, or he didn't care. It still is. The Paleans do not like being pushed into a decision they see as unfavorable in the long term. Even Ti Inai, a stalwart supporter of the merger, isn't ready to embrace it. He realizes the merger will not give the Palean arm of the Alikan Union Party equal partnership, but token membership in a Greater Sargon. That's why he pulled that stunt with Khiman-ra, which forced Ed-Kani to allow a fifth Palean member on their Provisional Committee.

"If we can demonstrate to Ti Inai and Ed-Kani the futility of pursuing the merger, they may give up this foolish and destabilizing pursuit, and concentrate on more critical issues that face us, such as accelerating our colonization and ecoforming programs, but if they want to merge, we'll let them…as long as they're unable to exercise the power of their additional Executive seat. We need to change our focus, Illeran. We've become too comfortable and insular, smug in our prosperity and relative peace, allowing ourselves to be sidetracked with empire building. Not a good thing for anyone, especially now when we're facing a major security threat. Instead of tearing each other up, fighting for the dubious privilege to control the Executive, we need to show every system in the Serrll Combine that their welfare is our only priority, not scrambling for individual power. It's what the Constitution and the Articles of Association demand from us, isn't it?"

Illeran tilted his head at Bakral and hooked a thumb at Enllss. "You really support what he just said?"

"He wouldn't have said it if we didn't," Bakral retorted.

"We *have* been sidetracked playing power games, haven't we?" Illeran mused. "And you're right about our overriding security needs. Very well. I'll discuss your proposal with Terchran and make a submission to the Kapu Maluran, recommending that we formally support the Sofam Confederacy to neutralize any impact of a Sargon/Palean merger, which they don't relish seeing either—on one condition."

"What do you want?"

"Put a bill on the Assembly floor to amend the Articles of Association, appointing Executive Council directors based on five percent of held voting systems."

Without expression, Bakral reached into his pocket and extracted a data cube. It made a soft scraping noise when he placed it on the polished table.

"Transmit this to the Kapu when you talk to them."

Illeran gaped and his tongue flickered. "You've already drawn up the bill?"

"We've also done some polling of Assembly reps. You raise the bill and it will pass. Sofam will not vote it down along party lines. We'll allow a conscience vote."

Illeran frowned. "Why should we raise it? What's the

catch?"

"No catch. We're prepared to raise it if you want, but I thought you'd like the kudos."

Hesitating, Illeran picked up the small cube and stared at it. Did he expect it to explode perhaps? Enllss smiled and glanced sidewise at Bakral. A lot of late nights were spent arguing with Sofam Assembly reps before agreement was reached, although most did not resist the notion, considering the change desirable in itself. What took time was convincing the reps why the bill had to be pushed through now. Anall-Marr would definitely like to see the bill pass, being one of his pet beefs. Twelve centuries ago the current arrangement was fair and equitable simply because the Serrll Combine was smaller. Growth eventually chafed the tight shackles. Changing the Articles might be the wisest thing Sofam had done in a while, and would leave a profound legacy, with a lot of goodwill for Sofam.

Illeran gave Bakral a speculative stare. "This won't change our basic policy or attitude toward the Sofam Confederacy, you know."

Bakral laughed. "I didn't expect it would."

"You're still a piece of worm slime, but I understand you better. I guess when all is said and done, we always understood you."

"More so now, I hope. The Celi-Kran don't care much for our politics, my friend. They'll be equally impartial as they devastate our worlds."

"Katan told me about the transport portal the Orieli are building and what the Fernai are doing for us. I can hardly believe it."

"Something has happened to change their isolationist policy. Whatever it was, I'm glad they did change it."

"Have you asked Alkarh Zor-Ell?"

Bakral frowned. "I'm sure it's not the whole story, but it appears the Krans can now emulate an interdimensional shell."

"You're kidding!"

"I wish I were."

"If they attack with ships using such a shield—"

"We'd be totally screwed, Fernai help or not. Worrying about Ed-Kani and Anall-Marr hardly seems relevant, wouldn't you say?"

"Ed-Kani is hoping the Krans will be dealt with and this will blow over. He's planning for what will happen afterward."

"I know, but we're also planning. That's why I gave you the data cube."

"You make it sound so simple."

"Just cutting through the fog," Bakral said and slapped the table. "This calls for some mutual congratulation. Enllss? Break out some of your better booze. I think we need to knock out your boss before he starts figuring angles."

Illeran hissed with amusement, his tongue flickering. "There are always angles, you know. Always."

* * *

Renlow sat reclined in the swivel-couch and allowed herself to drift. Even from here, far on her right some 120 lights away, the Karina Shield Nebula dominated the stars, an incredible sight. It hardly seemed possible that so much free hydrogen, oxygen, nitrogen and other gases could exist in a soup of metals and complex organic molecules. No wonder Karina spewed out new stars like a factory it was.

Around her, *Tureen 2* barely whispered as it trawled through the Navia sector. Brown and yellow gravity waves coiled in the ship's wake as its mass distorted the local spacetime continuum. Barely into her midnight watch—not really having to stand one, a privilege of rank—she had the ship ready at condition two: interceptor net fully modulated, safely tucked within its interdimensional shell, phasing randomly. The bulging brains at OSCOM were still to figure out how to see through a fully active barrier. She was happy with the system she had.

Guardians of Shadow

Sensor sweeps probed eight lights into the deeps and showed nothing unusual, which suited her fine. She wasn't looking for excitement. Their sister ship *Zadar* kept station a quarter of a million ampirs off their port quarter. A light-year behind them, Kardush glowed dull white. She disregarded two pairs of *Nasors* on the other side of the ecliptic who provided defense in depth. Four *Tangar* battlecrusiers patrolled the inner planets. A lot of ships to protect one star and its family of inhabited worlds, but OSCOM was not taking any chances.

Unfortunately, this protection was still woefully thin, spread across a 300-lights frontier. Ships were diverted from other duty, and the Orieli Cluster itself, to bolster support for the most vulnerable systems, but even using transport portals, full deployment would take time, as will installation of interdimensional shells, not only in ships, but on planets as well. A number of Klanina Caucus members were understandably disturbed, concerned about the safety of their systems. OSCOM was doing the best it could by degrading its defense posture in areas not under threat. However, since nobody was shooting at each other within the Technic Union, she figured most ship drivers would relish a change of scenery.

Fully settled into her role as executive officer, surprised to receive promotion after losing LTN-2, she took pleasure at locking horns with the Krans, enjoying running the huge assault ship. Karhide Resulan commanded, but she was responsible for the ship's readiness and its ability to execute whatever he demanded. Was she fast-tracked for a major command of her own? She wouldn't mind handling a *Tangar*. If this action continued, and she could not see it ending anytime soon, she might get one—provided she didn't screw things up somewhere.

Their last mission, destroying the Kran waypoint portal and its support complex, was almost an anticlimax. Secure within its defensive shell, *Tureen 2* devastated ships, planetary facilities and the portal before the horrid things could react properly. The ship took projector hits, the deadly beams disappearing as they touched the shell. Resulan may have been just a teeny bit apprehensive when two gravitic missiles streaked toward them, although he never admitted it afterward, but they were translated harmlessly far into space, the shell working as advertised. The Krans were not given another chance to launch further salvos. A textbook sweep, ideally suited for the ship's designed role.

Mission completed, they began a long voyage back to LTN-3, mopping up Krans along the way.

"For you, Tuval," Renlow remembered whispering as *Tureen 2* slipped into subspace, leaving behind broken hulls and debris.

Flicker...

"Tactical caution," Cent Comp announced. "A triad of *Fadhir*-class attack ships detected exiting subspace relational. Range, four point-two light-years on our starboard quarter. Caution, a second triad has dropped normal."

"Inform Karhide Resulan," Renlow snapped, clearing her mind, "and set condition three."

"Acknowledged. Warning! Contact lost. One moment...intermittent contact reestablished. Targets enclosed in an interdimensional shell, phasing in quarter-second intervals."

Renlow bit her lip. So much for cessation of hostilities. OSCOM was right. The Krans only held off until they could deploy their version of the shell. This could turn out to be a very bad day.

"Cent Comp? Send a sitrep to Navian Command."

"Acknowledged. Status. Condition three active. Status. *Fielder* and *Watice* changing course to intercept."

In the VI plot, six pulsing blue dots entered subspace, heading toward Kardush. Coming in at six lph, they would be within range in forty-nine minutes. There was no way for her to tell whether the Krans could detect *Tureen 2's* randomly modulated shell, their shields still phasing in quarter-second intervals. It appeared they were not able to see through their shells either. It gave her small comfort.

"Opturkarh Renlow, NAVCOM advises that Setlan Eleven and Heplon are under attack."

"Very well."

Wincing, she chewed her lip. It looked like the Krans were making a serious push, testing the limits of the Orieli defense posture at the same time. If this foray were successful, they might be prepared to open a whole front. She wasn't sure OSCOM could deal with such an onslaught. She also wondered where those ships came from. They obviously used a portal, but it could not be from somewhere close. It didn't matter really; the threat must still be honored. She hoped the pickets would be able to ward off the assault.

Alkarh Resulan looked fresh and relaxed despite having only two hours of sleep. He stepped out of the PT alcove, looked around quickly, and strode to his couch. He sat down and shot her a sharp look.

"Have the *Fadhirs* detected us?"

"No indication that we're sensor painted." It did not mean they weren't, she told herself. "The ship is phasing random, disengaging the shell for fifty milliseconds at a time."

Resulan nodded, not needing to have the obvious pointed out. At current closure rate, *Fielder* and *Watice* would close the intercept triangle in approximately eighteen minutes. The Karhide would want *Tureen 2* and *Zadar* there at the same time. When they engaged, it was preferable to do it as far from Kardush as possible, giving the two picket *Nasors* on the other side of the system time to position themselves along the line of advance if the Kran ships managed to break through.

"Cent Comp? Advise *Zadar* to synchronize our intercept with *Fielder* and *Watice*. Execute."

The stars drifted as *Tureen 2* changed course, heading toward a point in space where the Orieli ships would converge with the oncoming threats.

Resulan glanced at her. "If the *Fadhirs* maintain regular

phasing, our interceptor net will get a shot."

"One shot only," Renlow mused. "Hardly likely to be a disabling one. They'll stop phasing and ignore us."

"Not if we tandem our fire at one target at a time. Six collimated beams of 384 TeV will make an impression. They've got to drop their shell to engage."

"Unless they're prepared to bypass us, wanting to target Kardush, which after all should be their objective," Renlow said quietly and Resulan winced.

"Don't spoil what has so far been a fun day, okay?"

Renlow grinned. "Have you seen their formation?"

"Two triads. They might pull the same tandem stunt when we reveal ourselves, I know. Cent Comp? Advise all units to slave their fire control to us. If *Tureen 2* is disabled, *Zadar* will assume tactical command."

"Acknowledged."

"Once the furball starts, we'll have a barroom brawl," Renlow pointed out.

Resulan shrugged. "Death has no rules, Opturkarh. Whatever happens, we cannot allow them to close on Kardush."

Renlow quickly checked the manned watchstander stations. With everyone attending to their duty, silence settled over PFC as the minutes wound down, the level of tension rose and became palpable. The passive sensor array showed the Kran ships still phasing regularly, seemingly unaware of the Orieli pickets. A Wanderer on board would have been useful right now. All things considered, they were lucky to have one on Kardush and Heplon. Despite its scanner array, Setlan Eleven would have to take care of itself. There simply were not enough Wanderers to go around. When told what they were supposedly able to do, it seemed like black magic. OSCOM apparently thought the same and ordered all pickets to engage any contact rather than wait for some robe-wearing mystic to act. Not every sector commander agreed with the policy, but until these strange aliens were tested, standing orders would be carried out.

Guardians of Shadow

The Orieli ships closed the intercept triangle, still in subspace. If they dropped normal, they would be detected instantly, which would give away the whole game. Resulan ordered *Fielder* and *Watice* to target a ship in the second triad, while he and *Zadar* would tackle the first group to disrupt the Kran's tandem fire plan.

"Cent Comp? Set shell to maximum intensity with twenty-four-millisecond phasing," he ordered quietly. "Twin bursts at the leading *Fadhir* as it comes into range."

At half a million ampirs, *Tureen 2* and *Zadar* loosed continuous bursts that merged into a single 768 TeV beam, and mercilessly raked the leading Kran attack ship. The shell absorbed some of the enormous energy, but enough got through when it phased, which caused the shell to flicker and dissipate, indicating damage to the Kran ship. The insect-like forward and rear segments revealed, the *Fadhir* responded fiercely. The Orieli secondary interceptor nets easily absorbed what seeped through the 100-millisecond window when the shell disengaged. The computer needed that window not only to monitor the tactical situation, but also to fire out.

In the VI plot, Renlow watched as *Fielder* and *Watice* slowly dismembered their target, taking continuous fire from its two consorts in the triad. Backsurges tore away plating from the Kran ship, revealing the skeletal frames. Wreckage drifted from the stricken *Fadhir*, flickering as it dropped normal. The ship's field precursor failed and it too vanished.

Tureen 2 shuddered as it also came under attack while maintaining fire on its target. Badly damaged, the *Fadhir* dropped normal. *Tureen 2* immediately shifted its attention to another ship, the disabled *Fadhirs* no longer considered an immediate tactical threat. They would be dealt with later.

Raking beams lanced through *Zadar's* shell. It pulsed wildly and faded. Converging beams from two Kran ships ripped through its interceptor net and walked along the hull, shredding

Stefan Vučak

plating and venting atmosphere. Renlow pictured the torn interior, ripped bodies, screams, and the dead staring at nothing. She winced and concentrated on the job at hand.

Wounded, *Zadar* dropped normal. One disabled *Fadhir*, already in normal space, immediately squirted off a missile. At nine times light speed, it rapidly closed the distance between them and impacted before *Zadar* could evade. Its interceptor net flared a brilliant blue and Renlow held her breath. She watched in horror as the gravitational sink blossomed and began to consume the ship. A small cloud of escape modules sped from the doomed starship, but there weren't many.

She turned and looked at Resulan in dismay, the scene reminding her vividly of LTN-2's demise. He scowled and straightened. This was not the time to get emotional.

"Cent Comp? Cease fire and stop shell phasing. Intercept the closest *Fadhir*. Collision course."

"Acknowledged."

Without emission residuals as a targeting aid, the Kran ships lost lock. *Fielder* and *Watice* were still engaged in a furious exchange with two *Fadhirs*. At least they were both alive.

What Resulan contemplated was extremely dangerous—if it didn't work. Should *Tureen 2's* shell operate at a lower quantum level, part of the ship touching the Kran's shell would be translated. She tensed as the ship struck the *Fadhir* and staggered as *Tureen 2* shuddered violently. After two seconds, everything was still and they were in one piece.

Disabled, the *Fadhir* instantly dropped normal, most of its forward segment sheared off. The maneuver had worked, but Renlow did not plan adding it to her repertoire. For one terrible moment, she pictured a missile equipped with a shell striking a planet and her skin crawled. She shook off the momentary nightmare and realized such an impossibility. It took enormous power to generate an interdimensional shell and hold it open, not something able to be mounted on a missile, or even a medium-sized ship.

"Cent Comp? Resume phasing," Resulan ordered. "Close with the remaining *Fadhir*."

Even as the ship began to move, every watchstander gaped as a searing yellow bolt flashed past them and speared the Kran ship. It set off a cascade of arcing discharges as its shields failed. It immediately dropped normal. In quick succession, two more bolts destroyed the Krans battling *Fielder* and *Watice*.

Renlow and Resulan exchanged glances.

"I guess the Wanderers know how to do business," he said softly, his face tense.

"All the way from Kardush?" Renlow whispered, not believing what she saw, the images indelibly seared in her mind, but relieved the battle was over.

"We'll have an opportunity to recover more gravitic missiles from the wrecks. Pay them back with their own credits, I say."

Renlow smiled, liking it. It was about time somebody dished it out to them.

"Tactical caution! The damaged *Fadhirs* are launching missile salvos at Kardush."

Although wounded, the three surviving Kran ships had teeth and wanted to bare them while still alive.

"Cent Comp? Order *Fielder* and *Watice* to drop normal and engage the *Fadhirs*. We'll handle the missiles."

"Acknowledged."

Their interdimensional shells randomly phasing, the Orieli ships closed on the drifting Kran hulls. Before they could fire, three yellow bolts beat them to it, leaving behind dark wreckage. Although the *Nasors* were capable of taking out the alien warships, someone on Kardush decided not to risk a needless engagement, a decision Renlow approved. If OSCOM harbored any doubts about using the Wanderers, they were now firmly erased.

Tureen 2 overtook the deadly missiles and went normal. It

disengaged its shell and demodulated the interceptor net, allow-ing the missiles to lock. With the shell reengaged, the missiles struck and were safely translated.

"Operational caution. NAVCOM advises the attack on Heplon was repulsed. Two *Tangars* were lost. A damaged *Nasor* is under power and returning to Heplon for repairs."

"What about Setlan?"

"Two *Nasors* and a *Tangar* were lost in the engagement. One *Nasor* is disabled. A *Fadhir* bypassed the scanner array and col-lapsed Urunai's interdimensional shell. Maintaining its own shell, it descended to ground level. At 6,500 ampirs per hour average velocity, it proceeded to translate everything it encoun-tered. A collision with a *Tangar* destroyed both ships. Casualties unknown."

Renlow fought to control the sting in her eyes and bit her lip. She could clearly imagine the Kran ship carving its way over the landscape, through a city, peeling it flat. It hardly seemed possible. One moment, people would be going about their nor-mal lives, perhaps aware of the conflict in space somewhere above them, and then nothingness as the Kran ship swept over them, snuffing everything it touched out of existence. The de-struction must have been horrific. How could anything do such a thing?

Resulan cleared his throat, the horror reflected in his eyes. After a moment, he straightened and his features firmed.

"Order *Fielder* and *Watice* to resume their patrol positions if able. Otherwise, they're to return to Kardush for repairs," he said sharply. "Notify NAVCOM to send tenders to recover the Kran hulls."

"Acknowledged... *Fielder* is returning to her station and *Watice* is setting course for Kardush."

"Very well. Execute retrieval of *Zadar's* escape modules and reduce readiness to condition two." Resulan exhaled loudly and his shoulders sagged. "Prepare a sitrep for NAVCOM and ini-tiate necessary repairs."

"This is not the end of it, Da," Renlow remarked quietly, utterly weary. The intensity of the engagement had left her shaken. The weaponry they were playing with left little room for quarter.

"No, it isn't."

* * *

"Words are inadequate to express my feelings for your loss, master," Ronowan said softly, feeling uncomfortable. What could he possibly say to take away the hurt? He was not sure he even understood what his mentor was going through, never having experienced a personal loss.

Marrakan stood before the open window and gazed at the city as it emerged from a new dawn. Hands clasped behind his back, he remained silent, lost in thought. Ronowan wondered what went on in the old man's mind. Whatever it was, it wouldn't be pleasant.

Losing an old friend merely capped a disastrous time for Anar'on. All traces of devastation from the Kran attack were gone, except for empty lots where buildings and homes once stood and people lived. The dead were gone, cradled by the shifting sands, beyond pain and care. The living were left to mourn the loss of a loved one, facing an uncertain future and a life forever shattered. Painful as the losses were, life did go on as normalcy returned. Infrastructure was being rebuilt while sorrow slowly receded into memory.

Marrakan had more than Anar'on to contend with. As Prime Director of the Kaleen group, he was responsible for seven other systems. Diplomatic handholding took a significant fraction of his day. Then there was Captal, an increasingly complex dimension to be handled, and in many ways, not a welcomed one. Welcome or not, Anar'on was inexorably bound into the Serrll social fabric and could no longer remain aloof, especially now.

Given the threat facing them, Ronowan didn't know how the old man bore the strain. No, that wasn't true. He knew, all right, because he helped organize Marrakan's work schedule. His master did not manage, that was Ronowan's job, and the bureaucratic machinery supporting him, executing the normal mechanisms of administration across all departments. Marrakan set policy, in consultation with other controllers in the group. Lately, though, circumstances forced him to manage some things directly, security being foremost on the agenda. In an unprecedented environment, normal processes do not always apply.

"He will be missed," Marrakan said after a while. Turning, he walked briskly to his desk and sat down.

"Sidhara's body is on Captal. Director Bakral will transport it here once the portal is commissioned. A few days."

"Please send him a note expressing my thanks."

"Of course. The meeting with Prima Scout Servous—"

"Reschedule it for this afternoon."

"He won't be pleased, master."

"Send a memo to Commissioner Katan requesting a replacement. Servous is an adequate peacetime administrator, but he is slow to react under pressure. He also lacks the necessary diplomatic skills for the job, treating us like CAPFLTCOM is doing us a reluctant favor. I want him off Anar'on."

Ronowan nodded and suppressed a smile. The bombastic Prima Scout had ticked off his master more than once. Prodding a rock ray was always a foolish thing to do. Before the Krans showed up, they maintained a cordial, but distant relationship with the Kaleen Operations Command. Fast track officers regarded the Kaleen posting as something of a career stopper, and Servous hadn't been bashful saying so. Once Anar'on's strategic value was suddenly realized, everything changed, Captal and CAPFLTCOM became all smiles and fawning attention. It was pathetic to watch Servous preen with self-importance.

"It shall be done, master."

"Set up a meeting for me with Karhide Ventri at his convenience."

Nominally under KALOPSCOM authority, the *Nasor* commander wasn't happy with deployment of an M-9 and two M-6s, Anar'on's principal Fleet umbrella, and politely tried to point out to Servous that keeping one M-9 parked in close orbit was not tactically sound, but got nowhere. Not a military tactician or strategist, Marrakan nevertheless wanted to hear for himself what their important ally had to say.

"The power reticulation problem with the interdimensional shell facility is resolved?" Marrakan added.

"It is fully operational."

The old Wanderer snorted and shook his head. "A dimensional screen able to protect an entire planet. Remarkable."

"I hope we will not need it."

"You know better, my son. Thanks to the Orieli, our pickets can now modulate their shield grid. Ventri's ship is equipped with an interdimensional shell, but it is not enough. There are too many available targets and not enough assets to protect them. In reality, we're still very exposed."

"Karhide Ventri recommended to KALOPSCOM to adopt a more in-depth defense posture."

"And Servous wouldn't listen. I know. We can only hope our current deployment won't be tested anytime soon."

"Can we deal with the Krans, master?"

"If we can see them."

Ronowan did not comment. He didn't have to. If the Krans came cloaked behind their version of an interdimensional shell, Anar'on could be in serious trouble, planetary shield or not. Especially when the screen could be put up for only a few seconds at a time. Even the scanner array anchored to the sun needed to lock onto a target to fire. If the Krans remained outside the array's acquisition envelope, their movement would be totally unrestricted.

Marrakan bit his lip. "Bakral tells me the Fernai will deploy sensor pods able to neutralize these interdimensional shells. We could certainly use them to sanitize the system."

"According to BueDef, deployment and required modification to our sensor nets will begin in two days, master. We can also expect a courtesy call from a Fernai ship."

"The legends have come alive to haunt us," Marrakan murmured.

"Thanks to master Terr," Ronowan added with a broad smile and Marrakan laughed.

"He is an impudent scamp, all right."

"And perhaps a causal factor which tipped the Fernai into helping us."

"This monitoring system of theirs, truly almost beyond comprehension. Once in place, only then will I consider Anar'on and Kaleen safe."

"Tah, the gods will tell," Ronowan said.

"Indeed. What else?"

"The balance of trade with Orgomy..."

"Recommendations?"

They took a break after two hours of solid work and one meeting. Ronowan sat back in his formchair and sipped fragrant peelath tea. The air-conditioning whispered in the background, too hot now for open windows. Normally, he would not think about the heat, but living in an office had spoiled him, and changed his perspective of traditional Wanderer nomads. Had he become too paternal when considering policies affecting them, thinking his views were superior? A touch of hubris?

A warm cup between his hands, the redolent vapor evoked pleasant memories, he glanced at Marrakan.

"Master, does the Rahtir Council truly speak for our people?"

Marrakan raised an inquiring eyebrow. "Do I detect uncertainty?"

"When I sit here with you and we discuss issues and make

decisions that affect Kaleen and Orgomy, and to a degree the entire Serrll Combine, we seem to take it for granted that what we do is in the best interest of all Wanderers."

"Most of the time they are. When there is doubt, the Rahtir debate options before deciding on a course of action, which you know. With really important issues, we consult all the Rahtir. The process invariably gives rise to conflicting demands. It is up to us then to reach a workable outcome. We cannot hope to satisfy everyone. Attempting to do so would result in inaction."

"How is our wisdom superior to the village Rahtir?"

"You already know the answer, my son. Experience and accumulation of knowledge."

Ronowan thought about it. "Should one of them sit where I am, his perspective would also change."

"Just so. Why are you concerned?"

"That I might be wrong."

Marrakan smiled. "No one is infallible. It is only by erring that you gain wisdom."

"But at what price when I do err?"

The comms alert beeped and Ronowan glanced at the Wall pooling through soothing desert colors, wondering what errors led his master on a path to wisdom.

Marrakan reached across the desk and touched a pad on the inlaid console. "What is it, Henly?"

"It's Prima Scout Servous, sir. Six Celi-Kran warships were detected dropping normal two lights from the system and immediately went subspace."

Ronowan's stomach turned into an icy ball and he tensed.

"Tell him I'll hook into the Tactical Response Center from here." Marrakan cut contact and looked at Ronowan. "The gods may have spoken earlier than expected." He tapped another pad and faced the Wall. "Comsec? TRC link."

Clearing, the Wall displayed a full-dimensional view of the

KALOPSCOM nerve center. Servous turned away from a console.

"Mr. Controller, we have twenty-three minutes before the Krans reach the inner system. My forces are already closing to intercept. Karhide Ventri's ship will be in tactical command."

Servous had not liked the idea of an alien telling his ships what to do, but on this point, Ronowan knew his master remained unmoved. He did not want to repeat the mistake made last time.

"With the exception of Ventri's ship, you're not to engage if the Krans drop normal," Marrakan ordered. "Is that clear, Prima Scout?"

"Those were my instructions, sir," Servous said stiffly.

The reason was clear to Ronowan. In normal space the Krans would hold the tactical advantage where they could deploy their gravitic missiles.

"Prima Scout, order the orbiting M-9 to close with Karhide Ventri's squadron."

"Sir, I must protest! We need it to protect Anar'on."

"We have the scanner array and our interdimensional shell. You need to support Ventri."

"As KALOPSCOM—"

"As Controller, you act under my instructions. If you're not comfortable with that arrangement, you stand relieved, sir."

Servous bit his lip and stiffened, two red spots colored his cheeks. "Very well, sir."

One of his tactical officers stepped into view and pointed at the main display plate. Servous frowned, turned and looked at Marrakan, clearly puzzled.

"Sir, we detected another contact near the Kran vessels. One *Fadhir*-class attack ship apparently challenged and was destroyed. The others are withdrawing." Someone spoke to him rapidly and his eyes widened. "Sir, Karhide Ventri reports he is in communication with a Fernai vessel."

Ronowan tilted his head. The Fernai?

The comms alert beeped. "What is it?" Marrakan demanded.

"Sir, First Commander Shah Pak of the Fernai cruiser *Itaiah* requests permission to see you," Henly reported.

Pausing, Marrakan nodded to Ronowan. "Keep me advised of any developments…Henly? Please inform the First Commander he has my permission."

Vastly relieved, images of more devastation, more lives lost, coursed through is mind, Ronowan smiled. "It's one way to avoid an engagement."

"One we could easily have lost, my son. Our defenses are simply not secure enough."

A column of green radiance appeared in the middle of the office and coalesced into a short, powerful form dressed in a maroon uniform. His small black eyes were prominent against the sheen of his brown face.

He held out his arms palms down and bowed slowly.

"Thank you for seeing me, my lord Marrakan," the alien said in perfect Serrll interlingua. He sank to one knee, his bald head glistening. "I seek your blessing."

Frowning, Marrakan slowly stood and walked toward the alien. He stopped before the kneeling form and extended his right hand. It sank slightly through the projected image.

"You have my blessing, my son."

Shah Pak beamed happily, rose and nodded to Ronowan. "My lord."

"Please, take a seat." Marrakan pointed at a formchair, then smiled. "An isomorphic projection may not need to sit."

Shah Pak grinned. "Thank you, my lord. I will sit. My image is emulating what I do."

Marrakan resumed his position behind the desk. "On behalf of Anar'on, I should be the one thanking you, First Commander. Your timely presence has averted a certain loss of life, even a possible catastrophe for this planet."

"Nu. Until your defense systems are fully in place, the

Procurator Medala was obliged to extend its protection, my lord."

"For which I am grateful. Please offer my thanks to the First Procurator."

Shah Pak bowed. "I shall be honored to do so."

"The Kran force, are they retreating or massing to strike somewhere else?"

"They're retreating, my lord. I made sure of that."

"Are you the courtesy call BueDef told me to expect?"

"Nu. In a manner of speaking."

"I see. Tell me something, First Commander. Why did the Krans withdraw? I understand you presented only your ship to them."

"Extending a reminder, my lord."

Marrakan frowned. "And they will stay away?"

"Nu. For the time being, sufficient for you to complete your defense posture."

"I see."

"We will help the Serrll Combine and the Orieli defend themselves, but we cannot become involved, not unless the Krans choose to confront us."

"We all must follow a workable code of behavior, my son. Only you can judge its morality."

Shah Pak smiled. "Which my lord Terr has challenged somewhat."

Marrakan laughed. "Ronowan and I were just discussing him."

"His claim on our debt to you has raised ripples throughout the Medala."

"Apparently favorable ones, given what you're doing for us."

"My lord, I gave the Orieli location of the Zero Zero system."

"Sankri has the information?"

"Yes."

"He will use it?"

"Nu. I believe so."

"He must not, for the same reason you didn't."

"Perhaps we were in error," Shah Pak said softly.

"The Fernai cannot assume guilt for worlds the Krans destroyed."

"The Krans don't have a conscience, my lord. We do. We stood by and allowed a plague to spread. We should have acted to contain it."

"Meaning that Sankri should be allowed to act?"

"I cannot speak for him or the Wanderers."

"If he allows himself to give into the power lust, he could destroy himself."

"Nu. If I may be so bold, my lord. You could be underestimating his character."

"Perhaps. At any rate, there is nothing we can do to stop him. I can only hope he chooses wisely."

"By whose rules, my lord?"

Marrakan was silent for a moment. "What now, First Commander?"

"We will maintain watch to ensure the Krans have withdrawn. Day after tomorrow, one of our ships will begin deploying sensor pods and integrate them with your Tactical Response Center."

"Will this coverage include Orgomy?"

"It will not. Once BueTech has the manufacturing capability in place, the Serrll Combine can produce and deploy the pods as it sees fit. The critical path is integration with your defense systems and training of personnel, not manufacture."

Ronowan's immediate feeling of outrage that Orgomy would remain unprotected for some time faded as he thought it through. The Fernai probably had the capacity to completely shield the Serrll and the Orieli, but deliberately chose not to, and for a good reason—self-sufficiency. His reaction illustrated the point. Given a free gift, instead of being grateful, he resented it was not large enough.

"On behalf of Anar'on and Kaleen, I thank you," Marrakan said slowly. "You have done much more than we had any right to expect."

Some tension went out of Shah Pak and he nodded. "I am glad you understand, my lord."

"I understand, my son. We must be wary not to turn our gratitude into resentment because you did not do more. I trust the Serrll Combine will never descend into resentment."

"It has not. With your permission, my lord..." With a small bow, the alien's form shimmered and dissipated.

"Whatever debt they owed, master, the Fernai have repaid it in full," Ronowan remarked softly.

"Indeed."

"What Shah Pak said about Anar'on does not necessarily apply to the Serrll as a whole."

"I agree. The Krans may be logical, but they're not reasonable. Next time they strike, and they will, it won't be at us, but I fear for the worlds they might destroy. Even if CAPFLTCOM deploys sensor pods in every Serrll system, protectorate and outpost, they lack ships to ward off a concentrated attack, and we're not likely to have them for a long time to come, if at all. Not only because we cannot manufacture them in such quantity, we don't have the necessary personnel to man them. Logistics, my son. It has always been a deciding factor in any conflict."

"You're saying we cannot win this war, master?"

"Not winning, but containment. We need to deploy Discipline adepts on every Serrll world and on as many Orieli worlds we can, but even that might not be enough."

Ronowan stared. "You want to confront them?"

"A defensive war is a lost war."

* * *

"It is not right, Sankri!"

Terr stared at his brother and experienced a pang of genuine sadness. Being one, sharing everything each of them was, they were still different, which did not surprise him. When Dhar entered his mind and they merged, it did not mean they became a single personality in every respect. They remained individuals with distinctive traits, foibles, aspirations and failings. Once Terr woke from his madness and began to learn, bound to the Discipline, sharing the words of the *Saftara*, the words meant different things to both of them. Over the years, those differences became more pronounced.

As Dhar's ocher eyes probed into him, Terr was overwhelmed by a moment of poignant loneliness. He thought his brother would understand. Deep inside, he already knew the immutable answer. A Wanderer in spirit, Terr was not native-born. Having accepted this, he should have anticipated his brother's reaction. With Nightwings at his side for almost ten years, always supportive, sometimes critical, the chasm between them was now even more painful.

"When we confronted Zero Six, you were ready to unleash Death to see it destroyed. You didn't protest when I destroyed KP-001C. What has changed?"

Concerned at seeing them argue, Teena timidly touched Dhar's forearm.

"Remember what you said to Marrakan? 'The Krans will keep coming until we're all obliterated or they're scoured from the stars.'"

Visibly torn with inner conflict, Dhar clenched his fists. "Sankri, my brother, they must be scoured from the stars. I have no qualms seeing them swept into oblivion. My fear is for you!"

Rit!

"For me?"

"I fear the power you wield so recklessly. You use it with abandon, not realizing that each time you do so, you are eroding

331

Stefan Vučak

the fabric of your soul."

Terr gaped at him in disbelief and his eyes grew cold and hard.

"I may have indulged, Nightwings, and I came close to losing you because of it, but I'm no longer that person. Whatever Sidhara did to me before he died has indeed brought me a step closer to the god who holds his hand over me."

"He also called you Sarumajan."

"The wanton destroyer. Is that how you see me, without morals? Do you think the words of the *Saftara* mean nothing to me?" Terr swallowed hard and his shoulders sagged. "I'm sorry to be a disappointment."

Distressed, Dhar lifted his arm, palm up. "Touch my hand, Sankri," he whispered.

Slowly, Terr extended his arm. After a hesitant moment, the two aliens touched.

"Remember what I told you once? I said, 'No matter what'."

"I remember," Terr murmured and the memories crowded him. Old memories of a different life when things seemed simple and he could tell the difference between right and wrong. At least he thought he could. With Death in his hands, he was prepared to wade among the stars and right some of those wrongs, happy playing the avenger. He couldn't believe he was ever that naïve or trusting. His soul had hardened a lot since then, but despite everything, he remained true to himself, foibles and all, refraining from excess.

"Then believe me now, my brother," Dhar implored. "I stand with you now, no matter what, always."

Teena sniffed, her eyes glistening.

"But you still don't approve?" Terr demanded.

"I fear you will succumb to the power lust."

Terr withdrew his arm. "You fear the power in me because you don't understand it. It's all right, Nightwings. I don't understand it either, but I have reconciled myself to my duality.

Our master called me Sarumajan, and I know why the name sends shivers down your spine, but I am not him. He is someone from your past and his sins still reverberate through your psyche, through every Wanderer's psyche. I don't stand in his image and I won't accept the burden of his guilt."

He stood up and strode out of the room.

"Terr!" Teena cried out, but he didn't hear her, his thoughts dark.

He had failed his brother, not as someone who wielded Death, but as a Wanderer.

As the platform bore him toward the sharp hills, cleaving through pristine air, Tetra's rolling landscape slipped below him. Where the undulating land touched the faint green sky, they merged into a fuzzy ribbon, a doorway into another reality, one he longed to step into. He wanted to lose himself in a place where there were no cares, no problems to solve, no Krans, no missions, just restful peace if only for a little while. He wanted to lay down in deep grass, gaze at fluffy clouds, and imagine himself skipping with abandon over their bulging shapes, knowing he wouldn't fall through.

He wanted to lay beside the small pool at Katai Than, branches of taklan moss-palms cradling him in shadow, the white sands warm to his touch. He remembered the last time he sat there, Teena beside him, drinking in the jagged red cliffs towering around them, the smell of tarad grass and oily peelath strong in the still air. He had not wanted anything then, content to simply be. Freshly renewed after coming so close to losing everyone he loved, even himself, he thought he'd come to terms with what he was. Devon 3-VL4 then changed everything.

As the hills loomed large, it appeared his god was not quite ready to reveal his destiny.

The platform slowed as it shot through a canyon of greenery and emerged above a small meadow. A thin waterfall tumbled over its edge, casting a brilliant rainbow. The platform settled with barely a whisper and the nav screen faded. Terr drew a breath of crisp, sweet air, the sound of falling water a muted, hissing murmur. He stood and stepped into the short grass.

Nothing stirred, not even insects, as if the world waited for him to act. He raised his arms and faced the cliffs on the other side of the narrow gorge hidden in gloom where the sun was still to touch with light.

"I shall walk in the shadow of Death," he chanted forlornly, "and it shall be with me all the days of my life. With shadow shall I smite my enemies, and with thunder shall I purge their land. And all who stand with me in the shadow of Death…"

His throat tight, he could not finish the litany. He didn't have to, for the god already rested his hand on him. He lowered his arms and looked at them. There were no slithering lightnings, no overwhelming sense of holding infinite power ready to be unleashed; simply somber satisfaction. He could feel the power coursing through him, but instead of demanding release, it gave him strength and a sense of acceptance. Sidhara's doing?

He straightened, took a deep breath and exhaled. The god's words rang in his head. 'I am the harbinger of eternity.' The god undoubtedly was, but Terr certainly was not. He merely happened to be an imperfect vessel the god used from time to time.

Soft, smelling sweet, the grass cradled him as he lay down. Hands clasped behind his head, he gazed at the sky and listened to the waterfall. It helped still his churning thoughts.

He recalled an evening, a lifetime ago now, standing beneath the crest of a dune, the sands whispering to him, hands upraised as he cried out to the stars, 'I don't want to be a god!'

No, he was never a god, and he wondered how he could even think of himself as one. The words of his master rang loud and he smiled.

'Foolish creature, power magnifies our dark side, as well as the light we shine on others.'

He had not understood the words then, not sure he understood them now.

"Master..." he whispered, longing to have the wise old Wanderer with him now, for he badly needed to hear the wisdom of his words.

What sort of light did he shine on others? He'd walked away from Athal Than, his transgressions forgiven. So, there couldn't have been much darkness in his soul. He'd misused his power, an assassin guided by Anabb's hand, dealing out rough justice to those law could not touch. Was it wrong to cleanse out an evil? Given the multiplicity of norms followed across the stars, how was his yardstick superior, enabling him to arbitrarily hand out death as the final punishment? No, that was not quite true. He hadn't used his moral yardstick, but Anabb's. He could not blame the scheming old fart, though, happy to wield the lightnings.

"The gods are without morals. Ours, they leave to us," Sidhara once said, perhaps more than once.

Given free will, anything was possible, to everybody's regret.

"Tell me what to do, master."

Only the soft tumble of the waterfall disturbed the silence.

Zero Zero wasn't evil, even though he once thought so. The Krans were without morals, driven by a compulsion to destroy, helpless or unwilling to change. Tertulion and Shah Pak planned to seed the stars with killer nanobods and eradicate a plague that must have spread across an unimaginable distance by now. Surely their act would be no more horrendous than what he contemplated. If two acts achieved the same result, what was the difference? There was no difference, and Nightwings was wrong to voice moral concerns at the method used. Dhar's fear for his soul?

Even the presence of power is an influence, and unlimited power *could* lead to unlimited indulgence. On his return from

KP-001, sweeping everything in his path, he indulged just a little, but he was never tempted by the power lust of wanton destruction. Dhar's fears were mislaid because they were *his* fears. He feared what absolute power could do to him, dreading seeing Terr succumb like he might succumb.

"You should have had more faith in me, my brother."

Sarumajan? The thought made him smile. Somewhere in Anar'on's past, individuals had walked unchecked, dealing out wholesale death, and the Rahtir were justifiably wary at having another among them. Even Marrakan, wise and understanding, displayed an automatic reaction when Terr told him of his vision. But didn't the old Wanderer also say he should rejoice because he was a step closer to his god? They cannot have it both ways.

With shadow shall I smite my enemies…

And he had.

He stood and stretched his arms before him, strong with the power, creation lying at his feet. When he took on his aspect, he always reveled in the keen thrill and realization, were he to will it, he could shape reality. Perhaps he could, but that was merely arrogance and pride rearing their dark heads. Now, bathed in sunshine, he felt satisfied to have the comforting hand of Death rest easily on his shoulders.

No matter what Sidhara said, he was not a destroyer of worlds. He was not Sarumajan.

Yet, he *will* loose the lightnings.

His footsteps light, he stepped onto the platform.

With the sprawl of Tetra sliding beneath him, he wanted to face his brother and mend things. Dhar needed to loosen up and not take life too seriously. Everybody needed a good dose of fun now and then.

He left the platform in the parking lot beneath the apartment building, and hurried toward the PT alcoves. He stepped into the closest one and issued a mental command. He emerged in the lounge and shook off the tingling aftereffect.

"Teena!"

There was a squeal from the bedroom and she was in his arms, throwing kisses all over his face.

"Beast! We were so worried about you. Where were you? Dhar and I were beside ourselves thinking he has offended you. You ran off—"

"Can I get a word in?" Terr asked with a smile and her right cheek dimpled.

"You make my life a burden sometimes, you know."

"I am crushed."

She pressed her cheek against his. "It's all right. We don't make it easy for you either." She pulled away and turned her head. "You can come out now."

Dhar appeared in the doorway and stopped. Startled, Terr groped for the right words.

"What…"

"I was upset and we talked," Teena said soberly.

Without hesitating, Terr walked to Dhar, extended his arm and touched his brother's chest. "You have never done anything that would stand between us, Nightwings. I am the one who has made your life a trial."

Dhar swallowed and gave a lopsided grin. "You *were* a burden sometimes, Sankri. I am sorry for not believing in you. You are right. You're not Sarumajan, although your ability makes me go pale."

Terr smiled. "Me too. If you need moral reassurance, reflect what the Litany of Passage is really telling you."

Dhar assumed a vacant look, then his eyes widened. "With thunder shall I purge their land—"

"And with shadow shall I smite my enemies. Indulgence? Perhaps, but that's why we have the trials, to wash away indulgence. Whoever wrote those words was wise. An exercise in power can be an indulgence, but primarily, it's merely another tool to be used, no different from a ship's projector."

"Just a *little* bit different?" Dhar offered whimsically and

Terr punched his shoulder.

"Now you're being picky."

Teena beamed happily, walked between them, and her arms circled them. "How about dinner? You can discuss philosophy during drinks."

"Sankri…"

Terr tensed, sensing something bad was coming.

"The Krans have returned. They struck Heplon and Kardush. Ships were lost, but the situation is contained. Setlan Eleven wasn't so lucky. There is considerable destruction."

"Then we better move, my brother."

* * *

"Good to see you again, Illeran," Ed-Kani said with frosty dignity as he ushered his visitor into the office. He would rather not talk to the Karkan, not right now, but he did not believe that avoiding a problem would solve it. Besides, this was not the time for playing mind games. All the games were done.

Illeran smiled and his pointed tongue flickered. "That's not what you told me when you called."

"No, it wasn't, but I thought things over since then."

When he called, he wanted to rip out Illeran's heart, and the heart of every Karkan reptilian mud worm. If this is what they meant about finesse and subtlety, taking the long view, they can all slide back into their stinking swamps. Double-crossing bastards, that's what they were. Well, he was about to even things out. One way or another, he'll exact payment from the Karkans, and soon.

He waved a hand at loosely arranged formchairs surrounding an empty tea table. This wasn't a social call, and he did not feel forgiving or charitable. He wanted blood, and Illeran's would do just fine as an entrée.

"Make yourself comfortable."

He didn't wait for his guest to seat himself, a gross breach of protocol, taking the nearest chair, allowing it to mold itself to his body. He was being petulant, but petulance was eminently preferable to open hostility. After all, they *were* coalition partners, and partners should always be cordial toward each other—and trusting. However, like all commodities in Captal, trust didn't have much resale value, handed around like cheap confetti. He'd always known that, of course, but never expected to be shortchanged himself. Some hardboiled politician he turned out to be.

Illeran lowered his wiry frame, sighed and stretched his long legs. "We might as well enjoy the trappings while they last," he hissed as his eyes swept over the opulent office.

"A cheap bauble suitable for festive decoration," Ed-Kani growled, in no mood for mindless banter. "I want to talk to you man to man, no holds barred."

"I have always been straight with you."

Ed-Kani pursed his lips and admitted the worm turd was right. Illeran told it how he saw it, sometimes openly, at other times with gauzy veils and obscure hints. All Karkans relished playing their games of intrigue and elaborate deals, lauding their intellectual refinement and superiority. He often thought it was a defense mechanism against total despair, knowing their lofty political aspirations would never be realized. Now, he wasn't entirely sure.

"Most of the time. Today, though, you allowed your Assembly reps do your talking."

"You're referring to the Equal Franchise Bill?"

"It's the only one debated this morning!" Ed-Kani snapped and clenched his fists, irritated at this sidestepping. "We're coalition partners! Why didn't you talk it over with me before lodging it?"

"I thought you'd be pleased. Sargon and the Palean Union stand to double their number of Executive Council seats."

"As will everybody else."

"Sofam? They'll not double their seats. This bill will take

you a step closer to dominating the Servatory Party. That's what you wanted, isn't it?"

"Don't patronize me. You'd get four seats in your own right and our positions will remain unchanged. How would that help me? Worse still, the bill will give the independents three seats."

"Mmm, yes, an awkward situation, but not necessarily terminal. It simply means, to maintain their support, we must engage them in genuine diplomacy."

"You're not exempt from that problem either."

"Sometimes, my impetuous friend, you need to give in order to receive."

Ed-Kani grinned. "Is that why you're here?"

"Perhaps."

"We'd be subject to extortion."

"Not necessarily. After the initial rush of euphoria at this windfall, the independents might be tempted to run a bidding auction with us and the Revisionists in exchange for their patronage. Whoever is prepared to give them the largest slice of pie wins. Not a pleasant scenario, I admit, but I don't believe it will work out like that."

"Oh, and why not?"

"Think it through. With only one seat, they were careful not to irritate us to the point where we'd get tired of the game and annex them. With three seats, we can play another and more interesting game."

"Divide and conquer," Ed-Kani mused, not entirely sure Illeran was right. However, he *could* be right.

"Like all splinter groups forced into a union of convenience to survive, the independents aren't a homogeneous group. They have their differences and singular objectives. Differences we can exploit."

"If the bill is passed—"

"It will be."

Ed-Kani stared. "Sofam will support it?"

"And you know why."

"They'll lose their executive majority, and with it, control of the government! Sofam won't cut its political throat simply to give the independents three seats."

"They're not doing it because of the independents. Why the sudden concern for Sofam? I thought you'd be delighted. This bill clears the way for the AUP Provisional Committee to consummate the Sargon/Palean merger. With one of the three independent seats in your corner, you will become the senior Servatory Party member. It's what you sought to achieve all your life, isn't it?"

Ed-Kani hissed, hating being toyed with. "I won't need the independents."

"Ah, your plan to bring the Deklan Republic into your fold."

"What do you know about it?"

"Please, my friend. Karkan has a very good intelligence network."

"All right, I've had talks with Anall-Marr."

"So have I, and so has Sofam."

A cold lump materialized in Ed-Kani's belly and he tensed, expecting to hear the worst of bad news. "Who leaked?"

"If you're looking for a traitor in your midst, save yourself the trouble. Nobody leaked, but your overtures were impossible to hide. One of your staffers may have dropped an innocent word, or it could have been one of Anall-Marr's. It doesn't matter. Something as big as this cannot be contained."

"That's why the bigoted turd is vacillating. He waited to see who'll give him the best deal."

"He's not vacillating anymore. He has the deal he wants."

Ed-Kani snorted and shook his head in disgust. "He's staying with the Revisionists, isn't he? What did Sofam give them?"

"They didn't give him as much as we did," Illeran said softly, watching with amusement as Ed-Kani jerked upright.

"What did *you* give him?"

"Trade concessions, lowering of tariff barriers. Small stuff. Remember Anall-Marr's driver? He wanted to see the Deklan Republic playing a more prominent role in Captal, and we gave it to him. Sill-Anais will get the Bureau of Economic Affairs."

"My portfolio?"

"And Garnal-Tan will get the Bureau of Technology and Development. There will also be some commissioner appointments."

"These are critical portfolios, Illeran. Too important for trading as political favors."

"Both are good men, my friend. Besides, doubling the number of executive seats will result in more portfolio shuffling and position trading."

"It will mean splitting some portfolios," Ed-Kani said slowly.

"Not such a bad thing in itself. The executive is top-heavy with too much concentration of power."

"We'll be short of commissioners."

"There are enough senior ones to put where it matters."

Ed-Kani rubbed his hands, suddenly happy. "Anall-Marr supporting the Servatory Party. I cannot believe it."

His future looked immensely brighter. After all the hard negotiations and frustrated discussions, the idea of losing Anall-Marr to Sofam was initially a body blow, but if Deklan sided with the Servatory Party, everything he'd dreamed of could still be within reach. Sargon would swallow the Paleans and Greater Sargon would rule. With the Code, the Serrll would know order and discipline, and his name would stand enshrined forever in the Dumas.

"I can't believe we've got Sofam beaten! I've got to hand it to you, Illeran. I've never had much patience with your penchant for subtlety, but when it counted, you delivered. I cannot tell you how delighted I am to hear this news, but I'm surprised Sofam allowed Deklan to slip through their fingers. I thought they were astute political operators. This calls for a celebration!"

Illeran's tongue flickered. "I didn't say Deklan is joining the Servatory Party coalition."

Ed-Kani frowned. "They'll vote with the Karkan Federation?" After a moment, he waved a hand in dismissal. "Irrelevant. Whether they vote with you or are part of the coalition, it amounts to the same thing. The Servatory Party will rule and you'll be part of a majority government at last. From now on, we'll be the ones setting policy."

"We're setting policy now, my impulsive friend."

"But thwarted by Sofam in all strategic portfolios!"

Illeran sighed. "You weren't listening to me. When I said Deklan will vote with us, it didn't mean the Karkan Federation will vote along party lines every time."

Ed-Kani's mouth went dry and the heaviness in his belly became almost painful. From a vision of glory and adulation, his future lay shattered at his feet. He licked his lips and stared at the senior Karkan rep with intense hatred.

"You would side with Sofam? You're a traitor, you worm. Just tell me one thing. Why?"

"You really want to know?"

"Our plan for a Greater Sargon? That's it, isn't it?"

"You called me a traitor, while all along, Sargon used the Servatory Party machine to further its ambitions to topple Sofam. Your ambitions. You played the game well, but like I told you before, you lack subtlety, seeking instant gratification, refusing to see how a Greater Sargon would destabilize the entire Serrll Combine. We don't need that at any time, especially not now. Your martial philosophy would sweep aside centuries of development and prosperity, reducing everybody you touched to serfdom.

"We have our differences with Sofam, and we'll continue to fight them, but we won't risk social dislocation merely to further Sargon's dream of another empire. You had your glory days, and it makes for interesting classroom reading, but the Serrll has moved on. However hateful to your sensibilities, Sofam has the prosperity and stability of the entire Serrll Combine in mind, even Sargon's. As for you, my imprudent friend, you're prepared to plunge the Serrll into a possible war merely to advance a personal ambition and a place in history. The Karkan Federation couldn't simply sit back and allow that."

Torn with conflicting emotions, Ed-Kani glared at Illeran. "We were partners!"

"Only as long as it served your purpose. Look at the agenda of your Provisional Committee. You're a user, my friend, and so am I. We all are. That's how the game is played, and it's how you played it. It just happens you lost this particular round."

"Karkan Assembly reps will never support Sofam, nor will the Kapu!"

Illeran stood and patted down his pants. "It already has…where it mattered. I better go or I'll be late for the second reading of the bill. Coming?"

Ed-Kani's eyes were hard. "You enjoyed this, didn't you? You relished bringing me down."

"Believe me or not, there was never anything personal. I'll see you on the floor."

When the translucent panels clicked shut after the retreating figure, Ed-Kani sagged, totally dejected. He still couldn't accept the idea that Karkan would side with Sofam. Okay, they sometimes voted together, much to his frustration and annoyance, but to openly split from the Servatory Party? Or were they splitting? Illeran never said they would, but it amounted to the same thing—blocking Sargon from achieving greatness. Blocking *his* grab for greatness.

There must be a way to salvage victory from this mess, wishing for Keana's penetrating strategic insight, but his former aide was now in the Dumas, a powerful powerbroker in her own right.

He clutched his head between his hands and groaned, feeling old and unbearably weary.

"Director Takao. Your presence is required on the Assembly floor," Comsec announced in a pleasant female voice.

"Screw you!" he snarled at the computer.

* * *

Hands crossed, Terr stared into darkness and allowed his thoughts to drift. There was not any order to his thinking. His mind simply freewheeled, jumping randomly between ideas. He sought sleep, but rest eluded him. It was not merely what he contemplated doing that woke him. A nagging restlessness refused to leave him alone. No one particular thing chipped away at him, not exactly. A succession of past events paraded before him in review, a cold examination of what he was and what he had become.

Could he do this? Only a matter of will, his master said, and he had the will, all right. There would never be any security unless everyone was secure, and only by removing the threat would peace reign. What everybody did to themselves afterward, well, that wasn't his concern. He was not their guardian. Whatever injustice continued to exist would be a product of free will. Only as a collective whole, in agreement, can change be implemented. Peace cannot be enforced, only encouraged.

It can be a bitch sometimes.

Rit!

Given time, most problems tended to resolve themselves without having to do anything. It did not mean avoiding issues or abrogating responsibility. With enough information to understand the salient points that underpinned any problem, a solution was always available. It might not be accepted, but a solution was there. Gathering information could be the tricky part, and agreeing on an unbiased arbiter—really tricky as everyone harbored some bias. Only the gods were indifferent, but

345

there wasn't a channel to contact them.

They gave man freedom to act. No use complaining when things don't always turn out as planned.

He exhaled slowly and stared into darkness.

The warm bundle beside him stirred and Teena raised her head.

"Terr?"

"You expected someone else?"

"Only you, my brooding lord." She snuggled closer and threw one arm across his chest. "Thinking about tomorrow?"

"Not really. Just thinking about Zaron. We both studied its history and saw the holoviews, but it's not the same thing as being there."

"They had a nasty past for a while," she murmured.

"The Concordiat? They did well in the beginning, but maintaining order at any cost inevitably encourages formation of the very elements they tried to suppress."

"Totalitarian regimes always fail, no matter how benevolent. I learned that one going for my Scholar's."

Terr smiled. "They taught us the same thing at the Academy."

"Wise men."

"Actually, our coordinator for social analysis was really mean. Gave everybody a hard time. We got even with her, though."

"You played pranks on her."

He brushed a strand of hair from her forehead. "How did you know?"

"Oh, we did the same thing to an old coot I had. Juvenile, I know, but he deserved it. Terrible man. Like you."

"Like me?"

"You can be mean sometimes, you know."

"All right, lay it out for me. List my sins. Everybody else is doing it."

She scratched his chest and rested her head in the crook of

his arm.

"You cannot worry about everything, Terr," she whispered.

The words seared his heart, realizing she was right. He'd forgotten that an insightful analyst lay behind that enchanting face. Anabb did not pick dummies to work for him, not in areas where it mattered. It didn't mean Terr considered himself a brain. Anyone who can tell night from day can be trained as a field operative.

"You think I have a god complex?"

"I know you do. What's more, you also know it."

Not liking it, he conceded her point. They could have been on Zaron already, doing the cocktail rounds, but no. He had to save all creation from the Krans first, despite knowing Resnikan was here, capable of snuffing out Zero Zero. Why did he take it on himself to be the executioner?

"I do it for those who can't, my pet."

"You see? You need to allow us lesser mortals to solve our own problems."

He sighed because he'd been thinking along similar lines. Perhaps Nightwings also tried to tell him this, but he was too determined to follow what he considered the correct and only course. When he looked back on events, seeing some of Tertulion's reactions in a new light, he realized she saw it too, and gave him freedom to act because it was in her interest, and the Orieli's.

Perhaps he still had something to learn about pride and arrogance.

Teena lifted her head. "Why the silence?"

"Truth can be annoying, but coming from you, my pet, it doesn't sting so bad."

"Beast. Seriously, I didn't mean you shouldn't care, but you also need to leave some time for us. When we started this and you told me you wanted to share, I didn't exactly expect sharing it with the Krans."

Terr lifted his right arm, palm up. "I promise not to share you with the Krans again. Okay?"

"You're mean, and you're making fun of me."

He wished he could see her eyes. "I have never made fun of you. I have neglected you, for which I am sorry, and I made you cry. I'm sorry for that too, but I always respected and loved you. Tomorrow, we'll be on Zaron. No Krans there."

"I thought you wanted to go out after the Krans?"

"That's what I wanted once, but a lot has happened since then. This isn't my private war. Until I am told otherwise, we have a mission and it's high time we started it."

"I know you. It's not the mission. You like the idea of handling *Kara* again."

"Tertulion kindly gave us the S/12, and she is a sweet ship."

"With large sleeping quarters," she murmured.

"Adequate," he deadpanned and she giggled.

"You're crude."

"How am I to know if you don't remind me?"

"Beast!"

He slid down and gathered her in his arms, her warm body a poignant reminder that Death wasn't the only important thing in his life.

After a time, he slept and the dreams did not haunt him.

He woke feeling bright and chipper, eager to face the day, pleased with himself. Teena stirred beside him and blinked. After a lazy stretch, she lay on her back and sighed.

"Why can't our house on Taltair be appointed like this?" she demanded dreamily.

The apartment was luxurious, all right. On the first day here, he'd been startled to find himself in the diplomatic compound used by ambassadors, visiting OSA flag officers and dignitaries. It amused him to think the Orieli considered him a dignitary. Dhar protested at having a private suite, but Terr told him to shut up and suffer. They didn't want to offend their hosts, did they? Working for the Diplomatic Branch demanded some sacrifice.

"We can always move in here."

"Mmm. That would be nice," she purred.

During a quiet breakfast, Teena refrained from her usual banter. Perhaps it was his preoccupied faraway look. All done, she cast a critical eye around to make sure everything was tidy and wrapped her arm around his.

"We can go."

He brushed her cheek. "Ready to eat them raw," he said and they headed for the PT alcove.

He held her against him and slowly exhaled. "PERCOM main."

Tertulion stood beside the transparent wall, hands clasped behind her—no one could mistake her military bearing—and gazed at Tetra's sprawl.

"Beautiful morning. In many respects, a new dawn for all of us."

Terr stopped beside her and allowed his eyes to drift over the city. This early, colors seemed brighter and more alive. The pristine sky lay unbroken, bathed in sunshine.

"Thank you for everything, Dapata," he said softly.

She turned and smiled. "You're ready to depart?"

"Cent Comp has *Kara* preflighted."

"It was a unique experience having you here, Terr."

"But one you're glad to see the back of?" he ventured and she laughed.

"Teena, my dear, you need to work on his diplomacy. He will not succeed as an ambassador if he always tells the truth."

"I'm afraid, I'll be wasting my time, Dapata."

Nightwings stepped out of the alcove. "Alkarh Tertulion."

"Welcome, Da Dharaklin."

From a two-dimensional image, Resnikan's slightly stooped figure solidified. The old Wanderer paused as the aftereffect tingle passed, and then joined the group. In his presence, Terr felt the same calming peace as when he stood with

Sidhara. Except Dhar, the others could not see it, but he did. An almost invisible yellow radiance surrounded the Rahtir, which gave his craggy face a serenity that washed away cares, problems and pain. He exerted enormous influence simply by his presence. While on *Itaiah*—an astonishing ship, which Shah Pak politely did not allow him to explore—assimilating the dimensional sensor images, Terr talked to Resnikan more than once about what he intended to do. The Rahtir wasn't judgmental or overly helpful. He offered his blessing and simply said, 'Tah, the gods will tell'.

After exchanging pleasantries with Dhar, Terr was not surprised to see Sumen emerge. The deputy commander would surely want to witness the coming demonstration. For the next few minutes, the conference room buzzed with small talk. An auspicious morning, whatever tension lingered in the air quickly dissipated, at least superficially.

Tertulion strode to the head of the table, placed her hands on the polished surface and leaned forward. The atmosphere immediately became formal.

"Are you ready, Da Terrllss-rr?"

He expected to be somewhat apprehensive. It was not every day he participated in destroying a world, but he only felt a glow of wellbeing. He'd made his decision and it felt right. Nightwings would approve.

"With your permission, Alkarh." He turned and sank to one knee before Resnikan. Standing beside him, Teena gasped.

"Master, I am not worthy to stand in the shadow of Death. I crave that you absolve me from this burden."

Resnikan smiled faintly, extended his hand, and touched Terr's head.

"The god has cast a long shadow over you, Sankri. Rise, my son."

Terr stood and glanced at Dhar. His brother stared at him, mouth open in astonishment.

"My son, no one is really worthy to wield Death, but you

bear the gift well. You need not seek my absolution."

Terr didn't say anything.

Resnikan tilted his head, his sparse gray hair spilling across broad shoulders, eyes probing. After a moment, he nodded.

"You don't fear your power and you stand strong in its shadow. Yet, I sense a humility in you worthy of someone much older. You show wisdom, Sankri. Sidhara would be proud. Very well. I will assume this burden for you."

"Tabe," Terr husked, swallowing hard.

Sumen frowned, his yellow feline yes flickering from figure to figure. "What's going on?"

"We just witnessed a transformation, Alkarh," Tertulion said softly and gave Terr a whimsical smile. "It is a noble gesture to show restraint."

Slightly embarrassed, for it was not such a big deal really, Terr shrugged.

"It took me a while to get it, Dapata."

"And some never do."

Her eyes shining with adoration, Teena wrapped her arms around him. There was no need to say anything. He held her close and kissed the top of her head.

Dhar cleared his throat. "I do not deserve to have you as a brother, Sankri."

Terr touched Dhar's chest. "Your words told me what to do, Nightwings."

"Alkarh Tertulion?" Cent Comp queried diffidently. "First Commander Shah Pak requests permission to come down."

"Permission granted."

The alien's form shimmered and the image became solid. Brief pleasantries were exchanged all around. When Tertulion gave a small cough, Shah Pak looked at Terr.

"Our probes are linked to my ship and active, my lord."

"I will do this, First Commander," Resnikan said, his voice ringing with authority.

Shah Pak blinked, sensing something had happened, but

refrained from asking. Perhaps later, Terr would talk to him. The alien turned to Tertulion.

"If you please, Dapata. Instruct Cent Comp to establish the link."

After a few seconds, a holoview image wavered above the table, then firmed, showing two white stars. Pulsing blue dots represented eight planets. Terr still found it difficult to accept he was watching a real-time view of Zero Zero's home system some 11,200 lights away in another galactic arm. How the Fernai managed this, he wasn't sure he wanted to know.

Shah Pak glanced at Resnikan. "I regret we couldn't improve the resolution, my lord."

The old Rahtir smiled benevolently. "It is a remarkable sight. I feel I am almost there."

He stepped closer to the full-dimensional holoview and his features became grave. Not moving, he stared at the image. A soft blue glow enveloped Resnikan and Terr felt himself transported.

A gray crescent cut a swathe across an eternal blackness. Strings and pockets of light blazed on the night side. Two stars adorned his feet. He knew what he was looking at, Zero Zero's world lying naked before him. Simultaneously, he saw Resnikan level his arms. A prickle of power shot through Terr and he tensed, controlling an urge to raise his own arms.

With a shudder, Resnikan clenched his fists and a sheet of yellow light leapt into the holoview, accompanied by a crash of thunder. Everybody instinctively crouched, hands clamped against their ears. Terr saw the bolt appear above the crescent and run through the planet, spearing it, then fall back on itself. Bathed in a shimmering corona of light, the world tore itself apart. Fountains of magma shot into the sky as red chasms opened across the entire surface. Sections of crust heaved up in slow motion, only to fall back. In a sudden flash that made him stagger, only glowing debris spinning through space remained where a world once stood.

Terr found himself suspended in space with two stars at his feet.

He did not feel exultation or triumph, only indifference. What Resnikan had done was necessary. There was no question of ethics or showing mercy. Zero Zero was incapable of appreciating even this basic human trait. This was simple eradication.

Reality shifted. Resnikan lowered his arms and turned to Tertulion.

"It is done," he said softly and gazed curiously at Terr. "You were there."

In the holoview, points of light were expanding into space where the planet once orbited, and Terr realized that's all the others saw, an impersonal representation of a mere fact that didn't convey the full impact of the moment. He considered himself fortunate to be a witness.

Shah Pak regarded the old Rahtir with awe and gave a small cough. "Our sensor sweep confirms destruction of the fourth planet." He glanced at Tertulion. "Destabilized, it will take time for the system to reach a new gravitational equilibrium. The remaining planets will undoubtedly experience varying degrees of seismic activity. We will allow Cent Comp to link with our probes and access the data, which your astrophysicists will find useful."

"Thank you, First Commander. An opportunity rarely given." Tertulion looked keenly at Resnikan. "I never imagined…what did you mean when you said Terr was there?"

"I watched the planet destroy itself, Dapata," Terr said heavily. "If I wanted to, I could reach out and touch it."

"You did, my son," Resnikan murmured. "May you always stand in god's shadow, Sankri." He nodded to Tertulion and slowly walked toward the PT alcoves, leaving Terr gaping.

Did he somehow contribute to the event? Was it important to know? It made no difference, he decided. Like his discussion with Sidhara whether the gods were real, knowing the answer did not alter the facts.

"A short postmortem is in order," Tertulion said briskly and waited for everybody to get seated before doing the same. "First Commander, on behalf of the Klanina Caucus, I want to extend to you and the Procurator Medala our profound gratitude for your preparedness to assist us with information and technical support in our struggle against the Celi-Kran."

Shah Pak smiled faintly and bowed. "It has been a personal pleasure, Dapata."

"But the Medala has not stopped there. I was startled when you told me they're placing at our disposal three cruisers."

"Nu. With respect, you'll need them as a covering and scout force for your assault fleet."

Terr sat up. Assault force? He glanced at Tertulion. She smiled and locked her fingers above the table.

"Although we'll continue our research, we abandoned a response strategy based on invasive nanolites. The timeframe is too prohibitive, as are the associated risks. We're faced with an immediate threat, which we must honor now. Your technology transfer will in time enable us to adequately protect ourselves. However, this would be at best a standoff. Our worlds and those of the Serrll Combine will never have peace unless the Celi-Kran are eliminated.

"With the ability to track Kran movements and collapse their interdimensional shells, OSCOM has decided to mount a conventional eradication sweep. We shall assemble eighty-one *Nasor* assault ships at LTN-3, which will act as a logistical staging point. With a separation of five light-years between ships, the squadron will scour space along the Karina Shield Nebula in a nine-by-nine grid and penetrate three thousand lights. This will clear a corridor of Kran ships and ground-based facilities four hundred and fifty lights in three dimensions. The maneuver will be repeated until we clear this arm of the galaxy. As you suggested, First Commander, we shall use your ships as a covering and scout force for as long as they're made available."

Terr and Dhar exchanged glances, stunned at the sheer audacity and magnitude of the proposal. To conceive and execute such a mission was staggering, and brought into sharp focus Orieli's logistical ability. It would be a long time before they neutralized the Kran threat in this galactic arm, but everyone would be able to breathe a sigh of relief knowing that eventually they would be safe.

"An ambitious program, Dapata," Shah Pak murmured thoughtfully, "but you don't intend stopping with only one corridor."

"We're not. Attacks against our border systems and Anar'on were launched using transport portals. Given a range estimate of three thousand lights will utilize a substantial portion of our defense capability in search for those portals. Unless…" Tertulion paused, her eyes fixed on Shah Pak.

"Your operational timeframe would be shortened considerably if you had the location of those portals and key Kran support facilities."

"That is correct, First Commander. Without portals, logistical and maintenance support, their ships will be forced to withdraw, losing the initiative. We don't want to give it back to them. The Fernai have the necessary information. Your data feed from Zero Zero's home system proves it. It is only logical to assume you have sensor pods strewn through a substantial section of our galactic arm, and perhaps the neighboring one. It is inconceivable that your defense posture relies solely on the border represented by our Line Tracking Net."

Shah Pak nodded. "I find no fault with your reasoning, Dapata."

"Is the Procurator Medala prepared to share this information?"

"Nu. It is under discussion. With the manufacturing capability to produce and seed your own pods, some in the Medala feel they have done enough. However, it is recognized that it will take decades before you're able to accumulate sufficient information to be tactically useful, which you also appreciate, hence your front-on eradication sweep."

"The Orieli Technic Union has no right to expect anything from the Procurator Medala, First Commander. Should it decide to provide the information, it will be received with thanks."

Shah Pak stood and bowed. "My lord Terr…Dhar, I wish you a safe journey to Zaron."

"Until our paths cross again, First Commander," Terr said, his feelings mixed. In many respects, he would rather study the Fernai. In due time, perhaps.

"Nu. With your permission, Dapata, I shall return to my ship." The alien's image wavered and vanished. A moment later the holoview dissolved as the link with *Itaiah* severed.

Sumen crossed his arms. "Da Terr, we advised Captal of our intention, with one immediate action item. We're withdrawing from LTN-12 as it no longer fulfills the intended strategic purpose. Building it and revealing ourselves to Earth has generated a degree of social dislocation, for which the Klanina Caucus extends its apology. We acted in good faith, but that does little to repair the damage we caused."

"Thank you, Alkarh. Captal will welcome this development," Terr said gravely.

"You should also know, we'll not be rebuilding LTN-1 and LTN-2. The interdimensional sensor pods will assume their function," Sumen added.

Terr smiled at Tertulion. "What you omitted to mention to Shah Pak, Dapata, is your intention to extended your transport portal network on the other side of the Karina."

She returned his smile. "I'm sure the First Commander will arrive at this obvious conclusion. On behalf of the Klanina Caucus, Terr, I want to extend our appreciation to you and Da Dharaklin for your readiness to help us." She looked at Teena and sighed, her expression suddenly mournful. "I regret what you had to suffer, my dear."

Teena nodded. "As Terr is want to say from time to time, Tah, the gods will tell."

"And they have indeed," Tertulion murmured. "Echoing Shah Pak's sentiment, I wish you success with your mission."

Epilogue

Kara gently lifted off the apron, tilted and slanted into a clear sky. Tetra fell away as the ship gained altitude, eventually disappearing over the horizon, leaving the OSA complex far behind. Moments later, stars winked through the brilliant blue-green atmosphere curtain. Then they were through, surrounded by blackness, and the ship accelerated. A swirling cloud band smeared Perilia's northern hemisphere that stretched from the icy polar regions almost to the equator. As the ship drew away, landmasses became indistinct, dominated by brilliant greens of the southern ocean.

In the swivel-couch, hooked into the VI, Terr gazed nostalgically at Perilia retreating behind him. Many memories were left there. Poignant memories. He searched for a glimpse of Shah Pak's ship, but there was nothing out there, only emptiness. What did he expect, a sendoff band? The thought amused him immensely. He may have played a small role in recent events, but to Tertulion and Shah Pak, he was a curiosity, an oddity from their own more primitive past. He only needed to reflect on their last conversation. They talked in front of him out of politeness, not because he had something to contribute. Resnikan was right to walk away when he did. He had no pride to nurture, having already dispensed with such foolishness.

"Thinking again?"

He flashed Teena a smile. "Even as a kid, I always wanted to reach for those strange white points of light in the night sky, to hold them and see what they were." He pointed at the growing blue ring in front of them. "Beyond that portal, we'll find some very strange stars."

"We already have, Sankri," Dhar said beside him.

"Yeah, we did, but I hope these will prove more friendly."

"The Orieli, can they really do what Tertulion said?" Teena asked, not believing the outrageous notion. "Actually sweep this part of the galactic arm clean?"

"I don't see why not," Terr told her. "It will take time, but they now have the technology and the Fernai will give them the necessary intelligence."

"I get shivers just thinking about it. To have such power…"

"Makes me wonder about the Fernai and their capabilities," Dhar rumbled softly.

"Four hundred ampirs," the computer announced in her intoxicating voice.

"I cannot believe we're actually going to a galactic cluster," Teena breathed in wonder. "It's like a miniature galaxy."

"Interface charged and setting coordinates."

Terr glanced at Dhar and nodded to his brother, then reached to Teena and brushed her face with the back of his hand.

"We'll have time now for everything, my pet."

Eyes shining, she gripped his hand and nodded.

"Fifty ampirs." The S/12 slowed to a crawl. The portal's ring pulsed with blue fire. In its heart lay impenetrable darkness. "One hundred kanampirs…transiting."

Flicker…

About the author

Stefan Vučak has written twenty-one novels, which include eight SF books in the Shadow Gods Saga. His *Cry of Eagles* won the coveted Readers' Favorite silver medal award, and his *All the Evils* was the prestigious Eric Hoffer contest finalist and Readers' Favorite silver medal winner. *Strike for Honor* won the gold medal.

Stefan leveraged a successful career in the Information Technology industry, which took him to the Middle East working on cellphone systems. Writing has been a road of discovery, helping him broaden his horizons. He also spends time as an editor and book reviewer. Stefan lives in Melbourne, Australia.

To learn more about Stefan Vučak, visit his:
Website: www.stefanvucak.com
Facebook: www.facebook.com/StefanVucakAuthor
Twitter: @stefanvucak

More Books by Stefan Vučak

https://www.stefanvucak.com/Books/

 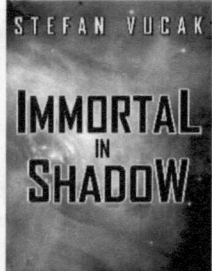 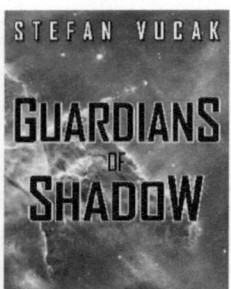

  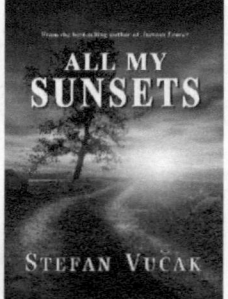